THE LAST VOYAGE
AND
HIGH STAND

HAMMOND INNES

Hammond Innes was born in Sussex in 1913. He wrote twenty-nine international best-sellers, all of which have been reissued by Pan. He also wrote a superb history of the Conquistadors, two books of his world travels and sailing, and an evocative illustrated book on East Anglia. It was in the early fifties, with books like *The Lonely Skier*, *Campbell's Kingdom*, *The White South* and *The Wreck of the Mary Deare*, all of them filmed, that he achieved international fame.

HAMMOND INNES

THE LAST VOYAGE

Captain Cook's Lost Diary

AND

HIGH STAND

PAN BOOKS

The Last Voyage first published in 1978 by Collins.
First published by Pan Books 1996
High Stand first published 1985 by Collins.
First published by Pan Books 1997

This omnibus edition published 2004 by Pan Books
an imprint of Pan Macmillan Ltd
Pan Macmillan, 20 New Wharf Road, London N1 9RR
Basingstoke and Oxford
Associated companies throughout the world
www.panmacmillan.com

ISBN 0330 34270 2

1 3 5 7 9 8 6 4 2

A CIP catalogue record for this book is available from
the British Library.

Typeset by Intype London Ltd
Printed and bound in Great Britain by
Mackays of Chatham plc, Chatham, Kent

THE LAST VOYAGE

CONTENTS

INTRODUCTORY NOTE

This manuscript, which only recently came to light in the cellars of the Old St James Club, is such an extraordinary document that I feel some explanation is essential. It appears to be in Cook's hand and style and covers his third voyage up to the time of his death, and to some extent it overlaps his official Journal, even to the extent of repeating passages almost verbatim. But unlike the Journal, which in the manner of those covering his earlier voyages of discovery was written more or less on a day-to-day basis, this was written spasmodically, presumably on those occasions when he had time for reflection.

As in a log, he heads each passage of writing with the day of the week and the date, and checking these against the official Journal, they coincide in the main with periods of relative inactivity. But as the voyage develops more and more of the writing seems to have been done on a Sunday, and since there is nothing in his journals to suggest that he regarded Sunday in any way as a day of rest from his main activities, I can only presume that he set this particular day aside for his private writing so that he would get into the habit of it. The necessity for this sort of discipline is evident from his official Journal, some of the passages of which are extremely lengthy, particularly those dealing with native customs and behaviour, so that he was already doing an immense amount of writing.

It has been said of Cook that, while we know every detail of his voyages, we know very little about the man himself. There are passages in this record that suggest he was in some degree conscious of this. His dislike of the two volumes Dr John Hawkesworth produced for the Admiralty from the Journal of his first voyage was such that he spent much of his time ashore after the second voyage trying to ensure that a more sensible and accurate account of his icy circumnavigation in the South Polar seas would be produced. That he should have decided to keep two journals on his third voyage – one the official record, the other a very personal account – is not, therefore, entirely surprising. He was the forerunner of all those great English writers on exploration that were to come in the next century – Livingstone, Burton, Speke, Baker, Thomson. What is surprising is the reflective quality of the writing – almost as though he had some premonition. And yet he was a man too sure of himself, and of his abilities as a navigator and a ship's captain, to contemplate death through disaster at sea.

The first page of the manuscript could be taken as an indication that the writing of it was suggested to him by Sir Joseph Banks. It appears to be a dedication of the work, but, like the rough canvas cover, it has been half eaten away, probably by rodents, so that all that remains are the following almost indecipherable words –

> *This personal hist. . .*
> *on board His Majes. . .*
> *my third voyage. . .*
> *to J. . .*
> *who made me acqu. . .*
> *certain facility I did not. . .*
> *Jams. . .*

In view of Cook's tendency to hark back with some nostalgia to his first voyage of discovery in the company of the young Mr Banks, and to the fact that Banks was a founder member of the St James Club, the work was most likely to have been dedicated to that 'Gentleman of Large Fortune' who was for three years – from 1768 to 1771 – his close companion on board the *Endeavour*. It was from him that Cook learned about science and the arts, and above all perhaps how to express himself. Even if it were Sandwich, First Lord of the Admiralty and his patron, who advised him to write a separate and personal record of his third voyage, it is still reasonable, and most likely, that he would have dedicated it to Banks, who was very largely responsible for his election to membership of the Royal Society Club,* an organisation

*On the resignation of Sir John Pringle, Banks was unanimously elected President at the Anniversary Meeting of the Society on 30 November 1778, 220 members voting.

for which Cook had great reverence. Certainly this would explain how the manuscript came to be in the cellars of 106 Piccadilly since Captain Gore, who brought the *Resolution* and *Discovery* home after Captain Clerke's death, noting the dedication, would have sent the bundle of papers, not to Cook's widow, but to Banks, either at the St James Club or at the Royal Society.

That it should have been left to rot in the Club's cellars may appear surprising, but it has to be remembered that at the time Banks received it he was already involved in the publication of the official account of Cook's last voyage; he certainly would not have wished the more personal journal to appear at the same time. Banks died in 1820 and under the terms of his long and complicated will he left his scientific collection and his manuscripts to his 'indefatigable and intelligent librarian', the botanist Robert Brown, for use during his lifetime, after which they were to pass to the British Museum. When Brown finally died 38 years later the intention of the will was overlooked and much of the material never came into the hands of the Museum's trustees.

In any case, there is some mystery about the rest of Cook's manuscripts. Dr John Douglas, Canon of Windsor, who was to edit the official journal of the last voyage, was sent three parcels of writing by the Admiralty Secretary which, according to a note dated 14 November 1780, contained Cook's journal, log books and loose manuscripts. Professor Beaglehole, who spent more than thirty years of his life seeking out and examining every document relating to Cook, states quite categorically that 'all such papers have disappeared', adding, 'how and when they disappeared it is impossible to say, except that it must have been after their arrival in England'. And James King, 2nd Lieutenant of the *Resolution*, in a letter to Dr Douglas says of his search for the missing loose manuscripts, 'They are not at the Admiralty, Mrs Cook has not got them and the Clerke knows nothing about them.' He adds that Captain Gore is out of town 'but it seems unlikely that he can give any account . . .'

If these official papers could disappear under the nose as it were of ship's officers and Admiralty servants, it is not surprising that a private journal left by Cook should have gone astray. Indeed, King's Journal, covering the later part of the Voyage when he commanded the *Discovery*, has only recently come to light, having been lost among Miscellaneous Sailing Directions in the Hydrographic Department at Taunton. Nor is it surprising that, after 200 years, the condition of the manuscript is now so very bad – all the pages mildewed by damp to a greater or lesser degree, some to the extent that they are almost illegible – that without the official Journal it would have proved impossible to reconstruct. Also the manuscript itself has been worked over with many alterations and additions which have added to its illegibility. This has not made my task an easy one.

I have put it all together to the best of my ability, relying on my knowledge and fascination with the subject to fill the gaps, using for reference Cook's official Journal as edited for the Hakluyt Society by Professor Beaglehole, also the journals of those who sailed with him, Clerke, Anderson, Edgar, Samwell, and others. And in reducing and editing the volume of the writing I have followed Professor Beaglehole in omitting the profusion of capital letters which would otherwise make it difficult to read, and again for ease of reading I have split the writing up into 52 sections under my own headings; however, I have kept largely to the original spelling and punctuation so that the style of Cook's writing is preserved as far as possible.

The last twenty or so pages proved the most difficult to edit as they had clearly been written in haste and had not been worked over. This is not surprising since they cover the period when Cook had ceased work altogether on his official Journal. Professor Beaglehole writes in his Textual Introduction: 'It is impossible to believe that he committed nothing at all to paper after his entry for Sunday 17 January 1779.' This private Journal fills the gap, recording Cook's personal reactions in the last month of his life.

Finally, in my selection of what shall be included I have tried to bear in mind that this is a very personal record and the story of Cook himself rather than what he did, which has already been the subject of innumerable books.

Hammond Innes
Kersey, Suffolk

PART ONE

A YEAR IN ENGLAND

CHAPTER ONE

START OF THE VOYAGE

Monday, July 22nd, 1776

Having had a day of calm weather now after the strong gale at South which forced me to stand to the Westward, I have an opportunity to begin this personal history, or Diary, of the Voyage on which we are embarked. The log book of my last voyage closed with the words: *Having been absent from England Three Years and Eighteen Days in which time I lost but four men and only one of them by sickness.* In circumnavigating the globe in those cold Southern Seas, and thereby disproving the presence of any great continent of land there, I thought I had been as far as a man may go. But now that I am away in search of the North West Passage, the which may well prove as elusive as that *Terra Incognita* of which men like Alexander Dalrymple dreamed, I fear I may be forced to go further than ever before. Pray God that it will not take so many years, and that at the end of it I may report as few men lost.

Much of my time since we sailed from Plymouth

on 12th of July has been devoted to this end, for with the Navy committed to the disagreeable task of convoying troops to America, the Men are not of the best and know little about how to look after themselves. Indeed, I have only just come from an inspection of the ship and its livestock, the which I could not do during the gale, and having ordered the smoking of all parts below deck and the scrubbing of tables and other flat surfaces with vinegar and gunpowder, I took this opportunity of demonstrating to Mr Bligh, the Master, and some others who have not sailed with me before, my customary routine of hygiene aboard ship and the methods I have ordinarily used to prevent disease among the men. We are altogether 113 souls on the *Resolution*, including myself and four officers, Mr Webber the painter and Omai, a native of Otaheite, also the livestock which is more numerous than on either of the two previous voyages.

During the month we were at Deptford due to delays in the fitting out and storing of the ships we had 30 desertions, all of which we have replaced. Fortunately I have with me on the two ships a dozen-and-a-half men who have sailed with me before, half-a-dozen of them on both voyages who thus have over 6 years service with me in the oceans, so that here on board the *Resolution* there has been no repetition of the difficulties experienced on the first voyage in persuading the People to a diet of portable soup, onions and fresh vegetables at regular intervals.

We were off Ushent on July 17th and 18th and are now almost across the Bay approaching Cape Finister. I intend putting into Tenerife instead of Madeira, it having been discovered that there is not a sufficiency of hay and corn on board for the animals to last us to the Cape and thinking to be better supplied at Tenerife. Thence we shall make for the Cape by way of the Cape Verde islands. I am not a little concerned about Capt Clerke, the one officer who has sailed with me on both previous voyages. He guaranteed the debts of his brother, Sir John Clerke, and on that gentleman's sailing off to the East Indies has been committed to the Kings Bench prison. If he does not get his release in time to take command of the *Discovery*, which I have left waiting for him at Plymouth having done all that is possible through my good friends, I shall not be so well served in that respect. I have every hope he may catch up with us at the Cape Verde islands or else in Table Bay where I propose to take on fresh victuals. If not, I have left orders for the *Discovery* to meet me in Queen Charlottes Sound in New Zealand which I know from past experience will provide us with all we need in preparation for our long voyage north through the Pacific.

Monday after Noon

We have on board a great deal of Instruments for Observations, more than I have had on any other voyage. As before, I am instructed to be present at the winding up of the Watch Machine, together with Mr Gore and Mr King, the first and second lieutenants, both of whom also have keys to the Box, all of us attesting the time and entering it into the Observations

Book. This procedure I have just carried out, following upon the noon observation for latitude, and because all these various observations, particularly those relating to longitude, take up a great deal of my own and my officers time, I think it of some interest to list the variety of instruments delivered to the two ships.

These are: – 2 Astronomical Clocks, one with an Alarum, an Astronomical Quadrant, a Hadley's Sextant by Ramsden and another by Dolland, an Acromatic Tellescope with a treble Object Glass 46 Inches Focus, a Reflecting Tellescope, a 4 feet hand perspective with large Aperture, a Marine dipping Needle with Six Magnetic Steel Bars, 2 Small Variation Compasses, an Azimuth Compass with a spare Card, a Theodolite and Gunters Chain, a pocket Pinchbeck Watch and Mr Bayly the Astronomer on board of the *Discovery* and I have a small Hadleys Sextant by Ramsden as well as logarithms and a variation chart.

The Night Tellescope I shall hope to use next week if the weather serves, there being a total Eclipse of the Moon on the 30th.

It is the necessity of making continual and accurate observations that caused me to choose in 1768 a cat-rigged collier, which was then renamed the *Endeavour*. Having been mate in these vessels and sailing out of Whitby on the Baltic coal trade before I joined the Navy as an able seaman, I understood very well their steady seakeeping qualities, they being three masted, very roomy and easy to handle. They are also shallow-draughted, enabling us to sail close inshore for the better observing of the coastline and being full-built can be readily careened, something we were very glad of after the damage we sustained when we grounded on the coral inside the Barrier Reef.

I had 2 such ships on the second Voyage, and now again I have the *Resolution* and another Whitby-built cat, the *Diligence* renamed *Discovery*. No better ships could have been devised for my purpose, except that the fitting out of the *Resolution* on this occasion has not been accomplished as well as I could have wished. The deck appears not very well caulked and after the gale on the 19th the Boatswain, who is an American named Ewin from Pennsylvania and was with me as Boatswains mate on the last Voyage, reported to Mr Bligh that there was some water in the forepart so that we had to pump. It may be that we shall discover further skimping of the work at Deptford. This poor workmanship may be due to the unreadiness of the Navy for the war against the American colonists, requiring the putting into service of additional ships and the repair of others. In the circumstances, I feel I am much to blame in that I could not look to the work myself to the extent I have done previously, the reason being that I was much engaged in the preparation of the Journal of my last Voyage for press.

There were many matters occupying my mind during the year I spent ashore between the last voyage and this. For the better understanding of the Narration I am embarked upon, I will attempt to inform the Reader of these matters later, my presence now being required on deck, and after the Cabbin will be set for dinner. Having recently butchered one of our sheep, we shall have roast meat again today.

CHAPTER TWO

THE YEAR ASHORE

Tuesday, July 23rd

I have said I will recount what transpired ashore between my ordering the anchor let go at Spithead July 30th 1775, on completion of my second Voyage, and my finally embarking again in the *Resolution* on June 24th of this year at the Nore. If I do not do this now, and also give some account of the feeling of my Lord Sandwich and others regarding the North West Passage, it will not be possible for the Reader to understand fully the circumstances of this Voyage and my offering myself for the command of it. Also, it is certain that once we clear the Cape and head SE into higher latitudes to chart the islands the Frenchman Kerguelen visited in 1772 the weather will be of the worst and my time much take up with the Navigation of the Ship.

At the time I completed my second Voyage I was not yet 47. I had then been 20 years in the Navy, first as an able seaman, then as Master's mate, then Master, finally as officer in command of expeditions of Discovery and Navigation. At the time of our arrival off Portsmouth I was feeling not a little anxious having returned a second time with no good report to make of that great Southern Continent of which several of my Lords of the Admiralty had entertained great hopes, believing that I would discover new and fertile lands in the Southern Ocean. Moreover, we had become separated from the second Ship under my command, the *Adventure*, off the coast of New Zealand and the last we had seen of her was at Midnight, October 30th 1773. I had heard, however, that Capt Furneaux had come safely home a year since and I now had that information confirmed and was told that the *Adventure* had arrived at Spithead on July 14th 1774.

Conscious of my duty to report to my Lords Commissioners as soon as possible, I left the *Resolution* in the charge of Lts Cooper and Clerke and hastened to London. I had much to think about on the journey, for now that I was clear of the Ship I had time to consider the reactions of the Board of Admiralty to the results of the Voyage. They would already have received copy of my Journal and the charts constructed partly from my own observations, partly from those of Mr Gilbert, my Master, also the Views, paintings and drawings by Mr Hodges and others; all these I had committed to Capt Newte of the *Ceres*, an English East India Company Ship from China which we had found anchored in Table Bay and which was bound direct for England. And by the *Dutton*, another Indiaman in whose company we had sailed to St Helena, I had sent a packet including some of the officers journals, so that my Lords would thus be prepared for disappointment in regards to the Southern Continent.

All the information I had from Capt Furneaux since parting company with the *Adventure* was the letter he left for me at the Cape in which, apart from the loss of Ten of his best men and a boat to the natives in Queen Charlottes Sound, some of the men being eaten, he stated that he had sailed over the position of Cape Circumcision. Thus even the land Bouvet saw is proved to be no continent. And at Portsmouth I was concerned to learn that my good friend and Benefactor, Lord Sandwich, was down channel sailing in a yacht accompanied by Miss Ray,* Mr Joseph Banks and others.

After being so long at sea it was not easy to adjust my mind to the hopes, aspirations and demands of those concerned with affairs of State in a Country from which I had been absent for more than Three years. There was also the matter of the book, the Admiralty requiring that the results of the voyage be presented to the Publick, but not I was determined in the loose and inaccurate manner in which the late Dr Hawkesworth had presented the first Voyage and for which his wife received the munificent sum of £6,000 after his death. I realised that I would have to look to this work myself even if there was no reward for it other than the satisfaction of the result being an accurate account and in this I would need guidance.

*Martha Ray was the First Lord's mistress.

And there were domestic matters to occupy my mind, my poor wife not having seen me since the morning of Sunday, June 21st 1772 when I had taken leave of my Family at Mile End and gone down to Sheerness in the company of Mr Wales the Astronomer. It seemed a very long time ago, so much having happened since. And there were the two boys, James who would now be eleven and Nathanial ten. I was most anxious to see them, hoping they were in good health, remembering that three of our children had died.

On arrival in Town I went straight to Mile End, my wife overjoyed at seeing me safe at last, and everybody well and in good heart. I being a Yorkshireman and born of the land, I fear I am not of the most demonstrative, but our sense of family is very strong and it was a great homecoming; better than the last time, which was in some part over-shadowed by the death of our daughter Elizabeth only three months before, and poor little Joseph, born just after my departure dead within a month of being baptised. On this occasion there had been no such misadventure in my absence so that the reunion between Mrs Cook and myself was one of the most complete happiness and content.

That same day Mr Wales brought the Watch to London by Post-Chaise. This was the duplicate of Mr Harrisons 4th chronometer made by Mr Kendall to the order of the Board of Longitude. It has proved a most excellent timekeeper throughout the Voyage and the following day he delivered it to Mr Maskelyne, the Astronomer Royal, at Greenwich, together with his observations, which were the purpose of our taking no less than four such machines – three by Arnold, only one of which had been properly tested for a year beforehand, and one by Kendall. Testing the accuracy of all the equipment, using at times portable observatories, had taken up a deal of our time during the Voyage.

There was much to occupy me during the next few days, apart from my family, for I had to report to the various Boards, notably the Sick and Hurt Board to give an account of the crew's health and effectiveness of such items as the inspissated Juice of wort in assisting my efforts to prevent scurvy. In this Capt Furneaux had not been so successful by failure to adhere to my practice of naval hygiene and the rigorous routing I had devised. He had been posted to the command of the frigate *Syren* and was leaving for the North American station, so I could not talk with him and had to be content with reading his journal, wishing to be assured that the massacre of his boat crew in Ship Cove had not been the result of any provocation on our part. This the journal seemed to confirm, and having in mind the warlike bearing of the natives and the trouble we had encountered on first setting foot on New Zealand in 1769, I accepted that and was relieved that he had taken no reprisals.

Lord Sandwich arrived at Admiralty House, he and Miss Ray having been so good as to leave the yacht and come to Town as soon as he knew I was returned. I spent some time with him and others, repeating to them verbally what I had already reported in my Journal despatched from the Cape regarding the Southern Continent. This I now restate for the benefit of my Readers, it being of the greatest importance that the results of so many weeks of sailing in mist and storm amongst floating ice be clearly stated and understood by the Publick:

I had now made the circuit of the Southern Ocean in a high Latitude and traversed it in such a manner as to leave not the least room for the Possibility of there being a continent, unless near the Pole and out of the reach of Navigation; by twice visiting the Pacific Tropical Sea, I had not only settled the situation of some old discoveries but made there many new ones and left, I conceive, very little more to be done even in that part. Thus I flatter myself that the intention of the Voyage has in every respect been fully Answered, the Southern Hemisphere sufficiently explored and a final end put to the searching after a Southern Continent, which has at times ingrossed the attention of some of the Maritime Powers for near two Centuries past and the Geographers of all ages. That there may be a Continent or large tract of land near the Pole, I will not deny, on the contrary I am of the opinion there is, and it is probable that we have seen a part of it. The excessive cold, the many islands and vast floats of ice all tend to prove that there must be land to the South and that this Southern land must lie or extend farthest to the North opposite the Southern Atlantick and Indian Oceans, I have already assigned some reasons, to which I may add the greater degree of cold which we have found in these Seas, than in the Southern Pacific Ocean under the same parallels of Latitude. In this last Ocean the Mercury in the Thermometer seldom fell so low as the freezing point, till we were in sixty and upwards, whereas in the others it fell frequently as low in the Latitude of fifty-four: this was certainly owing to there being a greater quantity of Ice and extending further to the North in these two Seas than in the other, and if Ice is first formed at or near land, of which I have no doubt, it will follow that the land also extends farther North.

To my great relief neither my Lord Sandwich, nor anybody I talked with, seemed unduly concerned that the Voyage had produced nothing in this respect to the Countrys advantage. Indeed, they had nothing but praise for the diligent manner in which I had proceeded, persevering to the limits that could be expected of both Ship and People in my attempt to discover this Land. I think it right to say that they found my detailed report more to their liking than Mr Dalrymples new book, just published, in which he had let his imagination overreach itself, still dreaming of command of an expedition and advising the setting up of a base at Cape Circumcision for the exploration of the continent attached thereto to the increase of our commerce in those parts – the very Cape the position of which Capt Furneaux had sailed over with no sight of land.

The *Resolution* was ordered up to Gallions Reach, the intention being to pay off at Deptford and lay up. On August 9th my Lord was kind enough to present me at St James's Palace where I presented His Majesty with various maps and charts. He expressed great interest in the plant specimens we had brought back, wishing that some of these should go to his gardens at Kew now in the care of Mr Banks. He also presented me with my promotion to Post-captain, I having been posted to a seventy-four, something I looked forward to with mixed feelings, never having been closer to action than when I was Master of the *Pembroke* and sounded the Narrows of the St Lawrence river opposite Quebec, so enabling General Wolfe to storm the Heights. But next day my posting was cancelled, it having been decided to lay the *Kent* up at Plymouth; as alternative I was offered the post of Fourth Captain at the Royal Hospital, Greenwich, the death of Captain Clements having created a vacancy there.

I was deeply disappointed, but on reflection my wife and I came to feel that this was for the best since it assured me of a pension of £230 per annum and free quarters with time to work on my Journal for publication. Accordingly, I wrote to Mr Stevens, the Admiralty Secretary, applying for the vacancy, but at the same time making it clear that I was ready at any time should my Country call me to more active or more essential Service, knowing myself still capable of ingaging in any duty which their Lordships might be pleased to commit to my charge. I had by then already in talk at Admiralty House had Rumour of such a duty and I had no desire to prejudice my chances of commanding another expedition, and one of such far-reaching possibilities. Mr Stevens was good enough to agree to this condition, replying that I would be employed whenever I asked to be.

So it was settled, and I had time to gather my thoughts.

Thursday, July 25th

Yesterday we had a fine gale at NNE which took us past Finister, the longitude of which Cape by the Watch and the mean of 41 lunar observations we made 9ϒ19′ 12 .* I do not intend to include in this Narration all our observations which are set down in the required Book, but only sufficient to remind the Reader of the purpose of the Voyage and indicate that I and my officers are constantly employed on this matter making the fullest use of the Instruments.

Capt Furneaux had brought back in the *Adventure* a native from Huahine, one of the islands which I had named the Society Isles. This had been somewhat against my wishes, knowing that this man would have to be returned there in due course. His name was Mae, but on my arrival in London I found he was known

*The actual position of Cape Finisterre is 9ϒ18′W, so that at this stage of the voyage a considerable degree of accuracy was being obtained with the improved instruments.

as Omai. Though far less intelligent than some that I could have delivered to London Society, he was of a most amiable disposition and had proved a great success, much as Ahutoru in Paris, whom M. Bougainville brought back. He has been presented to His Majesty, who has given him a sword and made him an allowance. He was lodged in Warwick Street, dined frequently in Society, stayed with my Lord Sandwich at Hinchinbrook Park, as well as with Mr Banks and Dr Solander, and various artists painted him, among them Mr Reynolds. They claimed he had even learned to skate. It really was most remarkable seeing him talking to the Ladies and remembering those jawbones hung up as indications of success in battle against the neighbouring islands which Mr Banks and I had seen on first going ashore from the *Endeavour* six years ago. But if any man should have been brought home by us it should surely have been Tupia without whose knowledge of those waters we should never have come safe through such a maze of islands and coral reefs.

He was in truth a strange and somewhat appealing figure, being so far from his native islands and trying without any great success to behave like an English gentleman, he not having much command of the language so that I was told he addressed His Majesty as King Tosh, that being the closest Otaheitan equivalent to King George that he could manage. The truth of this I am inclined to doubt, mentioning it only to show how there were stories current about him at the time of my return, Society being not so very different from a Ship and the currency of such stories a mark of popularity.

I do not myself possess these sort of qualities of publick appeal and never have, which is something always to be regretted by those whose nature is of a serious disposition and outwardly reserved. I was never regretful of this on board my ship, for a degree of remoteness is necessary to the command of men close confined. But since I could not change my nature and habit when ashore, I had some cause for regret at that time, my introduction to society again being not of the most successful.

I was much in demand it is true and paid the greatest attention and respect, but since it is not in my nature to be other than exact in answer to a question, I did find some time that when the Ladies enquired about even the most ordinary matters of seamanship, my explaining it to them was apparently so tedious that before I had finished they would have vanished from my side. At other times, while I was considering how I should reply to them in a manner that would be more easily understood, they would ask me about some other matter quite unconnected with the first. Something else of which I was always conscious was that, having no like background to the people I was meeting, I did not feel myself capable of engaging in general conversation and so was not at ease in their company.

I was, I must confess, more at home at the Mitre, the tavern where the Royal Society did used to dine, and I went frequently to Jacks Coffee House and

Young Slaughters to which Mr Banks had introduced me as a place frequented by artists and men of learning.

In November I was nominated for election to the Royal Society, something that was very close to my heart and a great honour. As well as Mr Banks and Dr Solander, also Mr Stevens, the Admiralty Secretary, there were no less than 22 other Members supporting me. It was March 7th of this year before I was finally admitted and in that same month my letter to the President, Sir John Pringle, on the health of seamen was reproduced in the Societys *Philosophical Transactions*. A great privilege.

Sir John Pringle, as well as being His Majestys physician, is also the authority on military hygiene and medicine. His was one house at which I greatly enjoyed dining, he being most hospitable to Mrs Cook and myself, and the discussions afterwards, and often at table, turning repeatedly to the problem of scurvy in ships at sea for long periods. We had, in fact, much to say to each other on this and similar subjects, and I greatly enjoyed these discussions, so full of facts and examples, in which I was able to explain the reasons for going ashore at each new anchorage to bring off vegetables and roots from which my crew might benefit by the improvement of their blood.

It was at one of these dinners that I met Mr Boswell, the friend of Dr Johnson, who listened most attentively to every thing I said. I met him again some two weeks later dining at the Mitre with Sir John Pringle and others of the Societys members. He seemed most anxious that I should take him on my next voyage, even though the discussion turned to cannibalism, a matter that was in everybodys mind and about which there was much curiosity after the bloody and unpleasant business at Ship Cove. Mr James Boswell was a writer with a most curious way of changing the meaning of words. At the end of the meal Sir John apologised for the poorness of it, whereupon Mr Boswell said laughingly something to the effect that he had had an excellent dinner because he had had a good cook, and he pointed at me, meaning I suppose that he had enjoyed our conversation. Everybody laughed heartily at this and we went on to Browns for coffee and then to the Royal Society.

Four days later he called upon me at Mile End, Mrs Cook giving us tea in the garden, and we talked for some time. Later he presented me with a signed copy of his book *Account of Corsica* in which he had written: *Presented to Captain Cooke by the Author, as a small memorial of his admiration of that Gentleman's most renowned merit as a Navigator, of his esteem of the Captain's good sense and worth, and of the grateful sense which he shall ever entertain of the civil and communicative manner which the captain was pleased to treat him.* I read the book immediately for what I could learn from it as to the best way to present travel to the Publick, it then being April and myself deeply engrossed in my own work, which I found no easy matter, the manuscript already so full of alterations and additions that it was difficult to read.

Wednesday, July 31st

We have been on deck the greater part of the night observing the Eclipse of the Moon through the Night Tellescope. By this means, and the use of the Ephemeris tables, our longitude was 15Υ35′30 , whereas by the Watch it was 15Υ26′45 . Clouds hid the Moon the greatest part of the time, particularly during the beginning and end of total darkness, so that our observations were not of the best. Tomorrow we shall anchor in Tenerife if the wind holds and there being much to do there, including the procuring of water as well as hay and corn and other articles we are in want of, also a description of the place to enter in my official Journal, I must now take this opportunity of giving some account of the work that occupied so much of my time ashore before the start of this Voyage.

Dr Hawkesworth, having died of a slow fever three years ago, I was spared the possibility of the preparation of my Journal being offered to him. In his account of the first Voyage, which I read at the Cape outward bound on my second Voyage, I found he had quite disregarded all my amendments and requests. He knew little of seamanship or navigation, had no knowledge or interest of the world I had explored, yet wrote as though he was the very person in command. A strange mannerism which I found most mortifying. And he adopted this mode of writing, not for my own Journal alone, but also for those of the other commanders* which were the subject of the first of his three volumes. He spoke thus with several voices, but it was all the same, his endeavour to entertain and thereby attract the attention and support of the Publick involving flights of fancy so that both I and the officers were for ever saying things we would never have said and in a manner foreign to us.

I was determined that this time the work should not get out of my hands. But I am not myself a writer, though I know very well what I wish to say and can set it down after a fashion. Three years in the Great Cabbin of the *Endeavour* in the close company of such learned gentlemen as Mr Banks and Dr Solander had much improved my ability to express myself. Whether my Lords, conscious of my lack of suitable education, had in fact proposed that Mr Forster should have charge of the work I do not know, but certainly that would appear to be his impression. Indeed, he went so far as to declare that he had made it a condition of his sailing with me on the second Voyage that he should write the history of it, receiving all the profits from the work in addition to a pension and the £4,000 voted by Parliament for the support of a man of learning on the expedition.

John Reinhold Forster had been recommended for the position by the Hon. Daines Barrington† after Mr Banks, Dr Solander and Dr Lind had all withdrawn

---

*The first volume of Hawkesworth's *Voyages* comprised three earlier voyages, those of Byron, Wallis and Carteret.

†A member of the Board of Admiralty.

from the expedition, the first in some dudgeon because he could not have the command of it. Many times during the voyage I had recalled with some nostalgia the pleasure I had had of the company of Mr Banks and Dr Solander in the *Endeavour*, and to have them replaced by this tedious, talkative, self-opinionated man so full of his own importance was hard to bear. And then, when we returned, to be faced with his arrogant demand that he, not I, should be in charge of the preparation of what was my own work. However, my Lord Sandwich conceived a neat solution to the problem. He requested Mr Foster to submit as an example of his work an account of our sojourn in Dusky Bay, that grim, forbidding inlet in the SW of the Southern island of New Zealand. He was given that section of my Journal to combine with his own recollections, and though it is generally supposed he got his son George Forster to do the writing, the specimen he finally produced proved less than satisfactory and was rejected.

This was in October of last year and I fear it was a terrible blow to his Vanity, for he at once indicated to Lord Sandwich that he could not be held responsible for the inaccuracies and vulgarities of expression he had found in my Journal. Lord Sandwich wrote immediately in my defence and afterwards there was some talk of a joint work, myself dealing with the navigation and Forster with the botanical material. But having lived with the man for so long I knew he would hang himself with the rope he had been given, and so from that moment I proceeded to work on the book in the certain knowledge that I should be sole author of it.

And so it turned out. But I was not so sure of my ability in this respect as to think it could be carried through without guidance. I discussed this with Lord Sandwich and he, having agreed, at once asked the Revd John Douglas Canon of Windsor to be my tutor. It is one thing to write day-to-day reports for their Lordships, quite another to prepare those same reports for press, even though they have been written in the form of a Journal. I have no proper command of grammar, spelling or punctuation, and for the Publick the work needs to be divided up into chapters, the longer sections into paragraphs, sentences shortened, and some rearrangement made in certain passages to give the Reader a sense of order. In part I was able to do this myself, but it would not have been so well done without the guidance of Dr Douglas, who was most helpful and painstaking, ensuring that any mention of the Amours of the People shall be unexceptional to the nicest of my Readers. And though His Majesty knew he was helping me, I do not think anyone except my friend Dr Shepherd was privy to the arrangement, Lord Sandwich making it very clear that it was best kept private. I think he was afraid Mr Forster would hear of it, he with his son George having been with me as naturalists and presuming he would have the writing of it. By then I fear my Lord Sandwich had had more than enough of that gentleman. Indeed, he once asked me how I had suffered him for three long years, but I said I had other matters to occupy my mind and scarcely noticed his presence after the first few days. The fact is that close contact with others and shipboard routine forces a man to keep a tight hold on himself. Forster was not a tenth as tiresome on the *Resolution* as he was ashore, perhaps because, like all of us, he had a settled position whilst he was on the Ship and work to occupy his mind.

That every man on board has activities to occupy himself even on long voyages seems to be something difficult of comprehension to those I talked with who have not been to sea. My attempts to answer them appearing tedious, I found they understood more readily when I indicated the crafts and trades represented on board. For example, on this voyage our total complement at present on board the *Resolution* is 114, which must appear a great number considering the size of the Ship and its ease of handling, but is not so great when it is understood how much of stores and gear must be seen to.

For the sailing of the ship, apart from myself and the 3 officers, Lts Gore, King and Williamson, there is the Master, Mr Bligh, 3 Masters mates and 50 able seamen. Of these last, 2 do duty as gunroom servants, 2 more are in the carpenters crew, one acts as cooks mate and Benjamin Lyon I can call upon when there is anything wrong with the Instruments, he being a trained Watchmaker. Also we have 7 midshipmen, and of course Mr Anderson and 2 surgeons mates. The Supernumaries on this voyage number only two, Mr Webber and Omai.

For other duties we have 5 Quartermasters, a

Boatswain and 3 mates, the Gunner with 2 mates, a Sailmaker and 1 mate, a Carpenter and 3 mates, a Cooper and Ships Corporal, and the Armourer and his mate. Besides which there is my Clerk, Alexander Dewar, and my servant, William Collett, who is also the Master at Arms. These are the men who look to the well-being of the Ship. For guard duties and for the maintenance of good order, and also for a disciplined show of our strength whenever it may be necessary among native peoples, we have a Sergeant, 2 Corporals and 16 privates of the Marines under the command of Lt Phillips.

All these men, together with our great quantity of stores, and also our livestock, would seem to make for some congestion on board. But they all have their place and duties, and with the seamen split into watches, so that there is never a time except in port when all are below, most do normally have more than the Navys allowance of fourteen inches space for each mans hammock. And the situation will be much improved when we are in warmer seas and many can find a place on deck to sleep without too great a disturbance. We had more on board last voyage and no complaints about conditions below, except the usual of wet quarters upon occasion.

CHAPTER THREE

A NEAR DISASTER

Monday, August 5th

We were in Tenerife some three days, anchored on the SE side of the Road of St Cruz. Being half a mile from the shore there was much work for the boats crews. I bought live bullocks, other cattle and poultry, also pumpkins, onions and potatoes which are the best keeping I ever had, but could wish for the Wine being near as good as that of Madeira, which it is not, though less than half the price at £12 a pipe. Of particular interest to me was the presence in the Road of the French frigate *Boussole*, Capt Bourdat* commanding, one of the Country's best navigators. In conjunction with a Spanish gentleman, Mr Varila, they made observations from a tent on the pierhead, comparing the Watches they had on board every day at Noon with the Clock on shore by signals.

Capt Bourdat was good enough to communicate

---

*His correct name was Jean-Charles Borda. He was well known as an experimental physicist and mathematician, also as an inventor of mathematical instruments.

these signals to us so that we could compare our Watch. The result was the same longitude within a few seconds, confirming that our Watch had not materially altered its rate of going. This is something that affords me considerable satisfaction for where we are bound on this voyage we shall have much need of an accurate timekeeper and no means of checking it. I have detailed all this more fully in my official Journal, being told by Dr Douglas that I should not in this more personal record involve my readers too much in the observations, they not being greatly interested in such information. This is something I find hard to understand, my whole life being so much taken up with astronomical observations and the mathematics of precise navigation for the purpose of determining any position accurately at all times and so drawing my charts correctly. Sufficient to say here that Capt Bourdat is charged with determining the exact position of the Peak of Tenerife.

I could have wished we had more of each others language, but not withstanding this difficulty I did enquire of him the latitude and longitude of the island his compatriot Capt Kerguelen had sighted in the S. Pacific and he did give it to me. It was not the big island, but a smaller island he had named Rendezvous. Its latitude by seven observations was 48ϒ26′S and the longitude by the same number of observations of the distance of Sun and Moon was 64ϒ57′E of Paris. By this means I shall be able to close the island even in Fog so long as I can obtain the observations required to establish my own position.

We weighed anchor yesterday, our course after clearing Tenerife SSW and helped on our way by a fine gale at NNE.

Sunday, August 11th

It is now 22 minutes after midnight and I have been on deck for the past 3 hours, the situation being for a short time most hazardous, and my own fault for believing we were well to the E of the Cape Verde islands with open water ahead of us. While I was here in the Cabbin writing my Journal, which I had been since shortly after sunset, I was conscious latterly of an increasing sense of unease. This is something that I have learned never to disregard for it has many times saved us from danger, though not on the occasion of our grounding on the Barrier Reef when I had no such feeling but was fast asleep.

I had left the navigation to Mr Bligh,* who at 21 may be regarded as very youthful to be Master, but he has proved a most excellent navigator and seaman, as indeed he was recommended to me. This unease that I have sometimes felt is a most strange thing, very common among masters and captains who have spent long periods at sea in the same ship. It is as though Captain and Ship were one and the Ship a sentient being aware of danger and capable of communicating

*William Bligh, notorious for his command of the *Bounty*, a brilliant seaman and navigator whose appointment as Master at such a young age and after only 6 years in the Navy is surprising and remarkable.

the awareness to the one person who can order action to avert it. The interest of writing caused me to ignore the message I sensed in the movement of the Ship and the sound of its timbers, so that I had almost left it too late, wishing to complete the official Journal to this date and continue my explanation of how it transpired that I was able to prepare my Journal for press and the guidance I had from Dr Douglas.

After the lamplight in the cabbin it was a little while before I had accustomed my eyes to the darkness on finally going on Deck. We were continuing on our course of SSW and I was peering to starboard, when suddenly land was sighted over the bow and I made out the unmistakable shape of Bona Vista island. I had not forgotten the SW-going current to be expected in the neighbourhood of the Cape Verde islands; indeed, I had warned Mr Bligh before going below, but either our position by the Watch at the noon observation was at fault or the set of the current was a good deal stronger than I had believed possible.

It is likely that both affected the present position of the ship, for on hauling to the Eastward, which was the best we could do to get out of the danger, it became clear that we could barely make enough speed through the water to counteract the current setting us down on to the island, and we had a very unhappy three hours of it, the island getting nearer all the time. Even when we appeared to be clear of it, this proved not to be the case, for I saw my surgeon, Mr Anderson, standing at the starboard rail staring intently, and when I joined him I also made out a loom of white extending beyond the last headland, which was the break of waves on a reef lying to the SE of the island.*

Our situation for a few Minutes was very alarming so much so that I did not dare sound the bottom for fear that the rocks would be as close under the keel as the coral had been on Endeavour Reef and that the leadsman crying the depth should cause so new and inexperienced a crew to lose their nerve. For those few Minutes I held my breath, as I imagine did the other officers, the white of breaking waves so close in the darkness and audible over the sounds of the ship driving through the water. Once we were clear, I noted that Mr Bligh was shouting his orders very loud, which though natural was regrettable, all of us feeling that same sense of relief, but not expressing it.

Now that I am back in the Cabbin again and the ship on its proper course of SSW I must give some thought to the Cause whereby the ship was put in a position of such hazard. I have not spoken with any of the officers on the matter, wishing them to regard it as of less importance than I know it to be. No doubt I have become so accustomed to this run down the Atlantic that I take our safe arrival at the Cape for granted. But to run so close to the Cape Verdes, presuming upon the accuracy of my position, and thereby placing ourselves at the mercy of the current, is something outside of my normal practice.

Is it that I have become too accustomed to relying on my officers and particularly the Master, being so

*This reef, called Domingos dos Sentos or Ninho do Guincho, extends some 2¼ miles south east of Bona Vista.

well served on my last Voyage? Or have I become less careful? If it is myself that is to blame in that I have become over-confident as the result of having been in so many dangerous seas and brought my ship through safely, then that is a serious matter that can be attributed to nothing less than some fatigue of the mind. So often I have seen bodily tiredness lead to a lack of mental alertness. I do not feel tired, though the last year has been a very full one and not at all easy. I recall that my Lord Sandwich and others of the Admiralty were most considerate in not proposing me for this command, but waited upon my offering myself, whereupon they accepted, seemingly with great relief.

I was certainly a tired man when we emerged from the Southern Seas more than two years ago now. We were altogether sixty-six days south of Latitude 60ϒ, reaching as far south as 71ϒ10′ on 30th January 1774, and during all that time I had very little sleep being constantly on deck. But I had fully recovered by the time we had completed the long voyage home from New Zealand. Indeed, it seems that I was looking a deal better than when I had left three years before, Dr Solander saying so in a letter to Mr Banks who passed on to me the good doctors estimate of my state of health, seeming much pleased that I was so full of vigour. But since then I have had much to do.

Apart from the preparation of my Journal, and all the difficulties with Mr Forster who was cutting his own throat and blaming everyone else, there was from as early as mid-December of last year the business of searching for a ship to accompany the *Resolution* on the Voyage, their Lordships having entrusted me with the finding of it. And about that time my wife discovered herself to be with child again. My dear Elizabeth is such a very comfortable, easy, companionable person, so efficient a housekeeper and so uncomplaining, that at no time did she give me any cause for alarm. But the fact is that this little boy, who was born only a few months since in May and baptised Hugh, though the fifth of my children, is the first at whose entry into the world I have been present. And knowing by then that I was shortly to leave on a further voyage I think we both had cause for feeling closer than ever to each other.

This is not a matter that should in any way have exhausted me, but it added to my responsibilities at a time when I was deeply committed to other activities, not least to my election to the Society and my writing of the paper on Hygiene at sea. And there was that dinner my Lord Sandwich gave when I said I would command the expedition with all the resulting letters and organisation, as well as the tiresome business of sitting for my portrait by the painter Mr Dance, which was kindly commissioned by Mr Joseph Banks, in admiration of me, he said.

All together there was so much to do, so many demands on my time and energy, that I may well be more tired than I feel myself to be. And then to find the ship ill fitted out and leaking, Clerke in prison and the *Discovery* left to follow after us. I must now watch myself, keep a hold on my temper and curb that irritableness which Mrs Cook has so often remarked upon. But at least I am not of a melancholy disposition though sometimes accused of it, those who do not like me mistaking silence and an inclination to careful thought for that condition of mind.

PART TWO

DOWN THE ATLANTIC AGAIN

CHAPTER FOUR

RUSSIAN MAPS

Friday, August 30th, 1776

Now at last we have picked up the Trade Wind, the interval since I previously wrote being full of disappointment and frustration. At day break following our being set so close upon that reef I hauled to the Westward to pass between Bona Vista and the isle of May intending to close the island of St Iago, I having told Capt Clerke he could meet up with me there at Port Praya. In this way we had sight of the rocks we had so nearly gone down upon and during that day and the next we made every attempt by sounding to determine the rate of the current, which we found to set SWbyW something more than half a mile an hour. We were off Port Praya at 9 o'clock in the morning of Tuesday 16th, there being 2 Dutch Indiamen anchored there, also a brig, but no sign of the *Discovery*, and having expended but little water we stood on to the southward.

We now lost the NE trade and there followed more than two weeks in which the condition of the ship rendered living on her very unpleasant, the wind being from SW blowing some times fresh and in squals, the weather generally dark and gloomy with frequent rains. These rains enabled us to fill those water casks that were empty, but that was all the good we got of them, the ship proving extremely leaky in all her upper works, the hot dry weather we had recently experienced having caused the bad caulking of the deck to open up, even the sides of the ship, so wide that the water came in as it fell. Not a man had a dry bed and the officers in the gunroom driven out of their cabbins.

It is on this passage that I find it particularly necessary to be on my guard against disease by obliging the people to dry their clothes and take every opportunity to air the ship with fires and smoke, which is never to their liking. I am glad to say that as a result of this, and despite the leaking of the ship, I have fewer men sick than on either of my former Voyages. And we had fresh fish, Omai proving very apt to the sport, catching twice as many of the small dolphin* that were about the ship than anyone else, he using a rod with a white fly.

Unfortunately, there was little we could do about the sails, they being very wet with the water getting in to the sail rooms and some quite ruined. Having experienced this problem on my previous Voyage I had made representation to the yard officers at Deptford, who undertook to rectify the matter, but it would

*This is almost certainly the true dolphin, which is a fish found in warm waters, not the relative of the whale which we generally called dolphin.

appear that either my representations were ignored or the work skimped. We shall I have no doubt a great deal of trouble with the Canvas and the sailmakers much unnecessary work in the future. And now that we have the SE trade and conditions more settled the caulkers are set to work caulking the decks and the inside Weather works of the Ship.

Having done all that is possible for both Men and Ship, I shall now have some time to write about the purpose of the Voyage and what I did while I was ashore to prepare myself for it. This being quite different to my official Journal I shall keep under Lock and Key, for I have no intention that the men shall learn about my innermost thoughts, and the knowledge that our ultimate destination is into the ice of the North Polar regions would be the surest way to induce desertion once we are in those friendly and hospitable islands of the Pacific. Ignorance of my intentions is I am convinced the best safeguard against the need to exercise the full penalties of Naval Discipline, something I am always willing to do for the good of the Ship and her People, but which I know from my own experience in the lower decks is in some degree to fail in the proper leading of the men under my command.

But I must leave this for a moment, it being close on Noon and my presence on deck being required for the Azimuth . . .

Saturday, August 31st

It is six months since I wrote that letter in the Admiralty office formally offering myself for command of the expedition, the which I had already and perhaps rashly done at my Lord Sandwich's dinner table. Between that date and the start of the Voyage among other matters that occupied me was the necessity of learning everything possible about the seas to which I have committed myself, my officers and my men, and to gather together such maps as exist, which is very few. This, as has been evident in the recent rains, proved greatly to the disadvantage of the Ship, for together with the preparation of my Journal, it left me little time for looking to the fitting out, victualling and all the other matters to which I have usually given close attention.

But first I must explain why I offered myself for the Voyage, or perhaps it would be more honest to say that I must now endeavour to explain it to myself, for now that I contemplate setting it down I find myself in some difficulty since I am not sure what it was that induced me to leap to my feet at the dinner table, fired by the nature of the arguments, hopes and speculations, to announce to the others, they being my Lord Sandwich, Sir Hugh Palliser, the Comptroller of the Navy Board, and Mr Stevens, the Secretary, that I would take command if that was their wish.

Undoubtedly it was to some extent due to the feeling that prevailed on this matter of the North West Passage at the time of my return to England last

August, particularly among the Members of the Board of Admiralty, the Government and the Royal Society. Since the arrival of the *Ceres* from the Cape with my Journal all had known that there was no Southern Continent offering the prospect of increased trade. This hope being finally dispelled, and the Prince Minister, Lord North, himself ignoring Mr Dalrymples request to be sent out at his own expense to colonise the Isle of Georgia* discovered by the *Leon* in 1756 and which I had described in such terms that made the prospect of colonisation unthinkable, all eyes were now turned once again to the North Polar regions and the question of the Passage through between the Atlantic and the Pacific oceans. Such a passage for ships trading to China, the Indies, and all the islands of the Pacific I had claimed for the Crown would be of great advantage to the commerce of our Country.

Belief in the existence of this Passage was of long standing. They tell me it is referred to in a posthumous Hakluyt which claims that a Greek pilot, Juan de Fuca, was sent in search of the Passage which was then called the Strait of Anian. North of Lat. 47° on the west coast of America he entered an inlet and after sailing for 20 days came out into the Atlantic and then sailed back again through this same passage. According to the Notes I have made, this was in 1592 and was the origin of this belief, which was held so firmly that in 1670 the search for it was written into the Charter for the setting up of the Hudsons Bay Company.

*The name Cook gave to South Georgia.

Saturday evening

The men who have searched for this Passage are very numerous. They include Frobisher, Davis, Hudson, Baffin. But except for Sir Francis Drake and some others, including the Spaniards sailing north from the Pacific ports of their American colonies, they have all approached it from the Atlantic. And the Hudsons Bay Company has only recently, and that under the strongest compulsion, undertaken exploration with this in view, and then all of them by land, except Govnr James Knight who took 2 ships up the west side of Hudsons Bay but found no tide to sweep him through to the Pacific. Though he lost his life in the attempt I do not think he was very serious in his endeavours being more interested in gold.

I did myself make representations to the Company, both personally and through my friends, but like the East India Company and other big City of London adventurers they proved most secretive, only pointing out that their Govnr after Knight, Henry Kelsey, got further than any man before him across the North American continent, but that there is no great hope of a sea route, the land being very bleak in its northern parts and Ice most months of the year. Kelsey wrote a Journal, the which an Irish gentleman Mr Dobbs has in his possession, this being the origin I am told of his extreme interest in the Passage.

It was Mr Dobbs who persuaded the Admiralty to obtain Royal consent for a naval expedition. This was in 1741, he having written a memorial on an easy sea route to China ten years before. Capt Middleton, late of the Hudsons Bay Company, was employed in this venture, but found the current from E and no way to the Westward from Hudsons Bay. And then in 1745 Parliament enacted a reward of £20,000 for the discovery of the Passage and some London merchants tried but failed. Finally one of the Companys servants, Samuel Hearne, put an end to hopes of a passage from that direction by journeying overland from Fort Churchill at the bottom of Hudsons Bay to the North Polar Sea without crossing any river or salt sea passage.

As with that great southern Continent, *Terra Incognita*, de Fucas Passage through the North American continent would appear another dream of those geographers and map-makers who let hopes rather than observations direct their pen. Nonetheless, Mr Daines Barrington, who is a member of the Council of the Royal Society and a friend of my Lord Sandwich, believes in it absolutely, so much so that in December of last year he persuaded Parliament to extend the Act offering £20,000 to him who first discovered the Passage and he also persuaded them to include a reward of £5,000 for all the People of the first ship to sail within 1° of the North Pole, being I fear one of those who believe that there is not any ice in the North Polar sea.

This matter of reward was the subject of some conversation between Mrs Cook and myself, since were I to discover the Passage it would be to the considerable advantage of all our household. I was never at any time offered any personal inducement, but in conversation with my Lord Sandwich and others before I even offered myself for the service, it was understood that whoever was successful would not be lacking advancement and afterward it was repeated. By which I understood there would be promotion from my present rank of Post-Captain and Sir John Pringle also hinting to me that there would be proper recognition of the achievement, I took him to mean that my service would merit some honour, the which I understood an honour bestowed by His Majesty.

Now that I am at sea, so far on my voyage that tomorrow we shall cross the Equator, I find I view this matter somewhat differently, being conscious of the Difficulties and Hazards that lie ahead. But at home in Mile End discussing it with my dear Elizabeth the prospect of position and the monies to uphold it quite dazzled us both. She, however, thought nothing of it so much as the danger to which I might be exposed and I do not recall that she expressed anything more than satisfaction that my Voyages be afforded proper recognition.

Thus I can say that it was not she who persuaded me to offer myself for the command of the Voyage. Nor I truly believe am I ambitious of such recognition or particularly desirous of the rewards. It was the challenge and the distress I felt ashore that my capability in Navigation was not being used for the service of my Country at a time when we were at war. It was not a sudden decision, though it may well have appeared so to Lord Sandwich and the other two gentlemen being entertained by him that day, but was come to gradually so that my leaping to my feet and declaring I would go if they so wished was well considered beforehand if abrupt in the stating of it.

Sometimes when I am alone in my cabbin I think about this and wonder if I was right. And since I never did such a thing before, accepting all my instructions as part of the service for which I had volunteered those years ago, I fear it is a mark of age. This Voyage will see me past 50 and approaching that I am aware that my mind is become more reflective, to which I attribute my committing my thoughts to paper in this way, something I would never have done when I was younger.

Now I must turn the Readers attention to the Russians, who for more than a century past have interested themselves in the northernmost part of the Pacific. The first voyage of discovery they undertook proved that Asia and America were not joined in the upper part, but the mapmakers taking no note of this the Czar ordered a ship out of the Kamtschatka river commanded by Behring who was a Danish captain in their service. He reached latitude 67Υ8′N and having no sight of the North American land presumed he was in a strait separating the two continents. This strait is shown in a map contained in a new book published 2 years since, also the many islands some of which Lt Sindo reported on his voyage some years ago.

This book, called *An Account of the New Northern Archipelago, Lately Discovered by the Russians in the Seas of Kamtschatka and Anadir*, was brought to the attention of the Royal Society by the Secretary,

Dr Maty, and an English translation having been made, I have it with me on board together with the map. It is the most recent and accurate I can get, including the observations of Behring and Tschirikow sailing from Petropaulowska in 2 ships. I also have on board the older book *Voyages from Asia to America* which includes a map showing Behrings first voyage, also that of Gvodzev, and was translated to English in 1761. Among the other maps I have are 2 French and John Greens of 1753.

But the map I must rely upon, in so far as I dare, is the new one, which the Society referred to me as the Stählin map because it was first printed by Jacob von Stählin of the German Academy of Sciences. It is much to be preferred to the Müller of 1758, being more recent and showing the NW coast of N. America much broken with islands, the largest of which are called Alashka and Unalashka, and there is also a line of smaller islands name Aleutskia.

CHAPTER FIVE

CROSSING THE LINE

Wednesday, September 4th

We crossed the Equator last Sunday and those
who regarded themselves as veterans of the
Equatorial Line, having for the most part crossed but
twice on the outward and homeward passage, did see
to the Ducking of all those who had never crossed it.
I know Capt Clerke will have none of it if he is on
board the *Discovery*, issuing Grog by way of compen-
sation, and my surgeon, Mr Anderson, has expressed
a strong view of this in my hearing, supported by Mr
Bligh to my great surprise. But it is the custom and
to my thinking customs are important, giving some
opportunity for merriment among the men. That there
is some danger in it I do not accept, believing there to
be as much hazard to the Ship and her company in
the issuing of spirits, there being at the time a gale
from SEbyS.

I well remember Mr Banks being greatly shocked
at the state of our crew during Christmas Day 1768
when we were running down towards Cape Horn, he

noting that by night fall all the crew were 'abominable' drunk and declaring his thanks to God for a moderate breeze since if it were otherwise he did not know 'what would have become of us, there being scarce a man sober enough to work the ship'. He did of course not fully understand how very easy these vessels are to work and that the officers could readily have handled her if the need arose.

I believe altogether upwards of 40 men were Ducked. All I wish to say on this matter is that men who have to live for months, indeed several years, close confined within the wooden sides of their ship are subject to as much despair, disaffection and enmity as any like number of prisoners, so that unless they are afforded excuse and opportunity for the release of their spirits they will make trouble. And this being something I do my best at all times to avoid, I consider it no advantage at all to save some from discomfort at the hands of others when all expect of the crossing of the Equatorial Line a day of frolicking. It is a break in the shipboard routine, they behaving like children let from school and the officers like tutors keeping as much apart from the activities as is conducive to the safety of Men and Ship.

During the last week or more we have had the pleasant distraction of watching the flying fish so common to this area and when we can catch them they are very good eating. We also have had a great number of porpoises around the ship which pleases everyone, also bonitos, puffins and boobies, and the men have had some sport catching sharks. Two days ago, and again this evening there has been a great display of luminosity in the water, the phosphorous clinging to the sides of the ship and to anything, even a line, that is wet. This is the same we saw in the *Endeavour* when there was great discussion as to the cause of it. But here again Mr Anderson, who is much interested in Natural History and has made a study of it, could find no small sea creature in the water that was lifted on board to explain it.

CHAPTER SIX

SECRET INSTRUCTIONS

I believe this to the most convenient place in the Narration to direct the Reader's attention to the Secret Instructions, which were delivered to me in a sealed package on board the *Resolution* at Plymouth by Butler, the Admiralty Messenger, on July 6th, four days before we sailed. Without sight of these the direction I am taking to achieve the primary object of the Voyage would not be clear. A copy of these Secret Instructions was also delivered to the *Discovery* with a note to Capt Clerke that he was not to open them unless he failed to meet up with me at any of the ports at which I had left orders for him to meet me.

Copy of Secret Instructions made by me
off the Coast of Brazil
Wednesday, September 4th

By the Commissioners for
executing the office of Lord
High Admiral of Great
Britain & Ireland &ca

*Secret Instructions for Capt James Cook
Commander of His Majesty's Sloop the
Resolution.*

Whereas the Earl of Sandwich has signified to us
His Majesty's Pleasure that an attempt should be
made to find out a Northern passage by Sea from
the Pacific to the Atlantic Ocean; and whereas we
have in pursuance thereof caused His Majesty's
Sloops Resolution & Discovery to be fitted in all
respects proper to proceed upon a Voyage for the
purpose abovementioned, and, from the experience we have had of your abilities & good conduct in your late Voyages, have thought fit to
intrust you with the conduct of the present
intended Voyage, and with that view appointed
you to command the first mentioned Sloop, and
directed Capt Clerke, who commands the other,
to follow your Orders for his further proceedings;
You are hereby required and directed to proceed
with the said two Sloops directly to the Cape of
Good Hope, unless you shall judge it necessary
to stop at Madeira, the Cape de Verd, or Canary
Islands, to take in Wine for the use of their Companies; in which case you are at liberty to do so,

taking care to remain there no longer than may be necessary for that purpose.

On your arrival at the Cape of Good Hope you are to refresh the Sloops Companies, and to cause the Sloops to be supplied with as much Provisions and Water as they can conveniently stow.

You are if possible to leave the Cape of Good Hope by the end of October, or the beginning of November next, and proceed to the Southward in search of some Islands said to have been lately seen by the French in the Latitude of 48Υoo′ South and about the Meridian of Mauritius. – In case you find those Islands, you are to examine them thoroughly for a good Harbour, and upon discovering one make the necessary Observations to facilitate the finding it again, as a good Port, in that Situation, may hereafter prove very useful, altho' it should afford little or nothing more than shelter, wood, & water. You are not however to spend too much time in looking out for those Islands, or in the examination of them if found, but proceed to Otaheite or the Society Isles (touching at New Zealand in your way thither if you should judge it necessary and convenient) and taking care to arrive there time enough to admit of your giving the Sloops Companies the Refreshment they may stand in need of, before you prosecute the farther Object of these Instructions.

Upon your arrival at Otaheite, or the Society

Isles, you are to land Omiah at such of them as he may chuse and to leave him there.

You are to distribute among the Chiefs of those Islands such part of the Presents with which you have been supplied as you shall judge proper, reserving the remainder to distribute among the Natives of the Countries you may discover in the Northern Hemisphere; and having refreshed the People belonging to the Sloops under your command, and taken on board such Wood & Water as they may respectively stand in need of, you are to leave those Islands, in the beginning of February, or sooner if you shall judge it necessary, and then proceed in as direct a Course as you can to the Coast of New Albion, endeavouring to fall in with it in the Latitude of 45Υ0′ North; and taking care, in your way thither, not to lose any time in search of new Lands, or to stop at any you may fall in with, unless you find it necessary to recruit your wood and water.

You are also, in your way thither, strictly enjoined not to touch upon any part of the Spanish Dominions on the Western Continent of America, unless driven thither by some unavoidable accident, in which case you are to stay no longer there than shall be absolutely necessary, and to be very careful not to give any umbrage or offence to any of the Inhabitants or Subjects of His Catholic Majesty. And if in your farther progress to the Northward, as here after directed, you find any Subjects of any European Prince or

State upon any part of the Coast you may think proper to visit you are not to disturb them or give them any just cause of offence, but on the contrary to treat them with civility & friendship.

Upon your arrival on the Coast of New Albion, you are to put into the first convenient Port to recruit your wood and water and procure Refreshments, and then to proceed Northward along the Coast as far as the Latitude of 65°, or farther, if you are not obstructed by Lands or Ice; taking care not to lose any time in exploring Rivers or Inlets, or upon any other account, until you get into the beforementioned Latitude of 65°, where we could wish you to arrive in the Month of June next. – When you get that length, you are very carefully to search for, and to explore, such Rivers or Inlets as may appear to be of considerable extent and pointing towards Hudsons or Baffin Bays; and, if from your own Observations, or from any information you may receive from the Natives (who, there is reason to believe, are the same Race of People, and speak the same Language, of which you are furnished with a Vocabulary, as the Esquimaux) there shall appear to be a certainty, or even a probability, of a Water Passage into the aforementioned Bays, or either of them, you are, in such case, to use your utmost endeavours to pass through with one or both of the Sloops, unless you shall be of opinion that the passage may be effected with more certainty, or with greater possibility, by smaller Vessels, in which case you are to set up the Frames of one or both the small Vessels with which you are provided, and when they are put together, and properly fitted, stored, & victualled, you are to dispatch one or both of them under the care of proper Officers, with a sufficient number of Petty Officers, Men, and Boats, in order to attempt the said Passage; with such Instructions for their rejoining you, if they should fail, or for their farther proceedings if they should succeed, in the attempt, as you shall judge most proper. But nevertheless if you shall find it more eligible to pursue any other measures, than those above pointed out, in order to make a discovery of the beforementioned Passage (if any such there be) you are at liberty, and we leave it to your discretion, to pursue such measures accordingly.

In case you shall be satisfied that there is no Passage through to the abovementioned Bays, sufficient for the purposes of Navigation, you are, at the proper Season of the Year, to repair to the Port of St Peter & St Paul in Kamtschatka, or wherever else you shall judge more proper, in order to refresh your People & pass the Winter; and, in the Spring of the ensuring Year 1778, to proceed from thence to the Northward as far as, in your prudence, you may think proper, in further search of a North East, or North West Passage, from the Pacific Ocean into the Atlantic Ocean, or the North Sea; and if, from your own Observation, or any information you may receive, there shall appear to be a probability, of such a Passage, you are to proceed as above directed; And, having discovered such Passage, or failed in the attempt, make the best of your way back to England by such Route as you may think best for the improvement of Geography and Navigation, repairing to Spithead with both Sloops, where they are to remain 'til further Order.

At whatever Places you may touch in the course of your Voyage, where accurate Observations of the nature hereafter mentioned have not already been made, you are, as far as your time will allow, very carefully to observe the true situation of such Places, both in Latitude & Longitude; the Variation of the Needle; Bearings of Head lands; Height, Direction, and Course of the Tydes and Currents; Depths & Soundings of the Sea; Shoals, Rocks &ca; and also to survey, make Charts, and take views of, such Bays, Harbours, and different parts of the Coast, and to make such Notations thereon, as may be useful either to Navigation or Commerce. You are also carefully to observe the nature of the Soil & the produce thereof; the Animals & Fowls that inhabit or frequent it; the Fishes that are to be found in the Rivers or upon the Coast, and in what plenty; and, in case there are any, peculiar to such places, to describe them as minutely, and to make as accurate drawings of them, as you can; And, if you find any Metals, Minerals, or valuable Stones, or any extraneous Fossils, you are to bring home Specimens of each, as also of the Seeds of such Trees, Shrubs, Plants, Fruits and Grains, peculiar to those Places, as you may be able to collect, and to transmit them to our Secretary, that proper examination and experiments may be made of them. – You are likewise to observe the Genus, Temper, Disposition, and Number of the Natives and Inhabitants, where you find any; and to endeavour, by all proper means, to cultivate a friendship with them; making them Presents of such Trinkets as you may have on board, and they may like best; inviting them to Traffick; and shewing them every kind of Civility and Regard; but taking care nevertheless not to suffer yourself to be surprized by them, but to be always on your guard against any Accidents.

You are also with the consent of the Natives to take possession, in the Name of the King of Great Britain, of convenient Situations in such Countries as you may discover that have not already been discovered or visited by any other European Power, and to distribute among the Inhabitants such Things as well remain as Traces and Testimonies of your having been there; But if you find the Countries so discovered are uninhabited, you are to take possession of them for His Majesty by setting up proper Marks and Inscriptions as first Discoverers & Possessors.

But for as much as in undertakings of this

nature, several Emergencies may arise not to be foreseen, & therefore not particularly to be provided for by Instructions beforehand; You are, in all such Cases, to proceed, as you shall judge most advantageous to the Service on which you are employed.

You are, by all opportunities to send to our Secretary, for our information, Accounts of your Proceedings, and Copies of the Surveys and Drawings you shall have made; and upon your arrival in England, you are immediately to repair to this Office in order to lay before us a full Account of your Proceedings in the whole course of your Voyage; taking care before you leave the Sloop to demand from the Officers & Petty Officers the Log Books & Journals they may have kept, & to seal them up for our Inspection, and enjoining Them & the whole Crew, not to divulge where they have been, until they shall have permission so to do. – And you are to direct Captain Clerke to do the same with respect to the Officers, Petty Officers, and Crew of the Discovery.

If any Accident should happen to the Resolution in the course of the Voyage so as to disable her from proceeding any farther, you are, in such case, to remove yourself and her Crew into the Discovery and to prosecute your Voyage in her, her Commander being hereby strictly required to receive you on board and to obey your Orders the same in every respect as when you were actually on board the Resolution; And, in case of your inability by sickness or otherwise to carry these Instructions into execution, you are to be careful to leave them with the next Officer in command who is hereby required to execute them in the best manner he can.

Given under our hands the 6th day of July 1776.

SANDWICH
C. SPENCER
H. PALLISTER

By command of their Lordships
Php Stephens.

On first reading these Instructions, and every time since, even now while I have been copying them, my mind has dwelt on those last lines. That their Lordships should require provision to be made in the event of the Commander falling sick or worse is normal practice in the Service. Nonetheless, it cannot but have the effect of causing me to think upon it, knowing that in the more than six years I have been at sea on two very arduous voyages I have been most fortunate, not only as regards sickness, but also as regards the safety of myself and the ship, we having been many times sailing close to most dangerous shores where no ship to my knowledge has been before, and some time have been ashore where the people are unfriendly.

From what I have learned, particularly from the Russian voyages, where we are intended to go now I may expect the worse as regards weather and ice, and both coasts and possibly the people also unfriendly. As early as February, just after I had been appointed to this Command, in a letter to Mr Walker of Whitby, to whom I was first apprenticed on board the *Freelove* and who offered me command of the *Friendship* when I was only 26, I did write something to the effect that I had quit an easy retirement for a Dangerous Voyage, adding that if I were fortunate enough to get safe home it would be greatly to my advantage.

There was never any other of those I corresponded with to whom I would have written thus, he being not only understanding of the dangers of the sea, but also a most benevolent person and to me something of a second father, having given me so much help and encouragement in what I most wished to do. Not even to Mrs Cook did I ever communicate my thoughts about the Dangers, nor shall do when I send to her from the Cape if there be some suitable ship at anchor to convey my report of the Voyage thus far to the Admiralty. It is something that is between me and my Maker, this feeling that no man can for ever be so fortunate as I have been until now and that a man approaching 50 cannot but view the hazards of attempting what so many others have tried and failed without some sober thought of the trials and difficulties ahead.

But I have said enough on this subject. I feel no different in myself than when I took the *Resolution* into those cold high latitudes of the Southern Ocean and so no cause to think we shall fare worse. Pray God Chas Clerke will catch up with me in Table Bay. At 33, he is the most experienced of my officers, devoted to his work and I believe to me, and what is more he is full of spirit and a goodly sense of humour, so making light of all difficulties. I should miss him greatly were he to be prevented from joining his ship.

CHAPTER SEVEN

A ROB OF LEMONS

Sunday, September 29th

All the remainder of this month there has been little to remark upon, save for the birds and the fish that are always with us. Also the seams have opened up again and when it rains water pours into the cabbins and the gunroom so that there is nowhere fit to sleep, all being wet. I keep the People as active and occupied as possible, but it being very warm there is little inclination to do more than is necessary. Now it is become a little cooler as we move into the S. Atlantic. As far as we can tell we have not been nearer than perhaps 20 leagues from the coast of Brazil, but nothing certain as we had no sight of land nor any bottom by sounding. Around 8°S, in the course we take for full advantage of the Wind, the land of Brazil protrudes so far to the Eastward that the danger of falling upon it at night is always of great concern, the current being an additional hazard. During three or four days we had it setting to the Westward and then for the period of at least a day it set strong to the

Northward, we being so much as 29 miles out in our reckoning.

But my greatest concern during the past weeks has been for the health of the People under my command, most of them quite unused to giving any sort of consideration to the state of their bodies until they have become diseased. Washing in sea water is done every day, and in this the officers as well as myself set the example, for the crowded state of the ship makes hygiene somewhat a case of the horse to water, for you cannot make him drink except you do it by example. This we learned in the *Endeavour* when they refused the portable soup, but when it was served to the officers, and they at my orders showing every sign of enjoying it, the men could not get enough of it.

We have this soup served on the Banyan Days which are the meatless days and in the Navy are Mondays, Wednesdays and Fridays, either with Pease or Wheat, which is to be preferred to the oatmeal we carried in the *Endeavour*. One ounce of the Soup is required for each man on those days, it usually taking about a quarter of an hour to dissolve, and it must be stirred all the time to prevent it burning to the copper.

I also ordered before we sailed the usual Sour Krout and Malt, also Sugar in place of Oil, a Rob of Lemons and Oranges which we had previously carried and an Inspissated Juice of Wort, which there is reason to believe from experiments may also be antiscorbutic. The Rob was made at the Apothecaries Hall and we had 5 chests of oranges and 5 of lemons delivered to the ships. The preparation of the Inspissated juice of

Wort was under the supervision of Mr Pelham and done at Mr Jacksons premises.

All this was arranged by letters from me to the Admiralty requesting that they instruct the Victualling Board accordingly. Thus far I am glad to say we have no sickness to speak of, every man being made to air his cloathes and bedding whenever possible and the ship aired throughout by ventilation as well as being cleansed by smoking pots set down in all the lower parts.

This is a rigorous routine and one that requires enforcement by firm discipline. Such discipline is more readily borne on the passage through the Atlantic Ocean both going out and returning since the men are fresh for the one and eager for home on the other. In the Pacific it is another matter, for there is always the distraction of the islands. The women are pleasing and all seem of the loosest morals so that it is hard to keep our Peoples hands off anything in the ship that can be traded for that which they most want. At the same time, we have the advantage of fresh food and an abundance of fruit and vegetables, something we never have in the Atlantic, not being able to call at any place and having to rely only on what we have in the ship. Thus it is on this passage that we most benefit of the Soup, Sour Krout and other items which have been specially prepared. It is to this, and the vegetables I purchased fresh before sailing into the heat and calms of Equatorial waters, particularly I believe the onions, that is the cause of the good health we enjoy. I am not speaking here of scurvy, which is a disease more common to the Pacific than to the Atlantic, though it is my strong opinion that the hygiene I do normally practise, and the fruits, roots and other fresh plants that I gather ashore at every opportunity and feed to the men is the cause of my being so free of this scourge.

I will have more to say of this later when I can describe the plants I shall bring off to the ship. There is always something to be found even in the bleakest places and it was Mr Banks and also Dr Solander with their knowledge of Botany that enabled me that first voyage to find everywhere something edible. Even when we were in the Le Maire Strait close by Cape Horn we found wild Sellery and scurvy grass and a sort of Cranberry but larger and the fruit of a bush which was very palatable with the shell fish that we prised from the rocks.

CHAPTER EIGHT

THE GREAT CABBIN

Sunday, October 6th

We are now far enough south to fall in with birds of colder waters and today we have seen albatrosses for the first time, Pintadoes and other Petrels, also 3 Penguins for which reason we sounded, but no bottom on a line of 150 fathoms. During this time I have given much thought and some study to the charts and maps of North America, something I could not do too openly and so had to see to it that the Cabbin was clear or at least the others so occupied that they would not take note of the work I was engaged upon.

I remember when the great Cabbin of the *Endeavour* was crowded with Banks, Solander and Spöring, who was their assistant, all busy studying and naming fish, birds, flowers and plants, and 2 artists, Parkinson and Buchan, engaged from morning to night drawing everything most exactly, so that often I had no place for my charts nor any room to do the work for which I had been commissioned. Now there is nobody on board to study specimens and only Mr Webber, who has been engaged as artist by the Admiralty at 100 guineas a year to make drawings and paintings, and those only of the places we shall visit.

So it is very quiet here in the cabbin in comparison to what it has been previously, for even on my late voyage I had among the supernumaries the Forsters and 2 draughtsmen who had been with Mr Banks on the expedition he made to Iceland. And there were always their servants in and out. For this voyage there is not even an Astronomer with me, Mr Bayly being posted into the *Discovery* for the better use of the instruments on board that ship. As a result I have quiet in the cabbin for my writing, but less time, there being a great deal of work for me to do in the care and setting up of all the varied astronomical and other Instruments and the observations to make, or otherwise to see to it that my officers do make them accurately.

I must confess, though I have learned to be solitary, and perhaps it is partly in my nature to be so or else has become so by habit, I do not entirely relish it. Thinking back to those times in the *Endeavour*, I find I enjoy the constant activity, the conversation and the excitement of new botanical discoveries and now miss it. Always I seemed to be learning something new. But not now, for there is nobody on board to tell me anything I do not already know, excepting possibly Mr Anderson. Mr Webber is a very quick artist and likes to draw birds as well as landscapes, but he is not very interested in the creatures we bring up from the sea in our net and so has little to do on this part of the voyage, there being few birds until now and no sight of land since we cleared the Cape Verdes.

Tuesday, October 8th

Today a Noddy was taken from our rigging, being birds that are very easily captured. Mr Webber is drawing it now and I have myself noted its arrival in my Journal, also the belief that they never fly far from land. This occasions us some concern since we are 100 leagues* at the very least from Goughs Island, which is a very precipitous and dangerous place being a volcano lifted up out of the sea and quite solitary in the great waters of this ocean. South of our present latitude being little frequented, there may be more islands than we know of.

One of the difficulties always to be faced in my voyage is the lack of any constant degrees of accuracy among sailors in the positioning of islands and coasts, they not having the benefit of the sort of instruments of navigation which I have on board, nor often the ability nor even the inclination to make exact observations of latitude and longitude. As for the mapmakers, I never can place absolute reliance on the results of their labours, excepting those charts of waters and ports that I know to have been properly surveyed. It seems that in their urgency to come out with a new Atlas or Map ahead of their rivals, they

*A league at sea is the equivalent of 3.18 nautical miles.

readily take supposition for observation and will draw in almost anything on the merest hearsay.

In regard to my Instructions, the maps I have most studied on the voyage thus far have been those of Müller* and Jacob von Stählin. The former is very open and honest in that he admits he has done no more than connect together by points according to probability the coasts that have been sighted. Both show the strait that Capt Behring claims to have sailed through reaching so far north as 67ϓ18' when he turned back, still having no sight of the shore. Both show the track of his ship the St Gabriel, the latter I think that more accurately. His later expedition with two ships did not progress so far north, but on this occasion both he and Chirikov separately did sight the N. American coast.

The other tracks shown on these maps are of Lt Sindos voyage in 1764–8 when he discovered and charted the Archipelago that is WSW from the coast of N. America, and the same is drawn on the Stählin map, the positioning of the islands of the Archipelago being in more detail, but a considerable difference in numbers, shape and position.

*Gerhard Friedrich Müller, official Russian historian.

PART THREE

THE CAPE TO NEW ZEALAND

CHAPTER NINE

TABLE BAY

Sunday, October 27th, 1776

We had sight of the Cape of Good Hope on the 17th, but did not anchor in Table Bay till a little after noon the following day, the wind blowing fresh the evening we arrived off Penguin Island. The *Discovery* is not yet arrived, the ships in the Bay being 2 French and a small Dutchman.

As soon as we were securely anchored in 4 fathoms, the Church bearing SW¼S, and had received the usual visit from the Master attendant and the Surgeon, I sent an officer to wait upon the Governor Baron Plettenburg, who had been most courteous to me on my previous voyage. On his return we saluted the Garrison with 13 guns, the like being returned. Afterwards, I went on shore with some of my officers and waited upon the Governor, his Second, the Fiscal and Major Prehn who commands the troops. All received me with the greatest respect and civility, promising every assistance.

I should I suppose feel flattered and indeed surprised

that my name and what I have done should be so widely known and so much acclaimed. And yet strange to say I am not, having now become used to it in a city so much bigger than Cape Town. I did not comment on this to the Governor, but 3 days before we came in here a French Indiaman parted her cable and drove ashore and the inhabitants far from helping plundered both Ship and Cargo. Such action is a disgrace to any civilised community and the Dutch it seems excuse themselves from being guilty of any crime by blaming the Captain for not applying for a guard in time, but when he did apply there were obstacles put in his way and on the guard finally arriving matters were not mended but worse than before. In short, Cape Town is a place where the Dutch regard all Strangers as fair game and as much to be got from them as is possible, whether the means are justified or not.

Having been told of these events by the French, I am now very careful, and constantly enjoin my officers to be on their guard, the which somewhat detracts from the civility and honour I receive officially. I had leave to set up our observatory wherever I wished, but the most suitable place was one where the Militia was exercising, so it was not until the 22nd that we had the tents for sailmakers and coopers ashore and all else we required, and it was the following day before we began to observe equal altitude of the Sun for ascertaining the rate of the Watch. Weather permitting this we shall continue every day until the time for our departure, the rate of the Timekeeper being of the utmost importance for the accurate determination of the position of the islands in the South Pacific that Kerguelen sighted and others nearer at hand that the French Lt Crozet spoke to me about when I met with him here at the Cape in March 1775.

Yesterday one of the French ships sailed for France and by her I sent a brief report to the Admiralty, also letters, my own and others. Whether they reach home safe I do not know, but am assured they will, the which I hope very much as I do not know when, nor by what means, Mrs Cook may hear from me again. The best hope is perhaps from some Russian port, and that a long way from England and not very reliable, since the Instructions I have for the Pacific and the route that I shall take makes the falling in with some other ship a most unlikely possibility.

On the 22nd I dined at the Garrison with the Governor and had 3 royal salutes of 21 guns and many Toasts.

CHAPTER TEN

THE DISCOVERY AT LAST

Thursday, November 28th

My anger and contempt for the Dutch is at times so great that I find myself almost shaking with it, they having behaved very perfidiously for all their protestations of respect.

But first I must state what has happened in the near 5 weeks since I last wrote anything here. I was ashore, and not in the ship, the better to overlook the observations and arrange all the stores we required. Apart from the arrival of the *Hampshire* Indiaman from Bencoolen, which saluted us with 13 guns, our replying with 11, no great event occurred until the evening of October 31st when it came on to blow exceeding hard from SE. This gale continued for 3 days and for that period all communication between ship and shore was impossible. The *Resolution* was in fact the only ship in the Road that did not drag her anchors. Ashore we had our tents and observatory blown to pieces and the Astronomical Quadrant was near ruined.

On November 6th the *Hampshire* sailed for England and I sent home in her the armourer Wm Hunt for trial, he being discovered making false coins. I handed him over to the Governor, since it was most like he made the money on shore and not on the ship. But the Governor would have none of it, so I had him disciplined and put on board the *Hampshire*, it not being my wish to have him cause any further trouble on the voyage and this being a civil matter. There were 3 men sick at the time which I would also have sent home, but that 2 of them, a carpenters mate and a quartermaster, I could ill spare and Mr Anderson had hopes of all three recovering.

Then on the 10th the *Discovery* came in. The sight of her that morning coming out of the rain and fog to anchor in the Road was a matter of great satisfaction and relief. It is never sensible, or at least should not be considered so, to take the risks necessary for the proper survey of unknown coasts but that there are two ships so that in the event one go upon a reef or be set ashore there is another to save the men in her. This was the situation on my first voyage, the *Endeavour* being alone in unknown waters for more than 3 years and when we went upon the reef off the north east coast of New Holland there was no other ship to help us and only good fortune and our own efforts saved us and brought the ship safe to an anchorage in the river further north along the coast.

My relief at the *Discovery*s arrival was the greater when Capt Clerke himself reported to me. He had sailed from Plymouth on August 1st, having got himself clear of the Israelites and out of that wretched prison into which he had been committed. He said he would have arrived a week earlier but that in a calm he was almost set down on Penguin Island, and having anchored was then forced by a gale of wind to fetch the anchor, a matter that took near on 2 hours such was the confusion on board. He had rode out the gale with North Passage open under his lee and had had good holding there.

He told it all so humorously that I felt the necessity of informing him what had happened to the Frenchman that was driven ashore and also that my need of a consort on the voyage was such that he must at all times exercise the greatest care for his Ship. In fact, I had not expected him earlier, for I had taken the most Westerly route down the Atlantic, sailing closer than heretofor to the coast of Brazil, thereby missing the Equatorial calms and having a reasonable fast passage.

The *Discovery* was also in want of caulking and this work being now finished on board of the *Resolution* I sent all my caulkers to work on his ship. I also gave him every other assistance to get on board his Water and the provisions I had already ordered. The bread I had ordered baked for the *Discovery* was not yet done for want of flour they said, but the truth of the matter was that the bakers had not thought she would arrive. This sort of pessimism is something that I have constantly to fight against. It seems to be in the nature of men that their spirits will not be lifted but the Commander is constantly letting it be known by the Rumours that are ever running between decks that he is sanguine of everything, including the outcome of the whole voyage.

CHAPTER ELEVEN

OF SHEEP AND GOATS AND THE WATCH

Now I must relate what has caused the anger to which I referred earlier. The night preceding the 14th some felons put dogs into the pen ashore where we kept our sheep, which numbered 16. They killed 4 sheep and the rest were broke out of the pen. Six were found next day, but 1 ram and 2 of the finest ewes were amongst those that were missing. The Governor being absent, I saw his Second and also the Fiscal, but their promise of action for the recovery of the animals was greater than their endeavours, so that I am not by any means convinced that some of the first people in Cape Town did not have a hand in the business.

This is a place where I am told that a slave with all his cunning and knowledge of the Country cannot escape from the Police, yet my sheep had no difficulty in evading the fiscals. I had recourse then to the scoundrels of the town, having been recommended to them by others who had suffered a like experience. These are men who for a suitable recompense will cut their

Masters throat, burn his house over him and bury his body and all his family in the ashes. Through them I recovered all but the 2 ewes. One of the rams being so badly injured it was doubtful he would live, Mr Hemmy, the Second Governor, offered to make good the loss, but I did not accept, satisfied that the Cape ram I had purchased would serve as well.

After this disaster I did not let those sheep that remained stay long on shore, but got them and the other cattle on board. And to the animals we already had I have now added 2 young bulls, 2 heifers, 2 young stone horses, 2 mares, 2 rams, some ewes and goats, also rabbits and poultry. They are intended for New Zealand and the islands of the Pacific, indeed anywhere where posterity may benefit from their being left.

The *Discovery* is now caulked and has got on board all her provisions and water. We have done the same, including everything I could think we might want in the next two years, for I did not know when we should come to a place where we could supply ourselves so well. This has been one of my chiefest concerns, for we sail in a day or two and once we lose sight of the Cape there is no turning back, and ahead nothing of certainty save the lands and islands I have already visited.

Much of my time has been taken up with the observations, but on the 23rd we got the Clock and the observatory on board having done I think all that we could to establish the rate of the Watch. I will not repeat the details of our calculations, which are all set down in the Book and also the Journal, only the results, which after 15 days of observations, taking the mean of them, we find the error of the Watch in longitude no more than 8'25 . Thus we had reason to conclude she had gone well all the way from England and the longitude that resulted nearer the truth than any other has given me. This is of great importance for the determining of currents, as off the coast of Brazil where from 2°N 25°W to 13°S 30'W in the space of 4 days we had an error in the Ships reckoning of 115 miles SWbyW the cause of which I now take to be a strong current setting in that direction.

Mr Anderson is now returned some days from a Wagon journey he made to Stellenbosh and other places in the vicinity of Cape Town. He is very full of all that he has seen, as are those that went with him, in particular the vineyards and orchards and the neatness of the farmhouses. His seeking for plants and insects was not well rewarded, but at Stellenbosh he and the others were entertained at a house that had a wine cellar and were received there with music, a band playing while they dined. Returning on the 20th much jolted by the Wagon he had all the insects he could wish, being much devoured by what he thinks may have been sandflies, the same we suffered from so badly last voyage when lying a month and more at Mr Pickersgills Harbour in Dusky Bay.*

---

*Dusky Bay is in South Island, New Zealand, a dismal place with a very high rainfall where I was plagued by sandflies on my visit there in 1970.

CHAPTER TWELVE

THE FIRST OBJECTIVE

Friday, December 6th

We are now at sea again and I back in the cabbin, having finally repaired on board the *Resolution* on the morning of November 30th after giving Capt Clerke a copy of my Instructions for the immediate voyage. I also gave him orders how to proceed in the event we become separated, the which I think less likely than happened with Capt Furneaux on the previous voyage, for though the *Discovery* is smaller and will sail slower, Chas Clerke is a much more tenacious man and understands my thoughts very well.

We had no wind on going aboard, but about 5 in the afternoon a breeze sprung up from the SE and we stood out of the Bay, saluting the Garrison with our guns and they replying. By 9 it was calm again and we anchored between Penguin Island and the East shore where we lay till 3 in the morning, when we weighed again with a light breeze at S. The wind remained somewhat light so that it was not until

December 3rd we got finally clear of the land with a fresh gale at WNW.

There is always a bad sea in the vicinity of the Cape and this occasion was no exception, the sea breaking with great violence over the ship and entering by way of the hatches so that all were very wet. But at the least the wind set us well on our way towards the first of the islands I wished to examine, which are those discovered by the French Capts Morion and Crozet in January 1772.

The fine start we had was something marred yesterday the 5th when we had the Mizzen Topmast brought down by a heavy squal of wind. The loss was not great, for it had given us cause for concern previously being a bad stick and we had another with which we soon replaced it.

Today we sailed through a number of small patches of sea that have a reddish colour. This was in the evening, our position being 39ϒ14′S, 23ϒ56′E, and when we brought up water in a bucket it had in it small creatures the size of a louse, which examined with the Microscope were like a kind of shrimp of a very red colour. These patches of red lie in streaks over the waves, even colouring the white as they break. I think them to be the same that Mr Banks and Dr Solander named when the *Endeavour* sailed through similar red patches coloured by minute crawfish in the South Atlantic. There was some talk then that they are the food of whales and porpoises for these animals were present in some numbers at the time.

Tuesday, December 17th

Though in the Southern Ocean, the weather we now have is such as we would expect in the north of England at mid-winter, very cold and thick with strong gales between north and west. Every man now has served out to him a good stout Magelline* Jacket and a pair of Fearnought Trowsers providing him with some protection against the weather, which though very indifferent, is not yet near as bad as we suffered on my late voyage when we sailed as far south as 71ϒ10′S among islands of ice, our rigging froze and watering the ship by sending boats to cut blocks of ice. Our clothing was ill-suited to those extremes of cold and I had a fire lit in the great cabbin.

Here we are no further south than Lat. 48ϒ25′S and it is the Fog that is my chiefest concern. Not a day passes but that we lose sight of the *Discovery* and it is only with the greatest difficulty and the most constant vigilance on the part of both that we are kept together. Conditions are most miserable for everyone, the ship leaking as before, all wet below and water getting in to the sail room, so that the sails must be brought out on deck to dry on every opportunity.

On the 12th we sighted the islands that Capt Crozet spoke to me of, there being two of them, the one larger than the other and very barren, the tops covered in snow. They were in Lat. 46ϒ53′S, Long. 37ϒ46′E. To distinguish them, they being unnamed on

*Presumably the jackets were named after Magellan, the Portuguese navigator, who entered and named the Pacific in 1520.

the French chart, I named the smaller Prince Edward Island, and that to the Southward, we passing between them, Morion and Crozet Island. Now my course is East for we are on the latitude given me by Capt Bourdat for the island Monsieur de Kerguelen named Rendezvous, though I do not know why since there can be no rendezvous here but for the fowls of the air. I am sailing a zig-zag course with the lookouts instructed to watch both ahead for the island and astern for the *Discovery* which we have again lost sight of, though continually hauling our wind to allow her to catch up with us.

It will soon be Christmas and a time when men who are at sea get drunk if they can, the reason I think being to dull the ache of thinking about their homes and families. When I consider how few Christmas days I have spent with Mrs Cook and our family it is not something I wish my mind to dwell upon and so shall keep occupied. There will be no great difficulty in this for we are searching blind for an island I sometimes believe does not exist. But this is only when the eyes get tired with staring into the white wall of vapour. I have the position, and I know it does exist, but reason is not easily sustained when for many hours at a time I am not able to see twice the length of the ship and we are firing a gun every hour so that we keep company with Capt Clerke by sound alone.

Any fears I have that we may suddenly find ourselves upon a reef I keep only to myself. Did the men, or even the officers, see how troubled I am, knowing there is a mass of sheer rock somewhere ahead of us, it would be instantly conveyed through the ship and everyone then afraid for their lives. Fear is something that is dreadful to contemplate on board of a ship, it being as contagious as the plague and equally dangerous since men are not then amenable to discipline, the marines equally so, with the result that there is nothing to prevent mutiny. Already the officers are talking among themselves. They do not see the purpose of exploring and charting these islands, not being privy to my Instructions and wondering all the time what the Plan of the Voyage really is.

CHAPTER THIRTEEN

CHRISTMAS, 1776

Friday, December 27th

Continuing to steer an Eastward course, the fog cleared somewhat and we saw land bearing SSE. This was at six on the morning of the 24th and the sight of it was the greatest relief, our navigation these past few days having been both tedious and dangerous, but as this is what I fear we shall have a great deal of in the northernmost limits of the Pacific I have considered it of considerable benefit to everybody, most particularly the officers.

Approaching the land we found it to be an island of some considerable height and about 3 leagues in circuit. There was another of the same magnitude to the east of it with smaller ones between, and with the fog breaking up we thought we could see land over the smaller islands. I had thought to steer between the two chief islands, but on approaching found it to be dangerous with the fog still about, they being to leeward and no way to run the ship off if we found no passage through. The wind was right on and a prodigious sea running that broke on all the shores of the island in a frightful surf. So I hauled off to wait for the fog to clear fearing we should become entangled among those islands in thick fog. Even so, we did but just weather the second of the larger islands.

By 11 o'clock, the weather clearing, we tacked and stood in for the land. At noon we had pretty clear observation, so that we were able to determine the position of the northernmost island as Lat. 48ϒ29'S Long. 68ϒ40'E. We were past the point of it which I named Blighs Cap by 3 o'clock in a fresh westerly gale and had land in sight, the same that we had seen above the small islands that morning. The left extreme of it appeared to be the headland Kerguelen had named Cape St Louis. It terminated in a perpendicular rock of some considerable height, and there appearing to be an inlet halfway along the coast, we stood directly for it, but finding it to be no more than a bend in the coast I bore up for the Cape and having rounded it, found the coast much indented.

I was seeking a harbour here for the night, but after making one board it fell calm, so I anchored off the first inlet in 45 fathoms black sand and sent Mr Bligh in to sound. He reported good anchorage, in every part a great plenty of fresh water and numerous seals, penguins and all manner of birds, but no wood. The *Discovery* was by then caught up. It being almost dark, both ships remained anchored in the entrance during the night, we observing that the flood ran at least 2 knots from SE.

And so on the morning of Christmas Day, with a gentle breeze at west, we worked to within a quarter of a mile of a dark sand beach, where we let go in 8 fathoms. I called this Christmas Harbour, though Capt Clerke had a poor day of it, he being very near set ashore on the southern point, his anchor starting before he could shorten cable and they having to sail with it still down, so breaking one of its palms. This appears to have been due to a fault in the metal.

It was very unlike other Christmases I have spent at sea, for we had no chance to celebrate, it being very urgent that we refill the water casks in case some gale of wind forced us to leave in haste. Water was very plentiful, as were the birds, and the seals being quite without fear we killed the number we required for the rendering down of their blubber into oil for our lamps. There were no trees nor a single shrub, and though the sides of the hills were a bright green, it was not grass, but a plant that grows very plentiful in these islands.

And after I had set all to work, I climbed a ridge of rocks that was piled up in stairs like the seats in a Roman amphitheatre. But having got to the top of it, saw nothing of the islands, the fog coming down so thick I had to call out for guidance otherwise I would have been lost. We had one of the seine nets the Admiralty had procured for me hauled across the entrance but with little success, so that we had to rely on birds for our fresh provisions and these we got in plenty.

The activities of both ships was so great that day that I doubt whether any man really believed it to be

Christmas Day. And the next day was no better, the filling of the casks with water having to be completed and all to be rowed back and forth between beach and ship, also grass for the cattle to be conveyed in the same manner after being cut from small sheltered areas at the head of the inlet where it did grow. All this work, and the killing of the seals and birds, was much hampered by rain, which was so heavy that the bare rock of the hillside was a sheet of water and every gully a raging torrent.

Thus it was not until today, the 27th, when I was fully satisfied that we were assured of a sufficiency of fresh provisions and water, that I was able to order the proper celebration of Christmas. Many of the men took this as an opportunity of exploring ashore and it was some relief in the evening to have a report that all were safe back on board and no-one lost. One of them brought a bottle to me he had found hanging to a rock on the north side of the inlet. It had a piece of parchment in it on which had been written:

> Ludovico XV galliarum
> rege. et d. de Boynes
> regi a Secretis ad res
> maritimas annis 1772 et 1773

thus making it clear that Kerguelen had used this same harbour when he first landed on this island February 13th 1772, which date is noted on the French chart of the Southern hemisphere. I did thereupon cause to be written on the other side of the parchment:

Naves Resolution
& Discovery
de Rege Magna
Brittanioe
Decembris 1776

and returned it to the bottle with a silver 2 penny piece
of 1772, which was Maundy money, two of which I
had of Mr Kings chaplain, my friend Dr Kaye. I had
the mouth of the bottle covered with a leaden cap and
tomorrow will erect a cairn in some prominent position at the head of the harbour as I have done at
various places on my voyages.

CHAPTER FOURTEEN

PLANTS AND SEAWEED

Wednesday, January 1st, 1777

Yesterday morning I was much relieved to have several observations of both Sun and Moon, something we had not been able to accomplish for some time due to fog and cloud. These showing no material error in the Timekeeper I am confident that we shall make our landfall correctly in Van Diemens Land,* which is where I am now headed, having left Kerguelens Islands on December 30th, the last of which I named the Island of Desolation it being even more bleak and sterile than the main land.

It is no way surprising that the first discoverers of it imagined this could be a cape of the Southern Continent, but we had a big swell from the south west, clear indication to anyone encountering it that there could be no mass of land in that direction. And Capt Furneauxs log, which I have with me, shows that after he had separated from me he sailed to the south of it

*At that time the name for Tasmania.

in such clear weather that he was able to establish his position by observation.

In the 6 days we were in the islands some considerable part of my time was taken up with examining such plants as there are, and also the numerous birds and the nature of the rocks, and in writing all this into my Journal. This is a labour I have come to regard as of equal, if not greater import than the preparation of accurate charts of the coastline, which had been my chiefest concern on previous voyages. The work that I did the year I was ashore in England preparing my Journal for press, the demand of the Publick for entertainment and information, and indeed the attitude of everyone I talked with, their Lordships and fellow members of the Royal Society included, has convinced me that, if I am to be suitably rewarded for all my endeavours, I have to use my time in the lands and islands I visit to produce a different sort of Journal, one that will appeal to the imagination and be ready for press immediately upon my return.

I shall be more than 50 years of age by the time I return. This will almost certainly be my last long voyage of discovery, my last and greatest opportunity to make my name and what I have done known to the larger world of the Publick. I have nobody, except my surgeon Mr Anderson, who is in any way understanding of natural history and must rely upon my own powers of observation, remembering what I learned from Mr Banks, Dr Solander and Mr Spöring, in the *Endeavour*, and to a lesser degree from the Forsters on my last voyage.

It is surprising that, even on these very barren islands, I was able to find plants that could be eaten to the benefit of everybody. Besides that sort of saxifrage, which made the hillsides so green they might have been covered by verdure, there was in the boggy declivities a plant growing quite plentifully about 2 feet high and not unlike a cabbage going to seed. It had 3 or 4 stalks growing separately from the root with long cylindrical heads composed of small flowers. It had the same appearance and the watery acrid taste of antiscorbutic plants, though being different it is to be regarded as peculiar to these islands. We all of us ate it raw, I firmly believe to the great advantage of our health, but when boild it had a rank flavour, though some of the men seemed not to notice this and thought it good whether boild or raw. Unfortunately, the seeds were not yet ripened, so that I could not take any with me to experiment with when Mr Nelson* the gardener is able to arrange the cultivation of kitchen gardens ashore for the benefit of the peoples we visit, this being I believe as important as the leaving ashore of our livestock in suitable places.

There was also 2 other plants growing by brooks or in bogs, one like cress but very fiery to the taste, the other quite mild. We did eat these as a sallad, and some also ate it boild when it too had a rank hot taste to use Mr Gores words who thinks it a good antiscorbutic. Altogether there are not above 18

---

*David Nelson, a gardener at Kew loaned by Banks, sailed in the *Discovery*, acting also as servant to William Bailey, the astronomer.

different plants, including various sorts of moss, a very pretty lichen and the grass we cut for our cattle.

I could wish that I knew more about the sea plants, and the uses to which they may be put. In particular, the weed that is like some form of kelp that we ran into after leaving Christmas Harbour, the same that we had encountered in the Le Maire Strait seven years ago and which Mr Banks identified as *Fucus giganteus*. Its stems are no thicker than a man's thumb, yet it grows to a most prodigious length, and not perpendicular to the sea bed, but at an acute angle.

We were steering SEbyS along the coast from the foreland I had called Hows after Admiral Lord How when we passed through a mass of rocks and islets, and afterward the sea ahead of us became chequered with large beds of this weed. The situation was hazardous, knowing the weed to be fixed to the bottom and always to grow upon rocky shelves, and the sea at the time being calm as a mill pond with no surge to reveal the hidden reefs. We steered through winding channels between the weed and after running in this manner for upward of an hour we chanced on a lurking rock just level with the surface of the sea right in the centre of one of these large beds of weed.

We were then about 8 miles off Hows Foreland across the mouth of a large bay with low islands and rocks in the entrance of it and more of these beds of weeds. After continuing our course half an hour I resolved it was so dangerous I hauld off to the Eastward to get into the open sea away from the land. But we were then into more weed and with the weather thickening, and we running over the edges of shoals with 10 to 20 fathoms depth, the moment we were over no bottom at 50 fathoms, I ordered Capt Clerke to lead in for the shore in search of an anchorage, the *Discovery* drawing less than ourselves. We were both of us anchored safely by 5 o'clock, just before it came on to blow so hard we had to strike our Topgallant yards.

I believe this weed to grow 60 fathoms* and more in length. Certainly we had no bottom on a line of 24 fathoms sailing through it and as I have indicated it grows at an acute angle to the bottom. Whether we shall encounter it with the same length of growth in the North Pacific as we do here I do not know, but encounter it I am sure we shall.

Sailing the ships along the dangerous coasts of these islands is a reminder to me of the hazards that lie ahead. It has had its uses, apart from observations and charting, for it has been a very practical warning to the officers, and I think to the men also, of the need of a constant watch and the readiness to handle the ships with the greatest alacrity.

*A fathom being 6 feet this gives the kelp a stem length of 360 feet and more.

CHAPTER FIFTEEN

ON BOARD
OF A CAT

I have always referred to the ease of handling these ships. There is none built anywhere that I have found so entirely suited to the purpose of surveying uncharted and dangerous coasts. This I have proved, never at any time wanting a better. Slowness of sailing is no disadvantage in this work. What is important is to be able to stop the ship dead and turn her in her own length, the which they do very readily. I am told they look clumsy, but that is only to those who have not sailed in them or who do not understand what is required of the work on which I have been so constantly engaged these last 8 years.

Something that was often asked of me ashore, particularly by the Ladies, was how big were the ships and what it was like to live so long on board of them. This was never an easy question to answer, for when I said the *Resolution* was of 462 tons berthen, it was immediately apparent that the tonnage gave them no idea of the size and all had to be converted into feet.

Thus we live on board of a ship that is almost 112 feet long at the level of the lower deck, 35½ feet at the greatest breadth and a little over 13 feet deep in the hold. The *Adventure*, my consort on the previous voyage, was of 340 tons, but in the *Discovery* Capt Clerke has one of the smaller colliers built at Whitby, the tonnage being only 298, the lower deck length 91 feet, breadth 27½ feet, depth 11¼ feet. When I arranged for their purchase the cost of the *Resolution* was £4151 and the *Discovery* £1865, but this was before the alterations necessary to fit them out for the purpose for which the Admiralty required them which was considerable.

They are, as can be seen from the measurements, very full-bodied and roomy with good Cargo space, the which is very necessary for we have of some provisions a full 3 years supply and are carrying a great number of livestock. So little room have we on board that Omai was forced to give up his cabbin to 2 horses when they were brought on board from the Cape, the which he seemed quite happy to do. But if we are more crowded than in some of His Majestys ships of war, at least we have the advantage of going on shore in various places and there is no threat to life and limb from the chances of battle. The leaking of the upper works had been a greater discomfort than the numbers that have to find room to lie in a small ship. At sea this is no great problem since watches greatly reduce the difficulty of accommodating the People below decks. And when we are at anchor in warmer waters, which we shall be after leaving New Zealand, the deck becomes a better place to sleep than below.

The question of what it is like to live on board these ships thus has no simple answer, but I can say that in all the years I have now been voyaging in them trouble with the men has never arisen on account of the confined space. There is most times plenty of work to keep them occupied, and when the ship makes no demands many follow the lead of myself and my officers and are busy writing their journals. Only when we are becalmed for too long a period do I have any reason to be concerned. And I know from all the reports of voyages that I have read that this is something that has been the bane of all commanders, most particularly in Equatorial regions where added to the heat is the dreadful presence of disease. This I am glad to say is something of which I have a different experience and I pray it will be so again on this voyage, which is why at every opportunity I bring on board fresh plants and roots and shall continue so to do.

CHAPTER SIXTEEN

VAN DIEMENS LAND

Sunday, February 9th

We have now traversed 105° of longitude in the 42 days since leaving the Island of Desolation, which is not much more than 100 miles each day though always carrying as much sail as possible. This we must do, for when we reach New Zealand, which we may do tomorrow if our observations are correct, we then have the whole Pacific Ocean ahead of us. From New Zealand to the Straits that Capt Behring discovered, and the sea passage across the N of America to the Atlantick ocean if any such Passage exist, it is 107° of latitude, a distance of some 2500 leagues in a straight line. But we cannot sail in a straight line, having to take advantage of the winds that prevail in the various latitudes. And we cannot sail continuously, there being our casks to fill with water, something that is very necessary for our survival, most particularly in the heat of the lower latitudes. Thus we must call at various islands, and discover others where there is water, in addition to taking the fullest advantage of any rain storms and squalls that are common in the central Pacific. We have with us on this voyage a still for making fresh water from sea water, the which we were not able to try until we reached Van Diemens Land, having found no wood in those barren Kerguelen Islands.

The delays we had at Deptford before we left on this voyage are now pressing upon me. The fitting out of the *Resolution* for a voyage to remote parts was ordered as long ago as 13th September 1775, but she was not ready to receive men until early January last year and in fact did not take in men till 10th February. For this, and the fact that she did not go down to the Norse until mid-June, I am in part to blame in that I was greatly occupied at home with my Journal and so not present as I was prior to the two previous voyages to give that sense of urgency to the preparations that drives men to their fullest endeavour.

Now we shall be hard put to make those distant Straits before the short northern summer is over and ice begins to form again. This I know from my own experience in the St Lawrence to happen very early, probably in late September or early October. After I was in the St Lawrence I was 3 years Master of the Flagship of the American Squadron surveying the Nova Scotia and Newfoundland coasts, and when the late War* ended in 1763 I was given my own command, the schooner *Grenville*, and was a further 5 years surveying those foggy Eastern Coasts of North

*This was the war that later became known as the Seven Years War.

America. I am thus very well acquainted with the harshness and length of the Winter and do not think from what I have been able to read that the conditions on the western coasts of that cold continent will greatly differ from those I experienced all those years on the eastern side.

It is thus very necessary that we do press on with the utmost dispatch, hastening our preparations in Queen Charlottes Sound and thereafter taking every advantage of the wind to make to the northward as rapidly as possible, I having no commitment in my Instructions other than to return Omai to his native islands and to make what new discoveries I can in our passage northwards. It was this necessity to carry all Sail possible that caused the loss of our Fore Topmast which carried away the Main Topgallant Mast with it at 4 o'clock in the morning of Sunday 19th January in a sudden squal of wind. This delayed us most of the day, clearing the wreckage and fitting another Topmast. The Topgallant we could not replace as we had neither spare nor any suitable spar on board.

During these days when we were sailing without sight of land on the voyage to Van Diemens Land, and also since, I have spent much time studying the two maps of the Russian and North American coasts and endeavouring in every way to prepare myself for the great opportunity that lies ahead. By constant study, and in the light of my experience, it does seem possible for me to form in my mind some semblance of a visual impression of what we may expect. This is something I have always been able to do, so converting the map

into an imagined reality of sea and rock and weather.
But though this has the salutary effect of preparing
myself for the physical eventualities, I have found that
the picture I have formed of it in my mind is never so
accurate that the reality of it does not take me somewhat by surprise, the unexpected resolving itself when
least expected so that once we are in unknown waters,
feeling our way along an unknown coast, I know there
will be no rest for me. Nevertheless, I have these past
weeks, and will continue to do whatever I can to
prepare myself, knowing that to arrive off those
northern coasts too late in the year is to put myself,
my People and my ships in the greatest hazard.

This is why, when we arrived at Van Diemens
Land, I went straight into Adventure Bay, where I had
previously anchored in March 1773, doing only what
had to be done and not making any further survey of
the coast. The officers, all except Capt Clerke who
knew very well the urgency of our sailing, could not
understand why, having spent time exploring the
Crozet and Kerguelen islands, I did not take this
opportunity to map the coast of Van Diemens Land.*
I could not tell them I was committed to the exploration of the former, but had no such order for the latter.
In any event, the time we were in those islands there

---

*If he had done so Cook would have discovered it was an island,
something which was not entered on any map of New Holland
(Australia) until after Bass had deduced the existence of the Strait
named after him and a year later had proved that his deduction was
correct by sailing through it with Flinders in the *Reliance* in December
1798.

was little wind with the fog so that it was no great loss of our progress Eastward.

We sighted the coast of Van Diemens Land bearing N½W at 3 a.m. on 24th January, but then lost the westerly wind and had in its place variable light airs and calm so that it was not until Sunday 26th at 4 in the afternoon that we anchored in Adventure Bay in 12 feet on a bottom of sand and owse. There was little grass, which was our greatest need for the cattle, and that not good, but an abundance of wood and water. The following day, whilst engaged on these duties, I posted a guard of Marines, having sighted smoke inland though no sign of the inhabitants, but Capt Clerkes Marines stole some liquor and got so exceeding drunk they were put into the boat like corpses. They received a dozen lashes each. That evening we had a great many fish in the seine net at the head of the bay, but an Elephant Fish broke it as it was being drawn ashore so that the catch was not so great and the Elephant Fish not much better eating than shark.

Mr Bayly had got the Observatory tent and all his instruments of navigation ashore, but it being cloudy all day he was not able to obtain observations, and in the evening I ordered him to get the whole on board again so that we were ready for sea. But the next morning there being no wind we continued loading wood and water and I sent the Carpenter ashore to cut spars, also Mr Roberts, one of the Mates, to survey the Bay. In the afternoon we had our first sight of the inhabitants, 8 men and a boy coming to us out of the woods, unarmed and with the greatest confidence.

They were quite naked, black with what I finally agreed with Mr King was hair as woolly as the natives of New Guinea. They are quite different from those I had met with previously in the north of New Holland, and not at all like the miserable desert people Dampier describes having seen on the western coast. One of them had a stick with him which he used as a throwing weapon, but he did not seem very good at it when a mark was set up at 20 yards and Omai told him to throw at it.

Fish and bread they threw away, though they understood that it was to eat, but when I showed them 2 pigs I had brought ashore they seized them by the ears like dogs and were for carrying them off immediately and would have killed them had I not stopped them. After they were gone I took the 2 pigs, which were a sow and a boar, about a mile into the woods and let them go beside a brook of fresh water. I would have left cattle, goats and sheep, but it was clear the natives would have killed them as soon as we had left. The pigs may survive long enough to breed, they being animals that soon revert to the wild and are naturally fond of the thickest parts of the woods.

We had no better fortune with the weather on Wednesday, the morning being dead calm, so we cut grass and wood again, the grass in one patch being plentiful and good. More natives came to the wooding party, including women with children, the women quite naked except for a kangaroo skin tied over shoulder and waist, but for no other purpose than to carry the children which had fine features and were quite pretty. The women did seem possessed of some modesty, for they rejected the offers of some of the *Discovery*s men. But this may have been through fear of displeasing their own Men, for an elder among them observing this ordered all the women and children away, the which order they obeyed with some reluctance.

The needs of our men, which are very natural after so long on board of the ships, is always a possible cause of trouble. In the islands of the Pacific this is not the case, the native men having not the same sense of possession of their women as seems to exist among races of colder climates. Much care has to be exercised in this matter by myself and the officers, for if the women are too forward in responding to the advances of our People, then there is jealousy which can transform a scene of peace so suddenly and so completely that our People have to be protected from the consequences of their own natural inclinations. This is something I am most reluctant to be involved in, since it can have fatal results and so affect the manner in which any ship that comes after me is received.

Calm and light airs from Eastward kept us anchored in the Bay until Thursday 30th when a light breeze at West enabled us to get to sea. Having done so, the wind veered to the Southward and increased to Storm. Of this we were warned by a fall of the Barometer, but then for a brief time it brought with it an intolerable heat when the mercury in the Thermometer rose in an instant from 70° to almost 90°.

The only captains to have visited this land before

were Tasman, who discovered it in November 1642, and Capt Furneaux, who was there in the *Adventure* after he had separated from me in October 1773.* I have given the Latitude and Longitude of this Bay and also the Capes and Islands in my Journal. I have also said that New Holland, of which this land is the most southerly part, if it is not a continent must be one of the largest, possibly the largest island in the World. We are now on the open sea passage to New Zealand where I shall hope to discover the exact cause of what befell Capt Furneauxs men. Some time during the night of the 6th and 7th the *Discovery* lost a Marine overboard, this being the second such man Capt Clerke has had the misfortune to lose since leaving England. He hailed me the following morning to inform me of the loss, the 2 ships then being in close company, both making very much the same speed through the water and this explaining why we had lost sight of his lights during the night, the which caused me some concern on being informed of it. There is nothing more disturbing when sailing in close company than to lose touch with the consort for no apparant reason.

*Cook did not know of Marion de Fresne's visit in March 1772.

CHAPTER SEVENTEEN

NEW ZEALAND

Monday, February 17th

This last week and more I have been much occupied ashore and with my Journal in which I have set down all that I have discovered from the Natives I encountered in Ship Cove. We are anchored in our old station in Queen Charlottes Sound, which we reached at 10 in the Morning of Wednesday 12th February, having first sighted the coast of the Southern Island of New Zealand on the Monday and rounding Cape Farewell some 45 miles to the north the following morning. No sooner had we anchored than several canoes came alongside, but few of the men in them ventured on board, they being afraid that we had come to revenge the deaths of Furneauxs men. This I learned from one of them whom I had befriended when I was last here, he having learned from a conversation he had had with Omai that I was well aware of the bloody affair. I did my best to reassure them and in this I appear to have been successful in that they laid aside the distrust they first had of me. This does not altogether surprise me for the attitude of these people to death is one of acceptance as something ordinary even though the means be violent, so accustomed are they to warring among themselves and to the eating of human flesh.

By the 13th we had set up our Observatory and begun making observations to determine the rate of the Timekeeper, as well as having the empty casks ashore for water and 2 men appointed to cut spruce and boil it to make an essence from which we shall have spruce beer to refresh us during the voyage ahead. A great many families came from different parts to reside with us, putting up temporary dwellings with remarkable facility, the which provided Mr Webber with abundance of subjects for his brush. Some of these natives went out fishing every day so that by exchanges we never wanted for fish, living with great enjoyment off something that was not unlike a small salmon. Every day Sellery and scurvy grass was boild up with the Portable Soup, Pease & Wheat for both ships companies, with spruce beer to drink. We had visitors in addition to those who resided with us, and these traded for curiosities, fish and women, so that all the time I had Marines posted to ensure that we did not at any time suffer the same fate as poor Capt Furneauxs men.

Because I cannot prevent it I allow my People to have intercourse with women when it is proffered and the Native men do not object. But I do not encourage it for though it is a sound practice for men settling amongst a people to take one of their women, we are not settlers but travellers and having connection with women with no regard for them, but only a selfish need to satisfy an appetite, there is always the danger of anger and betrayal.

Last Saturday I made an excursion by boat to look for grass and visited the Hippah or fortified village on the SW point of Motuara. This was where Mr Bayly had his observatory when the *Adventure* arrived first here in 1773. In their leisure hours they had planted gardens with seed brought from England, but no vestige now remained, they all being choked with weeds. Yet we found Cabbage, Onions, Leeks, Parsley, Radishes, Mustard and cress and a few Potatoes, these last being from the Cape and having been greatly advantaged by the change of soil. Husbandry, however, is quite foreign to these people, so that no attempt had been made to extend the gardens or to increase the produce we had been at such labour to bring them by planting of either roots or seeds.

CHAPTER EIGHTEEN

THE TRUTH ABOUT BLOODY COVE

Sunday, March 2nd

We are at sea again, having weighed and stood out of the Sound 10 a.m. Tuesday last 25th February 1777, keeping company with the *Discovery* and sailing E through the Strait to take our departure of the land at Cape Palliser 2 days later, which is the SE point of the Northern island of New Zealand. We had been anchored in the Sound 12 days, which is I would think the smallest number in which we could have expected to re-stock with fresh victuals by trade with the Natives, cut all the grass we required for our animals and otherwise prepare the Ships for the voyage through the Pacific. We took observations for 11 of the days and by a mean of these the Timekeeper was too slow, losing at the mean rate of 2 , 913 per day. The Astronomical Clock was also losing on Siderial time 40 , 239 per day and we had a difference of 6′45 by the Moon on the Longitude that Mr Wales had here last voyage, his being that much more to the West. Other opportunities will now have to be taken to make further observations.

Omai has added to our numbers on board by 2, he being from our first arrival in New Zealand determined to have servants with him to improve his circumstance and impress his grandness upon his return home. The eldest of these is a youth of 17 or 18 named Tiarooa and I thought little of it when he came on board, thinking that when we sailed he would return to his people. But this was not the case, he being the son of a Chief who was killed and eaten as is the savage custom of this Country. His mother is still alive and treated with the greatest respect, and she did come aboard just before we sailed to say goodbye to her Son and receive a last gift from Omai.

With this youth another came to be his servant, but having second thoughts he departed before we sailed, though he had slept on board all the time we were anchored. But the next morning his post was taken by Coaa, a boy of some 10 years old. He was delivered on board by his Father with as much indifference as he would part with a dog. This child was in tears before we left and was only prevented from abandoning Tiarooa by one of the Elders of the Tribe. Now they are both crying their hearts out, making of their tears a sort of lament in praise of their Country and their People, which is as much due to sea sickness as for their longing for home, and I think it very wrong of Omai to have told them that they will be returned later in the voyage, since I do not know what lies ahead or how I shall return, whether by way of New Zealand or by a more direct route, or by that North West Passage, the which I am instructed to discover. And if not the North West Passage, then perhaps the North East Passage over the top of Russia.

Since we sailed I have been much taken up with making my official report in the Journal of the true facts relating to the massacre of Capt Furneauxs men in what he called Bloody Cove. I have certain observations to make on this that are personal and not suitable to state in my Commanders Journal. But so that these be properly understood I must first relate the facts as I have discovered them from Kahoura, a Chief that sometimes visited us, and also an old friend of mine whom we called Pedro, a man who had been almost continuously with us the last time I had been in the Sound.

Kahoura had actually headed the party who cut off Capt Furneauxs boat. He had himself killed the officer who commanded it. I talked to him and to others through Omai, which is something strange, he coming from an island so many thousands of miles away, the which supports my belief that all these Peoples of the Pacific are of the same race, moving from one island to another in their big seagoing canoes in the same fashion that we do in our ships. He was not much loved, but greatly feared as a bad man, and many there were who importuned me to kill him, which is something that is quite natural to them, they believing in the Old Testament law of an eye for an eye, and if I had I do believe they would have eat him there in front of me.

The cove where the *Adventures* cutter was overwhelmed is on the E side of the Sound. We called it Grass Cove because of the abundance of that commodity. Here Pedro met us with another, both armed with Pat'too and spear, but nevertheless showing manifest signs of fear. Whether this was out of courtesy or caution, they expecting us to revenge our comrades deaths, I do not know, but their fear was quickly allayed by some gifts I made them. They told us in some detail the circumstances in which the massacre had occurred. Capt Furneauxs men, of whom there were 12, had paused at their work and were sitting around enjoying their victuals, several of the natives close about them, when some of them snatched some bread and some fish, for which the sailors did beat them, and this being resented a quarrel ensued. In this disturbance 2 natives were shot, and in the instant the natives sprang upon all of them, either seizing them or knocking them on the head with war clubs. This before the 2 muskets could be reloaded or another, if there was another, could be fired.

Pedro then indicated by pointing at the angle of the Sun in the sky the hour at which it had happened, which was in the late afternoon. He also showed us the exact spot where the crew had sat to eat and where the boat had laid about 200 yards away with Capt Furneauxs black servant in it. Later we were told that it was this man who was the cause of the trouble in that when a native stole something out of the boat he dealt him a heavy blow with a stick, whereupon the fellow cried out to his people that he was killed. There are other versions: that Mr Rowe, the officer, fired upon the thief and killed him and that this brought People out of the woods who got between our men and the boat, Mr Rowe firing and killing another of them before all were overwhelmed. Yet another, which were had from Kahoura himself, that on offering a stone hatchet for trade to one of the boats crew the man kept it without making payment, whereupon the natives snatched bread from them as recompense. This I believe to be a lie to make our People appear the cause. But the rest seems true enough, that Kahoura was hidden by the side of the boat and that when Mr Rowe shot the chief, he seized his opportunity before the musket could be reloaded to attack Mr Rowe, who drew his Hanger and wounded him in the arm before he was overwhelmed.

That the whole Melancholy affair was unpremeditated is clear and the Moral of it is in dealing with all Natives it is to be constantly remembered that our laws do not apply. Where there is no conception of property as we understand it, that is to say that there are many simple peoples to whom the possession and ownership of things has no meaning, then the greatest circumspection must be exercised. The use of force is seldom wise when ashore and faced with overwhelming numbers, though they be indifferently armed. The only sensible way to deal with any instance such as this I have recounted is through the Arees or Chiefs of the Tribe, by seizing upon their persons or persuading them of the trouble there will be for their people if items that belong to the Ship are made off with.

CHAPTER NINETEEN

THE NATURE OF TRIBAL WARS

There are I will admit great differences in the nature of Peoples and Tribes of different parts of the World. The tribes of these islands of New Zealand are the most warlike I have encountered, constantly fighting among themselves, each tribe so determined on the destruction of another that even in the short time I was in Queen Charlottes Sound I was constantly being importuned to go to war in aid of this village or that or to avenge the death of our People which they considered to be our natural duty and inclination, and I do believe that even when Omai explained to them why I did not do so, they did not comprehend. Omai himself did not understand, arguing with me that if a man kills another in England he is hanged, so why did I not hang Kahoura? He could not believe that I could forgive and wished my visit to be one of friendship, he being not over gifted with imagination and the total concept of our voyage quite beyond him.

This is a very different attitude to the peaceful

nature of those people I found upon the Society and Friendly Islands, which were the names I gave to those that were the furthest north I ventured in the Pacific on my last voyage, the which I shall certainly call upon again to re-victual upon our way north and to leave with them some of our animals.

I had intended leaving a bull and 2 heifers together with sheep, goats & hogs, in New Zealand, for the number of livestock we carry is a constant source of concern to me and the cause of much labour to the crews of both ships in cutting grass whenever we are anchored. I knew also that water would be an even greater problem when we got into hot weather latitudes. But I could find no Chief powerful enough over all the tribes to protect them, and of those I left there on my last voyage in West Bay and Cannibal Cove there was no sign, though I was told there was poultry gone wild in the Woods behind Ship Cove and I did hear that a Chief named Teratou had a great many Cocks & Hens and one of the Sows Capt Furneaux left ashore. Teratou was not there at any time while we were anchored and, as evidence of the unending struggle for power among the tribes and their terrible warlike nature, I learned that another Chief, Tringaboohea, was killed about 5 months before we arrived together with some 70 of his people. No man's property is secure in this country, but having before left upward of a dozen pigs in this Country I do not think they can have failed to breed and some survive. Two minor Chiefs soliciting me for pigs & goats, I let them go to take their chance hoping for the best.

On the matter of war between Tribes I would only say that it is a form of feuding, they being continually watching out for revenge, sometimes over many years, no Son ever forgetting an injury done to his Father. They creep up on the others when they are unguarded at night, sparing neither the Women nor the Children, and having slaughtered them they do then feast upon their bodies on the spot, gorging themselves sick, or sometimes taking away as many bodies as they can carry to their own home where they eat them, committing all sorts of brutalities upon the corpses. They take no prisoners nor give no quarter, but if they are discovered upon their raids they creep away and vanish into the woods. Thus all must be constantly upon their guard, having both Body and Soul to preserve, for should any man be eaten he goes straight to Hell, descending down into everlasting fire. But if he is killed and his body saved from being eat, then his Soul goes to Heaven, ascending upwards into the abode of the Gods. So their beliefs of Heaven and Hell are not much different from ours, and they also accept that a man has a Soul. Moreover, they bury their dead as we do and regard with abhorrence the thought of eating their own people after saving their bodies from the Enemy, but if they have more of the Enemy dead than they can eat, then they do not bury them, but throw them to the fish in the sea.

They have Priests who alone may speak with the Gods, but they do not gather together to worship in publick, the meeting house being for practical discussions. They cut their hair off and do sometimes fast with it, but for what reason I do not know except that it is connected with Eatua and is a ritual matter. But though they are for ever warring among themselves, a stranger journeying through their land is safe so long as his stay be no longer than that required to conduct the business upon which he is come. This ensures that they may trade their greatest possession, which is the green stone they call Poenammo which is found somewhere in the region of the southern island. There are many fabulous tales about this stone which is much prized, one being that it is a fish which when caught and brought ashore turns to stone. All agree it is fished out of a large lake or collection of Waters, the which I take to mean that it is a stone from the mountains that is brought down by torrents. All the southern island is known by the Stones name and called by the natives Poenammo.*

Of more interest to me were the stories I had of them about the medicines and unguants they extract from roots and plants, in particular a relief from the Pox. They say this disease was brought in a ship that came to their land only a few years before we first came there in the *Endeavour*. They called it Tupias Ship, but they may have confused the time or it is even possible they may in some polite way have been referring to our own ship, except that it would have meant a considerable elaboration of the tale in that they claimed the Captain during his stay kept one of their

*This greenstone, even now a tourist attraction and not unlike jade in appearance, is found in the Arahura river on the west coast of South Island.

women and had by her a son who was still living and now about Coaas age. It was by this ship they said they were infected with the Venereal Disease, but that it was now less common and the effect of it not near so bad as at first. Their method of cure was to wrap the sufferer in green plants that had first been laid over hot stones, thus forming a poultice that gave off steam like a bath.* I would much like to have gone further into this matter of medicine, having been somewhat troubled of late by pains in my leg which I fear is some form of rheumatism, due probably to the long months spent in the cold Southern Seas on my late voyage and brought on again by the damp of our quarters and the fogs we experienced after leaving the Cape. It is something I must keep to myself, for if I showed any of my People that I was in pain they would have less confidence in me than they do, the Commander always of necessity having to appear superior to those afflictions that do normally plague human beings. It is at these moments that I think with some longing of my home in Mile End Old Town and of my wife who would as always be of such great comfort to me.

*A hot poultice is one of the basic Maori medicines. The practice of medicine among the Maoris was sufficiently advanced for them to carry out trepanning operations. Discussing this with Hepe Te Hao Hao, one of their paramount chiefs, he told me he had been cured of terrible back pains by such a poultice after European doctors had abandoned his case as incurable.

PART FOUR

PACIFIC ISLANDS

CHAPTER TWENTY

SLOW PROGRESS

Tuesday, April 1st, 1777

All Fools Day and hoping the land we had sight of yday at Noon will afford us better prospect of an anchorage than at Mangaia, the island we reached on March 30th and which we found hostile both as to the coast and at first the people, for our beasts are in great want of food. But we have little wind and making up toward this next island is slow work. The wind had been very fitful and exasperating all this past month.

For a fortnight after leaving New Zealand we had the wind mostly between SW&N, some times Strong Gale with hard Squals, at other times moderate so that we made good progress in the direction we wished to go, carrying all sail on a course of NEbyE. We are thus in Lat. 39ϒ29′S and Long. 196ϒ04′E, our progress slow and all on board feeling the heat. The wind such as it was then veered between NE&SE so that we began to make too much to the Northward, our course for Otaheite* requiring as much Easting as Northing.

*Tahiti, the island group to which Cook was ordered to return Omai.

By March 16th the ships log records the wind veered to N so that I was able to tack and stand to the E, but very light and some times Calm. It then freshened at ESE so that we could again stand NE, but only for a short time as it often veered to E or even ENE so that we frequently made no better than N and even Westward of that course.

We did not cross the Tropic* until March 27th and then only in Long. 201ϒ23′E which was 9°W of our destination. I had thought all this time I would have been experiencing Westerly winds otherwise I would have made more to the Eastward after leaving New Zealand. The whole month has proved one of great frustration, always expecting winds we never got, and our progress so slow that I begin to have considerable anxiety about making the coast of North America in time to explore Northward before the ice begins to form.

I do not believe as some do that ice only forms from fresh water. It is true that the ice formed at sea, as we discovered in the Southern Ocean last voyage, yields fresh water when it is melted. But the sea does freeze off the E coast of North America. This I know, so that even though it be all water to the Northward of that continent, it will still turn to ice in winter and so stop our progress beyond Capt Behrings strait.

All March we saw nothing of any birds that would induce us to think we had passed close by any land, only a Tropic bird, also a large tree, but so covered in

*The Tropic of Capricorn which is Latitude 23½°S.

barnacles that it could have drifted on the currents from almost anywhere. The sellery and scurvy-grass &ca we took on board in Queen Charlottes Sound, together with the diet of Portable Soup and Sour Krout that we carry and also the hygiene I practise, all on board washing themselves every day in sea water and both ships constantly aired and the periodic smoking of all parts below deck, has preserved all in reasonable good health, only the animals being a matter for concern.

On the 29th the *Discovery*, which was to the NE of us, made the signal for land in sight. This was at 10 in the Morning. It was an island of no great size and by Sun set it bore NNE about 2 or 3 leagues so that we were forced to stand off and on until Day break when we could see a great surf breaking every where with great fury upon the reef and no way in to any anchorage. A great many inhabitants made their appearance out of the woods brandishing long pikes or clubs. After searching the N side of the island and finding no harbour of any sort, we turned back and met the same 2 men in a canoe that had come out to us before. This time they approached near enough to receive presents lowered to them on a line. I then had a boat lowered and went to them and they came alongside, stepping into my boat without any fear. I ordered Omai to question them about a landing place, but the two they indicated would have been a great risk to our boat, so we reconnoitred ourselves to within a cables length of the breakers when we had 40 to 20 fathoms depth over sharp Coral.

While we were thus engaged great numbers of the inhabitants all armed thronged upon the reef, but the man I had in my boat, who was some sort of Chief, ordered them back so as not to hinder our landing. This man came back with me to the Ship, but very uneasy all the time he was on board, which may be the reason that he expressed no surprise at anything we showed him, except that on leaving, as he came out of the Cabbin, he fell over a goat, staring at it astonished and asking Omai if it were a bird.

This island was called Mangaia and I departed from it with great reluctance, it being well wooded with Bread fruit, Cocoanut, Plantains & Tarra root so that it would have provided us with all fresh provisions of which we were in need. And the people not unfriendly, though their actions and language come nearer to the New Zealanders than the Otaheiteans, but their colour between the two and their ears pierced with large holes like the people of Easter Island, one with a knife stuck in the hole which Mr Webber did make a drawing of.

Now with another island in sight I am hoping that we shall not again be disappointed of a landing for we are in great want of refreshment.

CHAPTER TWENTY-ONE

THE COOK ISLANDS

Sunday, April 13th

We have now touched upon 3 islands and got very little for our trouble. Light airs all the time and so little water that I have had the still kept at work. Some improvement has lately been made to this Machine, but I do not regard it as such, it yielding no more than 13 to 16 gallons of water though it was at work one day from 6 in the morning till 4 in the After noon. My concern for the cattle is great, having transported them all this way and no opportunity to put them ashore, which was my intention. And the winds being so tedious I am now disappointed in my original intention, having in 2 weeks made barely 4° of latitude to the Northward.

The first of the 3 islands was Atiu, which Omai called Wenua-no-Eatua, meaning a land of Gods, for he said many of the men on it were possessed of the spirit of Eatua, the which causes a kind of frantickness common in Otaheite and neighbouring islands. The 2nd was Wennuaete, which signifies little island; and the 3rd was Manuae, which I had visited on my last voyage and called Herveys Island after my friend of the Board of Admiralty Capt Augustus John Hervey who is now the Earl of Bristol. There was no anchorage at any of these, but at Atiu Mr Gore with Omai, Dr Anderson and Mr Burney from the *Discovery* were ashore in a canoe, in some peril of their lives they thought, being surrounded by a multitude of people, then pent up for the whole day and in the evening much alarmed when a fire was made, Omai in particular being afeared they were to be roasted and eat. But it was only to roast a hog and all were returned safe to the ships well fed, but nothing in the way of trade.

It was on this island that Omai met with some Otaheiteans who, sailing in their canoe to the island of Ulieta, had missed it through poor navigation or other adverse circumstances, and after being at sea a great number of days, their canoe was oversent. Only 5 out of the 20 men and women survived, they being much weakened by lack of water and victuals but still clinging to the side of the oversent canoe until it was drifted toward Atiu, the people of which sent out canoes to bring them in. This I believe is the way in which these people, who all speak and behave in much the same manner, have progressed through the Pacific, their colonisations being not so much by intent as by chance. Omai offered these castaways a passage back to Otaheite with us, but they declined, saying that they were better suited where they were.

Mr Gore also landed on the small island, this time in our own boat which I had ordered ashore if it were at all possible. Despite the great surf breaking upon the rocks he, with the Jolly boat as well, brought off Scurvy Grass and Palm leaves, about 90 Cocoanuts and branches of the Wharra tree,* which being of a soft spongy juicy nature we fed to the Cattle who did eat it very well though it was much like feeding them billit-wood. We made no landing on Herveys Island, for after I had sent Mr King to reconnoitre in one of our boats, he was met at the outer edge of the reef, which was a quarter of a mile from the shore, by some of the inhabitants armed with long pikes and clubs, and observing that their women were very busy bringing down more spears and darts, he returned. We were in great want of grass for the Cattle and also of water, neither of which could be procured from any of these islands without great labour and some danger.†

*Pandanus.

†This small group of islands, at which Cook had so little luck, are now named for him the Cook Islands.

CHAPTER TWENTY-TWO

AN INEVITABLE DECISION

Reluctantly I made the decision to bear away from the Easterly wind and make for the Friendly Islands,* which were to the W, knowing from my previous Voyage that they would give me good anchorage and provide us with all that we were in such urgent need of. It was not a decision arrived at on the spur of the moment, the which I fear some of my officers will have a misapprehension of when they learn of our ultimate destination. But none of them have experience of the North American coast and so cannot understand how early and how suddenly the Winter does come upon that land. For some weeks now the realisation has been growing on me that we were too late in starting upon this Voyage and the Summer already too far advanced in the northern Hemisphere to enable us to prosecute those discoveries in high northern latitudes for which I am committed, we not yet being across the Equator,

*Now known as the Tonga Islands.

after which we have no less than 60 and more degrees of Latitude to make to the N.

The decision I have now made, which is to postpone the search for the North West Passage until next year when we shall have the advantage of all the time we require, is a great disappointment to me. I could have stood back to the S until I had the advantage of westerly winds, but it would have meant the loss of all the Cattle, which I still have hopes of landing to the advantage of the peoples of the islands, and even then I think we would be too late in arriving in the Strait, so it is likely no advantage gained and the animals all lost. Besides which, in our haste to make to the Northward, I fear we should consume too much of the Ships stores and provisions. I do blame myself, not for the decision, nor for any failure to make as much haste as possible on the Voyage, the winds having been more contrary than I had expected, but because I failed to appreciate when I was in England how urgent it was to get to sea betimes and make a start upon the Voyage.

It is better, I am convinced, to proceed upon this expedition with caution rather than to endanger all our lives with reckless haste. And there is some advantage to me personally in that I can now utilise the summer months for a proper study of these island People, the which I have not had the opportunity before. There is so much about them that fascinates me, they being navigators of no mean sort and their customs, nature and practices being all so interesting. This I shall set down in my Journal with as much detail, and I hope with the greater facility that comes with the practice of writing to which I was at one time quite a stranger, that it will be very acceptable to that larger Publick which requires always to be entertained with details of the life of the people, their religion, morals and most intimate practices. For the next few months therefore I will concentrate upon the Journal with the intention of setting down the fullest possible record of these People, the which has not been done by any person heretofor.

I shall not write any of it here that is not to my purpose, this being a very private account of my thoughts and deepest concerns, but if at the end of the Voyage this record should be considered worthy of publication, either during my life or perhaps more properly after my death, then whoever shall prepare it for the press can add as much to it as is thought necessary from the official account in my Journal. It was Dr Douglas who made this suggestion to me that I should set down my most intimate thoughts, so that there was more in it of the person I am, and something also that Mr Boswell said to me. I have had in mind therefore that I am writing to that kind and considerate friend and employer of mine Mr Walker of Whitby. And if there is any choice of who should correct all my various mistakes in spelling and punctuation, and give to it that polish of phraseology the which he has achieved in his own writings, I would hope perhaps I might prevail upon Mr Banks, with whom I am glad to say I was during my stay in England on the most friendly and even affectionate terms despite all that had gone before when preparing for my second voyage, he being disappointed of the command of it and much angered thereby.

CHAPTER TWENTY-THREE

PLANS FOR THE NORTH

Wednesday, November 19th, 1777

We have now been in the Friendly and Society islands all of 6 months and with Winter coming on I think it time for me to leave Omai and proceed upon the main purpose of my voyage. Accordingly I have this day delivered my Instructions to Capt Clerke how he should proceed in the *Discovery* in the event that we become separated after leaving these islands. We will shortly be exploring coasts that few if any save the Greek navigator Juan de Fuca have touched on before. And since I cannot know whether I, or any of us if the truth be admitted, may survive I am copying my instructions to Capt Clerke into this record, as I did my original Instructions, so that if the *Discovery* be lost and I not survive, it will be known how I made provision for our meeting up upon the coast of New Albion.*

*The west coast of America north of California, which was then occupied by the Spanish and which the Admiralty had expressly ordered Cook to avoid. It was named Nova Albion by Drake who discovered it in 1579.

By Capt James Cook Commander
of His Majesty's Sloop Resolution

Whereas the Passage from the Society Isles to the Northern Coast of America is of considerable length both in distance and time, and as a part of it must be performed in the very depth of Winter when gales of Wind and bad Weather must be expected and may possibly occasion a Separation, which you are to take all imaginable care to prevent. But if notwithstanding all our endeavours to keep company, you should be separated from me, you are first to look for me where you last saw me, not seeing me in five days, you are to proceed, as directed by their Lordships Instructions (a Copy of which you have already received) for the Coast of *New Albion* endeavouring to fall in with it in the Latitude of 45°; in which latitude, and at a convenient distance from the land, you are to cruze for me ten days.

Not seeing me in that time, you are to put into the first Convenient Port in or to the North of that latitude, to recruit your wood and water and to procure refreshments. During your stay in Port you are constantly to keep a good look out for me, it will therefore be necessary to make choice of a Station situated as near to the sea-coast as you can, the better to enable you to see me when I appear in the offing. If I do not join you before the 1st of next April, you are to put to Sea and proceed northward to the latitude of 56° in which latitude, and at a convenient distance from the coast, never exceeding fifteen leagues, you are to Cruze for me till the 10th of May.

Not seeing me in that time, you are to proceed Northward and endeavour to find a passage into the Atlantick Ocean through Hudsons or Baffins Bays, as directed by the above mentioned Instructions. But if you should fail in finding a Passage through either of the said Bays or by any other way, and the Season of the year may render it unsafe for you to remain in high latitudes, you are to repair to the harbour of St Peter and Paul* in Kamtschatka, in order to refresh your people and pass the Winter.

But, nevertheless, if you find you cannot procure the Necessary refreshments at the said Port, you are at liberty to go where you shall judge more proper, taking care before you depart to leave with the Governor to be delivered to me on my arrival, an account of your intended destination. And in the Spring of the ensueing year 1779 to repair back to the above mentioned port, endeavouring to be there by the 10th May or sooner.

If on your arrival you receive no orders from, or account of me so as to justify your pursuing any other Measures than what are pointed out in the before mentioned Instructions, your future proceedings are to be Governed by them. You are also to comply with such parts of said Instructions as

---

*Petropavlovsk, or as Cook spelt it, Petropaulowska.

have not been executed and are not contrary to these orders. In case of your inability by sickness or otherwise to carry these and their Lordships Instructions into execution, you are to be carefull to leave them with the next officer in command who is hereby required to execute them in the best manner he can.

To

Captn Charles Clerke Commander of His Majesty's Sloop Discovery	Given under my hand on board the Resolution at Ulietea* the 18th day of Novr 1777

            J. Cook

Now I must recount some of my chiefest concerns during the half year we have sojourned in the islands above mentioned.

*Cook's spelling of Raiatea.

CHAPTER TWENTY-FOUR

WOMEN AND THIEVES

First as regards the People under my command. Such a long period of relative inactivity must always put a strain upon the Discipline of the Ships. I do know that they look upon me as a man of undoubted severity and this I have never discouraged. Indeed, it is something I have at all times fostered, both in my manner and bearing, my officers all being much younger men and only myself by practice and experience able to enforce Discipline by a glance. I am seldom able to relax, nor have been these many years, so that when I see myself in the mirror I am forced to the realisation that by habit my features have become set into an expression that is something severe. Capt Clerke manages to temper this with his humour, but I lack this advantage, and if I be not much liked by some it does ensure that I am always obeyed and so absolute master in my own house, though living in close company with others long years at a stretch. Nevertheless the strain of it is at times almost beyond bearing and when I see the flaunting, libidinous behaviour of some of the women of these islands, they so handsome and free with their favours, I confess there are moments when I would be happy to exchange the isolation of command for the carefree abandon of a Midshipman's life.

It is this knowledge of my own weakness that causes me to turn a blind eye to the presence of females on the ship. I do not openly condone it, but pretend not to know. There are two or three living aboard at this present time, one of them seemingly with such great attachment to Mr Edgar that I do believe he is half in love with her, so that if he were not the *Discovery*s master but only a seaman he would desert the ship. Others will certainly attempt it now that everyone knows our destination and the conditions that will face us during this Winter and next Summer in the high latitudes of the Northern Hemisphere. But I have not lost a man yet by desertion, nor do I intend I shall on these islands or at any place we touch upon on the American coast.

It was but last week we had the latest desertion. Moored at Haamanino Hbr in the Otaheitean island of Ulietea I had the Observatory set up and all the instruments taken ashore so that Mr Bayly and I could observe the Suns Azimuths both on board and ashore to discover the Variation. This we did on the 7th and 8th November and on the night of the latter observed an occultation of S. Capricorni by the Moons dark limb, Mr Bayly using the Acromatic Tellescope, Mr King the Board of Longitudes Reflector and I my own 18 inch Reflector. And then on the night of the 12th and 13th the Marine posted as sentinel over the Observatory deserted taking his Musket with him. Having myself discovered which way he went, I sent a party after him, but they returned in the evening without seeing or hearing anything of him.

In such circumstances it requires that I go ashore, talk with the Chief and apply to him to send a party of his own people after the deserter. This I did, and because there were many natives around the Ships engaged in their usual thievery, all were taken with *matau*, which is to say a dread of my presence, and vanished, including the Chief. I had intelligence that the man was at a village called Hamoah on the other side of the island and I went there with 2 armed boats, apprehending the Chief on the way. This was all that was necessary, our party beaching the boats a mile and a half away and marching briskly over land, whereupon they took me straight to the deserter, whose name was John Harrison. He was in one of the houses, sitting between 2 women who burst out crying at my arrival, and his Musket was lying on the ground.

I have ordered him to be disciplined with a dozen lashes on each of 2 days, this being the maximum allowed per day for a single Crime. Two dozen lashes is not a great punishment, my anger and annoyance being tempered by the circumstances that he had stayed at his post till within a few minutes of his time of release. I do believe that had I gone ashore alone, without any armed party with me, it would have been sufficient for me to apprehend him, for the natives of these islands do hold me in great dread and awe, but whether from my manner and habit of command or for fear of the reprisals I may inflict upon them I can never be sure. My purpose, however, in recounting this escapade is to indicate how troublesome are the natural desires of my men, requiring of me time and energy that would be better employed in observations and all the other objects of the voyage.

Discipline and punishment is something all men on a voyage of this nature learn to accept, recognising the need for it if we are to return safe to our own Country. John Harrisons desertion was a momentary lapse, largely on account of the lure of those women and the attractions of this place. It is something I can understand and forgive. Thievery I can never forgive because, while desertion affects only the deserter unless he be allowed to get away unpunished, the theft of Ships stores affects the safety of us all and endangers the voyage, Nails and other larger items not being obtainable anywhere and therefore irreplaceable. The temptation thus to satisfy their lust is understood by Capt Clerke and myself, this being the price the Women demand for their favours, and having suffered such deprivation from previous voyages we take great care to guard against it. But whilst thievery of this sort I can understand, I was myself appalled when we were bearing north from New Zealand to have the midshipmen and some others of the crew complain that their victuals were being stolen.

This is something I had not suffered on previous voyages and it is the most damnable thing. It is like a sore, the thieves feeding upon the body of the crew and if unchecked the whole infected with suspicion and anger. Since we could not discover who the thieves were, I had recourse to something that is the last resort of those in command; I had the whole Ships company assembled and told them that unless the thieves were informed upon I would on the next occasion that meat was stolen reduce the Allowance to $\frac{2}{3}$rds the following day. This having no effect, I did reduce the Allowance, whereupon the men refused to eat it, complaining of the injustice of being punished for a crime they did not commit, all of them being entirely honest. Considering their behaviour near mutinous I informed them the $\frac{2}{3}$rds allowance would continue indefinitely and that thereafter the meat would be issued after it was cooked and not raw. That ended the matter, but it was not to my liking since it confirmed the poor opinion I had of some of the men shipped for this voyage, the thieving being secret and without the knowledge of the rest.

This was in April when we were very short and only the week before I had had my own sheep killed, and also those belonging to the gunroom gentlemen, so that the men should have some variety and the officers not appear to be better supplied in this respect. But while the men behaved unreasonably and very near to a mutinous proceeding on this occasion, they behaved most sensibly when on our arrival at Otaheite I called all hands together and having acquainted them with the purpose of the voyage and the improbability of renewing any of our Provisions, I did suggest to them that it would be better for the present to discontinue the daily issue of

Spirits and preserve our Grog for those colder climates which were our destination the following year.

It is not my normal practice to submit my intentions and desires to my crew, this being a Navy ship and not a private venture, as was the case with many of those earlier Discoverers who deferred to a Council for the wishes of a majority. However, the issue of rum and other spirits is a Custom that gives every man something to look forward to each day, a relief from the burden and routine of his close confinement, causing him to relax and so enjoy the company of his fellows instead of becoming resentful and argumentative. On this occasion I had the considerable satisfaction that no sooner had I put it to them that they saved their Grog for when the harshness of the climate made the issue of it more necessary, they without the least hesitation or a moments consideration did agree and consent to it immediately.

I have written of thieving on board, but much more difficult to deal with and most troublesome is the thievery practised by the natives of all the islands we have visited. It seems common throughout the Pacific, and though I go ashore everywhere and arrange the trade, putting an officer in charge of it as I did Mr Banks on that first voyage in the *Endeavour*, and setting the terms of that trade, the thievery continues very troublesome so that everything must be secured and the People watched at all times.

When we were at Nomuka in the Friendly Islands we caught one of the *eiki* or chiefs making off with the bolt of the Spun yarn winch, for what purpose I do not know since it was little use to him but of importance to us as it was upon this machine we made our ropes. I ordered him a dozen lashes, then took him ashore securely and most uncomfortably tied to the place where we traded and did not release him until I had a hog given me for his liberty. Thereafter no Chief engaged in thievery, but always they employed their servants or slaves for this dirty work on whom a flogging made no more impression that upon the Main-mast, and when we caught them as often as not their masters advised that we kill them. This I would not do and since my customary punishment had little effect I often did not bother to punish them at all. Capt Clerke conceived of a better idea and had their heads shaved, or the half of it, so that they were marked out and as a result derided.

However, there is no stopping their thieving, and not only in the Friendly Islands, but in the Society Islands also and at Otaheite itself, so that the constant necessity to keep watch on everything about the Ships when there were natives on board or in their canoes which so often swarm around us proved most wearying, and always I did my utmost to maintain a degree of impartiality between the islanders and my own People, so that I found myself as previously in the Pacific having to stand in judgment whenever there was conflict between the two. This was sometimes to the disadvant-age of my seamen, particularly when it involved the women who infested the Ships, as was the case when a Tongan chief whom I greatly respected came on board of the *Resolution* and wanted to take away a

Girl he found with one of my sailors between decks. The man had paid the price for her favours for the night, which was a hatchet paid to her father who had delivered her on board, and so refused to give her up. The Chief insisting and attempting to drag her away, the man struck him, whereupon the Chief made complaint to me. I had no alternative but to order the man a flogging, this Chief being second in importance on Nomuka and my orders being very strict that no man shall strike a native of any degree for whatever reason. This is a most necessary regulation for the avoidance of provocation and the attendant danger of stirring up enmity and so endangering all our lives, for we are most times greatly inferior in numbers. Our superiority in weapons is something to be relied upon only as the last resort, since knowledge of our actions and behaviour travels fast by canoe through these islands and we greatly depend upon the goodwill of the natives for our Provisions, thereby saving the Ships stores for our greater need in the Northern Hemisphere.

Thievery and women are a constant annoyance to me and the greatest disadvantage of these most salubrious attractive islands, the former having to be guarded against at all times for the danger it may inflict upon our enterprise and the latter accepted by me because I must. If the men were not contented in this manner there would have been Mischief, by which I mean desertions even Mutiny, for having lost this year I had no alternative but to stay in these islands where we had all we needed in the way of Provisions.

The constant intercourse with the women, both

ashore and on board of the Ships, some of them even voyaging with us from one island to another, is a danger both to themselves and my own People. I have always ordered that no man shall be permitted to stay a night on shore who has the Venereal, but there is always the difficulty that neither Mr Anderson, the surgeon, nor, I declare, any member of his Faculty, can truly declare a man free of the disease, since it is so normal a complaint of sailors and they, though possessed of it, often appearing able-bodied in every respect. In cases we know of my orders do ensure that it is not communicated to the islanders. But the native Chiefs are not so concerned and I have no means of enquiring into the health of all the Women that come aboard.

The discovery I made upon visiting the Friendly Islands this time that the people there were infected by the disease indicates how impossible it is to prevent the spreading of it. Some of our own People were so infected of the Venereal after we had left and I did myself see when I was ashore natives who had ulcers on their bodies, others with the nose or parts of it missing. They do not regard it of great account, which surprises me, so that I am inclined to think that they were inflicted of the disease prior to my visiting the islands on my last voyage since such a short interval of time would seem to be insufficient to produce so dreadful a disfigurement.* When the swellings are sufficiently big to cause a tumour they make deep gashes

*Possibly yaws or even infection from cuts caused by the coral when swimming.

across it with a sharks tooth or other sharp instrument. Some have swellings of the legs and arms for which they apply a piece of sinew tied very tight to prevent it spreading. This is not the Venereal but something else, very near as shocking to look upon.*

Whatever the cause of these people being infected with Venereal I intend to hold very strict to the precautions I have always taken wherever we may anchor so that so far as is possible I cannot be accused of having brought our own disease to the islands. I can do no more, and if the Spaniards or the Russians, or anybody else, have been there before me my conscience in this matter will be free of any guilt.

*Obviously elephantiasis.

CHAPTER TWENTY-FIVE

A CURE FOR RHEUMATICS

I was myself suffering at this time from the rheumatics, the pain beginning at the hip and extending right down to my heel. Though I kept more than usual to the Cabbin it was not possible for me to hide my affliction from the Ships company, the pain being very great and myself unable to move without limping. Then in September, when we had been among the Otaheitean islands a little over a month, I was forced by my affliction to decline an invitation made to me to attend a *Morai*, which is a thanksgiving to the gods of Otaheite. The invitation came by Messenger from Towha, who had returned with his fleet of war canoes after concluding a Peace with Mahein, a rival Chief. I would much like to have attended this ceremony, but instead sent Mr King and Omai, myself returning to the Ship. With me in my boat came the Mother of Otoo, another chief, and his 3 sisters with 8 other Women. I thought at first they had come on board to take passage with me to Matavai Bay, but so soon as we were on board they said they were come to sleep there and to cure me of my pains.

Many who read this will profess astonishment that I accepted their offer, but my voyages have revealed to me that there are many peoples who we would regard as primitive and uncivilised that have developed most remarkable cures from the plants and roots that grow in their lands. I had beds made up for the women in the Cabbin and submitted myself to their ministrations, though I would have thought twice about doing so had I known what they intended. I was desired to lie down in their midst, the which I did, whereupon as many as could get at me began to squeeze my flesh, using both their hands and working upon my whole body, though more especially upon the area of pain in my leg. They made by their onslaught a perfect Mummy of my body, squeezing me till my bones cracked. This first attempt lasted a full quarter of an hour and when it was done I was much relieved to be rid of them. Nevertheless, the pain was less and before I retired to bed they were at me again so that I had a fairly comfortable night. The cure was repeated in the morning before they went ashore and again in the evening when they returned to the Ship, and after that I had no more pain.

This operation they call *Romy* and though sometimes performed by men, it is more usually the women. They use it upon themselves whenever one of them is overtired or languid and this has a very good effect, particularly upon the legs, as I discovered myself, always thereafter benefiting from this treatment.

These people, whether of the group of islands I called Friendly, or that I named after the Society, or here in Otaheite, are not at all like their distant relatives in New Zealand in that they do not appear to practise cannibalism, but the gods they worship are similar and they are warlike, on certain occasions as I witnessed making human sacrifice at their *Morai* or secret place, but using a corps and not killing a man for the purpose . . .

CHAPTER TWENTY-SIX

TAHITIAN NAVAL TACTICS

Monday, November 24th

Having been moored to the shore at this place, we took the opportunity the ground being good to heel the Ship and scrub both sides of her bottom, so that I could not any longer write unless I went ashore to do it. At the same time I have had them fasten some Tin plates under the bends, which are the thick planks that do girdle the sides of her just above the waterline. These plates were provided by the ingenious Mr Pelham, Secretary to the Commissioners of Victualling, as a substitute for Copper. The Copper sheath is laid over the extra planking that is studded with large-headed nails to give something of an iron protection, but since those parts of the Copper that are worn or damaged cannot be replaced, Mr Pelham thought to try Tin as a protection against the worm. Whether it will serve the same end as Copper we shall only discover by attempting it.

The work is done now and as well as it is possible to do with the men clinging like flies to the slanted sides of the ships. The worm does not seem to affect the native canoes, of which there are very many, this being their mode of travel, of transporting people and goods, and of fishing along the outer edges of the reefs. Either the material of which they are constructed is not to the taste of this pest that seems to inhabit all the warm waters of the Globe or they discard their canoes or repair them as soon as ever the worm infects the wood. The canoes are double-ended and vary from the smaller *va'a*s or *proeses* to the great war canoes which are 60 or 70 feet long with a rounded bottom made of large logs hollowed out to a thickness of about 3 inches, the sides being built up of planking of similar thickness.

Some 2 months ago I was offered one of the former by Otoo just before we sailed from the island of Otaheite to go to Moorea. It was about 16 feet long and having all those pieces of Carved wood upon it that they do fix upon their war vessels I thought at first it was a model of one such, but it was a *va'a* and being much decorated I would have taken it with me except that it was too large to be conveniently stowed. Their war canoes are of great interest to me and a little before, when all of those at Matavia were paraded for a general review, the Royal family having arrived with presents for our Ships so bountiful that we had more on board than we could dispense with, I took the opportunity to get some insight into the manner of fighting them.

I having made my request, 2 of the fleet were ordered off, Mr King and myself with Otoo in one and Omai in the other. When we were out in the Bay, we faced about, both canoes advancing and retreating by turns as quick as the paddlers could move them. The warriors upon the Stages or fighting platforms brandishing their weapons and displaying all sorts of Anticks, the purpose of which seemed to be to arouse their fighting passions. Otoo stood at the side of the Stage giving the order when to advance and when to retreat. After moving thus backwards and forwards upward of a dozen times, the 2 vessels closed bows-on so that the Stages were held fast together and after a mock fight it was declared that all our men were killed and Omai and his group boarding us, Otoo and all the paddlers leaped into the sea at the very same moment to save their lives. Omai informs me that this is not always the tactic employed, but that sometimes the 2 canoes are lashed together head to head, in which case they fight until all the warriors in one or the other of the vessels is killed. It seems that if this is the method adopted, they never give any quarter unless it be to hold an enemy for a crueller death next day.

For their safety these islands and each community relies upon its Navy of war canoes, never fighting upon land but only upon the water so accustomed are they from birth to the sea and the manoeuvring of their vessels. The night before a battle is given over to feasting, the place of the engagement having been agreed by both sides in advance, and since the victor spares neither women nor children, those who have lost can only save themselves by fleeing into the mountains. This is the manner in which lands and sometimes whole islands change hands, and after the slaughter the winners all assemble at the *Morai* to give thanks to their gods and to Sacrifice the Corps of those that are slain and also the prisoners if any be taken. Omai declared that he was once taken prisoner by the men of Bolabola* and would have been put to death next day if he, and the others with him, had not contrived to make their escape.

Our mock battle over, Omai donned the Suit of Armour he had brought with him from England and mounting a Stage on one of the canoes had himself paddled all along the shore. But though he was standing in full view of all I think he was much disappointed in the attention paid to his demonstration.

I will write more about Omai, but cannot now as I have just heard from Capt Clerke that 2 of the men in the *Discovery* are missing and must go ashore to enquire of the natives. I would not mind so much except that one of them is Mr Mouat, Midshipman and son of Capt Mouat who was a commander at Quebec in 1759. Though but 16 years of age the boy should have learned better from his father than to desert ship, if that is what he has done, led astray by some Woman.

---

*Cook's spelling of the island now known as Borabora.

CHAPTER TWENTY-SEVEN

ALARMS, EXCURSIONS AND A PLOT

Wednesday, November 26th

Having been up much of the Night observing an Immersion of Jupiters 3rd Satellite with Mr King and Mr Bayly, they using the 3½ foot Gregorian Reflector, I am in no mood to accept any longer this delay in getting the 2 deserters back. It seems that Mr Mouat had publickly expressed his desire to stay in the islands and that the evening preceding Capt Clerke informing me they were missing, they had gone away from the *Discovery* in a canoe. Of this we were informed by the Natives as also that they were at the North end of the island. Capt Clerke immediately went after them with 2 armed boats and a party of Marines, returning that same evening without even any certain intelligence as to their whereabouts. By this conduct he assumed that the Natives were harbouring them, they sending him off here and there in what can only be called a wild goose chase.

Next morning, which was yesterday, we were informed they were at Otaha, whereupon I decided I must go after the 2 deserters myself, knowing full well that there were others in the Ships desirous of setting up their home ashore in the islands and if these 2 Miscreants were not quickly apprehended there would be more desertions. Also the Natives, holding me as they do in very great awe, seldom venture to deceive me with false information. Accordingly I set out with 2 armed boats, having the Chief with me so that he could direct me, the which he did so that we did not stop until we reached the middle of the East side of Otaha. There we set a man on shore to go before us with orders to have the deserters seized and held until we arrived with the boats.

All of this proved a great waste of time, for when we arrived there we were told our men had left the day before to go to Bolabola. I thought it less than prudent to follow them in the boats and so returned to the Ships, resolving to adopt my usual practice of making the Chief responsible for seeing that they are brought back. So this morning, when he did come on board, together with his Son, Daughter and Son in law, I arranged for the 3 last to be detained, Capt Clerke luring them on board his ship with the offer of knives, where he confined them in his Cabbin. When their Father heard of this, he protested to me, thinking it was done without my knowledge, and when I undeceived him on the matter, telling him it was done on my orders, he made great haste to leave my Ship. I did not have him seized, but told him he was quite at liberty to leave but that the others would be held until the Deserters were returned to me, and if they were not returned, and the enticement of others to leave the Ships did not cease, I would not hesitate to carry his family with me when I sailed, which I was already preparing to do.

The whole matter was a most tiresome business, for though the Chief sent at once to Bolabola requesting Opoony, the Chief there, to apprehend the deserters and send them back, a party of natives seized upon Capt Clerke and Lt Gore who were walking ashore a little way from the Ships. This was between 5 and 6 this evening. I was myself ashore and noticed all the natives who were in and about the harbour and the Ships suddenly moving away as though in a panic. The reason for this was not clear to me until they called out to me from the *Discovery* and told me what had happened. This was my own plan in reverse, the tables turned upon me. With no time to deliberate what to do, I instantly ordered the Ships companies to arm and within three or four minutes had despatched a strong company under the command of Mr King to rescue them, also 2 armed boats I sent after the fleeing canoes, and another party under Mr Williamson to cut off their retreat to the shore.

The seizing of our People or the sudden killing of them by these hot-blooded and sometimes warlike people is something I do often dread and fear may happen as it did to Capt Furneauxs people. But on this occasion it was a mistake, or not all of it as I discovered later when I had sent to recall both men and boats. Capt Clerke and Lt Gore were safe, but only because a fat jolly girl that was on board of the *Discovery*, having been brought by one of the officers from Huaheine, overheard some of her country men plotting to seize them and ran at once to inform our People. Also when the alarm was given and I had despatched armed boats after the dispersing canoes some shots were fired to stop them, and on hearing the report of the Muskets the party of natives armed with clubs that was coming up to Capt Clerke and Mr Gore turned on their heels and dispersed.

When I enquired into the circumstances of this plot, I discovered that the true intent had been against my own person. It was my custom every evening to go for a bathe in the fresh water that came down from the mountains, and in this exercise I was often alone and unarmed. They had expected me to go this evening and would have seized me then, and Capt Clerke if he had accompanied me which he sometimes did. But after I had confined the members of the Chiefs family on board of the *Discovery* I resolved not to go and cautioned Capt Clerke and the officers to keep close to the Ship for fear of some reprisal. The Chief came to me several times, asking if I would not go to the Water, but when he realised that I would not he went off with the rest of his people and nothing I could say would stop him, which I now realise was because he was a party to the design, if not the instigator of it.

This affair gives greater credence to the story that was whispered to me when we were at Lifuka in the

Friendly Islands. I did not believe it at the time, partly because I did not wish to, thinking perhaps the people more friendly than they were, and partly because I would have had to forego a *bomy* or night dance with torches which I greatly wished to attend for the purpose of my Journal. It concerned a native named Fenough who had first presented himself to me as the Chief, but who I later discovered was no more than the 2nd and regarded by many of his people as a bad man. Whether there was a plot or not I do not know, it being something I heard later and the dance proceeding as I have described in my Journal without anything untoward happening. The supposed plan was to cut down myself, my officers and the guard of Marines at this dance, this being proposed by the Chiefs, but Fenough objecting on the grounds that it was better done by day when detachments could be led astray in search of me until the Ships were so weakened of their complements that they could be taken by assault. Fenough had that Morning desired to see the Marines go through their exercises, and he being gratified by me in this and the Marines firing off several volleys, he may have been discouraged. But if I listened to all the tales that were current in the Ships I would have become so feared of the Natives that I would have had to forego all opportunities of studying them and their customs, which was my purpose in these islands.

That the people in these parts are warlike and sometimes treacherous I do not doubt. Oft times they behave like children and yet they are men and have their politics and the Naval power to force their will upon others of their country men. I enjoin caution upon all my People, but mixing so close with them as we must it is difficult to maintain such a guard that would keep us safe against all surprises and I rely greatly upon the awe in which all natives of the islands that I visit do seem to hold me, treating me always as a great Chief or even some sort of god. But whether that is because of my nature and behaviour or because of the power I have in my Ships and the discipline of my men I must leave to others to judge. At all times I endeavour to mingle friendliness with severity, main-taining absolute impartiality as between the natives and my own people, but it is their thievery that I do find most tiresome, so that I am not so much troubled for my own safety as for the property that is on board of my Ships and without which if they had taken something important we could not very easily continue our voyage.

CHAPTER TWENTY-EIGHT

TWO DESERTERS

Sunday, November 30th

We got away from Ulietea on the 27th, having carried everything that was on shore on board of the Ships, with the intention of following the Chief Oreo to Bolabola in search of our deserters. But the wind did not serve and the same wind that kept us in harbour brought Oreo back from that island with both men, who instantly had irons put upon both their legs and will stay confined while we continue in the islands. Shaw, who is aged 23 and a Gunners Mate, Capt Clerke has ordered disrated and he has been given 2 dozen lashes laid on very hard. Mouat will do duty before the Mast for the rest of the voyage. And that is the end of it, the vexation being more than the men are worth, particularly the boy, whom both Capt Clerke and I looked upon something as a son and who will now, by this one stupid action, make his distinguished father miserable.

The only good to be got of the affair is that the capture of them and the severity of the punishment meted out has had the effect upon everyone that I desired, the seamen petitioning their Capt to excuse Shaw further punishment and all hands promising to behave exceeding well for the future. One other good has come of it also, that Mr Webber has had the opportunity whilst she was held hostage to paint the Chiefs daughter, Poedua, who is very beautiful. And I am glad to say that some friends of the girl who gave the alarm, when the attempt to seize my two officers was made, carried her off in the middle of the night and took her to a place of safety until they could arrange for a canoe to take her back to Huaheine, the men charged with the execution of the design having threatened to kill her if she had gone openly ashore.

CHAPTER TWENTY-NINE

OMAI ABANDONED TO HIS FOOLISHNESS

Before all this happened I was intending to write something about Omai who we have now finally bid farewell to and left behind, not in his own island of Otaheite where he made too many enemies and had so much of his possessions taken from him, but at Huaheine. About this he seemed never able to make up his mind, for no sooner was it settled and the Chiefs met that could give him some protection than he desired to go on with me to Ulietea. This I would not permit, since it required that the Bolabola men that were in possession of the island be driven out and I told him bluntly that if he went there it must be as a friend and not an enemy. Whereupon I was told by one of the Elders that the whole island of Huaheine and everything in it was mine and I might give any part of it I wished to Omai. That settled, Omai began to behave in a more sensible manner, tending seriously to his affairs and seemingly to repent of the prodigality of his behaviour at Otaheite, which was the cause of so much envy and so much loss of his property. Nor did he show off by dressing up in every thing he possessed.

Accordingly I had the Carpenters set to work to build him a small house, and since the relatives he had upon his island, which was a Sister and Brother in law, were not of a standing to protect either him or his property, so that he was liable to lose everything as soon as we had gone, I advised him to take a good part of his possessions to the principal Chiefs. Had he done this he would have ensured their protection, but I heard later he did not heed my advice and so is dependent for his protection against the envy of others less well endowed than himself upon my threatening to return to the island later, when those that were his enemies would feel the weight of my resentment. And so we left him and the natives in no doubt that I would return, which is something I cannot be sure of.

He did not seem at all disposed to take a wife, though the house we built him was 24 feet by 18 and 10 feet high, fashioned out of boards with as few nails as possible so that there might be no inducement for them to pull it down. He still had of his possessions a Musket, Bayonet and Cartouche box, a fowling piece, 2 pair of Pistols and 2 or 3 Swords and Cutlasses. I gave him about twenty pound of powder, some Musket cartridges and pistol balls, though I think he would have been better without them. He was such a silly fellow in many ways so that I often had cause to regret that Capt Furneaux, if he must bring a native back to England and with so many good youths to choose from, had not carried off a more sensible. Yet he had his good points, being very likeable and sometimes useful since he could inform us what the people were saying and was always grateful of the favours he received in England.

I have written this of him in my Journal: He had a tolerable share of understanding, but wanted application and perseverance to exert it, so that his knowledge of things was very general and in many instances imperfect. He was not a man of much observation, there were many little arts as well as amusements amongst the people of the Friendly islands which he might have conveyed to his own, where they probably would have been adopted, as being as much in their own way, but I never found that he used the least endeavours to make himself master of any one. This kind of indifferency is the true Character of his Nation, Europeans have visited them at times for these ten years past, yet we find neither new arts nor improvements in the old, nor have they copied after us in any one thing. We are therefore not to expect that Omai will be able to interduce many of our arts and customs amongst them or much improve those they have got, I think however he will endeavour to bring to perfection the fruits &ca we planted which will be no small acquisition. But the greatest benefit these islands will receive from Omais travels will be in the Animals that have been left upon them, which probably they never would have got had he not come to England; when these multiplies of which I think there is little doubt, they will equal, if not exceed any place in the known World for provisions.*

The two boys that Omai took on board in New Zealand I would have taken with me, this being their wish, but that I did not entertain much hope of another ship being sent out from England to bring them home. So we left them also, one of them being so attached to us that he had to be carried ashore by force. Before we left we exhibited some of Omais fireworks, much to the delight and wonder of the great crowd of natives that were gathered to see them, and also some expressions of fear.

It was two days later, some time between 12 and 4 in the Morning, that a man who had made himself a mortal enemy of Omai, and who for Omais safety I had in confinement, contrived to make his escape, taking with him the shackle of the bilboo-bolt that was about his leg. Upon enquiry I discovered that not only the Sentry, but the whole watch on the quarter-deck had laid themselves down to sleep, so that he was able to take the Key out of his irons from a drawer. It was clear no proper lookout was being kept at night and for an example to the others I had the Mate of that watch, Mr Harvey, disrated and sent on board of the *Discovery* as a midshipman and Mr Martin, one of Capt Clerkes midshipmen, brought on board the *Resolution* and rated Mate. Mr Mackay, the midshipman of that watch, I sent before the Mast, he and Mr Harvey being both in bed during the watch,

*This was not the case, Bligh recording on his voyage in the *Bounty* that all but the pigs and dogs were dead.

and since the Sentry and the Quartermaster appeared guilty of aiding the escape they were flogged a dozen lashes on each of several days. In this manner some of the Marines were also punished, this being something that cannot be overlooked if we are to have a safe voyage.

The night before we left Huaheine, I and all the officers, except Capt Clerke whose health was very poorly,* dined ashore with Omai, when we were served with the very best the island afforded. Before we departed I had this Inscription carved upon one end of his house: *Georgius tertius Rex 2 Novembris 1777 Naves: Resolution Jac. Cook Pr, Discovery Car. Clerke Pr.*†

---

*He was already suffering from the tuberculosis he had contracted during his period in prison.

†Pr is short for *Praefectus, praefectus naves* being the Latin for Captain of a ship.

CHAPTER THIRTY

THE COMMANDER'S RESPONSIBILITIES

It is with relief that I am now able to turn such energies as are left to me towards the object of this Voyage. My enforced stay in these islands, though of benefit to my official Journal, has proved most fatiguing and a great burden upon my resources, the which has been increased by Capt Clerkes sickly state of health, though in all other respects I could not wish for a better nor a more pleasing officer to have with me in command of our consort. All these six months I have felt the weight of my responsibility to maintain discipline among my own People as well as to ensure their strict behaviour towards the natives, so that there be no reason or excuse for them to fall out with us. During such a long period with oft times so little for our men to do the danger is boredom. This is something that seldom occurs on a Vessel of War, not even during a blockade, for they are at sea and the crew in watches and so pretty fully engaged.

On this voyage that I am sent upon the temptation

to desert and otherwise behave in a manner that is contrary to the Navys practice and discipline is very great and it is upon the Commander that rests the whole weight of maintaining that sense of purpose and endeavour that alone can carry the voyage to a successful conclusion, and this as much by his own self-discipline and manner at all times as by the strictness of his regime. Yet he must at the same time consider the happiness of his People, so that they do not hate him to the extent of conspiring to mutinous proceedings, but only respect him and hold him in some awe. I do relax sometimes, when I am bathing or feasting with the natives, their manner being so exceeding cheerful and friendly that on occasions I attend wearing nothing but my breeches, unarmed and with my head bare so that my hair, which is now bleached almost as white with the sun as the coral sand, hangs down to my shoulders. Officers of a seventy-four or some such ship of the line would be very surprised to see me then, but I cannot always be on my guard, month after weary month.

And it is not only the maintaining of proper discipline and constantly looking to our safety ashore or at anchor that is tiresome. I am informed by the people of these islands that there are sometimes great storms that come tearing down upon them with very huge dangerous seas and I have seen some evidence of these where palm trees have been snapped off and whole villages destroyed and abandoned. This gives me some cause to believe what they say and, besides maintaining our observations, must always have an eye to the weather so that we may take action in advance to save our ships, the anchorages not always being very secure, though the best we can find in islands that are more often than not surrounded by coral reefs.

However, the health of my People is very good and except for the Venereal and those diseases of the Tropics that are to be found here we have suffered very little Sickness. They have the advantage of all manner of fruits and vegetables, also fish from the sea, including turtle which they have much sport in catching, so that I have at no time had difficulty in the provision of a proper diet. I hope I will find as good upon the American coast, but knowing the scarcity of such provisions on the East side of that continent, I do not think it very likely.

CHAPTER THIRTY-ONE

AN ISLAND FOR CHRISTMAS

Tuesday, December 30th

We are now at a very barren low island with but a few shrubs and plants growing out of a black soil that would seem to be composed of the dung of birds and decayed vegetables mixed with the coral sand. In places it is bare of anything but coral stones and shells thrown up in long narrow ridges. These are like fields ploughed parallel to the coast, but sometimes well back from it so that I think it incontestable that the whole island is formed of Marine productions and continues in a state of increase. There is no water to be had here and those who have drunk of the Brackish pools have suffered bad results of it. The island is some 16 miles long and almost as many across, which is larger than I have seen before of islands formed totally of Marine creatures. But at our first sighting of it, which was on the 24th about half an hour after day breake, it appeared only as a low bank with a few Cocoa nut trees enclosing a lagoon.

This sort of island is very common in the Pacific,

and a great contrast to Bolabola which was a very high mountainous island. After leaving Bolabola I steered to the Northward close-hauled, the wind being generally between N and NE, and some time in the night between the 22nd and 23rd we crossed the Equator in the Longitude of 203ϒ15 E. Before leaving the Society Islands I enquired of the inhabitants whether there were any islands to the N or NW of them, but they declared they knew of none. It is thus evident, though they progress 2 or 3 thousand miles southward across the Pacific, that for some reason they do not sail their canoes in this direction, for on the 24th about ½ an hour after day breake this land was sighted. The wind being ESE we only had to make a few bords to get up to the lee of it when we anchored in about 14 fathoms fine sand some ½ a mile from the breakers.

The next day being Christmas Day I named this island Christmas Island as I had called the place where we spent Christmas last year in the Kerguelen Islands Christmas Harbour. I sent a boat from each ship to seek out a landing place and 2 others to fish. These last caught 2 hundred weight of fish between day breake and 8 o'clock. After breakfast I sent them out again and myself went in another boat to search for a way through the reef, but found none. About noon Mr Bligh returned with the first 2 boats I had sent and reported a Channel into the lagoon about a league and a half to the N of us, but only fit for boats, the whole lagoon being very shallow.

As the previous year, we could not hold our festivities on the proper day but kept Christmas Day on the

26th, the People being served with fresh pork from the Hogs we had from Bolabola, also fish and a double Allowance of Spirits. Having reports of turtle in the lagoon, and of the green sort which are very good eating, I ordered Capt Clerke to send a boat out hunting for them in the SE part of the lagoon while I, with Mr King, went each in a boat to the NE part. We saw but one, which we caught, then waded through the water, which was not very deep, to the small sand island that is at the entrance to the lagoon. Afterwards I left Mr King to observe the Suns Meridian and went inland, walking to the sea coast where I saw 5 turtle swimming close inshore, only one of which we caught, but it was the exercise I enjoyed after the hot tedious passage to the Equator.

The men are in great spirits, there being no inhabitants here and no need for any strict regulations. As many as can be spared from the Ships are sent out hunting for turtle, which gives them good sport, so that they forget what lies ahead on the voyage and give themselves up to the full enjoyment of this most barren island. I and Mr Bayly have been occupied in other directions, for this morning there was an Eclipse of the Sun to be observed and we began our preparations 2 days ago. This was the chief cause of my anchoring at this island for such a length of time.

The results we obtained this morning were not very satisfactory, the Sun being clouded at times and toward noon the heat of it reflected from the sand very great. Also there was a protuberance in the Moon, which escaped my notice, so that though Mr Bayly and I

were both observing with the large Acromatic Tellesco-
pes which are of the same magnifying power, there
was a difference in the time between us of 26 seconds.
Mr King was observing with the reflector and Capt
Clerke would have assisted but that he was in such
poor health that he was incapable of the effort. I am
greatly concerned about his condition, there being
nobody with his experience among my officers and if
anything should happen to me the great weight of
responsibility for the conduct of the expedition falls
upon him; if his health do not improve I am doubtful
that he can survive the rigours of the fog and ice we
shall encounter to the N of North America.

CHAPTER THIRTY-TWO

FUN AND STUPIDITIES ASHORE

Sunday, January 18th, 1778

We weighed from Christmas Island at day breake on the 2nd and this Morning raised an island bearing NE by E with more land bearing N seen shortly afterward. But we have light airs and calms now so that it will be some time yet before we make up to it and discover what sort of a land this is.

During the week we were anchored off the lagoon at Christmas Island we took on board of the 2 ships about 300 turtles, which is a most providential addition to our provisions. They weigh about a hundred pound apiece with the shell and all the people engaged on the hunting of them had the greatest sport in getting them. With those that are on the shore sleeping it is but a simple matter to turn them on their backs and leave them thus helpless for the boats to collect. But when they are in the water, where they are to be found waiting in deep pools for the return of the tide, they are in their own element and very powerful so that often they escape into deep water beyond the reef.

Most of our men though not myself included are the best of swimmers and there is much merriment over the chase. There is some danger also, for there are numerous sharks, they being so voracious that they bite at the oars and even the rudders. The men who are fishing go armed with long pikes to hold these creatures off, and on board of the ships, when they are caught by those that are fishing with lines, they sometimes lash two of them together by the tails so that they cannot dive, which is called spritsail yarding them and causes great merriment.

It is very fortunate that we have not lost any men to these sharks, the biggest damage any has suffered being from the coral, the cuts being most difficult to heal. We did nearly lose 2 men, but only from the helplessness of sailors on shore who never seem able to look for what is obvious to any sensible man but become totally confused. The men were missing the last two days of December, the one for 24 hours, the other for 40 hours. The former saved himself by killing and drinking the blood of a turtle, which he also gave to his companion, but seeing that he was too weak to wander any further, he left him and finally joined one of the *Resolution*s boats. A search party found the other after walking some dozen miles or more across the island. He was in such great distress from the heat and lack of water, and also the burns that the sun had inflicted on his skin, that though revived with some bread and weak Grog he could scarce travel back to the boat.

Of this incident I have written in my Journal that it was a matter of surprise to every one how these men contrived to lose themselves, the land over which they had to travel from the sea coast to the lagoon where the boats lay was not much more than three miles across, and it was a plain with here and there a few shrubs upon it and from many parts of which the Ships masts were to be seen; but this was a thing they never once thought of looking for, nor did they know in what direction the ships were from them, nor which way to go to find either them or the party no more than if they had but just dropped from the clouds. Considering what a strange set of beings the generality of seamen are when on shore, instead of being surprised at these men losing themselves we ought rather to have been surprised there were no more of them; indeed one of my people lost himself in the same place, but happening to have sagasity enough to know that the ships were to leeward, he got on board almost as soon as it was known he was missing.

The Latitude of Christmas Island is 1ϒ59′N and the Longitude 202ϒ30′E, which was established by as many observations of the Moon as there was time for. Besides Marine animals, there was on the island land crabs, small lizards and rats, and of birds Men of War and Tropic birds, Boobies, Terns, Curlews, Sand pipers and a small land bird like a hedge sparrow. Before leaving I had planted some Cocoa nuts and yams that we had on board and some Mellon seeds, and I left a bottle containing the inscription *Georgius tertius Rex 31 Decembris 1777* with the name of the ships and their captains as I had done at Huaheine. Most of the time we were anchored there we had fresh Easterly gale, but always a great swell from the Northward which broke in a very big surf on the reef, and this swell remained with us 2 days after we sailed, though the weather was fine with but a gentle breeze from the Easterly direction.

Not expecting to sight any land between Christmas Island and the American coast of New Albion, the day we sailed I set the Carpenters to work upon the caulking of the main deck and the following week once again had the Fearnought jackets and trousers served out. I also put the Ships companies to an allowance of 2 quarts of water a day per man, the wind being contrary and fearing a slow passage. Between Latitudes 10 and 11 we sighted several turtle and there have been birds with us every day, both which usually indicate land in the vicinity, but none that we saw until this Morning, when our position was 21ϒ12′N, 200ϒ41′E.

CHAPTER THIRTY-THREE

THE UNEXPECTED ISLANDS

Thursday, January 22nd

Our situation last Night and this Morning was none of the safest, the wind between SE and S with constant rain and ourselves so anchored that our stern is little more than 2 cables* from the breakers. We did not get to this anchorage on the second of the 3 islands† we had sighted till the 20th, having stood off and on all night. By then we knew the islands were inhabited, canoes having come out to us, and everyone surprised and gratified to find the natives had many words that were the same they spoke at Otaheite and the other islands we have visited so that our People could make themselves understood. And they had the same aptitude for thievery, or rather they thought they had the right to whatever they could lay their hands upon. Of

---

*A cable is 100 fathoms – i.e. 200 yards.

†These were the western islands of the Hawaiian group.

this we had immediate example, the first man that came on board making away with the lead and line with which we had been sounding and taking it into his canoe. Another took the Butchers cleaver and leaped over the side with it.

This same desire to possess whatever they could get hold of was the cause of an accident ashore that was quite contrary to my orders and as a result not reported to me at the time by the officer in charge, which was Mr Williamson. Attempting a landing, he was prevented by the great number of inhabitants that came down to the boat. They pressed so thick upon him, laying hold of oars, muskets, anything to hand, that he felt obliged to fire and so killed one of them. Mr Williamson is not the best of my officers and when I questioned him closely on the matter, he admitted that the natives did not seem intending any harm to our people, but were chiefly excited by curiosity and it was probably this that caused the man he killed to lay hold of his pistol.

It was such an incident as I have always used my best endeavours to avoid. I was very angry when I knew about it. These islands had water and we had taken on none since leaving Bolabola, which was 2 months since, and not to be told of it at once made it a worse offence. Finding the people friendly on our first acquaintance I did not order the degree of protection to those ashore that I would have done had I known of this incident.

There was at that time something I felt more important weighing upon me, not knowing that a man had been killed. When we arrived at these unexpected islands there were on board of the ships some that were suffering from venereal complaints, they having contracted the disease from the Women they had connection with in the Society Islands. There may well be others that we do not know about, for there are always some who will do what they can to conceal it from their fellows, being ashamed. And there are always men that do not care that they communicate it to the natives. We had an instance of this at Tongatapu in the Friendly Islands. The Gunner of the *Discovery* was put ashore by Capt Clerke to conduct trade with the natives and even when he knew he had contracted the disease he continued to sleep with different women, thereby giving it to them, or so they supposed. He continued in this manner despite the expostulations of his companions until Captain Clerke heard of it and recalled him to the Ship.

Accordingly, on our arrival here I gave strict orders prohibiting all intercourse with native women. No women are allowed upon the ships and no man is to go ashore in whatever capacity if he has the disease, is in any way suspected of it, or is off the Surgeons list as recently cured of it. The more serious of the men understand the reason for my orders, but the most of them have thought only for the moment and the pleasure they are deprived of, being quite incapable of imagining how others that come after us will regard our behaviour if they find we have introduced this foul disease to people that were previously free of it. I have enjoined all the officers to maintain the utmost vigilance to prevent any intercourse whatsoever, but I doubt if we can prevent it entirely for some of these girls are exceeding wanton and abandoned and I have been told of occasions when they have endeavoured to drag our men into their houses by force.

I had reports of water here in ponds or shallow wells and as soon as we were anchored I went ashore with three boats to examine the supply and test the disposition of the natives. There were several hundred of them gathered on the sandy beach before the village and the very instant I leapd from my boat they all fell flat on their faces before me and did not rise until I had made a sign for them to do so. They then came to us with an abundance of provisions for the which they seemed not to want anything in return except my good opinion of them. From their behaviour it would seem the power I command of men and ships makes me appear to them a great chief or king.

The watering proceeded without any obstruction, the natives even assisting in rolling the casks to and from the pond. I took a walk up a valley accompanied by Dr Anderson and Mr Webber and a considerable retinue of the inhabitants, and everywhere I went the people prostrated themselves, lying with their faces to the ground till I had passed. There was in this valley a pyramid about 20 feet high which was some sort of temple, being in a *Morai* much like those of Otaheite with the same carved boards, but part covered by a thin grey cloth; something similar to this had been thrust upon me as I came ashore from the boat. Mr Webber made a good drawing of this edifice and later we saw others at every village along the E coast of the island. And at all these villages there was also many plantations of Tarra and Plantain, Sugar cane and the Chinese paper Mulberry tree or cloth plant, so that, the people being so friendly and good natured, and so much in awe of me, we are not likely to go in want of provisions, pigs being in great plenty also.

CHAPTER THIRTY-FOUR

SERGEANT OVERBOARD

Sunday, February 1st

Tomorrow I intend to sail. We are not yet full up with water, there being not too much of it to be had here and all to be carried off to the ships in the boats, but as we progress Northward into Winter there will be less consumed than is required in the vicinity of the Equator. We have a full 3 weeks of provisions and a good diet to maintain the health of our People. This continued exceeding good considering all the circumstances, except that we have had an outbreak of the Yellow Jaundice. However, those that suffered from it show every sign of recovering fast and we have only lost one man, which is Roberts, the Quartermaster.

This man died the Morning of January 27th, having been sick of a Dropsy and unable to do any duty since we left England. I wish now that I had sent him home from the Cape for his death was very long drawn out and a sad sight to watch. I am also concerned for the health of Dr Anderson. He is in the same Consumptive state as Capt Clerke, and though both are at times sufficiently recovered to take a little exercise with me ashore, they are at other times so incapable that they are scarce able to undertake their responsibilities. Both would be a great loss to me, and not only for what they contribute to the expedition, but also for their companionship, so that oft times when I am alone in my bed I think of this, and about the meaning of death. This voyage is not like the others, for it has afforded me in my loneliness on board a great deal of time for reflection on matters that are too private to mention even here.

One thing I should mention is that on the following day I persuaded myself once again to carry my son Nathanials name on the Ships books as an able seaman, having carried both him and his brother James on the pay and victualling roll on my two previous voyages. This earns them time and myself something extra, and though some people may regard it as fraudulent, it is nevertheless very general and the custom among most captains. I had forgot to do this previously, James being now at the Naval Academy at Portsmouth and no longer needing to earn his sea time in this manner.

A more amusing matter to reflect upon occurred the Night of the same day Thos Roberts died when I was woken with the report of a man having fallen overboard from the *Discovery*. This was the Sergeant of the Marines who, being a little drunk with liquor, laid himself down upon the gangway to sleep it off. Both ships were under way at the time coasting along the islands and he slipping off the side of the *Discovery* into the sea one of the watch with great presence of mind seized upon a Machine that had been sent aboard in England to try, it being designed for just this very purpose. It is a pole with a weight at one end, a bell at the other, and corks to support a man in the middle. It was intended that the man that is overboard should sit in the corks and the movement of the waves would ring the bell, so enabling his rescuers to come to him. I had already tried out this Machine with our best swimmers, but they could never sit in the corks and the bell had to be rung by shaking the pole, the which the Sergeant did so bringing the *Discovery*s boat to him.

CHAPTER THIRTY-FIVE

OF GODS AND THE POLYNESIANS

This morning I got off Mr Gore and his party that was marooned ashore. I had sent them to trade with the natives on Friday and a gale springing up they were kept there 2 days by a very heavy surf falling upon the beach. This was the thing I had most wished to avoid, there being some 20 men ashore 2 nights including the Marines to guard them and as a result intercourse with the women very likely. Even the natives durst not venture out to us in their canoes and I only rescued our people by ordering Mr Gore to march his men to the SE point where they could be embarked. I took this opportunity to give some Goats, Pigs and seeds to a man who seemed to be in some command. At the same time I took a little walk into the island and when I stopped to look around a woman called to the natives that were with me, whereupon the Chief began muttering something like a prayer, and the 2 men that were holding the pigs walked round and round me. Thereafter many natives came to me from all parts of the island and all at a word from those that were with me laid down and remained with their faces to the ground until I was out of sight.

This behaviour of the natives of these islands is very strange. It is also somewhat disturbing, for in their manner they have raised me to a station that is entirely beyond capability of fulfilment. Their gods I know to be strange gods and something beyond my understanding, but that my person should be regarded in this fashion is to place me in the awkward position of not knowing what I am in their eyes and what they would have me be.

In the circumstances, I was not a little relieved that the gale forced me to get under way. This happened about 7 o'clock this evening, the anchor starting so that the Ship came off the bank on which we were anchored and no alternative then but to get the cable in and hoist sail. Now, thinking back to the visit we have made to these five islands, I have to remark upon the similarity of their people to many others of the South sea islands. They have a darker hue than the Otaheiteans, which may be because they wear less clothing, but I have no doubt they are of the same nation. So how shall we account for this nation, finding them as I have from New Zealand in the south to these islands in the North, and from Easter Island to the Hebrides? They are thus stretched out over 70° of latitude north and south, and 83° of longitude east and west, and how much farther I do not know, but west beyond the Hebrides I have no doubt; a great square of some 1300 leagues each way.

It is a most extraordinary range of ocean for any people and considering the nature of their craft and the squals that infest the whole region, there can be little doubt that these are the greatest navigators of any race, not excluding my own, our ships being so much bigger.

PART FIVE

AMERICA AND THE ARCTIC

CHAPTER THIRTY-SIX

DOUBTS AND HOPES

Sunday, February 15th, 1778

It is now two weeks since we left the islands, the longitude of them having been fixed by a total of 72 lunar observations. The *Discovery* had caught up with us by the 2nd and though the course I wished to make was NE we were forced to stand away to the Northward, the wind being Easterly and very fresh. On the 7th the wind veered south easterly so that we could steer our course, but on the 12th it veered round by S and W back to NE so that I had to tack and stand to the Northward again, our position then being 30°N, 206°15′E. We have had no sight of any further land and the temperature seeming very cold after so long in the Tropics, though the Thermometer still reads about 60°.

During this time there has been much preparation on board of both vessels for the harder conditions that lie ahead. The Carpenters have been working on the Boats, which were badly stove in the surf, the Armourers forging new keel bands, and I have the Sailmakers busy at the sails. A strange matter, and one that is very revealing of the manner sailors have of settling to a habit, the Ships company petitioned me to serve them Sour Krout, which I did, though for their health there was no need of it for they still had plenty of the provisions we got of the islands, particularly Yams. The cockroaches we got of the Friendly Islands will I hope disappear as soon as we are in colder waters, but the rats that came aboard of us more recently are a serious matter, Capt Clerke reporting that he is having to make good a large hole eaten by them in the Quarter Deck where he had Yams stored.

The handling of the Ship being taken care of by Mr Bligh, and I only concerned with the Noon observations according to my Instructions, this fortnight has been a time for reflection upon the matter on which I am sent on this Voyage and what may lie ahead for us all. The two maps* lie constantly before me, and I giving so much attention to them that I have every detail of the supposed coastlines of Capt Behrings straits clearly imprinted on my mind. More particularly I have lately been examining closely the map which Müller included in his *Voyages from Asia to America*, the which he has called *A General Map of the Discoveries of Admiral De Fonte and other Navigators, Spanish, English and Russian, in quest of a passage to the South Sea*. It is described as being by Mr De Lisle and dated September 1752. This shows a

*Those of Müller (1761) and Stählin (1774).

lake that Bernarda sailed across stretching 436 leagues in a NEasterly direction and also the Passage that De Fuca discovered ending in the so-called West Sea, the eastern extremity of which is blocked by a great range of mountains extending from California to about latitude 65°N. And there is Admiral De Fontes route across the North American continent, entering it by way of a river called the De Los Reys and proceeding by way of Lake De Fonte or Mishinipi through Ronquillo Strait & Lake to Hudsons Bay. And in the far north of the Map at about latitude 80° are printed the words *Mountains of Ice*.

The more often I look at this Map the stranger it becomes, there being some of it that I must accept, though the exactness of the positions of rivers, lakes and mountains must be in some doubt, and there is much else that I fear is no more than a part of the mapmakers art, being based as I know them often to be on reports that are not in any way confirmed and sections of coastline drawn in for no other reason but that they wish to publish a complete map and not a collection of unconnected sightings of land.

How is it possible to put any faith or credence in this pretended strait of a Spanish Admiral or the long voyage across an inland lake of his Captain Bernarda when by all accounts these Spaniards will claim anything to their own personal advantage and glory and for the satisfaction of those in Madrid who have sent them north from the Pacific colonies? The voyage that De Fonte made in 1640 I have no reason to doubt, but until I see his passage with my own eyes I will believe his Discoveries to be no more than vague and improbable stories.

What then am I to think of the voyage of the Greek Capt Juan De Fuca, which was even earlier, being made in 1592? His claim to have sailed across the American continent from one side to the other in 22 days is not something that I can believe to be in any degree accurate. But their Lordships do believe there may be something in it and being a Greek and his people so much of a seamanlike disposition, I cannot dismiss it entirely. But in all of this I fear there is too much of hope and too little of reality, all our own people having failed to find a way through from the Atlantic Ocean or, from the Pacific side, even to approach the latitude of De Fucas strait, the which is about 45°N.

Only the Russians, and in particular the Danish Capt Behring, have succeeded in proving anything substantial in this extreme north part of the Pacific. I have myself great hopes and expectations of finding a Passage. But all that has been said of it was, previous to my last voyage, said and claimed for the Terra Incognita of the Southern Hemisphere, and it may be that this will prove to be as great an illusion as the Southern Continent.

If that is the case, then I intend to prove it to be so, as I did with the other, so that no man will ever thereafter have to be sent north again on another such voyage.

And though I doubt the validity of anything printed upon the map of De Fontes Discoveries and do fear I may find that the Mountains of Ice may prove, to my great discomfort, to be the one exact and correct statement thereon, I shall still press forward into the Arctic Sea to the utmost of the Ships capabilities and my mens endurance. There is such a deal to be gained for my Country if I discover the Passage, and much that has been offered to myself if I am successful. Time will give me the answer, not these maps, not even Dampiers dream, who is a man for whom I have considerable respect.

Saturday, March 7th

This Morning at day breake we raised the Coast of New Albion, which is that part of the western coast of America that is north of California. The land is about 8 miles distant extending from NE½N to SEbyE, of moderate height and well wooded. Our position by the Noon observation is 44Υ33′N, 235Υ20′E. Prior to our sighting of it, we had seen few birds or Oceanic animals that would indicate land anywhere in the vincinity until yesterday Noon when we sighted two seals and a whale.

Now that we are upon the Coast of North America I feel a great uplifting of the spirits, having wasted half a year, or so it seems, and now at last finding myself set upon the threshold of that purpose for which I am come here. The wind is light and variable and we are standing NE to close the coast. From hereon we shall have it always off the starboard side until we are through those Straits and can turn our bows to the eastward towards home.

Tonight I am thinking of my Elizabeth and the family, praying that I have the good fortune to return to them direct across the North of the World. What a peal of bells would ring out, what honour I would have, and some fortune too ... but my hopes run faster than this sun-dried leaking ship can sail and I know from experience there are more foul winds than fair and nothing is ever achieved but that you force it through against much difficulties.

CHAPTER THIRTY-SEVEN

AMERICAN INDIANS AND SPARS

Tuesday, March 31st

These last weeks have not been of the best, the weather proving very foul for which reason I have now named the first point of land sighted Cape Foul Weather. My greatest difficulty was to discover a safe harbour, our search for it being hindered by the weather and by that natural caution that besets the Discoverer closing with an unknown land. No sooner were we near to the coast than the wind came to NW in Squals of hail and sleet, the weather thickening so that I considered it best to stand out to sea again.

We made several attempts to explore the coast more closely, but the wind was generally from the westerly direction, hard gale at times with heavy squals, sometimes with snow showers, the land here still being in the grip of Winter. In this searching for some suitable harbour, which is very urgent now for the water we need and also to repair the ships after so long at sea, we made nothing to the Northward and at one time were pushed so far to the Southward that a Cape we sighted was most probably that called Cape Blanco, which was discovered by Martin de Aguilar in January 1603. During all this period we suffered extreme discomfort, the ship leaking at her upper works and all feeling the cold.

The wind continued between W and NW, storms and moderate calms succeeding one another by turns, until the 21st when it backed to SW becoming fairer and enabling me to stand to the NE, so recovering the ground lost and closing the land again. The sails were got out to dry and the Bread Room smoked with Sulphur to kill the cockroaches; there was also rats to hunt, which kept the men busy and entertained. Two days after the wind was back at W and NW, moderating at evening and veering S, which was always the prelude to storm with rain and sleet. These southerly blasts, which lasted but 4 or 6 hours before we had another gale from NW, was the only means we made up to the Northward at all.

It was not until the 29th,* when we were standing to NE, that we saw the land again. It was of very different appearance, full of high mountains, their tops white with snow, and as we closed it we sighted what appeared to be two inlets. I bore up for that which

---

*It was during this night that Cook sailed past the entrance to the Straits of Juan de Fuca. He had no means of knowing that the land he closed next day was not the mainland or that the 'Passage' de Fuca had discovered was in fact the seaway between Vancouver Island and the mainland.

was in the NE corner of the bay we were in and after entering it and being twice becalmed, we finally anchored just before night fall so close to the shore as to reach it with a hawser. This coast is inhabited, the which we discovered even as we closed the inlet, having at one time as many as 32 canoes full of Indians about us and almost a dozen of these remained along side most part of the night.

They appear a mild inoffensive people and very ready to trade, mostly the skins of such animals as Bears, Wolfs, Foxes, Dear, Polecats, Rackoons, Martins and in particular the Sea Beaver.* In exchange they take knives, chisels, pieces of iron and tin, nails and buttons, in fact anything of metal pleases them greatly. But here is the same problem as we had in the islands, they being as light-fingered as any we had met with. We have had them with us all this day and on board they mingle with our people with great freedom and lack of restraint, but with their knives they can cut anything free that takes their fancy. Our boats are stripped of everything in a moment, and in a very wily manner, one fellow amusing the guard while at the other end his companions are pulling it to pieces. If discovered at once, and we usually did so for they appear very ready to impeach one another, the thief is very reluctant to return the article, often being induced to do so only by force.

If this is the measure of all the Indians we shall meet with on this coast, then we shall have much

*Probably otter.

trouble securing our belongings and all that is on board the ships. At this present time it is near impossible to keep a guard upon everything, for I have had the Topmast struck and the Foremast unrigged in order to fix a new bibb in place of that which was decayed so that the deck is much littered with the rigging.

Sunday, April 19th

The condition of the masts, the which I last wrote about, is causing us all great concern. It is not only the sticks that are decayed, but also the lower standing rigging. After getting the Main rigging set up on the 11th, we next day attempted to get the Mizenmast out, but it was so rotten it fell while the mast was in the slings. I spent a whole day in the woods with a party that was sent ashore to cut down a suitable tree and next morning we dragged it to the place where the Carpenters were working on the Foremast. But when the work on the new Mizenmast was almost half done, the stick was found to be sprung, which was doubtless caused in the felling of it, so that we had to cut down another tree and start again.

Today, being the first fair day we have had for a fortnight, we got up Topmasts and Yards and set up the rigging. This was the most of the heavy and difficult work done and if the weather holds I feel sufficiently at ease with the state of the ship to have a look at the Sound in the morning. I shall be glad of the opportunity to be free of the Ship for a day, my energies having been so much directed toward the problems of refitting, and the Indians having to be guarded against all the time. Every day we spend here is a day lost in making to the Northward, not knowing what we may expect there except that the Summer will be very short lived.

CHAPTER THIRTY-EIGHT

THE PEOPLE OF NOOTKA SOUND

Sunday, April 26th

At last we are ready to sail, but this morning Tide and Wind was against us. After we had got the Sails bent on and the Observatory with all our Instruments back on board, it took two more days to put the Ship in a condition for sea and bring on board small spars and timbers we have cut for use during the voyage. When we could not sail I was so frustrated with the trick the weather played on me I took Capt Clerke ashore to visit an Indian village at the mouth of the Sound, where we were received in a most friendly and hospitable fashion.

Their houses are communal, and since they use them for cooking, sleeping and all natural functions the smell inside of them is most disagreeable, being a mixture of rotten fish, sweat and urine, and far worse than anything we experience on board of our ships even when, because of bad weather, we are unable to ventilate or even to smoake below decks. As in other villages, we were offered food, but what they eat and the manner in which it is served is not to my liking. Capt Clerke, who seemed very cheerful today, said if anything happened to us upon these shores it might be to our advantage to accustom ourselves to the diet, but he also refused to partake of what we were offered.

We came back to the ship about noon with a boatload of grass and it was shortly after our return that one of the Indians that was on board jumped into his canoe with a piece of iron he had stolen. He refused to give it up even when I seized a Musket from the Marine that was on guard and threatened him. In the end I was so angry with the stupidity of the Man, he knowing full well what damage the weapon could inflict on him, that I fired it down into the canoe. In accordance with my orders it was loaded only with small shot so for his stupidity he and several others had their backsides peppered with it, and so we got the iron back and they left us in a less friendly manner than was usual.

It always seems to be the same, in every place we anchor, that sooner or later an example has to be made to protect our stores and teach the natives to respect our property. Shortly after this it fell calm so we let go our Moorings and proceeded down the Sound with the boats towing. About 4 this afternoon we were able to hoist in the boats and proceed under sail, a breeze coming in from the North and a very thick haze with it. I expect a storm shortly for the Mercury in the Barometer is unusually low.

Sunday, May 17th

The Sound we left on the 26th April I named King
Georges Sound, but the Indians called it Nootka
Sound.* We were in that Sound near on a whole
month, the which I fear I may regret, so much time
having to be spent on work that should have been
done at Deptford before we left England. Now the
question in my mind is the same as it was last year,
shall we be able to get far enough to the North to
open up the Passage in time to have full advantage of
the short Summer? I think it necessary to have discovered the entrance to the Passage, if such exist, by
the beginning of August at the very latest, the which
is no more than two and a half months away.

I fear we may soon have to rely upon the antiscor-
butics that are among our provisions, for we found
but little in the way of fresh vegetables in King Georges
Sound. The most benefit we had was from the forest
spruce trees from which we made beer, though a tolerable quantity of wild garlick was brought us by the
natives and this sweetens our broth, and there was a
firm root which is edible though like to liquorice in
taste. Of fruit I found Raspberry, Currents and Goose-
berry and will hope I can rely upon them and possibly
others to be ripening as we proceed North.

Some account of the Nootka Indians was written
in my Journal while we were in the Sound. They are
a very different people to all those we have previously

*Nootka Sound is the name by which it is now known. It is halfway
up the west coast of Vancouver Island.

encountered in the Pacific, most particularly for what they cover themselves with in this colder climate and in their gods. For their cloathes they depend greatly on the animals of the spruce forest, but they eat mainly fish and other Marine animals, these being coast Indians and most certainly different in their customs and behaviour from those described by Hearne and others of the Hudsons Bay Company that have explored the interior. Though friendly, they are very dirty both in their Persons and in the manner of preparing their Victuals, but of their gods I understand very little. They most commonly have in their houses very large images carved of wood and in human form of which they speak in a most mysterious manner, and when Mr Webber was intending to draw one of these there was a man who seemed very displeased, but later for iron or brass they would have let me walk away with any I wished for. If these are their gods they hold them very cheap for I now have 2 or 3 of the smaller.

The cause of my failing to learn much of the Government and Religion of these people is that I have none with me who can speak their language, and because it is of the greatest importance that I be able to communicate with them, I spent considerable time while at Nootka making a list of some of their words and the meanings thereof. This I did chiefly by signs, writing the answers down as best I could by the sound of the words they spoke. But while this may help to make our requirements known to other Indians we shall meet with, it will not suffice for me to make enquiry of them what ships have been on this coast and where I may find the entrance to the Passage leading through to the north and east.

This is my greatest difficulty and one that I am not likely to overcome.

CHAPTER THIRTY-NINE

REPAIRS AND A POSSIBLE PASSAGE

For the last day of April we were in 53ϒ22′N, which is the latitude of the pretended Strait of Admiral de Fonte. But it would not have been prudent to keep in to the coast, the weather being very tempestuous, and so I cannot state with absolute authority what I believe to be true, that the Geographers have been misguided about the very existence of the Los Reys river.

All the beginning of May we had fair weather, the calms on occasion of such absolute serenity as I have seldom seen, sky and sea appearing as one and everything reflected with the clarity of a mirror, so that our progress has been slow. Not until the 6th did we arrive at what I think to be Capt Behrings anchorage, the latitude being 59ϒ18′N which corresponds pretty well with the Map of his Voyage. This was after we had sighted a most remarkable conical mountain which I named Mt Edgecombe, the snow pouring down from its top like cream on a cake, all of which Mr Webber drew most perfectly. At this point the coast began to trend more and more in a westerly direction and at the same time our fine weather gave way to fog and excessive hard squals from SE.

All this time we had the coast close aboard and not only for the purpose of mapping it. The ship had developed a leak and I wanted to get into some anchorage where it could be stopped. This I was finally able to do in a large bay or inlet, heeling the ship at her mooring by Kedge anchor and hawser. In laying out the Kedge one man had his legs fractured, being carried out of the boat by the buoy rope and dragged straight to the bottom. It is difficult to protect men from their own carelessness, but at least he had the good sense to disengage himself from the rope and come to the surface again. The Carpenters, on ripping off the Sheeting, found the leak to be in the seams, those both in and under the wale being very open and in some places devoid of Oakum.

On our anchoring in this inlet and my sending a boat to sound the head of it, there was an attempt by Indians armed with spears to take it. This being prevented, they moved to the *Discovery* and on climbing aboard and finding only the officer of the watch and a few others on deck, the ship appearing otherwise deserted for it was early morning and most were still asleep below, they drew their knives, making signs to the officer and others to keep off, and began looking for what they could take. They had already tossed the rudder of one of the boats down to their canoes when the men below, alarmed at what they could hear on deck, came up armed with cutlasses. That was sufficient to discourage the Indians and no Musket shot was fired.

It would seem from their boldness that these people have no knowledge or experience of firearms, otherwise they would not have dared attempt any such thing, which leads me to think that no other ship has been upon this coast.

We weighed at 4 o'clock this Morning with a light breeze from ENE and meeting with a good deal of foul ground and the wind failing us, we had considerable difficulty extricating ourselves from the danger that threatened. The Channel of this inlet is about 6 leagues across and wide enough to be the entrance to some Passage, which I intend to explore, having now anchored again under the eastern shore.

CHAPTER FORTY

DISAPPOINTMENT

Monday, May 18th

There is no passage here, or very doubtful. I sent Mr Gore with 2 armed boats up the northern arm and he reported it extending a long way to the NE. I then sent Mr Roberts one of the mates to sketch it and he was of the opinion he had sighted the end of it. Mr Bligh with 2 more boats returned from the arm that was easterly in direction to tell me that it connected with the inlet we were last in and one side of it was only formed by a group of islands.

Early this morning the wind came favourable for getting out to sea, so weighed at 3 a.m. resolved to waste no more time here. We are more than 500 leagues to the Westward of any part of Baffin or Hudsons bays and it is my opinion that any Passage must lie North of latitude 72°. The Indians have indicated that there is a way Northward to the sea that will take us 2 days, but this information being got by signs I cannot rely upon. Nonetheless, the Russians have indicated a line of islands to Westward and no doubt there is a passage through them to the N.

We are now seeking to get to sea by way of a Channell other than that we entered by, hoping it to be shorter, but there being many rocks above and below water we shall not have much rest tonight though it be fairly light.

Tuesday, June 2nd

This is the greatest disappointment yet. On May 26th we headed north into what I took to be another inlet, but some believed otherwise despite the high mountains ahead that were all capped with snow. Now I am proved right and no alternative but to turn back, the Master having returned after exploring all night with 2 boats and reporting the water ahead of us perfectly fresh. Much debris is also floating past on the ebb so that, though the distance between the two shores is still a league as far as Mr Bligh went, and still navigable, it is nevertheless a river. By this and its several branches it is clear a very extensive inland communication lies open, for already we have traced it as high as 61ϒ30′N, to 210°E, which is over 70 leagues from its entrance. I shall call this the Turnagain River, for we have now weighed and are proceeding south on the ebb . . .

We have been stuck fast on a bank in the Middle of the River these last 3 hours all because of the inattention of the man that was heaving the lead. There is no damage that we know of and the ship will float off on the flood. It is a reminder to me and to the officers that the men must constantly be watched over, many of them not having the sense to understand the dangers of a coast such as this. The need of a consort is very apparent in our loneliness and in an area where the constant sudden gales seem always to blow onshore. And if both ships were driven on to the rocks I do not know what we should do.

It is constantly in my mind, the thought of wintering here in the manner of the early Hudsons Bay people. I do not think many would survive. There are forests here from which we could fashion some sort of boat, but as we proceed north I think the barrenness of the land, which is already to be seen in some of the rocky islands, will increase and the trees grow smaller until there is nothing to our purpose in the event of disaster.

I have been on many hostile coasts, but never on one that continued for such a great length. Constant vigil is our only safeguard, the which means little sleep and the danger of officers, not excluding myself, making wrong judgments and decisions through weariness.

The one gain as we go Northward is that the nights are already become very short. Soon there will be no darkness. But then the decision that I dread will be close upon me, for I am in command and whether to proceed or turn back will be for me to decide. I fear I am a man of too little imagination to have fully understood what a burden of responsibility for mens lives I was laying upon myself when I jumped to my feet at my Lord Sandwichs dinner party and said I would go upon this expedition. Pray God that when the time comes I am strong enough to make the right decision.

CHAPTER FORTY-ONE

ALASKA AND A RUSSIAN NOTE

Sunday, June 28th

Today we broke through to the Northward of that great archipelago of islands that the Russians discovered running so far to the Westward. We came through a Passage close by Oonalaschka Island, having a breeze at S and the tide with us; but the *Discovery* was not so fortunate, being carried back by the ebb into the race where the tide ran 6 knots. Even near the shore where we are now anchored it runs $5\frac{1}{2}$.

We had a great deal of fog and mist this last month and 2 days ago, when we were off the NE shore of Oonalaschka, what I feared most did very nearly happen. The weather was so thick that we could scarce see the length of half a cable and hearing breakers on our starboard bow I had the anchor let go and called for the *Discovery* which was close by us to do the same.

When at length the fog cleared I perceived that we had sailed between two high rocks. I would not have ventured into those waters or anywhere near those rocks on a clear day, yet providence had guided us through in dense fog. I hope I may regard this as a good omen, but we were all of us a deal shaken by the sight of such dangers so narrowly missed and I am reminded once again that the fogs on this coast present the gravest danger, so that however much I desire to make the Northward with all speed, I must take the greatest care if we are to return to those we love.

A few days previous to this, when we had passed through a narrow Channel between the land and a group of rocks, the *Discovery* suddenly fired 3 guns. Fearing she had suffered some accident and sprung a leak I immediately sent a boat to her. It returned soon after with Capt Clerke who showed me a small thin wood case that was proffered him by an Indian in one of the several canoes which were following the Ship. This case opened in 2 halves and in it was a piece of paper with some writing which we took to be in the Russian language. There was nothing we could make of it except a date which was 1776. Capt Clerke thought it might be word from some Russian sailors ashore that had been shipwrecked, but in that case they would undoubtedly have come out to the ships themselves and I considered it to be a note of information left by a Russian trader for the advice of the next one of their ships that came this way. On my supposing this, and Capt Clerke finally agreeing it to be most likely, we had some comfort of it, that if our ships were destroyed and we marooned ashore there was some hope that we might be rescued by a vessel trading out of Russia.

All to the N of us is now open sea, which if the maps are to be believed will lead us direct to the Straits that Capt Behring discovered. Nevertheless, I intend to said N Eastward along the N shore of these islands until I come up with the mainland coast again, so that I can map it and be sure there is no passage through it to the NE.

CHAPTER FORTY-TWO

FOG AND MORE FOG

Sunday, August 2nd

For a month past we have had calms and fogs, these last being at times so dense we could not see the length of the ship, so that progress has been slow and wearisome. But at least I have been able to correct some of the misapprehensions contained in Mr Stählins *Map of the New Northern Archipelago* in that the islands of his Archipelago run out continuous from a long narrow peninsula of the Mainland, rather in the manner of Mr Müllers map. But that is all of my achievement, there being no passage through this part of the Continent to the NE, though we had hopes that were proved false when we settled into a wide river entrance just Northward of the Alaschka Peninsula.

This river I called the Bristol and a few days later, when we had so little wind it was only the strong tide that moved us, I sent Mr Williamson to climb an elevated promontory the better to see the form the coast took to the N of us. There he took possession of the Country in the name of His Majesty, left a bottle with a piece of paper in it giving the name of the ships and the date, and returned on board with the information that the coast bore nearly N, also the country inland of it was without any tree or shrub, the hills naked and only the lower ground bearing any grass or other plants.

From this I conclude that we have progressed N of the tree line and shall find none hereafter, nor any shelter if we are driven upon the coast. Shortly after I last wrote anything here I was brought another piece of paper written upon in Russian and a young Indian who came aboard very wet after his canoe was upset put on dry cloathes I gave him with such ease I was assured that he was no stranger to our sort of apparel, so that by this and other signs it is clear the Russians come to this coast more often than was generally supposed. But I do not think they will have come N of the Alaschka peninsula and islands for there is nothing of trade to draw them to these coasts.

We are now in latitude 61°N with no sight of any passage so that I do not think any such exists south of Capt Behrings straits. So much slow wearisome toil in diligently searching this coast and all of it to no purpose other than to prove that what has been believed for so long is no more than the vague hopes of men who have let imagination run beyond the reality of it, as was the case with that Southern Continent.

Am I destined to return home again with nothing to show for this expedition but proof that a connection between the two great oceans of the Atlantic and the

Pacific is no more than a dream? There will be no reward for me in that, nor any advancement. Men do not much favour their dreams being dashed to the ground; all I shall then have is my own satisfaction in the knowledge that I have pressed the matter to the limit and done what no man has done before, that is to map this coast in as much detail as the wretchedness of the weather with its fogs, calms and sudden gales has allowed.

Already I have abandoned the coast and am making up towards the straits. But I have little hope that the seas beyond will be open and free of any ice, for beyond the straits we shall be above 70° latitude N which is more than I ever sailed to the southward in the Southern Hemisphere without meeting up with ice floes.

Tuesday, August 4th

My Surgeon, Mr Anderson, having died yday, I have now had the *Discovery*s Surgeon, Mr Law, transferred to my own ship and discharged Mr Samwell into the *Discovery* to be surgeon there, he having been previously my Surgeons 1st mate. Mr Anderson who had been lingering under a consumption expired between 3 and 4 of the Afternoon and he being such a loss to us all, and particularly to me for his discourse and knowledge of natural history, I named the land we sighted to the Wward shortly after his death Andersons Island.

CHAPTER FORTY-THREE

THROUGH THE STRAITS AND INTO THE ICE

Monday, August 17th

We are now through the Straits and in latitude 70ϒ3′N. This position, together with our longitude of 197ϒ41′E. We got by some flying observations, both Sun and Moon shining out at intervals towards Noon. At the same time we perceived a brightness on the Northern horizon, which I think to be the blink that is reflected from large fields of ice. We hardly expected to meet ice so soon, but the weather has been very gloomy these last days and there is a sharpness in the air, so that I fear that it will prove to be ice that is ahead of us.

I have explored both shores of the Straits insofar as the weather permitted, naming the most Westerly extremity of all America hitherto known Cape Prince of Wales, and I have myself landed on an island on the Western side to see an Esquimaux village, the which together with the people and their weapons I have described in my Journal. They are very similar in all respects to those we have met with on the American coast. But what to make of the land we have seen beyond in comparison with the maps I have on board I do not know, the conditions of the weather making exact observations extremely difficult. I am inclining to the opinion that the maps are exceeding erroneous even to the latitude and have written thus in my Journal. If as I now begin to fear we are forced to come back this way I shall endeavour to make closer examination of this shore.

The two coasts in the Straits were distant from each other some 7 leagues and when we returned to the American side the trend of the coast forced us in a NWesterly direction. We were leading for depth of water all the time and I had little or no sleep, not knowing what I might expect. Yesterday we came round to a more Easterly course, Fog and the Wind strong with it, which made it very dangerous, for the little we had seen of the land had shown it to be low, the which suggests there may be banks off it.

Since we are making steadily to the N Eastward I do believe that we are now upon the Top of the American Continent. My officers and others of the men who have also been excited by the thought that they may be the first to sail N from one Ocean to the other have been in great spirits since passing through the Straits and finding open water to the N.

If it is ice ahead, the disappointment will be very great. It is cold now and all of us are very tired who have the safety of the ships in their care.

Presuming that it is ice and we find there is a gap between it and the shore through which we may proceed, the decision whether to go on or turn back will be a very difficult one. I must not then through weariness or fatigue make a wrong decision, for in that lies the greatest danger. And I cannot sleep, for there is very little night and the safety of the ships my responsibility . . .

At 10 p.m.

It is ice. I was called up from the Cabbin about 1 p.m. with the information that a large field of it was sighted from the masthead. Shortly after I was on deck we could all see it and by ½ past 2 we were up to it, tacking close to it in 22 fathoms water, the latitude 70Υ41′N and the icefield extending from WbyS to EbyN and seemingly impenetrable. There being no way through to the Eastward I turned to the W. We had an abundance of Sea Horses* around the ship and I would have hoisted out the boats to improve our diet but that the wind freshened.

*Walrus.

CHAPTER FORTY-FOUR

THE DECISION
TO TURN BACK

Tuesday, August 18th

The Noon observation showed that we had gained nothing sailing to the Westward since our position is now 5 leagues further to the E then it was yesterday, the latitude being 70ϒ44′N. We have 20 fathoms water and are close to the Ice which is 10 or 12 feet high and as compact as a Wall; further to the Northward it appears even higher though with pools of Water.

I turned S and after sailing 6 leagues found the Water shoaled to 7 fathoms. We were in this depth for ½ a league, after which it deepened very slightly. The haze, which had been thick, then cleared slightly so that we could see land 3 or 4 miles distant, all of it very low and much encumbered by ice, because of which I named it Icy Cape.

Sunday, August 30th

I have now been to the Westward as far as I may. Yday we were within 3 miles of the Asian shore with the depth of Water decreasing very fast to only 8 fathoms. We had no Noon observation, the weather being hazey with drizzling rain, but the previous Noon our latitude was 69ϒ17′N so that we were to the southward of our furthest position on the American shore and all to the N great masses of ice.

Our spruce beer is finished and we have great need of Wood and Water. There is no Wood to be had here, the coast which trends in a Westerly direction being the same as the American shore, barren of everything but a sort of Moss.

I have informed the Ships company that I am now turning back for the Straits and that we will try again for the Passage next year. There was much relief at this, for the last 2 weeks have been very wearisome and full of peril to our safety, and though I took good care to warn them that everything on board must be considered of the most urgent necessity to our purpose, I fear they do not think ahead so far as a year, but consider only the moment and that we are turning Southwards.

My reason for turning back is chiefly that the Season is now too far advanced. Soon the sea will start to freeze again, which is one thing I have proved, that the sea does freeze, and freezes to a most terrible extent. I am also greatly concerned at the state of the ships, the rigging, sails and masts in particular, as well as the leaks. Navy ships are never put to such desperate hard work and their gear never intended to last so great a length of time. Everything is rotten and giving way, all except that which the Navy Yard condemned and the Boatswain with great good sense got back, the which is clear proof that *Resolution* was better fitted at Whitby for the coal trade than ever a Navy ship for battle.

One other matter that concerns me is that Mr Stählins Map shows 2 passages to the N between the American and Asian continents, one either side of the great island of Alaschka, and Behrings route through the Western passage. When I turned back from my farthest N I thought Icy Cape to be a part of the Mainland of America. I do not think I was mistaken in this, but I intend to assure myself that it was not a part of the N coast of Alaschka Island by further examination of the American shore S of Cape Prince of Wales.

If my view of the matter is correct, and there is no way through to the N, then I must be sure to arrive at the Straits at least 2 months sooner next year and endeavour to work the Ships between the Ice and the American shore, so reaching Baffin Bay before the seas start to freeze again. From all that I have perceived so far I fear this may prove a most desperate venture, but since I am sent upon this Voyage for one purpose only I intend with the help of Providence to carry it to a successful end. I do but wish we had been more fortunate this year, for another Winter spent in the islands will contribute nothing to the good of either ships or men, and if I stay the Winter upon the Asian side, it will be worse, for we would be forced to lie idle at Petropaulowska in Kamtschatka 6 or 7 months.

Sunday, September 13th

I have now cruzed down the Asian shore as far as the Straits, and after passing through these and crossing to the American side, we discovered a big Sound trending NE which gave me hope that Stählins Map was right and there was another way through to the north. When we were well into it, and still hoping that the larboard shore might in truth be that island of Alaschka, we came into shallow water with only 3½ fathom and the ship stirring up Mud from the bottom. I called this Bay after Sir Fletcher Norton and the Sound also, my having no better opinion of either than others have of the man.

Sunday, September 20th

On Thursday last Mr King returned from the expedition into Norton Bay I had sent him upon. He confirmed there was no way through even for the boats, having discovered it to terminate in a small river about 3 or 4 leagues beyond where our ship nearly took the ground. So the Stählin Map is a fraud and Mr Müllers Map nearer to the truth.

CHAPTER FORTY-FIVE

THOUGHTS OF WINTER AND FAILING GEAR

Sunday, October 25th

Tomorrow **I** intend to depart from our anchorage here at Samgoonoodha, which is the same we were at on our voyage N. We have been here more than 3 weeks, which is scarce enough to do all that we had to do, which is to repair the leaks under the Sheathing where the seams were quite open and clear the Fish and Spirit rooms, also the after hold, and re-stow in such manner that if we suffer further leaks the water will find its way freely to the pumps. We have replenished the store of vegetables which we previously got here and are now decayed, and have taken on board plenty of fish, some including Salmon both fresh and dried we had from the Natives, but the most we caught ourselves with one Halibut that weighed 254 lb.

My greatest interest at this place was the meetings I had with the Russians who are resident here. They know nothing of the Continent of America to the

North or of my Maps or of Lt Sindo, but have a great reverence for Capt Behring. Having set down all that they told me, more particularly my discourses with the chief among them, a Mr Ismyloff, in my Journal I will not repeat it here, except to say that the conclusion I have reached from my own observations does not vary greatly from the view expressed by Mr Ismyloff. This is that there being no tide nor any current to be discerned in the Straits and no hollow seats that I would expect with the Wind at N, the two Continents are either joined by land or ice, and the latter most likely having ourselves seen such a mass of it spread across a full 20° of longitude.

The information I got of Mr Ismyloff about the Kamtschatka coast, and also of Jacob Iwanowitch, another Russian who was Capt of a small vessel at Oomanak, together with the 2 charts I was shown, will relieve me of much anxiety when I fall in with that coast.

This is now my intention, to return to the Sandwich Islands for some of the Winter months, then to proceed to Kamtschatka to be at the harbour of Petropaulowska by the Middle of May. I shall give Capt Clerke these two objectives as our rendezvous in the event of the Ships become separated, and when we have purchased what we may urgently need of the Russians at Petropaulowska I shall make to the Nward with as much speed as the Weather allows and hope that providence will be with us in the Year 1779 and lead us through into Baffin and Hudsons bays.

Meantime there is the Winter ahead of us, which

offers nothing but months of wearisome waiting with all that it entails of labour to keep the ships in a sufficient state of readiness and the men reasonably content. Boredom I do know to be very destructive of that necessary determination and high spirit, so that discipline may not be enough and all my endeavours will again have to be directed to keeping my People fully occupied. And, wherever we are, constant guard will have to be kept against the thievery of the natives, for we have all too little now of those necessities on which the state of our vessels depends. This I find most irksome, since it depends so greatly upon myself and upon my standing with the island chiefs. Harsh measures may have to be taken, the which I do not like, since they are innocent of malice and their going off with whatever takes their fancy something quite as natural to them as the behaviour of children.

Sunday, November 8th

On the 30th of last Month we sailed through the pass between Oonalaschka and Oonalla and have since sailed S from the Archipelago as far as latitude 40°. The day before we made through the pass we sighted an elevated rock like a tower, the high seas nowhere breaking except against its shores, so that it must be very steep to. Its appearance was a dreadful reminder of the dangers of sailing in waters that are not properly charted, for it is marked on the Russian Map and we must have passed very near to it during the night.

Yesterday Capt Clerke came on board, there being little wind, to report the failure of more gear. On the night of the 2nd, when there was a Storm that blew very Violent and we heard the *Discovery* fire 3 times, it was apparently the Signal to bring to because of damage to sails and ropes. But much worse, the 2nd night after we left Samgoonoodha the Main tack gave way in a squal killing one man out right and wounding the Boatswain and some others.

This news was a most terrible reminder to me that there is a great deal of work to be done on the ships before they face the Ice again and if the Sandwich Islands, for which we are now headed, do not provide a sufficient shelter I do not know what I may do for the best. To go further south means a greater distance to sail when we turn north again, and if we were to encounter one of those great storms of which we had information in the Society Islands and again at Bola-bola it is very doubtful that we could ride it out in the present state of the ships. I could wish that those men whose responsibility it was to fit our ships for sea were with us now. They would then learn what poor material and workmanship means in lives, discomfort and danger.

PART SIX

HAWAII: PRELUDE TO DISASTER

CHAPTER FORTY-SIX

A STUPID MUTINOUS BEHAVIOUR

Thursday, November 26th, 1778

Land was sighted this morning at day breake, the which I take to be some part of the Sandwich Islands, though not any we know since we are now approaching these islands from E whereas when we discovered them in January we were to the S and W of them. The temperature is now over 80° which is a great change to our condition since but a month ago it was little above 40°. The relief I felt at our arrival was somewhat lessened by the nature of the shore which everywhere appeared steep to and rocky with a great sea breaking and a hill like a saddle disappearing into Clouds. Nowhere did I see any good bay or anchorage which was my most urgent need, though for days past both ships had been hard at work repairing sails, gear and boats.

At Noon we were close in to an isthmus that run out from the heights, but though the land was low it was still rock bound. This was the more tiresome since I could see there was wood and water ashore, also people and plantations to supply our needs. Canoes now came off to us and the natives came into the ship without the least hesitation, all of them most friendly and of the same Nation we had met with when we were in this area before.

In the excitement of their arrival a black cat that was with us fell overboard, but instead of drowning, which some might have regarded as ill luck, it was brought back on board by one of the canoes which had picked it up about 2 miles astern of us.

I had already given orders that all men were to be examined for that disease which I am determined they shall not communicate to these islands. But on their coming on board I learned from the natives that they already had the disease and they spoke of it being past on to them by the people of Atowi where we had been before. However, I do know if there were Spaniards here before us we may not be the cause of their complaints; but I cannot be sure for the need of our People is such that whatever my orders and however strictly enforced they will always find some means of getting at the women and the women themselves ignorant of any sense of chastity are quite free with their charms.

I have also given strict orders that there is to be no trading other than through those appointed by me or Capt Clerke. I have already exchanged Nails and pieces of iron for Cuttle fish and am informed there is plenty of fruit and roots ashore, also hogs and fowls, and these they will bring off tomorrow so that we shall have the benefits of fresh provisions to our diet, which recently has been none of the best.

One thing I can say for this place, the natives appear more honest than anywhere I have been in the Pacific Ocean, not one of them making any attempt to steal from us.

Sunday, November 29th

We have had much difficulty with women here. They come out to trade their bodies and when sent away they turn quite nasty as though it was a slight upon their charms when it is only for their own and their peoples good, and so that we shall not be accused later of carrying the disease. We did a good trade on Friday getting of them bread fruit, potatoes, tarra roots, a few plantains and pigs for which they seemed satisfied with nails and pieces of iron which is about all we have left to trade with. Our decks were quite crowded with them and when the trading was done they were dancing and singing for us, everyone seeming happy.

The land to the Westward of us appeared to be another island and since we were drifting to windward though lying to I decided to ply to windward and so get round the E side of the island into its lee, the seas here being very big.

Now that I am back in warmer climate with the prospect of re-fitting the ships and another attempt to find a way through to the Atlantic next year, I find my mind dwelling upon the time spent on that fog bound coast and in close proximity to the northern ice with something that is near foreboding, knowing how fortunate we are to have got S again without damage to our ships or any disaster. I fear the long hours on constant watch for real and imagined dangers have tired me more than I dare admit even to myself, for I never felt like this before. It is something I cannot communicate to any living soul, not even to Capt Clerke, who being sick is in less condition than myself to face the perils of another season in the north.

I have constantly now to keep a hold on my temper for I am at times very irritable, the smallest matters upsetting me most. The keeping of my official Journal has become a wearisome business, not being able to write what I do in truth feel since those who would read it in the safe security of the Admiralty Office would not understand, they never having spent years at sea in total isolation from their fellows nor carried upon their shoulders the weight of responsibility for an expedition engaged for so long in such hazardous exploration. Only here can I express my thoughts freely and these are of the most gloomy, for there is the Winter before me, the same endless routine keeping men and ships in condition, and ultimately the ice again and the constant watch as we search for a passage I no longer believe exists. But it must be done if I am to report on my return that there is no such passage, the which they will not accept, and blame me accordingly, unless I can prove to the satisfaction of my officers and all who keep their own Journals on board that we have pressed the search with so much diligence and determination that nobody, however hostile to me personally, can doubt the truth of it.

When I was in England there was some curiosity expressed as to my state of mind sailing in seas where no man had been before and charting the shores of unknown lands. Even my Lord Sandwich asked me once was I never afraid? In such circumstances no man but a fool is a stranger to fear. But all I said was, not that I was aware of. And this was the gist of the reply I gave to all that asked me, the which they accepted as the proper reply of a naval officer and the truth too since it is my nature to appear unemotional. But it is not the truth, nor ever can be, for a man who knows exactly the risks he is taking, and because he is the commander, and by his direction putting all the men that sail with him at similar risk, the fear of what may happen is something he has to live with day and night.

And particularly at night, for on deck or at work in the cabbin the mind is occupied with the active details of navigation and mapping. But in the night imagination is free to consider all desperate possibilities, which I do believe to be some necessary preparation of the mind for the instant action that must be taken in the event of some disaster overtaking one or other of the ships. I did not sleep much during the long period we were off the American coast, and now that the nights are so much longer and myself less extended, I have more time to indulge myself, yet sleep does not come readily as it used to. My chief concern at the present is that the coast of these islands we are come upon is hostile in the extreme and the

seas very big, so that I fear I must wait upon a change
in the weather before we can come to a satisfactory
anchorage.

Wednesday, December 2nd

Something no one of us had expected so far S as Lat.
20°, the mountains of this larger island which we have
stood off and on from all night are covered in snow,
some of it appearing deep and to have laid there some
time. The island we were previously off is called
Mow'ee and this one O'why'he.* The wind remains
at SE and while still off the NE end of the former
island we received a visit from the Chief of these parts,
who is called Terreeoboo. The natives of O'why'he are
for some reason very shy of us, but in the end we were
able to persuade them to bring off all that we needed
and our trading with them did not cease until it was
getting dark. I am now plying to windward again with
the intention of rounding the island and shall soon be
much occupied with Mr King in preparing for Fridays
eclipse of the Moon.

Friday, December 4th

By the Eclipse just observed the mean longitude was
204ϒ35'. On reducing all observations to the Timekeeper at 4h30' it was 204ϒ04'45 E.

* Cook's phonetic spelling of Hawaii.

Monday, December 7th

I can scarcely control my temper for the behaviour of the men, and also the apparent loss of the current we had previously observed setting us to windward. Of the behaviour of the men in refusing even to taste the sugar cane beer I have had brewed in order to save our Spirits I have written at some length in my Journal, for it is not to be borne, and my Lords and the Publick must understand that my insistence on their drinking home brewed beer is for their own good and to save their Grog, the which is now very precious, there being so little of it remaining, and that their behaviour has become close to mutinous and my anger at it wholly justified.

But though I can discipline the men, I cannot discipline the wind or currents, so that though we ply constantly to windward we make little progress, the which is an aggravation to the men who have little in their minds but to get on shore where I know they will make free with the women and following upon that they will begin to desert as happened before.

We have three months at least to wait until we begin to work N again along the Russian coast of Kamtschatka, and if there is to be such thoughtless mutinous behaviour this early in the Winter it is evident I cannot indulge them, but must speak out to the assembled men and enforce my will with the most strict discipline.

Added to this annoyance and the contrariness of the weather, the ship is leaking, and not as before from the upper works, but from her bottom. If it opens up worse we may have to attempt a forthering such as we did after hauling the *Endeavour* off the reef.

Sunday, December 13th

Still plying to windward off the NE coast of O'why'he, regularly coming in to trade with the natives. Today we stood in again, but had only made 6 leagues to windward, so that I and all on board begin to tire of our continued beating and fear some devil is at work to prevent our turning the End of the island, so enabling us to work round into the lee. Nowhere in the Tropicks have I met so high or so troublesome a sea as we have had these last weeks on the E side of these islands, and though the direction of the wind shows frequent shifts of 4 or more points, allowing us some progress, there is never any reduction of the sea, which makes living on board exceeding unpleasant. And if it adds to my temper, I can sometimes understand how the men feel, deprived of the promise of terra firma and the hope of women after being so long upon the desolate shores of North America.

But though I can understand their mood, I cannot, and dare not, condone it or in any way indicate sympathy with it. The stupid mutinous behaviour they showed in refusing the sugar cane beer we brewed, which had hops in it to give it some sharpness and flavour, was followed later by their delivering to me a most impudent letter. In this they did not only declare their refusal to touch the decoction because they did not like it, but complained of the scanty provisions I was allowing them. This was not to be borne with since the allowance of provisions was that commonly served while the ship was among the islands of the Pacific. However, I was more concerned to save us our Spirits for the colder climate N of Alashka and so had all hands mustered aft, when I spoke to them fayre on the matter of the allowance, telling them it was the first I heard of it being in any way scanty and that they should have more allowed to them if that was what they wished. But on the matter of Grog, I told them bluntly they would get none at all other than they drank the cane decoction every other day. And on they declaring the brew to be unwholesome and injurious to health, despite the fact that they had last year in the islands been stealing sugar cane from the plantations at any opportunity and eating it raw, I said it was nothing of the kind and if they would not drink it then I would have the Brandy Cask struck down into the hold and they can make do with water and nothing else.

I gave them 24 hours to consider my offer, and when they would have none of it, refusing absolutely to drink of the decoction, I kept my word and had the Brandy Cask sent down. That was not the end of it, Wm Griffiths, a cooper, taking the matter into his own hands and starting the cask in which was the cane beer so that it went sour. He was punished yday with 12 lashes and I took the opportunity of the crew being assembled to speak to them again about the stupid and mutinous nature of their behaviour.

This, and the desertions that I know will be attempted when we finally come to an anchorage and the time draws near for the ships to head N again, causes me constantly to consider how best I can deal with the men, it being a fine point how much they must be forced and how much indulged. The *Resolution* and *Discovery* are both Navy ships and the officers and men in them subject to Naval discipline, but in voyages of discovery of the length of 3 years the enforcement of discipline is not something that can be taken as granted, being dependent on the acceptance of it by all, not as of right but for the greater good of everybody. This is most particularly so at the mid point of the voyage, the which we are now at, for it is then that all, myself and my officers included, are feeling the greatest degree of weariness, our homes still perhaps eighteen months away and more hardships and dangers ahead of us before we may turn the ships for England.

No mention of these doubts and concerns of mine can be made in my Journal, the which makes it tiresome to work over, and the Publick when they read it will have a very false impression, all seeming so much more simple and straightforward than it really is.

Facing the assembled men yday after Griffiths had been flogged and understanding their mood very well from the time I had spent in the Navy as a seaman, I felt very much alone, conscious that the custom of obedience and my own demeanour was but a very thin wall to the dam of their feelings bursting and a mutiny breaking out. There was no reasoning with them and no logic in the faces I looked down upon. This was evidenced by their total rejection of the beer I had had brewed, though 12 months since all had accepted the spruce decoction with evident enjoyment, and also by their being incapable of looking to the future and how they would manage on the edge of the ice with no Spirits to warm their bellies, which was again very different to last year when they had so readily accepted that the Grog should be saved for when we were in colder climates.

This wretched big sea and the Wind always in the same quarter is the chief cause of their complaint. I cannot expect them to understand that I must continue to make to windward when even my officers find some difficulty, only Capt Clerke really seeming to understand that if we turn downwind we shall probably never regain our position. It is very essential to our safety that we are not blown from these islands where, once we can round the E point of O'why'he, we shall have a lee and smoother water, also the prospect of some suitable anchorage for repairs. This we are in increasing need of, the leak in our bottom so bad that water has got into the Gunners store room making it necessary yday to try and stop it with oakum in a net drawn down by ropes in the hope that the pressure of water entering the hull would force the fothering to hold.

CHAPTER FORTY-SEVEN

YARD OFFICERS CONDEMNED

Sunday, December 20th

Yesterday we came very near to weathering the
island, which the natives have confirmed to me
as the most windward of the group. We also came
near to being set on shore, for after a week of variable
winds in which it sometimes blew hard in squals,
and at other times fell calm with thunder, lightning and
rain, it suddenly fell quite Calm. This was at one
o'clock in the morning with a big NEasterly swell
which set us down so fast upon the land that though
we were at first some 5 leagues off, we were very soon
barely a league from the shore and could see lights.
Again the calm was accompanied by thunder, lightning
and rain, the night being very dark.

To our great relief a breeze then came in from SE
by E, but then we had squals with rain and were in
some peril when the Main topsail leach gave and the
sail rent in two, and then the 2 topgallant sails went
the same way. At day breake we saw we were off the

E point of the island at last and everywhere a dreadful surf breaking.

I fear that what I wrote in my Journal about the failure of the sails, I being very angry at the time, may have to be reconsidered. But the blame does lie with the Navy yard* for the bolt-ropes are not equal to the strength of the sails. Indeed, what I have said is that nothing of the Navy's gear is the equal of that in general use by the Merchant service and the Yard officers seem to have had no consideration for the time their gear would be required to stand up, though they knew very well we would be away upwards of 3 years. It makes me very angry to think upon it, that for lack of consideration or any imagination these men ashore set my ships and the lives of my men at risk. Again I do wish they were on board to stand with me and see the surf breaking upon the rock shores of this mountainous island. Did they thus know what a danger they put us to they would quake in their shoes and their conscience be overcome at the risk to their own lives. But the men who order the gear and rig our ships never sail in them, which is something I greatly regret, wishing with all my heart that I had them with me, not only here but in the far N among the ice fields.

* Sir Hugh Palliser, Comptroller of the Navy, who was responsible for the Navy yards, proved very touchy about Cook's reference to this in his official Journal and requested Dr Douglas to suppress it in the book, pleading somewhat speciously that Cook did not know what he was talking about – 'It would need a long Note to explain Capt. Cooks Error it being out of his line.'

Sunday, December 27th

Another Christmas is gone and I barely noticed it,
except to say a prayer for my family at home and
think briefly of their celebrating it again without me.
My concern is for the *Discovery* which we lost sight
of on Thursday morning.

CHAPTER FORTY-EIGHT

AN ANCHORAGE AT LAST

Sunday, January 3rd, 1779

A **very hard** rain ushered in the New Year. But we are finally round the E point of the island, still plying and trading when close to the shore. Some of the hog bought I have salted for use when we are upon coasts where none is available. The natives are hard bargainers and maintain the price of their provisions even when they bring off more than we need, being quite prepared to take all back to the shore again whatever the difficulties of landing. I never could persuade them to bring off sufficient only for our immediate requirements. Either they brought too much or too little, and if we purchased more than our requirements the nature of the roots and fruits is such that in the temperature prevailing they instantly rot, something that the men through perverseness refused to comprehend so that they imagined they were justified in their complaint that they had too little allowance of fresh provisions, which on some days was undoubtedly the case.

Sunday, January 10th

Today the Wind has veered, the easterlies giving way to light airs from NW and SW, finally blowing fresh from WNW with rain. We are now off the SW shore of the island, having passed the S point of it on Tuesday where we could see a large village. The following day I sent Mr Bligh away in a boat to sound the coast with orders to land and look for fresh water. His report was far from encouraging, he finding no bottom with a 160 fathom of line as close as 2 cables from the shore and on land only rainwater in rock pools made brackish with sea spray and the country composed of large slags and ashes partly covered with plants.

I am at something of a loss now where to go for an anchorage, the island being much broken up and half destroyed by volcanic disturbance, so devastated in fact that it is a matter for wonder where the natives grow all the abundance of fruit and vegetables they bring off to us. Can the mountain that is covered with snow be the Volcano that has caused all this devastation? It does not appear like any I have seen before, yet the destruction that is everywhere visible to the naked eye must have occurred not very long ago.

There is a strong current setting SE and the only good thing that has happened in this past Week is that the *Discovery* has rejoined us. This she did at 1 p.m. on Thursday, 7th January, Capt Clerke coming on board and informing me that after we parted he plied round the E part of the island, but then had unfavourable winds and was carried some distance off the coast, all the time with one of the islanders on board who had remained there at his own choice.

It is a great relief to have Capt Clerke with me again, for I am heartily sick of standing off and on this wretched island not knowing what best to do. But though we discussed the matter of an anchorage he had no other information to offer and so we reached no conclusion. This lack of any prospect that would make a decision possible is having a very bad effect upon me personally and upon everyone on board of the ship.

Sunday, January 17th

We have been up to the NW of the island, the weather being sometimes Calm, sometimes fresh gales. On the night of the 13th the Wind veered westward and by morning we had been set back all we had gained. Yday, when plying to the northward again and within 3 leagues of the coast, I sighted what looked like a bay and sent Mr Bligh in with a boat from each ship to look at it. Shortly after he had left, about 10 o'clock, we had the most extraordinary sight, our 2 ships being quite surrounded by a dense mass of canoes filled with all manner of produce so that it must have been gathered from every part of the island. I think there were not less than one thousand canoes massed about the ships.

Today it has been the same. At first we counted

500 canoes about the *Resolution* and another 300
around the *Discovery*. By the afternoon so many had
joined them that we quite lost count. Mr King
reckoned at least 1500 and with a generality of 6
natives to each, the population around us was something close to 10,000 allowing that women and young
boys were swimming off to us from the shore. They
were like a shoal of fish in the sea about us, even men
on pieces of wood. This is the greatest number of
natives I have seen assembled in one place in the whole
Pacific Sea, the shore at times being quite thick with
them. And all unarmed. The women also very bold.

This was after we had at last come to anchor,
which we did at 11 a.m. in 13 fathom a quarter of a
mile off shore, the bottom sandy. We then immediately
unbent the sail and struck yards and topmasts, hoping
our anchors would hold us if it came on to blow from
SW. This bay is called by the natives Karakakooa.*

Unfortunately the people on this side of the island
are different from those on the N, they being as thieving as any we have met with, to the extent even that
some of those that are swimming about the ship have
equipped themselves with a stone headed stick for use
as a tool to extract the nails out of the sheathing under
water. And their desire to stay the night on board is
not for the sake of curiosity but what they might take
in the darkness.

However, this appears a very disciplined and
organised society in that they accord their priests

* Kealakekua Bay.

and their chiefs absolute obedience. One of the latter, a man called Parea, who said he was a servant of King Terreeoboo, when I appealed to him instantly drove them all off the ship. Before this I had observed the *Discovery* with so many clinging like flies to one side of her that she was actually heeled over, because of which and the difficulty they were having to keep more from entering the ship, I sent the Chief Parea to get them off her.

CHAPTER FORTY-NINE

TREATED AS A GOD

The chief priest of the place came to me with a piece of red cloth, which he wrapped round me, also a large hog, two cocoanuts and some fruit. All the people of Note introduced themselves in similar manner. Then Touahah the Priest and Parea invited me to go on shore with them, the which I did accompanied by Mr King and Mr Bayly, and as soon as we landed we were conducted to a large *Morai*, which was the sacred place of one of their gods. This was after I had entertained Touahah, Parea and 2 other chiefs, Kaneina and Koah, to dinner. Here Koah, and a grave young man with a long beard called Kaireekea, took me by the hand and led me to the top of a Scaffold that was somewhat ricketty and had at the foot 12 images and offerings of a hog and fruit much rotted, and all the time muttering a prayer. Also in the village where we had been before coming to this sacred place everybody prostrated themselves at the sight of me as they had done before at the island of Atowee to the Westward.

There was now a sort of ceremony, some 10 men in procession and again this business of the Red Cloth, they all prostrating themselves before me, then handing the Cloth to Kaireekea who carried it to Koah and he wraped it round me and afterward gave me the hog they had brought, and all the time prayers being said in constant repetition. I was finally brought down off the Scaffold and taken to each of the images where words were said that appeared derogatory, except only to the Centre Image which was about 3 feet high and was the only one wraped in a Cloth. Before this image they fell prostrate and desired me to do the same, the which I did, the image being called Koonooakeea.

The Ceremony continued with another procession bearing gifts and a great repetition of prayers and the crowd constantly repeating Erono, Erono. A chewed cocoanut was then wraped in a cloth and rubbed all over me including the face and after that we were invited to eat, something I found difficult being handed the food by Koah and remembering that in the first ceremony he had been fondling a hog that was quite putrid while repeating the prayers. Seeing my difficulty the old man went so far as to chew it for me first so that I was glad finally to excuse myself by making a small speech and handing round gifts of iron and nails.

We left then, 2 men with wands going before and repeating again and again the word Erono and at the sound of it everybody prostrating themselves. What can this mean? That I am viewed as some sort of god? Is it their desire to propitiate me for this reason, or would they do this with anyone who came with the might of two ships and armed with cannons? I do not know and can only accept it as the work of Providence, it being so much to my purpose, and am resolved to play the part I am assigned to. For there is a proper social and religious structure in their society that enables discipline to be maintained so that orders when given are obeyed by all the people, and whether I am regarded as a God or a Chief does not concern me very much so long as they bring us what we need.

CHAPTER FIFTY

KING TERREEOBOO AND CEREMONIALS

Sunday, January 24th

We got our Observatory and Tents ashore the day after we anchored, choosing a field of Sweet Potatoes close beside the *Morai*, which at my request the priests then tabooed. Nevertheless I put a guard upon it of six Marines and a Corporal under their officer with orders to wear Regimentals on duty, which always ensures a certain respect, and not to allow the natives to handle their Muskets. This was not necessary for the taboo was so strictly enforced that no Women would come near whatever the inducement for fear, I was told, that either God or the King would kill them. It is for this reason that these people are the most amenable we have met with, that is so long as we hold the respect of the Chiefs and Capt Clerke and I continue to represent whatever it is we do to the priests. For this purpose, whenever I go ashore, I permit myself to be supported under the arms as is their wont and to go through the same ceremony of the priests singing and chanting some words and all prostrating themselves before me.

Parea was generally on hand when I came ashore and I understand that it is to the Chief Priest whose name is Kao and who will come with King Terreeoboo that I am indebted for all the presents of hogs and fruit and roots. Parea was often very hard on his own people, which is no doubt the reason they obey their Chiefs without question. The first day, or the day after, I cannot recall which, a native who had stole something out of the *Discovery* was discovered by Parea, whereupon the man jumped overboard and the Chief after him. They were both under water a long time and when finally Parea alone came up half drowned he said the thief was dead, presumably throttled and most probably held down by one who undoubtedly had greater under water prowess.

Discipline seems better among the natives than among my own People. My orders to prevent the spread of the Venereal are more honoured in the breech, if that be not a rude way of putting it. I blame the women flaunting themselves and thus making contact between my men and themselves so easy, and if it is done too blatant and the man has not been cleared by Mr Samwell then I must discipline him. So tomorrow I will have 4 men flogged, Bradley with 2 dozen lashes for intercourse when he knew that he had the disease, the others 1 doz each of absenting themselves or for disobedience. I fear I may have more of this before I leave. Why cannot men perceive that orders are not given but for the good of all? Instead they give rein to their natural desires without thought for the future or for others and without the slightest degree of common sense.

Today there is peace round the ships. It seems that a taboo has been placed upon us, the natives being kept in their villages and no canoes allowed to put out. All this I believe because Terreeoboo is on his way to visit us, he being held in great awe and the same man that came on board of us off Mowee who I thought then to be just an ordinary Chief. This second meeting will be of more interest since I now know in what great awe he is held by people and understand very well that the manner of his signalling his coming is to impress me. How he will behave toward me will perhaps give me some clearer idea of how I am regarded by his people, whether as some god or emissary of a god or simply as the Commander of ships representing a powerful King across the ocean.

Monday, January 25th

The King has just left, it being after 10 at night and he having come on board in great state accompanied by an endless concourse of canoes.

I had been informed of his imminent arrival shortly after the disciplining of the men aforementioned and after I had been forced to order a Musket to be fired over a Chiefs head to make him desist from driving off the few canoes with which we were endeavouring to trade for much needed provisions. Towards evening a long line of canoes came round the N point of the Bay and I understand more were still coming in until it was too dark to see.

Terreeoboo treated me with the greatest respect and was accompanied by Kao who I think to be the High Priest of these parts.

Tuesday, January 26th

King Terreeoboo came out again today about Noon in great State but did not come on board. He had with him a canoe with 4 images and the priest called Kao, and another filled with hogs and vegetables for gifts, and the priests that were with Kao, if they were such, kept up a solemn chant. The images were of basket work and covered with feathers of red, black, white and yellow, with strangely distorted mouths full of dogs teeth and eyes of Pearl Oyster shell, and the Chiefs that were with the King resplendent in feather cloaks and caps.

After paddling round the ship the 3 canoes headed for the Observatory. I immediately followed in the pinace and was glad to see that Mr King had the Marines drawn up as a guard of honour. I met Terreeoboo in the Markee and at my entrance he rose and threw over me the very cloak he was wearing, placed a feathered cap on my head and handed me a feather-crowned fly-flap which I take to be a symbol of power. Afterward, when we had renewed our friendship, there came a procession of priests headed by the emaciated figure of Kao who wrapt a piece of cloth round me as before and presented me with a pig. After the usual religious chanting, everybody joining in the responses, I took the King and as many others as the pinace would hold back to the *Resolution* where I gave them all presents, some beads and iron things that I knew they valued.

In so many islands I have had to behave in such fashion that I now find it a wearisome business, their customs always of such serious formality though at other times they appear like children. But here the formality and discipline is very great and I cannot be sure if the real power is with the King or the Priests. And if I am regarded as some sort of god, a god called Lono or Erono, then is this because Terreeoboo has declared it so, because I have power greater than his and by making me a god my power does not detract from his in the eyes of his people, or is it to the Priests with their chants and cloth wraping ceremony that I owe my elevation?

Sunday, January 31st

Yesterday the Rudder was finished and sent on board, and today I have sent the Carpenters into the Country to cut timber for the head rail. Every time I go ashore the natives prostrate themselves as they did for

Terreeoboo and the Priests. Kao, who lives in some religious houses close by where we have the Observatory, is always there to greet me with gifts, given with the usual Ceremony. But god or not it does not discourage these people from thieving and it is the Chiefs who are at the back of it. A box of knives, forks and pewter plates had been taken from the Markee though Mr King was sleeping there and a Marine sentry on guard. Capt Clerke has ordered a native flogged for stealing and this morning Mr King tells me he was astonished to have one of the greatest Chiefs come to him with gifts and tied to his wrist was our Gunroom carving knife. He had much difficulty persuading him it was not his property.

I shall be glad when all is repaired and we are at sea again, fee of the constant ceremonial, the thieving, and the temptations of women. My greatest fear, which was desertions, has not been realised, but I believe this is only because the men know that the Chiefs and Priests have such power over the people that they will be returned immediately. The matter of provisions also causes me concern. My Gunner and Mr Vancouver from the *Discovery* headed a party to the interior of the Country to botanise, and also with the intention of reaching the top of the Snowy Mountain. They report the land very difficult and full of the crumbling remains of Volcanic action, so that I begin to wonder how long the natives can continue to trade with us, the area of land they have for plantation being so circumscribed by slag and ash. Already I have been approached by some of the Chiefs to enquire when we will depart. I believe them to begin to resent our taking so much of their provisions even though we do always trade fairly with them.

Thursday, February 4th

We are now at sea again having weighed and sailed out from Karakakooa Bay early this Morning.

We made our farewells yday, I accompanied by King Terreeoboo going to the abode of the High Priest Kao where parcels of cloth and a vast quantity of red and yellow feathers was laid out, and beside this a great number of hatchets and other iron pieces which was our contribution. All this was for the King who then selected a goodly portion and offered it to me. I took but a small amount to show my appreciation so that the many hogs and other provisions were given to the Common People of the village. We took away in the boats a few of the largest hogs and only as much of the bread fruit and sweet potatoes as we could eat since they would not keep.

The priest Kao seems to have taken a great fancy to Mr King, who was my only companion on this occasion, for both he and Terreeoboo asked me to leave him on the island. Apparently they took Mr King for my son so that I had to excuse my taking him with me on the ground that I could not spare him, but would consider the matter again when I returned next year. He told me afterward that they had already pressed him to elope, promising to hide him in the hills till the Ships had sailed. I suppose I must take this as a compliment, but poor King was not a little put out at the time having to explain it all to me.

We had already got the Observatory and tents on board that morning and in the evening were entertained with boxing and wrestling, which was followed by the letting off of the rest of our fireworks.

The Wind is light, but we are now clear of the Bay and before it wax dark could see Mowee, which I intend to visit from the western side, and afterward we will map the rest of this island archipelago and get what provisions we can before heading for the Russian coast. There will be opportunity enough then to work on my Journal, something I seem not to have had either the time or the stomach for these past few weeks for I see that my last entry in it was for 6th January.

Sunday, February 7th

Mr Bligh has returned safely with the pinace, which is a great relief as we have had such heavy squals from off the Snowy Mountain which is distant from us barely 5 or 6 miles that I was forced to furl the sails and bring to under Mizzin staysail. I had sent him away yday to explore the bay we are now off in hope of water, a native who was on board at his own insistence and who called himself Brittanee having said there was a good supply of it there and also shelter. But the Master reports nothing to our purpose, neither shelter nor water, and the native has stayed ashore. I think

Mr Bligh may have upbraided him very severely for so misleading us.

On his way back to us, when he had a fayre wind, Mr Bligh was able to save an old woman and 2 men who had their canoe overturned in a squal while trying to get ashore. There were other canoes about but they offered no assistance. It was not possible to save their canoe. The severe weather came on yday so that many canoes that had put out to us as they had done the previous day were forced to turn back. As a result of the suddenness of the tempest we have a number of women stranded on board so that the ship is somewhat overcrowded. It is this constant traffick with the natives and the sense of their being always about us crowding in upon us that makes life in these islands so very restless. It is hardly surprising that I get so little writing done.

Tuesday, February 9th

Yday Evening it came on to blow very fresh so that we reefed and got the Topgallant yards down and by Midnight it was Strong Gale. This morning at 6 it was reported to me that the head of the Foremast was sprung. It was still blowing very strong, but moderated toward Noon and I then had a full report of the damage. It appears that the mast is sprung at the point where we fished it in King Georges Sound, the fishes being made out of driftwood which the Carpenters did not much like at the time. The cause of its springing is undoubtedly the slack in the Fore topmast rigging which I had commented upon on our leaving Karakakooa Bay.

The question now is whether to continue in the hope that we may find suitable anchorage in some suitable bay in the islands we have not visited or return to that we know of? I fear it must be the latter, for to continue in our present state is too great a risk, and yet I am most reluctant to put back having taken our departure of those people who will again have to supply us while we make repairs. It was perhaps unfortunate that just before we sailed William Watman, who had been 21 years a Marine and one of the Gunners crew, died of some sort of Paralytic stroke. If I put back some of the men are sure to comment on this, believing such is their superstitious nature that the ghost of poor Watman has called us back, and he buried at the *Morai* by request of Kao and his priests.

Wednesday, February 10th

Last night I finally gave the order to bear away for Karakakooa, a decision I arrived at with the greatest reluctance. But perhaps it is better that the mast should have gone now rather than later on when we may be upon an even more hostile shore. The wind being now light and variable some canoes have come off to us enabling us to rid ourselves of the natives that were stranded on board by the bad weather.

Friday, February 12th

This morning at daylight we were anchored in 24 fathoms in Karakakooa Bay and very sorry I was to see the place again as also was the Ships company knowing there was much hard work ahead of them and my orders that no-one was to go on shore save he had orders to do so. By night fall Fore and Main topmasts were down and prepared as Sheers for getting the Foremast out of her. We will need to have Carpenters and Sailmakers ashore and Marines to guard their tools from thieving, all the difficulties we had before and more besides since I do fear we have ate out this part of the island of most available provisions. Very few canoes have come out to us and nobody seems rejoiced that we have returned.

CHAPTER FIFTY-ONE

TROUBLE BREWING

Saturday, February 13th

Entertained King Terreeoboo on board this morning, he and some of his Chiefs being as I feared much displeased at seeing us returned and very searching in their questions, though they can see very well the reason, the mast being ashore and all the Carpenters working on it. The foot of it is rotten as I saw when it was stepped, but it will have to do. I wish the Yard officers were here that they could see how the failure of their work endangers us at the hands of these people and the elements. I shall make a very full report to their Lordships, but by then we may have lost the ship as a result of the ill equipping of us for a voyage of this nature and duration.

After the King had been we had a great number of canoes about the ships, which had been tabooed until he had been on board. But they now insist on pieces of iron about 2 feet long for trade, like the 2 I gave to the King, I suppose for the purpose of hammering into daggers which they call *pahooahs*, and though we now have hogs and other provisions aplenty, with the canoes and the people comes thievery. This appears worse than it was before, the chiefest impudence occurred this morning when the Armourers Tongs on board of the *Discovery* was stolen. Capt Clerke had the native that did it seized and given 40 lashes, then strung up to the main shrouds till such time as the Tongs may be returned. There was more trouble in this connection this Afternoon, and to my mind much more serious since it involved one of the Chiefs.

It was reported to me by Mr King on my going ashore that this man had made trouble with the natives who were employed and had been paid for assisting in the filling of the casks with water from the well at the far end of the beach. Mr Hollamby, recently appointed Quartermaster in the *Discovery*, who is in charge of the work, had requested a Marine whom Mr King sent back with him but only equipped with side arms, which was not sensible since by then the natives had armed themselves with stones. It was not until Mr King had spoken with the Chiefs, he being accompanied by another Marine armed with a Musket, was the work able to be continued without hindrance.

No sooner was I informed of this and myself engaged in inspecting the work of the Carpenters than there was Musket fire from the *Discovery* directed at a canoe which was being paddled towards the shore. I immediately set off along the beach to intercept it in company with Mr King and one of the Marines. There was a great crowd of people gathered and a good deal of noise, and though they gave back whenever the Marine presented his Musket, I noticed there was also laughter at the threat, and I do believe that the name Erono was more potent than the Musket, for mention of it caused the crowd to fly back some distance from me.

We proceeded in pursuit of the canoe until it was almost dark and then, being some 3 miles from the tents, we were led back by another route that was further from the sea than we had come by, and I believe this to have been done with intent, for when we returned to the Markee we were informed by the Coxswain of the Pinace of a more serious outbreak of violence against us. The pinace having gone to assist the *Discovery*s boat that was in pursuit of the canoe, on reaching the shore the chief Parea had roused the people against those that were in the pinace and they having no arms with which to defend themselves all the oars got broke and our men thoroughly beaten.

I was very angry at the Coxswains stupidity in going unarmed in pursuit when there was such an immense crowd of natives gathered and all showing signs of hostility, and he knowing very well that I had given orders before setting off in pursuit myself that the Marines were to fire if there was any more hostility against us.

The whole troublesome affair was due to the Tongs and the lid of a cask that contained salt horse, both being handed over to another canoe which returned them to the *Discovery*s Master who was in pursuit. There followed a most unfortunate misunderstanding, the Coxswain of the pinace thinking to capture the canoe that had made off with the Tongs and the natives that had stolen them leaping overboard and swimming ashore. Mr Vancouver got into the empty canoe and was just starting to paddle off with it to the *Discovery* when Parea, whose canoe it was and who was going ashore to recover that which had been stolen from us, got hold of it and hauled it back on shore, taking hold of the paddles so that the canoe could not be taken off to the ship, he fearing for the loss of it. Whereupon Mr Edgar tried to wrench it out of his hand, but being not so strong as Parea was pinned down. On assistance being sent, Parea let go and ran away, but towards the pinace, where he was struck by an oar wielded by one of our men.

This as far as I can learn from those that were involved was the true cause of this most unfortunate affray, the which has taken me some time of patient enquiry to unravel. It was Parea who made the mob desist, but on his going to get back the oars that had been taken, the crowd knocked Mr Vancouver down and would have stripped him of his cloathes and also got the ring bolts out of the pinace if Parea had not returned in time to stop them.

All this confusion is as much the fault of our people as of the islanders and I fear it may not end there, for Parea went off in his canoe to the Town of Kowrooa where the King resides and has said he will come on board of the *Resolution* tomorrow doubtless to lay complaints before me. I have ordered all the Women out of the ship and told Mr King to have his centries keep a close watch ashore on the tents tonight and to open fire in the event any native attempts to creep up on them in the dark.

Tomorrow I will use my best endeavours to satisfy Parea for he is the one Chief who has at all times been at great pains to help us and I am very much disturbed by the rash behaviour of our People, fearing it may have antagonised him.

The generality of Chiefs is no longer friendly towards us and it is now my belief that only the Priests and the standing I have as some sort of a god that prevents the great mass of the people from arming themselves with their weapons and attacking us. This, and the use of our firearms, is I think sufficient to hold them in subjection for the time that it is necessary to complete the repairs to the mast and ship it. But from this moment forth a bold front is become necessary and in the event of more trouble I shall seize upon the person of the King himself and hold him until we sail, the situation being I fear more dangerous than it has ever been, so that I have no alternative but to employ force. And this largely because the officers and men act without thinking and do not seem to understand that once raised to a frenzy the numbers of these people is so vast and their canoes so numerous that even though we use cannon they could readily over-whelm us.

I have seldom felt more alone than at this moment, knowing that our safety may now depend more upon the manner in which I face them than upon the weapons we can bring to bear. Whatever happens tomorrow, whatever the aggravation with which I am faced, I must not lose my temper, but must act as though I had a power over them . . .

I have just been on deck, having heard Musket fire from the shore where we have our tents and Observatory. It is now almost Midnight and this is the second time the centry there has opened fire, the first time being about 10 p.m. All is quiet again now and I pray Mr King and his people are not overwhelmed in the night. I have ordered a sharp lookout kept and the boats to be held ready. But I do believe matters have not yet reached the point where a show of force and my own presence are no longer sufficient to keep the situation within my control, and it will not be long now before we are at sea again.

The diary or personal record ends there.
The next day Cook was dead.

PART SEVEN

COOK'S DEATH

It was Sunday 14 February 1779, and what happened ashore that morning in Hawaii is covered by most of those who kept journals. In describing the manner of his death I have drawn particularly on the Journal of Captain Clerke who succeeded to command of the expedition.

HAMMOND INNES

COOK'S DEATH

It was the theft of the *Discovery*'s cutter that started the events that led to Cook's death. At daybreak that Sunday morning Lt Burney, Officer of the Watch on board of the *Discovery*, observed the cutter no longer sunk at her mooring buoy and reported its disappearance to Capt Clerke. Close examination revealed that the 4'-rope securing it to the buoy had been cut. The fact that it had been filled with water, to tighten up the planking which had been opened by the heat of the sun, had made the theft easier, the look-out being unable to see the sunken hull in the dark. In view of the previous day's trouble Clerke reported the loss to his Commander, and, after some discussion, he and Cook agreed that the *Discovery*'s boats should head for the SE point of the Bay and the *Resolution*'s for the NW point with the object of seizing all the native canoes and holding them until the cutter had been returned.

The time was then something before 7 a.m.

According to King, who had come out to the *Resolution* to report that natives had been seen skulking round the shore base during the night, Capt Clerke was 'too unwell to go on shore to Terreeoboo'. Burney, the 1st Lieutenant of the *Resolution*, says much the same thing, that Capt Cook 'desired Captain Clerke to go on shore to the old King Terreeoboo, to endeavour to prevail on him to use his authority and influence to have the boat restored. Captain Clerke was in too reduced a state of health for so much exertion, and was obliged to excuse himself.'

Cook was well aware of Clerke's condition and since King reports that when he came on board of the *Resolution* 'they were all arming themselves & the Captn loading his double Barreld piece' it is likely that the instant Cook heard of the theft he had decided to go himself and had already made up his mind to seize the king as a hostage as well as any canoes the boats could lay their hands on.

Clerke returned to his ship and sent Lt Rickman away in his two remaining boats, a launch and a cutter, with their crews and some marines, all well armed, to the SE of the Bay. After seeing them on their way, he had himself rowed back to the *Resolution* in the jolly boat with the intention of discussing the matter further with Capt Cook. On arrival he was informed that Cook had himself gone ashore in the pinnace, accompanied by the launch and small cutter, and had headed straight for Kaawaloa, the town or large village on the NW point where King Terreeoboo lived. Clerke then returned to his ship in the belief that everything would be all right and that the cutter would be quickly recovered once Cook had seen the King.

Everything at that time seemed reasonably normal with quite a few small canoes trading with the ships. However, shortly after his return, Clerke heard musket fire from his own boats and sent the jolly boat away to the SE to discover the cause of it, which he could not see from the *Discovery*, and also to bring back any captured canoes. It was most probably the news that they had shot and killed an Aree, or chief, named Kareemoo that was the cause of all that followed. The time was then just on 8 a.m. and shortly afterwards those on board the two ships heard a volley of shots and a great uproar from the mass of natives gathered around Cook's boats at the NW point opposite the town of Kaawaloa. Clerke, looking through his telescope, says that he could clearly see 'our People were drove off to their Boats'. He could not see Cook or identify any individual. But his first lieutenant, Burney, who was on deck beside him looking through his own glass, says he could 'see Capt Cook receive a Blow from a Club and fall off a Rock into the Water'.

At this time both the pinnace and the launch were firing and the *Resolution*, which was moored close off the landing beach, opened fire, throwing shot into the crowd milling around the beach. With all their boats away there was nothing else the ships could do and Clerke had to look helplessly on until the shore engagement was called off for lack of ammunition and Lt Williamson, who was in command of the boats, had reported to him from the *Resolution*. It was then that he heard definitely that Cook was dead and himself now the Commander of the Expedition.

He immediately transferred to the *Resolution* and despatched a strong force to protect the observatory and all that were ashore working on the mast. Four marines had been killed and three wounded, including Phillips, their 2nd Lieutenant, who had been stabbed in the shoulder with an iron spike and was badly bruised with stones. It was Phillips who gave Clerke a blow-by-blow account of what had happened, and though it is inevitably a little confused in places it is the most personal information we shall ever have of the untimely and quite unnecessary death of England's greatest navigator.

Capt Cook landed at the Town situate within the NW point with his Pinnace & Launch, leaving the small Cutter off the Point to prevent the escape of any Canoes that might be dispos'd to get off, at his landing he order'd 9 Marines which we had in the Boats and myself onshore to attend him and immediately march'd into the Town where he enquired for Terre'oboo and the 2 Boys (his sons had liv'd principally with Capt Cook onboard the Resolution since Terre'oboo's first arrival among us). Messengers were immediately dispatch'd and the 2 Boys soon came and conducted us to their Fathers house.

After waiting some time on the outside Capt Cook doubted the old Gentlemans being there and sent me in that I might inform Him. I found our old acquaintance just awoke from Sleep when upon my acquainting him that Capt Cook was at the door, he very readily went with me to Him. Capt Cook after some little conversation observ'd that Terre'oboo was quite innocent of what had happen'd and proposed to the old Gentleman to go on board with him, which he readily agreed to, and we accordingly proceeded towards the Boats, but having advanc'd near to the Water side an elderly Woman whose name was Kar'na'cub'ra one of his Wives came to him and with many tears and intreaties beg'd he would not go onboard, at the same time 2 Chiefs laid hold of him and insisting that he should not, made him sit down, the old Man now appear'd dejected and frighten'd.

It was at this period we first began to suspect that they were not very well dispos'd towards us, and the Marines being huddled together in the midst of an immense Mob compos'd of at least 2 or 3 thousand People, I propos'd to Capt Cook that they might be arrang'd in order along the Rocks by the Water side which he approving of, the Crowd readily made way for them and they were drawn up accordingly; we now clearly saw they were collecting their Spears &c, but an Artful Rascal of a Priest was singing & making a ceremonious offering of a Coco Nut to the Capt and Terre'oboo to divert their attention from the Manoeuvres of the surrounding multitude.

Capt Cook now gave up all thoughts of

taking Terre'oboo onboard with the following observation to me, 'We can never think of compelling him to go onboard without killing a number of these People,' and I believe was just going to give orders to embark, when he was interrupted by a fellow arm'd with a long Iron Spike (a pahoa, or dagger) and a Stone; this Man made a flourish with his Pah'hoo'ah, and threaten'd to throw his stone upon which Capt Cook discharg'd a load of small shot at him but he having his Mat on the small shot did not penetrate it, and had no other effect than farther to provoke and encourage them, I could not observe the least fright it occasion'd; immediately upon this an Aree arm'd with a Pah'hoo'ah attempted to stab me but I foil'd his attempt by giving him a severe blow with the Butt End of my Musket, just at this time they began to throw stones, and one of the Marines was knock'd down, the Capt then fir'd a ball and kill'd a Man.

They now made a general attack and the Capt gave orders to the Marines to fire and afterwards called out 'Take to the Boats'. I fir'd just after the Capt and loaded again whilst the Marines fir'd; almost instantaneously upon my repeating the Orders to take to the Boats I was knock'd down by a stone and in rising receiv'd a Stab with a Pah'hoo'ah in the shoulder, my Antagonist was just upon the point of seconding his blow when I shot him dead, the business was now a most miserable scene of confusion – the Shouts and

Yells of the Indians far exceeding all the noise I ever came in the way of, these fellows instead of retiring upon being fir'd at, as Capt Cook and I believe most People concluded they would, acted so very contrary a part, that they never gave the Soldiers time to reload their Pieces but immediately broke in upon and would have kill'd every man of them had not the Boats by a smart fire kept them a little off and pick'd up those who were not too much wounded to reach them.

After being knock'd down I saw no more of Capt Cook, all my people I observ'd were totally vanquish'd and endeavouring to save their lives by getting to the Boats – I therefore scrambled as well I could into the Water and made for the Pinnace which I fortunately got hold of, but not before I receiv'd another blow from a stone just above the Temple which had not the Pinnace been very near would have sent me to the Bottom.

This account, which I give in full because it is the only one we have from a witness at close hand, cannot be taken entirely at its face value since Lt Phillips knew perfectly well that at home it would be thoroughly scrutinised for any evidence of failure on the part of his marines to do their duty and protect the Commander of the expedition with courage and discipline. And though Midshipman Harvey supports him, another midshipman, Watts, gives a somewhat different view of the marines' behaviour. 'In the mean time,' he writes in his journal, 'the Marines with the same undisciplined infatuation began a fire also and the Attack on both sides became general.' Watts claims that the 'undisciplined' firing by the marines was after Cook had waved his hand at the boats and ordered them to stop firing – they had apparently opened fire immediately the huge crowd had started stone-slinging. He also says that it was whilst Cook was getting down the beach to the boats to stop the firing that he was stabbed 'somewhere near the shoulder blade upon which he staggered a few paces and fell into the Water where two or three of the Natives Jumped upon him and beat him about the head with Stones until he expired'.

Samwell, who had been promoted to surgeon in the *Discovery* six months previously and who, like Anderson before him, kept a very full journal, is even more damning in his comments on the behaviour of the marines. He says that after the first volley the natives fell back and a 'vigorous push at this juncture would have put them to flight; but no sooner had the Marines made the general discharge but the body of them flung down their pieces and threw themselves into the water, on this all was over . . .'

He makes the point that natives of the Pacific, however numerous, will never stand and fight in the face of a group of 'resolute Men with fire arms who will firmly maintain their Ground'. He not only blames the marines for not standing their ground, but like Bayly and Watts, who refer specifically to Lt Williamson's order forbidding the boats, other than the cutter, to close the shore, even to embark men that were in the water, he finds it extraordinary that the three boats, which were all under the command of the *Resolution*'s 3rd Lieutenant and contained upwards of 40 seamen, most of them armed, did not take more resolute action. Thus Williamson's part in the affair becomes 'even more irresolute and unsatisfactory than the marines'.

Something of Cook's sublime confidence in his ability to maintain command of the situation is indicated by Harvey's statement that when Phillips informed him that the natives were arming, which was surely something he could see for himself, 'the Captn made light of the intelligence, and from his actions, I imagine he thought that they were only arming themselves to act upon the defensive, that is to say, to protect the King from being taken off by force'. Again, when Phillips kept urging him to embark Cook merely agreed to his drawing his marines up on the rocks of the foreshore and himself still standing there 'permitted the greatest insults from them to such a degree that for the security of his own person he was obliged to shoot two of them . . . even after this by an infatuation that is altogether unaccountable he continued to trifle away his time on shore and did not attempt to recover the Boats until the attack was begun . . .'

Clearly Cook was not 'trifling away his time'. Throughout three expeditions he had succeeded in dominating every situation that had faced him and in the Pacific had grown accustomed to the excitability of the native peoples. Usually his own presence had proved sufficient to quieten them, particularly when backed up by a show of strength. Use of firearms had been a final resort and this had never failed, but in this instance, though he had ordered the marines to load their muskets with ball before leaving the ship, he had loaded one barrel of his own twin-barrelled piece with shot. It was this barrel that he fired first and since the man he fired at was wearing a protective mat, which was their armour against slung stones, it had no effect. His action was thus discredited in the eyes of the mob. They are reported as laughing at it, so that instead of subduing them, it only served to embolden them. Edgar, the *Discovery*'s master, is probably right in saying that 'had Capt Cooke come down to the boats directly as he was advised he most probably would have saved his life . . .' But it was not in Cook's nature to run from a native mob, and if he thought it an ugly situation and one that might get out of hand, the more reason for him to stay and outface them.

That it was an error of judgment is obvious, but I do not believe it was caused by fatigue. This is a recurrent theory, that Cook's judgment was impaired at this time by exhaustion due to the eight years he had spent in arduous ocean exploration, and particularly by his disappointing and wearying voyage into the Arctic. My own sea experience gives me a little understanding of the nervous tension and fatigue that results from inshore navigation on a hostile and unfamiliar coast in poor weather conditions, but I also know the recovery rate, and Cook had had plenty of time to relax and unwind after the strain of navigating to the edge of the Arctic pack ice. The increased irascibility revealed in his official Journal is not in my view due either to fatigue or age, but to his feeling of frustration at having to spend another winter in the islands, and also to his growing facility in the use of words and the sense that he now had sufficient standing to express his irritation officially, even to the extent of criticising yard officers senior to himself.

Nor do I think it true to say that Cook was unaware of the almost godly status accorded him by the priests and the extent to which the resources of the island had been plundered to support his ships. He was not a sensitive man; few sailors are, their lives being mainly concerned with practicalities, and Cook in particular had spent the last 17 years largely immersed in the exact science of surveying and charting. But he certainly was not unaware of the strain his ships had imposed on the islands' economy and resources and the effect upon the people of his sudden and almost immediate return after the elaborate farewells.

That Cook was a changed man, however, I accept. Not in any fundamental sense, of course, but there is no doubt that on this third voyage his reactions to things were different, and they were different because his whole attitude, even his objectives, had been changed by the year he had spent ashore in England. He was a more ambitious man, or rather he was ambitious in a wider sense. His election to the Royal Society had opened new doors and prospects, and the time he had spent learning to write up his Journal for publication under the tutelage of Dr Douglas had given his precise and determined mind a new direction.

Like most eminently successful men, Cook possessed that quality of single-purposed drive that can ride roughshod over all opposition, sometimes with complete disregard for the feelings of others. On the enforced return to Kealakekua Bay his concern was the repair of the mast, nothing else. He was urgent to get to sea again, to explore Kamchatka and the Russian coast and make an earlier and more thorough search for the North West Passage. The grumblings of his own men on not being allowed ashore, the reluctance of the Hawaiian people to continue to supply his ships and their thieving propensities all served to increase his irascibility. He was never the easiest of men and his temper could be very short indeed. At times he could be quite unfeeling. The punishment of men meant nothing to him so long as it was deserved and for the good of the ship, or in the case of a native for the advantage of the expedition. The theft of the cutter, which could not readily be replaced and was essential to his operations in the north, was the last straw – in modern terminology he blew his top and went storming ashore, determined to put an end to these constant pinpricks by seizing upon the person of the King as a hostage.

The fact that he took only nine marines with him out of a total of 31 is a measure of his hastiness and his supreme confidence in his ability to carry out his purpose by his own presence and if necessary a small show of force. And in this he would undoubtedly have been successful had not the news of Rickman's action with the *Discovery*'s boat at the south east point and the death of one of their chiefs been brought to Kaawaloa just as Cook was leading the old King to the boat. It was this which sent the King's wife rushing to her husband with entreaties to him not to go on board and others of his entourage to restrain him from proceeding. Up to that point everything was so normal that one of the King's two sons was already in the boat, and only left it on the advice of the sailors after the firing had started, for the pair of them spent a good deal of their time playing about on the *Resolution* and were very popular with the men.

Samwell with his eye on publication gives by far the most vivid and poignant account of Cook's death, but since he was on board of the *Discovery*, which was stationed further from the scene than the *Resolution*, we must accept that the account is based on general talk and conversations he may have had with those seamen who were in the boats. This is his account of Cook's end:

Captain Cook was advanced a few paces before the Marines when they fired, the Stones flew as thick as hail which knocked the Lieut. down & as he was rising a fellow stuck him in the back with a Spear, however he recovered himself shot the Indian dead and escaped into the Water.

Captain Cook was not the only Man on the Rock, he was seen walking down towards the Pinnace holding his left hand against the Back of his head to guard it from the Stones & carrying his Musket under the other Arm. An Indian came running behind him, stopping once or twice as he advanced, as if he was afraid that he should turn round, then taking him unaware he sprung to him, knocked him on the back of his head with a large Club taken out of a fence, & instantly fled with the greatest precipitation; the blow made Captain Cook stagger two or three paces, he then fell on his hand & one knee & dropped his Musket, as he was rising another Indian came running to him & before he could recover himself from the Fall drew out an iron Dagger he concealed under his feathered Cloak & stuck it with all his force into the back of his Neck, which made Captain Cook tumble into the Water in a kind of a bite by the side of the rock where the water is about knee deep; here he was followed by a crowd of people who endeavoured to keep him under water, but struggling very strong with them he got his head up & looking towards the Pinnace which was not above a boat hook's Length from him he waved his hands to them for Assistance, which it seems it was not in their Power to give.

The Indians got him under water again but he disengaged himself & got his head up once more & not being able to swim he endeavoured to scramble on the Rock, when a fellow gave him a blow on the head with a large Club and he was seen alive no more.

They now kept him under water, one man sat

on his Shoulders & beat his head with a stone while others beat him with Clubs & Stones, taking a Savage pleasure in using every barbarity to the dead body; as soon as one had struck him another would take the Instrument out of his Body and give him another Stab.

The disparity between the various versions of what happened ashore that day is clearly due to the fact that the only man on the spot who wrote an account of it had reasons for representing his own men in the most favourable light. All the others wrote from hearsay and what they had observed of the confusions ashore from a distance. There is no doubt, however, that Cook's death was the result of his failure to appreciate fully the changed mood of the Hawaiians and of course to the violence of his own reaction to the theft of the cutter. This quick temper of his, exacerbated in this instance by the frustration he felt at having to put back to the same bay and deal once again with the same people, emerges very strongly in the first biography of the navigator written by Andrew Kippis and published only nine years after his death.

Describing Cook's character and getting much of his information from Banks and Samwell, Kippis writes: 'With the greatest benevolence and humanity of disposition, Captain Cook was occasionally subject to hastiness of temper. This, which has been exaggerated by the few (and they are indeed few) who are unfavourable to his memory, is acknowledged by his friends.'

Elaborating on Cook's character he quotes firstly from King, by then a Captain: 'The constitution of his body was robust, inured to labour and capable of undergoing the severest hardship. His stomach bore, without difficulty, the coarsest and most ungrateful foods; great was the indifference with which he submitted to every kind of self-denial. The qualities of his mind were of the same hardy and vigorous kind as those of his body. His understanding was strong and perspicacious. His judgment, in whatever related to the services he was engaged in, was quick and sure. His designs were bold and manly and, both in conception and in the mode of execution, bore evident marks of a great original genius. His courage was cool and determined, and accompanied by an admirable presence of mind in the moment of danger. His temper might perhaps have been justly blamed, as subject to hastiness and passion, had not these been disarmed by a disposition the most benevolent and humane.'

Kippis also quotes Samwell on Cook – 'His constitution was strong; his mode of living temperate. He was a modest man, and rather bashful; of an agreeable lively conversation, sensible and intelligent. In his temper he was somewhat hasty, but of a disposition the most friendly, benevolent, and humane. His person was about six feet high and, though a goodlooking man, he was plain both in address and appearance. His head was small, his hair, which was a dark brown, he wore tied behind. His face was full of expression; his nose exceedingly well shaped; his eyes, which were small and of a brown cast, were quick and piercing, his eyebrows prominent which gave his countenance altogether an air of austerity.'

Both men refer to his single-purposed determination. King writes: 'But the most distinguishing feature [of Cook's character] was that unremitting perseverance in the pursuit of his object, which was not only superior to the opposition of dangers, and the pressure of hardships, but even exempt from the want of ordinary relaxation. During the long and tedious voyages in which he was engaged, his eagerness and activity were never in the least abated. No incidental temptation could detain him for a moment; even those intervals of recreation which sometimes unavoidably occurred and were looked for by us with a longing that persons who have experienced fatigues of service will readily excuse, were submitted to by him with a certain impatience, whenever they could not be employed in making a further provision for the more effective prosecution of his design.'

Samwell puts it more elaborately: 'With a clear judgment, strong masculine sense, and most determined resolution – with a genius peculiarly turned for enterprise, he pursued his object with unshaken perseverence; – vigilant and active in an eminent degree; – cool and intrepid among dangers; patient and firm under difficulties and stress; fertile in expedients; great and original in all his designs; active and resolved in carrying them into execution.'

These examples give some indication of how he was regarded by those he commanded. No seaman ever had better epitaphs by those who sailed with him.

PART EIGHT

THE END OF THE VOYAGE

Captain Clerke's initial and natural reaction, on succeeding to the command of the expedition, was to send a force ashore, burn the town and avenge Cook's death. But after thinking it over, he came to the more sensible conclusion that any further loss of men would be to the detriment of the voyage. He posted Lt Gore to the command of the *Discovery* and having got the mast aboard and all the men that were ashore re-embarked, set about getting the *Resolution* fit for sea as soon as possible.

His acceptance of the situation without any reprisals was not to the liking of his men. It was bad enough seeing a chief parading ashore with Cook's hanger, or sword, but when another of them came out in a canoe and had himself paddled around the ships flaunting Cook's hat on his head and slapping his backside in contempt of the sailors, they went to Clerke in a body and requested revenge. He agreed to land a force and burn the town, but this had to be postponed as Gore was not ready to have the *Discovery* warped in to cover the landing.

There followed almost a week of provocation by the natives and periodic skirmishing ashore due to the fact that water had to be brought off to the ships. The native weapon was the sling, and so ignorant were they of firearms that, because of the flame and smoke, they thought they were being killed by burning and as a protection soaked their body armour of mats with water. All this time the *Resolution* was very vulnerable to attack, her decks being littered with spars and cordage, but the *Discovery*, with two more guns brought up from the hold, was warped in to cover the watering and on 17 February Kealakekua, the village nearest the watering point, was set on fire, some 50 or 60 houses being destroyed including that of the priest who had been their most consistent friend. Feeling among the men ran so high that the heads of two of the natives they had killed were cut off and mounted in the boats lying off to protect the watering parties.

All this time Clerke was endeavouring to recover Cook's remains, the Hawaiians repeatedly trying to lure him or his officers ashore to receive them. In the end they appear to have become frightened that further reprisals would be taken and on Saturday the 20th they made their peace, handing in to the pinnace a large bundle wrapped in a cloak of black and white feathers. This bundle, which contained all that remained of Cook's body, was unwrapped in the great cabin of the *Resolution*, and Samwell, who presumably examined it in his capacity as surgeon, gives the following description of its contents:

> We found in it the following bones with some flesh upon them which had the marks of fire. The Thighs & Legs joined together but not the feet, both Arms with the Hands separated from them, the Skull with all the bones that form the face wanting with the Scalp separated from it, which was also in the bundle with the hair on it cut short, both Hands whole with the Skin of the fore Arms joined to them, the hands had not been in the fire, but were salted, several Gashes being cut in them to take the Salt in. Tho we had no doubt concerning the Identity of any of the parts contained in the bundle, every one must be perfectly satisfied as to that of the hands, for we all knew the right by a large Scar on it separating for about an inch the Thumb from the forefinger. The Ears adhered to the Scalp, which had a cut in it about an inch long, probably from the first blow he received with the Club, but the Skull was not fractured so that it is likely that the Stroke was not mortal.

The same day the *Resolution*'s mast was stepped. On the Sunday Cook's hanger was brought out to the *Resolution*, also the two barrels of his gun which 'had been taken asunder and the end of one of them beaten flat intended to be made into Daggers or small adzes'. The following day his underjaw and feet were delivered, together with his shoes and a bit of his hat. And on that day Monday, 22 February, just one week after his clothes had been sold in the great cabin to his fellow officers as is still the custom in the Navy, what was left of Cook was committed to the deep 'with all attention and honour we could possibly pay it in this part of the World'. At five in the afternoon both ships had their ensigns and pennants flying at half mast, their yards crossed, and at 5.45 the *Resolution* tolled her bell and fired a 20 gun salute in slow time as the remains were slid over the side into the Pacific.

The following day Clerke sailed in an endeavour to succeed where Cook had failed the previous year, and before their departure the ships were once again crowded with Hawaiians, gifts being exchanged and all on the friendliest terms, even girls living aboard. He spent three weeks exploring the remainder of the Hawaiian Group and then headed for the coast of Kamchatka, which he reached on 23 April after a night of frost, snow and sleet.

He was too ill to explore ashore as Cook would have done, but he sent his officers, and while the ships were making up the river to Petropavlovsk the Governor, Major Behm, paid him a visit. This most helpful and generous official, who was later treated so callously by his government and Prince Potemkin in particular, was on the point of returning to St Petersburg. To him Clerke entrusted Cook's journal for delivery to the English Ambassador, also reports from King and Bayly and his own journal since succeeding to command. By this means, and after an interval of seven months, the news of Cook's death reached the Admiralty in London.

Clerke remained with his ships harboured at Petropavlovsk for the better part of a month, sailing on 16 June, having got on board the stores he needed, much of which were at Major Behm's personal expense. By the first day of July he was into the Gulf of Anadir, through the Bering Straits by 6 July, and from 7 July to 27 July he probed northwards, all the time either in the ice or on the edge of the pack. But at no time did he get further north than Cook.

On Wednesday, 21 July, he wrote in his journal: 'It is now clearly impossible to proceed in the least farther to the Noward upon this Coast and it is equally as improbable that this amazing mass of Ice should be dissolv'd by the few remaining Summer weeks which will terminate this Season but it doubtlessly remain as it now is a most unsurmountable barrier to every attempt we can possibly make. I therefore think it the best step I can take for the good of the service to trace the Ice over to the Asiatic Coast, try if I can find a Hole that will admit me any further North, if not see whats to be done upon the Coast where I hope but cannot much flatter myself with meeting better success, for this Sea is now so Choak'd with Ice that a passage I fear is totally out of the question.'

This was his last journal entry. He had pushed himself and his ships to the limit and was totally exhausted. He turned south, was back through the Bering Straits on 30 July, and the day after they sighted the coast of Kamchatka again he was dead. He had been totally confined to his bed since 16 August and died at 8.30 a.m. on 22 August. It is a pity Anderson was not alive, or somebody on board to give a proper obituary to so conscientious a man. In King's recently discovered Journal the entry for 22 August reads: 'Captn Clerke dyed on the 22nd Augst. when we were almost in sight of the bay of Awatshka; his disorder was a consumption* of which he had lingered during the whole voyage & his decay was so gradual, that he did the duty of his station till within a week of his death, when being no longer able to come on deck, he desired the officers to receive my orders & gave the command up to me . . .' Later King wrote what can be described as a brief obituary: 'He had three times encircled the World, & attempted a fourth, In the pursuit of which for the last half year, he commanded the expedition, nor did he swerve in any instance from persevering on account of his health, preferring his duty to his Country, to even his own life.'

Samwell, though a surgeon, is less than generous in his final comment, but does give a fair character sketch:

> Captn Clerke was a sensible Man & a good Sailor, but did not possess that degree of Firmness & Resolution necessary to constitute the Character of a great Commander. He was ever diffident of himself & consequently wavering and

*King himself was to die of consumption in November 1784 aged 34.

unfixed in his Conduct, except where a certain Line of Action was chalked out to him & then no man was readier to pursue it than himself; he was fitter to be second than first in Command, fitter to execute than to plan. However his Perseverance in pursuing the Voyage after the death of Captn Cook, notwithstanding his own bad state of Health will ever reflect Honour upon his Memory. The most remarkable part of his Character was his happy convivial Turn & humourous Conversation in which he excelled most Men; these, joined to an open generous Disposition, made his Company universally caressed and engaged him in excesses which laid the Foundation of the Complaint of which he died.

Thus both Commanders were lost in a voyage that finally extended to four years and three months. But in spite of all the ships had been through, indifferently rigged and fitted out, ranging the Pacific, exploring new islands and the northern coasts of America and Asia, and twice spending weeks on the edge of the Arctic pack ice for which they were not equipped, they lost only 12 men of a total company of 194, including those who joined at the Cape. Of this total only five died of disease during the voyage, and in the case of Clerke at any rate this was from tuberculosis which he had contracted before sailing. A great tribute to Cook's routine of hygiene, something that was not fully recognised at the time and is one of the most important aspects of this and his earlier voyages.

His achievements as a navigator, however, were recognised, both in his own country and abroad. The standing and regard with which he was held in England is indicated by the official reaction to the news of his death. The Royal Society had commemorative medals struck in gold and silver with Cook's head in profile and round it *Jac. Cook Oceani Investigator Acerrimus*; and on the reverse Britannia holding a globe and the words: *Nil Intentatum Nostri Liquere, Auspiciis Georgii III*. One of the gold medals was given to Mrs Cook. The King granted her a pension of £200 a year and £25 a year to each of her three sons, also a family coat of arms. And the Admiralty allocated the profits of the book of the voyage* almost entirely to the families of those officers who were dead by the time it was published, one half going to Mrs Cook and her family, a quarter to King's heirs, an eighth to Clerke's and the remaining eighth to Bligh, less 100 guineas to Anderson's heirs; a most unusual action by a Board that was never distinguished for its generosity.

Abroad his standing was such that though France had joined the United States in their war against England, both countries ordered their warships to grant safe conduct to the *Resolution* and the *Discovery*. Benjamin Franklin instructed his privateers: *A*

---

*A Voyage to the Pacific Ocean . . . was published in 1784, the first two volumes being credited to Cook, the third to King. The first edition priced at 4¼ gns sold out in three days. The second and third editions did not appear until 1785 by which time the first edition was changing hands at 10gns. The Cook family share of the profits according to Prof. Beaglehole, 'certainly amounted to over £2,000'.

Ship having been fitted out from England, before the Commencement of this War, to make Discoveries of new Countries in unknown Seas, under the Conduct of the most celebrated Navigator and Discoverer Captain Cook . . . he earnestly entreated them to *treat the said Captain Cook and his people with all Civility and Kindness, affording them as common Friends to Mankind all the Assistance in your Power which they may happen to stand in need of.* These instructions were signed *B. Franklin, Minister Plenipotentiary from the Congress of the United States at the Court of France.*

Finally, Sir Joseph Banks, who as President of the Royal Society had sent the gold medal to Mrs Cook with a note saying 'His name will live for ever', initiated and encouraged Kippis to write his biography. This was the first of the many volumes that have been written about Captain James Cook RN in the 200 years since he was killed in Hawaii. In 1874 a concrete obelisk was erected in Kealakekua Bay; and in 1928 a small bronze plaque was set into the seabed below the water near the spot where he fell. But his real memorial is the great multiplicity of islands, headlands and bays he discovered and named, the charts he drew and the work of the naturalists and painters who sailed with him.

AUTHOR'S NOTE

This self-revealing account of Cook's search for the North West Passage, written as a diary or personal record of the great navigator's last tragic voyage, is something that I feel is within the bounds of possibility. Even his official journal, so different from those of the two previous voyages, reveals his newly awakened interest in writing.

In presenting the main body of this work as Cook's own writing I am conscious of having taken a great liberty for which I hope those who are as fascinated by the subject as I am will forgive me. I have done it for two reasons:

Apart from my writing, I have had sixteen years of sailing my own boat on the coasts of Europe. I know the sea at close quarters and as a result I felt it was possible to imagine myself standing in Cook's shoes on board of the *Resolution*. Also, in my travels I have gone out of my way over the years to visit places that Cook visited, even his passage through the

Great Barrier Reef and the almost inaccessible Dusky Bay in New Zealand. The fact is that I seem to have been living with Cook a very long time now.

Captain Cook's journals tell us nothing about the man himself. They are official journals, as were those written by the men who sailed with him. If, therefore, I have succeeded to any degree at all in bringing this great navigator to life I shall be happy, the work having been done as a labour of love and in an honest endeavour to set right the impression left by those official journals. Cook was neither a dull man, nor unemotional and inhuman. He could not have been, or he would not have achieved what he did.

Addendum

Apart from my indebtness to the late Professor J. C. Beaglehole for the years of dedicated research that has made this book possible, I would also like to express my thanks to Dr Helen Wallis, Map Librarian of the British Library, for finding the time, in the midst of preparing her paper on Captain Cook for the Vancouver Symposium, to check my manuscript and put me right on a number of points. It was Dr Wallis who informed me that Captain King's journal for the latter part of this voyage has only recently come to light after 200 years – among Miscellaneous Sailing Directions at the Hydrographic Department, Taunton. A most extraordinary coincidence!

HIGH STAND

TO
ALL MY FRIENDS
IN
WESTERN CANADA

CONTENTS

PART ONE

THE GOLDEN PLAYBOY

CHAPTER ONE

My mind didn't register for a moment. It was nine-forty, a Friday in mid-August. Everything was always a rush on a Friday and I was trying to complete the draft of an affidavit before my first appointment at ten. 'There's a Mrs Halliday to see you.' My secretary was on holiday and the girl standing in for her got the name wrong.

'I told you, I don't see people without an appointment.'

'She said she was an old friend.'

It took a moment even then ... My God! I thought – Miriam. I looked out of the window, at the long sweeping back of the downs running towards Ditchling Beacon, a smooth flowing line against a cloudless sky, streaks of cirrus forming in the west. More than a year ago, April or May, driving back late at night from a dinner party ... May. It must have been May, the hedges long lines of white in the car's headlights. 'Tom

Hall'day's wife,' I said. 'You typed that codicil for him to sign. Remember?'

'It's spelt Halliday,' she said firmly, putting a slip of paper in front of me. 'And she says it's urgent.'

'They pronounce it Hall'day,' I told her, wondering what the hell Miriam wanted. Did she know he had changed his Will? I pushed the draft affidavit aside, my mind searching for an answer. Miriam I had liked more than most, but it was the cognac and the May moon, that was all, the only occasion, in fact, we had ever been alone together. The last time I had seen her had been about six months ago, at a dinner party at their house just after Tom Halliday got back from another of his Yukon trips. I told the girl I would ring when I was ready and leaned back into the shaft of sunlight streaming in through the open window, bracing myself for an awkward interview. She hadn't told her husband, I was certain of that. If she had he would have behaved quite differently. So it was either the Will, or else her sex life had suddenly become so complicated she needed advice. That was a development of the practice I hadn't expected, women whose husbands had found them out, or who had got themselves pregnant, or, even worse in a way, men whose involvement with somebody else's wife had come out into the open.

I picked up my pipe, but I didn't fill it. I just sat there sucking at it and thinking of Halliday, remembering how he had looked, sitting in the chair opposite me – a compact, nervously tense man with a shock of black hair and a small moustache, the eyes bright, intensely alive, and the hands restless. Miriam was a lot younger and I had wondered then if his hair wasn't dyed, it was so uniformly black.

Why had he done it, adding a codicil that switched the forestry property in BC from Miriam to the younger of the two sons by his first marriage? And that nervous tension. He wasn't normally tense – a rather extrovert man with a fondness for good wine and showy cars. Bit of a show-off really, with an unpredictable streak that seemed to go with the fact that he was rich and had not had to earn a penny of it. I sucked at my pipe, staring out towards the downs, brown in the sun. I could almost smell the scent of the grass, but the picture in my mind was of Tom Halliday sitting over the port at the end of that dinner talking compulsively about his father, about Dawson City and the dreadful haul up from Skagway, talking so fast that the words seemed to spill out of him. I had heard most of it before, the incredible story of the phoney gold mine, but never in such detail and never told with such a sense of excitement. He had seemed lit up by the memory of it, and then he had taken us through into his study where the walls were hung with pictures and relics of the gold rush, a great moose head over the fireplace. But it was the faded photograph of his father that remained most vividly in my mind, a photograph of his father as a young man, with a drooping moustache, braces and a battered hat, standing against a rickety wooden sluice box that was half-covered in snow and ice, holding in his hand a panning dish, his mouth wide open and his teeth showing in a grin as he danced a jig over the contents. Strange to think that all his life Tom Halliday had been living off that pan. Well, at least Miriam had still got the mine, so what was she worrying about? Or hadn't she realized it was only the trees he had come to see me about?

I put down my pipe and reached for the intercom. Better get it over with, whatever it was. 'Show Mrs Halliday in, will you.'

She wasn't pregnant, that was my first thought, every detail of her revealed by the close-fitting jeans and her stomach flat as a boy's. And though the sight of her made my blood run faster, I knew at once that the reason she was here didn't concern me, for she'd taken no trouble with her clothes – just the jeans and a pair of sandals, a chequered cotton shirt, hardly any make-up and her hair straggling in wisps across her face. She smiled at me, briefly and without any special warmth, her eyes blank. She didn't even say she was glad to see me again, her mind totally preoccupied as she took the chair I indicated.

Even then she didn't look at me. She just sat there across the desk from me, staring blankly at the wall behind my head. She seemed at a loss for words. 'This isn't a social call, I take it?' I tried to keep my voice light.

She shook her head. 'No. I need some advice. Your help, Philip.'

The large eyes focused suddenly and I felt something stir in me and was surprised that just a glance and the knowledge that she needed my help could do that to me. 'What's the problem?'

'Tom,' she said. 'Have you seen him recently – since he got back?' And when I didn't say anything she nodded to herself. 'Tuesday, wasn't it?' And she added, 'About his Will?' She was staring at me, teeth clamped on her lower lip.

'You know I can't give you the reason for his visit.' He could have phoned me about it, but he'd been in a hurry, wanting the codicil typed out there and then while he waited, and then the temp and I had witnessed it. 'You're his wife, I know, but a solicitor –'

'Rubbish.' She shook her head quickly, a gesture of impatience. 'I knew you'd say that. He came to you about his Will. There's no other reason he would have come here. Is there?' It was said as an afterthought, almost under her breath, and she added, 'I don't care about the Will, but how did he seem?' She leaned suddenly forward so that I could see the swell of her breasts in the V of her shirt, her hands clasped, very tightly. 'You've met him a number of times over the last two or three years. Was he any different – worried, upset, tense? Was there tension?'

'Why?' There was an edge to my voice. If it wasn't the Will, then why was she so upset? 'He seemed just the same.' I said it quickly, angry with myself, and with her for the effect she had on me.

'Then why change his Will? Just then – right after his return.' Her voice faded, became uncertain. 'I don't understand.'

'No need for you to worry,' I answered her, thinking of the trees and that son of his. 'You're very well provided for.'

She brushed that aside. 'I can always look after myself.' I thought I caught the glimmer of a smile. 'But

I happen to be very fond of Tom and there's something wrong.' Her eyes flickered round my office as if searching for some indication of what that something might be. 'Did he give any reason?' And when I didn't answer, she said, 'It's Brian, I take it.'

I didn't say anything, wondering how she had guessed. I had asked him about that – why the younger son? But when he said he had had the boy trained in forestry I could see the sense of it from his point of view. Miriam still got the mine, which was what really mattered. And the elder boy, Martin, inherited all the shares in Halliday Special Bodies, which was presumably what he wanted since he more or less ran the works for his father. 'Martin's an engineer,' Halliday had said. 'He doesn't know one end of a tree from the other.'

'Was it the mine or that land in British Columbia?' She was watching me closely, her eyes searching. 'Not the company, surely. That wouldn't suit Brian, it's been losing money for years. It must be the trees – that land Tom's father planted fifty years or more ago.' Her eyes, still fixed on me, caught the light, a sort of turquoise blue with flecks of green, very striking. I hadn't seen them so clearly before, the sun straight on her. And that hair of hers, almost red. 'Did he give any reason? Brian has a feeling for trees, I know that. But there has to be a reason, something that impelled Tom to come and see you – right then, just after he had got back from Canada.'

'I'm sorry,' I said. 'I can't discuss it. I really can't.'

'Balls! Really, Philip . . .' She was suddenly more like herself – vital, very alive, with that sharp intelligence that had so attracted me. 'He came here last Tuesday, and Brian came back about a month ago, straight from some Godforsaken village in the Himalayas where he'd been sitting at the feet of a Muslim fakir – a guru, a wizard, I don't know what you'd call him.' And she added, quite softly, 'He's wild, that boy, always has been. Tom said once he ought to have some trees of his own. The only trees he could give him are on the Halliday Arm. One of the finest stands of western red cedar in BC. That was how he described it to me once, and the only business he had with you was his Will.' She stopped there, almost breathless, for it had come out in a rush, her eyes still fixed on mine. She seemed on the point of saying something more, but then she turned her head away, locking whatever it was up inside herself, the silence dragging.

'Suppose you tell me what the problem is?'

She gave a slight movement of the head, a negation. 'I thought you might be able to help, that he might have told you something.' Another long silence, and then suddenly she had turned to me again. 'He was in Canada, a longer trip than usual, and when he got back . . . That was the weekend – Sunday morning. He saw you on the Tuesday and left for London that same evening. I haven't seen him since.'

'So he's been gone two and a half days, that's all.' I didn't understand why she was so concerned. London, his club, the company, which was at a place called Haverhill near Cambridge, old car rallies and motor shows. Miriam was the daughter of a professor of archaeology at Cambridge. She was interested in ancient buildings, timbered buildings in particular. She knew a lot about hammerbeam roofs and old oak carvings. Nothing about cars, except as a means of getting somewhere. As a result she was often on her own, which was how it had happened, the two of us paired at a dinner party, and then the starter motor of my car packing up just as we were leaving. 'Did he say why he was going to London?'

She shook her head. 'No, he wouldn't tell me anything.'

I reminded her then that she had told me herself he would quite often leave at a moment's notice to meet some fellow car enthusiast at his club, see an old crock that could be rebuilt in the company's works or go off to a show he'd only just heard about, but again she shook her head. 'He's sold his fleet of old cars, you know. There's only that lovely Rolls tourer left.' And she added that she had tried the RAC in Pall Mall, all his usual haunts, the works at Haverhill, even Beaulieu where she knew he was trying to get the Rolls put on display.

Another woman, then? There was always that possibility, particularly at his age. But when I hinted at some personal attachment, she brushed it aside. 'No!' She said it explosively, adding with a little smile, 'Whatever you may think, Tom and I are very close.'

I hesitated then, not sure how serious this was. 'Can we go back a bit?' I said. 'He returned from Canada at the weekend, you say?' She nodded. And he had seen me on the Tuesday. 'Did he have any meeting, anything he didn't tell you about – did anybody come to see him?'

'No, nobody. I picked him up at Gatwick early Sunday morning and the rest of that day we spent at home. He slept a lot of the time. Monday we were at a drinks party in the morning – the Griersons, do you know them? Lovely place near Firle. That afternoon he dealt with a pile of post that had accumulated, dictated a lot of letters, then in the evening we dined out at a nearby restaurant.'

'And he saw nobody between his arrival back in England and last Tuesday when he left for London. By car?'

'Yes, by car.'

'And nobody had contacted him?'

'Not as far as I know – nobody who was a stranger to me, if that's what you mean.'

'Telephone calls?'

'Yes, several.' She hesitated, then said, 'There was his accountant, I know. Otherwise they were social calls.' And she added, 'He never talked to me about money. Never needed to, I suppose. He was a Canadian citizen, as you probably know, and we'd always had what we needed. But I had the feeling – I've had it for some time now – that things were getting a little difficult. And there was one call, just before he returned – a man named Josef Wolchak, an American I think. He wanted to know when my husband was expected back. He had to see him – urgently, he said. I remember the call because I'd never heard of the man before and when I mentioned it to Tom he seemed quite shaken for a moment.'

'Perhaps that was why he went to London,' I suggested.

But she didn't seem to think so. 'I'm sure he would have mentioned it. And why hasn't he phoned me?'

I didn't tell her he had mentioned Wolchak at our meeting on Tuesday, asking whether anyone of that name had contacted me. And when I had said no, he had seemed relieved. Even so, it wouldn't account for his sudden silence. I could still see him sitting there in the chair where his wife was now seated, his features so strained, and his manner, that sense of tension. 'This son of his,' I said, thinking of the codicil. 'I've met the other one, Martin, but not Brian.'

'He's wild, like I said. Suddenly turns up at the beginning of the month looking like death. It was dysentery, but he still insisted on seeing his father. Money, of course. He wanted money for this guru he'd been with in the Himalayas. It's always the same, always money. Whenever he turns up. Though I'll say this for him, it's not for himself, always some cause.' And she added, 'It was trees this time. Before that it was seals. He wanted Tom to produce something in the works that would jam the Canadian sealers' instruments. He's crazy,' she added softly. 'Quite crazy.'

'But you like him?'

'Oddly enough, yes.' She nodded. 'Yes, I do. He's a very strange, very exciting person to be with.'

That was something, I thought. At least she wouldn't go to law when the time came and she discovered the land and the trees in British Columbia really were going to another woman's son. I was trying to recall Tom

Halliday's words, everything he had said. But it wasn't much. He had virtually written the codicil himself. All he'd wanted was for it to be drawn up properly. There'd been no discussions, no explanation. I'd simply done what he'd wanted and that was that. True, his features had looked drawn and rather tense, and he seemed to have a cold. But people often pick up a germ at the end of a long hard trip. 'His health all right?' I asked.

She looked at me quickly. 'Why? Did you think he looked ill?'

'No. A bit strained, that's all, but one always wonders when a man starts fiddling about with his Will.'

'Physically he's all right. I had him go for a check-up before he went to Canada this last time. We were in London, one of those receptions to launch a new car.' She hesitated, then went on, 'Dr Wessler's report arrived just after he had left: all systems functioning normally, only the cholesterol slightly high. More exercise and lay off the fat. That was all, bar a reference to nervous tension and the suggestion that I should get him away for a holiday somewhere in the sun, preferably an island with no roads and no cars.' She gave a snort of derision. 'Seychelles. That was what he advised. Boat to hotel by bullock cart, can you imagine?' She looked down at her hands, that warm Titian hair of hers falling across her face. 'We've never had a holiday together since our honeymoon, and that was at Brighton. We drove there in a 1913 de Dion Bouton.' She gave a suppressed giggle. 'It's almost as ridiculous as the colonel, married to his regiment, who took his bride round the battlefields of the Second World War.'

The girl came in then to tell me my ten o'clock appointment had arrived. Miriam didn't move. 'What am I going to do, Philip?'

I didn't know what to say. It wasn't really my problem if the man hadn't been home for a couple of days. I'd heard talk that he had been away a good deal these past few months, so she ought to be used to it by now. But when I said as much, she insisted he always rang her every evening when he was away. 'Always,' she insisted. 'Even in the Yukon, when he's visiting the mine, he still telephones me most days – they've got radio-telephone in the trucks up there. And if he can't get hold of me he gets quite upset. Sometimes,' she added, 'he forgets the time difference and wakes me in the middle of the night.' She smiled. 'He did that twice on the last trip when he was down in BC.'

'Could he be suffering from amnesia, then?' I suggested. But she brushed that aside. 'Not Tom. He can remember every old crock he's ever seen.' I was on my feet then and she muttered something about ringing round some more people who might have some idea where he was. 'I'll give it another day, then if I still don't know – ' She left it at that and got slowly up from the chair. 'At least I know now why he came to see you . . . But to change his Will and then go off – I don't like it, Philip. Do you think something's happened to him?' And when I didn't answer, she added, 'You're sure he didn't say anything – about where he was going? Not even the vaguest hint?' I shook my head and she said again, 'I'll give it another day.'

She turned then, very abruptly and without another

word, and after she'd gone I went back to my desk and sat there for a moment thinking about Halliday, trying to imagine what must have been going on in his mind as he'd waited here in my office for the girl to type the codicil. He hadn't talked. He'd just sat there, his grey eyes staring out to the high ridge of the downs, quite expressionless, so that I had had the feeling he was mentally far away.

It was about an hour later that a freelance journalist based in Brighton phoned me to enquire whether it was true Tom Halliday had left his wife. He wouldn't say where he had picked up the information, only that it was another woman, and he then suggested that Halliday had 'gone walkabout' – did I have any information on that? I said no, I had not; that in fact I had seen Mr Halliday as recently as last Tuesday and there had been nothing to suggest my client was going 'walkabout', as he put it. He then asked me a lot of questions, personal questions, mostly about money, which I refused to answer. Finally I put the phone down.

I found that call very disturbing. For one thing, it was a reminder of how little I knew about Tom Halliday; I knew more about his father. But my main concern was the fact that a journalist was taking an interest in his movements; it suggested that there really was something seriously wrong. I must have smoked most of a full pipe while thinking about it. In the end, I put the thought that he might really have disappeared out of my mind and got on with the day's work. I had been in Ditchling now three and a half years and in that time I had built up a thriving practice based largely on the precept that when it comes to Wills people want a solicitor who is of the locality and readily available, but not living in the same town and thus a part of their own community. Ditchling was perfect, being little more than a village and removed from the seaside towns of Eastbourne, Brighton and Worthing that were my main catchment area by the downland barrier. And now that I'd taken on a junior partner, my weekends were beginning to be my own. I had just bought my first boat, a junk-rigged *Jester*-type craft, and with it the dream of going trans-Atlantic had come one step nearer.

Next day, Saturday, I was into Shoreham early, driving the long dock road out to the east harbour entrance where I had left my pram dinghy on a dirty patch of gravel among a litter of old rowing boats, rusting buoys and baulks of timber. The boat was over on the far side of the harbour on a borrowed mooring. There was still a lot to be done and I stayed the night on board so that I was there to give a hand when the moonlighting engineer arrived on the Sunday morning to install the single-pot diesel I'd finally bought in preference to an outboard motor. I worked with him for a couple of hours or so, then rowed over to the yacht club for a drink. There was some sort of race on that afternoon and the bar was fairly crowded. I found myself next to a man with one of the Sundays spread out in front of him; that was how I heard about it – not from Miriam or the police or any official communication, but haphazardly, peering at a headline over another man's shoulder:

GOLD MINE OWNER DISAPPEARS –
MILLIONAIRE'S CHEQUES BOUNCE –
'COULD BE SUICIDE' SAYS SON.

Good God! I must have said it aloud, for the man
looked up. 'Do you know him?' And when I nodded, he
pushed the paper across to me. 'Help yourself, I've
finished with it. But a man with a gold mine in the
Yukon – you'd think he'd have more sense than to let it
run through his fingers, all of it, so that he's dead broke.'
He turned the pages, laying the paper flat where a large
headline screamed across two pages: GOLDEN PLAY-
BOY COMES TO GRIEF – *His Three Loves: Beautiful
Cars – Beautiful Women – and Speed.* The full story of
the 'lush life' of Thomas Francis Halliday and his 'Klondike Gold' was carried over from the front page to
almost two full inside pages. The three investigative
journalists involved had clearly been putting in a lot of
overtime, for it was a very full, very colourful account
of the life of a gold-rich playboy, and it made good
reading, the sort of life-style that half the commuters in
the country would give their souls for.

Poor Miriam! They had treated her kindly, but it
was hard all the same: names, and sometimes the
addresses, of several of the girls who had claimed his
attentions, including one he had talked to in a club bar
in Brighton on the Tuesday evening. A reference to
drugs, too, and how he had gone into silver mining in
Peru and failed. But the main story was his disappearance, speculation as to the reasons for it and whether he
was alive or dead. Somebody answering his description

had taken the late night Townsend-Thoresen ferry from Felixstowe to Rotterdam on the Wednesday. He was also thought to have been seen at the Aust service station by the Severn Bridge. That was on Friday. There was a quote from a garage owner at Polegate and a builder at Lewes, both of whom had presented cheques on a joint account signed by Miriam and had been told to refer to drawer. The Hallidays' bank manager had, of course, refused to comment. The journalists had then gone on to discuss the possibility of suicide and the article finished up with a quote from his doctor – 'Nothing organically wrong with him, nothing at all.'

'Well, what do you make of it?' the owner of the paper asked as I folded it up.

'Sorry,' I said, 'can't discuss it.' I was thinking of Miriam alone in that big flint house below the downs surrounded by the relics of a long-dead gold rush. I couldn't remember whether her family were still in Cambridge, even whether they were alive and she had someone to fall back on. I knew, in fact, less about her than I had known about her husband, only that I felt impelled to see her and make sure she was all right. Those newspapermen, they would have been on to her, and now there would be others, the phone constantly ringing.

I thanked the man, tucked the paper under my arm and pushed my way out of the crowded bar, running down to my pram dinghy and rowing fast across the harbour to where I had left my car. In Brighton I stopped at a callbox and rang the Halliday home. There was no answer. It crossed my mind then that perhaps somebody had found the body, in which case it would have to be identified. I drove out past the marina, taking the coast road through Rottingdean and Peacehaven and up by Westdean Forest above the Cuckmere.

It was just after twelve-thirty when I reached the old flint farmhouse nestled into a hollow of the downs not far from the Long Man. Being the weekend, there was no one about and the place had a sleepy look, cows grazing in a paddock of lush grass and everything very still in the leafy shadow of Bull's Wood. Miriam opened the door to me herself, her face pale and set. 'Philip!' She didn't smile. She just fell into my arms, clutching me tight for a moment. 'God! I thought you were another reporter. I've had two this morning and the phone . . . You've seen that paper, have you?'

'That's why I came.'

'They must have got it from the police. I notified the police the day after I saw you – Saturday.' She shook herself free.

'I didn't realize you could cause such a stir just by walking away from everything. That's what he's done, isn't it? Just walked out and left other people to pick up the pieces. Unless he's killed himself. D'you think he's killed himself?'

'No, of course not.'

But she didn't seem to hear me. 'I should have got it out of him,' she went on quickly. 'I knew there was something . . . But to go off like that – without a word. Why?' And she repeated it, her voice breaking and a little wild. 'Why, for God's sake why?'

'Would you like to have lunch somewhere?' I

thought it might relax her a little to be away from the house.

She nodded, and when she was in the car and we were out on the Lewes road, she said, 'We had a row. No, not a row. That needs two. He just exploded, a nervous, end-of-his-tether sort of eruption. I thought he was going to have a heart attack, his face all suffused, his hands trembling. He was quite overwrought, so I didn't press him.' And she added slowly, 'Perhaps I should have, but at the time . . .' She left it at that. 'Did you come straight from your boat? I heard it was finished. You never asked us to the launching.'

'We just dumped it in the water.'

I took her to the Tiger Inn, and because I knew she wanted to be taken out of herself I talked to her about the boat, all my plans. It wasn't until we had sat down to eat that we got back to the subject of Tom Halliday, and it was she who insisted on talking about him – not about what had happened, but about the man himself. Quite why she decided to tell me about him I'm not sure. Perhaps it was an attempt to explain, even justify, his action to herself. Whatever the reason, once she had started the words seemed to pour out of her, so that I had the feeling she couldn't help herself, and at the end of it I was just thankful I hadn't been born with a gold mine round my neck.

He had had everything, the whole world handed to him on a plate. I could see him now, sitting at the end of the table, the little brushed-up moustache picked out in the candle light, his high cheekbones flushed pink as the port made its vintage ruby way round the table, telling the story once again of how his father had gone out to the Klondike as a young man, up the White Pass from Skagway all the way to Dawson, then along something called the Dalton Trail where the wild man who had hacked it out of the bush rode shotgun to keep out intruders who hadn't paid his toll fee. Somewhere along that trail, or else in Dawson, Josh Halliday, who was the son of an insurance man in San Francisco, was sold that mine. 'Lucky' Carlos Despera. That was the name of the man who sold it to him, and the name of the mine was Ice Cold Creek. I remembered the names because of the way Tom had rolled them off his tongue, laughing as he did so – the Noisy Range, too. Then he was telling how his father had packed in to that mine and found it high up near a great mountain mass that roared with the sound of glaciers on the move.

'Tom was like a little boy.' Miriam was leaning forward then, her elbows on the table, her chin resting on her hands, which were closed fists, the knuckles white, her eyes staring at nothing. 'A brash show-off. It was part of the attraction, that extraordinary charisma of his, all his energy – and he was tireless, quite tireless, bubbling over with vitality – all of it with no outlet. No positive, real, constructive outlet.'

I could see him, so full of himself – and that picture of his father. The mine was a dud, of course. 'Josh knew that as soon as he'd packed in to the white glacial heart of the mountain. There were men working claims lower down the creek, just managing to pan enough to give them hope, and they all said the upper end of Ice Cold Creek was worked out, gone, finished.' And still, in desperation, the poor devil had gone on shovelling rock, working his guts out while the food lasted and he still had a few dollars left. Then, the day he decided to pull out – that was probably apocryphal, but when his money was just about gone – suddenly he struck lucky. 'Not just ordinary pay dirt, but small nuggets of gold.' And the way Tom said it, you could see the stuff there in the calloused hand, the mouth open in a great cry, the feet pounding to the excited, boisterous jig of joy.

'Cars, speedboats, Le Mans, the RAC – aircraft, too. He flew his own plane. And women. I didn't understand that at first. His need of women. I think he'd have liked to bed every one of them that took his fancy. Just to prove something. That he was a man, I suppose.' She gave a quick shake of her head, smiling. 'He wasn't homosexual – I don't mean that. But when you've got a pot of gold up there in the Yukon, where nobody can see it . . . It's different for you, Philip. You can take people along to your office and say, Look, this is what I've done with my life. I've built a practice. You are possessed of an expertise that brings people to you, for your advice, for your help. But Tom had nothing like that.'

'The factory,' I said.

She shrugged. 'It wasn't his. It was Martin's. Martin ran it. The thing was his idea. Tom paid for it, that's all. Just as he paid for his cars, his plane, a speedboat that could flash him around the Royal Yacht at Cowes and into an occasional picture in one of the glamour mags. But nothing of his own, nothing he had created himself. It all came from the mine, everything he possessed.

Periodically he'd go out there. I don't know why. He had an excellent manager. Jonny Epinard. Absolutely straight. But every so often he'd take off for the Yukon. Sometimes I thought it was just to make sure it was still there, that it was real.'

She shook her head slowly. 'I wondered myself sometimes. All those years – through his father's lifetime, and now his – all that time and steadily yielding its golden harvest, keeping the Hallidays in the manner to which . . .' She laughed, a mocking sound. 'But, oh, the damage a thing like that can do to an insecure youngster! He went out to South America once, did he tell you?'

I shook my head and she smiled. 'Peru. He bought a silver mine ten thousand feet up in the Andes, just above Cajamarca where Pizarro murdered the Inca King's helpless retinue. But he didn't have Pizarro's luck. He was there several years, the mine steadily yielding less and less, and when it finally petered out he came home. That was the only time he ever made a serious attempt to build an empire of his own. It was just toys after that, playthings. All he got out of Peru was a sense of failure that increased his already well-developed inferiority complex – and a bitch of a wife to make sure he never forgot it. A termagant. That's Brian's view of her, not mine. I never met the woman, thank God. She was a *mestizo*. Mixed Spanish and native Indian blood. She claimed descent from an Inca chieftain slaughtered by the Conquistadors. That's why Brian is the way he is, why he looks a little strange – those ears, the nose, those broad cheekbones. And his temperament, his hot aggressive, solemn manner, the lightning changes of mood . . . ' She shrugged. 'A little of his father – the machismo, the panache, the determination to project himself as an image, a figment of his own imagination if you like.' She sighed, a deep breath. 'But Tom was still a wonderful person to be with. All that vitality, and now and then the stars in my lap like a gift from heaven. He plucked them out of the night in the early hours, made me feel I was riding the world – a whirlwind. Sometimes. At others . . . ' The corners of her lips flickered, a glint of amusement at her own ingenuousness. 'At other times . . . ' She turned, her face to the window, her eyes towards the downs humped above the houses and the sea. 'I could have killed him for his brazen stupidity, his insensitivity, his total involvement in himself – his bloody-minded selfishness. His egotism. Christ! what a bastard!'

She laughed. 'Then – when I thought I couldn't stand it any longer' – she was shaking her head, as though in wonder at her own behaviour – 'then there'd be flowers, champagne, and the man, that mercurial, impossible man at my feet, the stars in my lap again.' She leaned forward, her large eyes suddenly staring at me, almost imploring. 'Do you understand, Philip? He was so alive, so wonderful to be with. When he was on top of the world.' I couldn't help noticing that she was talking about him in the past tense, and she went on, still in a rush of words, 'Then, when he'd taken too much – flown too high – the reaction would set in, everything crashing down – from the stars to despair in one quick devilish leap – Christian's Slough of Despond.

'My God! Living with a man like that, knowing it was that bitch Martina who'd introduced him to the stuff, and nothing I could do about it. He wouldn't listen. Said he'd been taking coke off and on ever since he'd gone to South America in his early twenties. At times he even had a little mini-spoon, silver-gilt I think, hung round his neck on a thin golden chain. All part of the mystique. Oh, I know, I shouldn't be telling you all this, but I've got to talk to somebody about him.' And she went on, 'Cocaine has always been an élitist drug, and it's not really addictive. Least, that's what he said, not the good stuff. He had me try it once or twice and I didn't get hooked. But the way he's been taking it recently . . . I don't know, perhaps he'd reached the age when he found himself looking over the edge and not liking what he saw, his sexual prowess declining, his competitive spirit flagging. Even his interest in cars had lessened and he hadn't visited Martin at the factory for ages, the mine taking up more and more of his time, his temper short, his face strained, that little stutter of his suddenly noticeable, and sometimes at night I'd hear him muttering to himself. Do you think he's had a nervous breakdown?'

But I had only seen him a couple of times in the past year and I had had no idea he took drugs until I had read the piece in that Sunday paper. 'I don't know,' I said. 'I'm not sure how people behave on the verge of a nervous breakdown.'

'No, nor do I. I can only guess. And his doctor didn't say anything about a breakdown – I phoned him last night. He said he thought his nerves were on edge, that he needed a rest. From what? That's what I said. What the hell did Tom need a rest from? And he repeated what he'd written in his report – get him out somewhere on his own to lie in the sun, swim, do nothing and take the minimum of food – healthy, natural food – no alcohol. I don't think Tom had told him about taking cocaine, but he probably guessed. He was overfed, he said, depleted, suffering from nervous exhaustion.'

I didn't understand it either, and I said so – a man with all the money in the world, a lovely wife, a beautiful home, cars, interests, a man who'd never had to work in his life . . . he'd no bloody right to be suffering from nervous exhaustion.

'It's all very well for you,' she went on. 'You're so solid, so dependable.' I could have slapped her face the way she had been talking about her husband, but she went on, the words still tumbling out of her – 'Tom was just a child. A spoilt child, yes. But something more. A sort of real life Peter Pan, with all that creature's selfishness, and fascination.' She nodded, her hair glistening reddish in the sunlight. 'Yes, that's it – a fair simile – and if Peter Pan had suddenly found himself growing up . . .' She sat for a while, her head bowed, thinking about it. 'But to take off like that, without a word – to me, to anyone. He told nobody, nobody at all. He's just thrown off everybody, his whole life – like a snake discarding its old skin . . .' And suddenly she was crying, her shoulders shaking, but no sound coming.

I took her home then. I think at that point she was just about emotionally and physically drained. I didn't realize it at the time – though the newspaper article had hinted at it – but it wasn't only that Tom had disappeared, there was the financial mess he had left behind.

This only became apparent in the following week, the bills rolling in and no cash at the bank to meet them.

CHAPTER TWO

Never having been dependent on money I didn't
earn I always find it difficult to appreciate how
frightened people can become when the source of their
income shows signs of drying up. It was the following
Tuesday before I began to realize that this was what had
probably happened to Tom Halliday and by then his
son Martin had been on the phone to me twice. He
employed almost a dozen people at the works and their
pay was five weeks in arrears, his own salary too; the
rent was due, electricity, gas, rates, water, telephone,
and in addition he owed several thousand for materials.
He had one car ready for delivery, but that was all. He
wanted money to tide him over, but I had to tell him
that there wasn't any at the moment and it would take
time to sort things out. 'But I have to have some money.'
That anguished cry from a man who all his life had lived
off his father . . . I had told him, quite bluntly I'm afraid,
that he'd better think in terms of selling up and standing
on his own feet. I was more concerned with Miriam.

She had phoned me on the Monday asking me to deal with the financial problems arising from her husband's disappearance. They had a joint account at the Lewes branch of his bank, but this was only for convenience, the account being fed from the head office branch in the City. It was the Lewes branch that had refused to cash the two cheques referred to in the newspaper report. Tom Halliday had apparently drawn out the entire balance of the account the very day he had come to see me. It seemed likely, therefore, that his disappearance was a deliberate act and not due to any accident.

This became more apparent after I had talked to his London bank. Apparently they received the profits of the mine half yearly. Sometimes his account was in balance from one half year to the next, at others it was overdrawn. The overdraft arrangements had been generous because of the regularity of the half-yearly payments. However, these had recently become less regular and Halliday had been making use of the overdraft facility. In other words, the bank had been advancing money in anticipation of the income from the mine. The latest half-yearly payment had been due almost two months ago and the manager had let the overdraft run for that length of time because his client, before leaving for Canada, had assured him he would be dealing with the matter while he was there. However, a fortnight ago he had begun to make his own inquiries. These had been complicated by the fact that the payments did not come direct from Canada. Instead, they were routed through a Swiss bank, payment being made half-yearly through their London office. He thought this was probably for tax reasons, the Zurich bank informing him that it was a numbered account and they were not in a position to divulge any information.

I tried contacting them myself. I was, after all, one of Tom Halliday's executors, but it made no difference. They refused to discuss the matter until there was some definite news as to what had happened to Halliday, and if it did turn out that he had had an accident, or had killed himself, then it would be a matter not for his executors, but for whoever inherited – Miriam, in other words.

I had the distinct impression, however, that they were going through the motions rather than protecting an important account, and it was after talking to them that I telexed the Mines Department of the Yukon Government in Whitehorse. Two days later I received this reply: GOLD PRODUCTION ICE COLD CREEK MINE FOR PAST THREE YEARS RECORDED AS FOLLOWS: 60.236, 27.35 AND 43.574 OZS. FOR FURTHER INFORMATION REFER JON EPINARD, TAKHINI TRAILER CRT, WHITEHORSE.

It didn't make sense. Yields of that sort couldn't possibly have been covering even the cost of production, let alone producing the sort of half-yearly payments the English bank had referred to. It was the younger son, Brian Halliday, who first made me realize where the money might have been coming from. He phoned to ask whether an American named Wolchak had been in touch with me. And when I said he hadn't, he asked if I had the deeds to his father's BC property.

'No,' I said, 'the bank has them. Why?'

'Wolchak wants to buy. He's acting as agent for an American company and says they're willing to pay cash for an option to purchase.' And then he asked me straight out whether the BC property had been left to him. 'Miriam says I get the trees, that right?'

'There's no reason to suppose your father isn't alive,' I told him.

'Of course. But what about the trees – do they come to me or don't they?' He had a rather deep, soft voice, his manner on the phone slightly abrupt so that I formed the impression of a man who needed to assert himself.

There seemed no point in not telling him that the BC property would be his should his father suddenly die. 'Subject, of course,' I added, 'to settlement of any outstanding debts.'

'Meaning your fees, I suppose,' he said rudely. And when I told him there would naturally be solicitor's fees, he said very sharply, 'Well, I'm not selling. Just understand that, will you. The Cascades is not for sale – not now, or ever.'

'You've had an offer, have you?' I was wondering what sort of figure Wolchak had put on the property.

'Not me. Miriam. She told him to see you. That's why I phoned – to warn you, and to make my position clear. He saw her this morning and she says he was in touch with her last week, wanting to see Tom and then asking when he would be back.'

'Did he see your father after his return from Canada?' I asked.

31

'Yes. On the Monday, here at Bullswood. The Monday morning.'

And the following day Tom Halliday had come to me to change his Will. I could accept that people did get scared when the source of their income dried up, or when they had lost their money in some financial disaster. I had seen it happen to elderly people – one of my clients had committed suicide for just that reason. But Tom Halliday was still a relatively young man and he had disappeared owning a slice of land in Canada that was apparently saleable. And what was even more extraordinary, he had altered his Will so that the land went to his son instead of his wife, and his younger son at that. Either Miriam had been wrong when she had said, 'Tom and I are very close', or else this stepson of hers had put quite exceptional pressure on his father.

'If I do hear from Mr Wolchak I'll be in touch with you,' I told him, and I put the phone down. My secretary was back from her holiday and about an hour later it must have been she came in to say Wolchak had been on the phone to her and she had arranged an appointment for Friday afternoon at four-fifteen. 'Ten minutes, that's all.' She knew I wanted to try the boat out at the weekend. 'He says, incidentally, he appreciates your difficulties and is prepared to offer a solution.'

I had already arranged with the bank for them to take Bullswood House as security for the overdraft. Fortunately Tom hadn't mortgaged it. He couldn't very well without it becoming apparent he was in financial difficulties for the freehold was in his wife's name as well as his own. But the house and its contents, that was about all there was left. They had had a 99-year lease on a big flat in Belgravia and a villa in the Algarve, but he had sold those over the past two years, and very recently he had parted with the all-cream Rolls tourer that had been the pride of his collection of old cars – 'built for a maharajah just before Partition,' Miriam told me, 'door handles, headlights, all the trimmings gold-plated.' And she had laughed. 'Trouble is it needed mink or leopard skin, something like that, and nothing would induce me to have some poor wretched animal wrapped around me.'

With my partner on holiday the amount of work crossing my desk pushed the Halliday problem to the back of my mind, so that when I received from the bank the photocopies I had asked for of the deeds they held I had no time to do more than check that they included the deeds of the BC forest land and that it hadn't been mortgaged or otherwise encumbered to raise a loan.

Wolchak was late that Friday afternoon and I had to keep him waiting. 'What's he like?' I asked my secretary as she came back from showing my four-thirty appointment out. She hesitated, then smiled, the corners of her mouth turned down. 'You'll see,' she said, and she showed him in.

He came bustling across to my desk, hand out-stretched, a short, thick body, a large, square head, and a smile that flashed like a beacon, eyes lighting up, a switched-on incandescence, and the teeth very white against a tanned skin. 'Josef Wolchak,' he said as he shook my hand. He had a slight accent that was difficult to place.

I sat him down and he said, 'You're busy, so'm I. I'll be brief. It's about this Halliday property in British Columbia. I'm acting for an American company. They want to buy it. You got the deeds here?'

'They're at the bank.'

'But you've seen them.'

'I have photocopies.'

'And there's nothing in them to preclude a sale – a mortgage, anything like that?'

'Not that I know of.'

'Good, good. It's the trees, Mr Redfern, not the land. My clients don't necessarily want the land. It's the trees they're interested in.' He took a wallet from the pocket of his jacket, produced a card and passed it across the desk to me. 'That's the company. You'll find they're an old-established timber and saw-milling outfit. Been in existence more than half a century. Anybody in Seattle will tell you.' The card simply gave the name of the company – S V L Timber and Milling Inc. – and the address in Seattle. 'It's north along the waterfront, out on the Everett road,' he said. 'They've already been in touch with lawyers in Vancouver who've had dealings with Mr Halliday. But now that he's reported missing . . .' He gave an expansive shrug. 'I was advised I should contact you.'

'Who by?' I don't know why but I was sure from the way he had made such a point of informing me about the company that there had to be an individual involved. 'Who are you really acting for?'

There was a fractional hesitation, then he said, 'Bert

Mandola. He has interests in a number of companies, Chicago and out west.'

I wrote it down on the back of the company card, just in case, at the same time pointing out to him that I was in no position to dispose of any part of my client's property. And I added, 'You will appreciate that Mr Halliday may turn up any moment.'

'Yes, of course. But suppose he doesn't, eh?' He had already talked to 'young Halliday'. And he added, 'There's a problem there, but if the man's dead and the estate's in debt, and it will be, your English tax boys will see to that ...'

'I'm sure Mr Halliday's alive and in good health,' I said, not liking the way he was trying to rush me.

'Yes, yes, but as I was saying, if he's dead and the estate is in debt, or there are financial difficulties ...' He wasn't smiling now, his small mouth a thin, hard line. 'You've been out there to see the Cascades, Mr Redfern?'

I shook my head.

'Well, I have,' he said. 'Mr Mandola and I took a look at it a while back. Quite a nice looking place, but very remote – about eighteen and a half square miles, that's counting the mountain tops and the waterfalls that give it its name. There are some timber extraction roads in poor condition, the remains of an old logging camp at the head of the Halliday Arm, an A-frame drilling truck that looks like it dates back to the Red River oilfield days, and a lot of mosquitoes. There's nothing much there of any value except the timber in the bottom.'

'So why's your client interested in it?' I was still trying to make up my mind what all this was about. Wolchak himself, I thought, probably belonged to one of those ethnic groups that stem from America's flood of refugees. There was an accent but, as Brian Halliday had said on the phone, it was more an undercurrent, difficult to place. He could be Irish, I thought, or equally from one of the Mediterranean countries; there was a quickness about him, and the tanned face, the nose, the dark eyes. But definitely a man who had lived quite a bit of his time in America, fortyish and well fleshed, the face a little leathery from the sun. California perhaps. But that was only a guess. I'd never been to California – or anywhere very much for that matter.

'It's the timber in the bottom. All the rest of the property has been cut over, nothing good left, but down by the river and round the lake expansions there's a stand of real good timber, and all of it western red cedar. SVL Timber specializes in western red cedar, either putting the logs through their sawmill or trucking them to other outfits in the States. It's just that bottom stuff, otherwise the property's ripped out and not worth a damn. So we're talking about a square mile or so of top-grade timber.' He glanced at his watch and got to his feet. 'I've kept you long enough.' That smile beaconed out. 'Think it over. Have a talk with Brian Halliday – that's if he comes into it, as I understand he does.'

'Did he tell you that?' I asked.

'He didn't deny it.' He produced his own card and flipped it onto my desk. 'I'm staying with friends in

Brighton over the weekend, back at my London hotel Monday. Get in touch with me when you've made up your mind.' He held out his hand. 'I take it you'll be contacting the lawyers in Vancouver and arranging for a firm of forestry consultants to make an independent valuation. If so, kindly put it in hand right away, then as soon as you have it we can start talking figures. Option money ten per cent of agreed total, management in the SVL Company's hands from date of signature.' The smile flashed out again. 'When you get the valuation you'll be pleasantly surprised, I think. That bottom stand should see you out of any difficulties with a good margin.'

'Supposing the worst has happened and Mr Halliday is dead,' I said. 'I think the executors might well decide to put the property up for auction.'

He looked at me sharply. 'Timber is an up-and-down business. It's down at the moment, so there aren't many buyers around over the other side and this Cascades place is up north so it's a long haul down to the markets. Also, auctions aren't sure money, and they don't produce cash on the nail for an option. If Halliday is dead, then I guess you'll be needing cash very badly, and that's what I'm offering you.' He nodded and was about to walk out when he looked back at me. 'I'm in this for the commission, you understand.' His eyes, sharp and grey, were fixed on mine. 'I'm sure you and I can come to a sensible arrangement.' He nodded, smiling confidently, as though bribing lawyers was all part of the day's work. 'Just so long as the deal goes through. And don't be too long making up your mind,

Mr Redfern.' His eyes flicked wide in a stare, and then he was gone, a broad, neatly suited man of uncertain age with something near to a bounce in his walk.

Three hours later I was on board my boat and getting ready to make Littlehampton and back over the weekend. It being new and everything to be checked out by trial and error, my mind was so concentrated on the business of sailing that I thought of nothing else until I walked into my office on the Monday morning and found Brian Halliday sitting in the little waiting room that was really a part of the old entrance hall when the house had been a private residence. He had no appointment, but that I presumed was typical. I wasn't at all pleased as I was due to appear in court in Brighton that morning for a client who was up on a drink-driving charge.

He was short and dark, a long face with a long beak of a nose and big ears, high cheekbones – not exactly ugly, but definitely an odd appearance, his hair black and somewhat lank. He was wearing jeans and a T-shirt with Greenpeace on it, canvas shoes on his feet. He seemed very agitated and I thought at first it was because Miriam had gone. He blurted this out almost as soon as we were into my office and I thought at first it was why he had come to see me. With feminine practicality she had apparently gathered up some of the more portable valuables in the house, silver chiefly, also the gold cigarette box I had seen on the dinner table and the silver-gilt chamber pot that had been the centre-piece. She had taken them off in her car on Saturday –

'presumably to flog them to a dealer for some ready cash. Have you seen her?' he asked me.

'No.'

'She hasn't been here, then?'

I shook my head, and at that moment my secretary came in and handed me a typewritten slip. 'It was on the phone tape. I thought you'd like to see it right away.'

It was a message from Miriam. She had phoned on the Sunday morning to say she was flying to Canada that day and would be away a week, maybe ten days. *I'll be staying part of the time at the Bayshore, Vancouver. Very extravagant of me. But what the hell!* And she had added, *I'll be in touch with you if I have any news of Tom.*

I showed it to Brian Halliday and he said, 'Do you think she's going out there to sell the Cascades? You saw Wolchak, did you?' And when I nodded, he added, 'I haven't had a word from him since I phoned you. Do you think that's what Miriam's up to?'

'She can't sell it,' I told him.

'You're sure?'

'Of course.'

'Then what's she going to Vancouver for? It's just across the Juan de Fuca Strait from Seattle with a daily ferry service and Wolchak said he was acting for a timber company in Seattle. If Miriam can bugger off with the silver like that . . .'

'You shouldn't jump to conclusions.' I could see the makings of a vicious family row and, noting the almost wild light in the very dark brown eyes staring at me across the desk, I added quickly, 'You seem to forget your father is reported missing, nothing more. And in any case, a slice of timber land in British Columbia is a very different matter to a few items of household silver.'

He nodded slowly, sitting back, but still tense. Finally he said, 'I'd like to see the deeds. If it turns out that I now own the trees . . .'

'I told you, the deeds are at the bank.'

'Your secretary said you had photocopies.'

I hesitated, not sure I would be justified in refusing him. And then he said, 'Tom said there's a curse.'

'A curse?' I stared at him, wondering what he was talking about. 'How do you mean, a curse?'

He shook his head. 'I don't know, not really. It's quite a time back. Eight years almost. We were chewing coca together in an Indian hut, not the leaves, but the powdered sort they call *patu* – ' He smiled, a sleepy, almost feline smile. 'It was real potent stuff, like dust – took your breath away if you inhaled it before you'd got enough spittle worked in to make a masticating ball of it . . .'

'Where was this?'

'In the Andes. Below the pass that leads to Cajamarca. Anyway, that's what he said.' And he added, 'He hadn't seen the deeds. Not then at any rate. He wasn't much interested in trees. But he said his father had told him he'd put a curse on anybody who cut them.'

'Why?'

'He'd planted them, hadn't he? Not all the trees, but the real good stuff in the valley bottom, the area

Tom always refers to as High Stand. Planted them with his own hands.'

'And this curse is in the deeds?'

'I think so. I don't know. I wasn't that interested, you see, not at the time. I was still in my teens, and though I was engaged in forestry – we were doing a lot of planting for the Peruvian Government – BC seemed like a million miles away, and anyway the chances of my ever being involved with the curse seemed very remote, my father just divorced and full of energy again. Didn't you feel that about him?' Again that strange, almost secretive smile. 'All that machismo, the adrenalin flowing – ' The smile became a laugh as he added, 'And then suddenly you'd see it was all a sham. He was just a kid, nothing for real, the world a toy.' The face became solemn, a sadness in the eyes, so that I had the impression he was fond of his father.

I picked up the intercom and asked my secretary to get me the file. 'It's very unusual,' I said, 'something as personal as that incorporated into a land deed.'

He nodded, his eyes fastening on the papers as soon as she brought them in, his expression intent, almost avid. I don't think it was greed, more the excitement of getting to grips with something he wanted to be involved in.

There were three documents altogether, an original purchase of Indian land, a conveyance of that land to a logging company and a further conveyance from the company to Joshua Francis Halliday. The curse was appended to the last page of this final document. Below all the signatures and government seals, a slip of paper of a different shade and consistency had been gummed on. Even on the flat surface of the photocopy it showed as something added later. 'I'll read it out to you,' I said, and he nodded, sitting hunched forward, his eyes fixed on the page I had opened out and laid flat on the desk before me. 'It's side-headed – *To all who come after me and inherit or in any other way acquire this land: Know ye*' – his choice of words indicated his intention of making it as solemn a declaration as possible – '*Know ye that when I bought this land, which I call Cascades, the logging company who sold it to me had ripped out all the big timber in the valley bottom alongside the Snakeskin River, above the gorge and beside the lake expansions in the flats, everything that could be got out easily. They said it was big stuff, western red cedar mainly and Douglas, like the Macmillan outfit keeps preserved close west of here on the Port Alberni road . . .*' I glanced across at Brian Halliday. 'Where was he living when he wrote this?'

'Vancouver Island probably. That's where he died anyway. Near a place called Duncan just north of Victoria.' His eyes gleamed brightly for a moment. 'Nice country, good forest land. And he had a fishing boat.' And he added almost dreamily, 'I went there once, just to look at where he'd lived, and then I went on out to the west coast, a hell of a road, more of a trail really. Cathedral Grove.' He nodded, as though confirming the name to himself. 'That's what the Macmillan Bloedel logging people call it. There's trees there four, six hundred years old. *Thuja plicata* – that's western red cedar – standing two hundred feet and more, one of the last remaining stands of primeval coastal forest, some of them with a bottom bole circumference of anything up to thirty feet or so. Cathedral Grove.' He smiled, an almost dreamy expression. 'I wonder what the Cascades trees run to now. Does it say when he planted them? Does it give a date? They'll be getting quite a spectacle now, something worth seeing.'

I glanced back through the conveyance. But I could only find the date he had bought the land, and I twisted the deeds round so that he could see.

'That's over seventy years ago. They could be a hundred and fifty feet now. More maybe.' He turned back to that last page, reading on, his lips moving. 'You see, he says it here – he planted it all himself. Had Indians in, cleaned off the scrub, had seedlings brought up from Duncan and planted it up, the whole area that had been devastated by the loggers.' He sat back, looking straight at me, eyes wide under the lank black hair. 'One man marking out the future, ensuring a lasting monument to his life on earth.' And he added, 'My God! What a Herculean task – more than eight hundred acres, he reckons. That's over three hundred hectares. A plantation like that, it must be unique. No wonder he put a curse on anyone daring to take a chainsaw to any of his trees.' He suddenly laughed. 'No, of course, it must have been back around the First World War. He wouldn't have had an inkling then that thirty, forty years on chainsaws would make it possible for one man to fell a three-hundred-foot Redwood giant that had been growing five centuries and more in a matter of hours. But hours, days – it doesn't matter. He saw the threat and did the only thing he thought might deter a future owner greedy for money . . .' He was silent for a moment, his lips moving as he read. Then he sat back. 'Have you read it? The curse, I mean.' And when I shook my head, he passed the deed back to me. 'I think,' he murmured, 'if I had read that and was thinking of felling High Stand, compartment by compartment, I think I'd have second thoughts. Either that or . . .' He paused, shaking his head again and muttering something to himself.

I read the rest of it then: '*However long I live there will come a time*' – this was the final paragraph – '*when my physical presence will no longer be there to guarantee the safety of my trees. But you who read this Declaration be warned – I am the man who planted them, they are my family, and my spirit. As his ancestor is to the Indian, so will I be to my trees. They are my Totem. Let any man fell even one of them, other than in the interests of sound forestry, then with the first cut of the saw or swing of the axe my curse will be upon him.*' Finally, as if pointing an accusatory finger, he switched from the third to the first person: '*Do that and I will never leave you, day or night, till your nerves are screaming and you are dead by your own hand, dead and damned for ever to rot in Hell.*' And it finished with these words: '*This curse stands for all time, to be renewed with my last breath, and may the Good Lord help me to my purpose.*' No date was given.

'He doesn't rule out thinning, you see, or scrub clearance, or anything that will encourage the trees to achieve maximum growth. *In the interests of sound forestry*. That's modern terminology, which shows how involved he was in the business of forestry.'

'When did he die, do you know?'

He moved his head, a dismissive gesture, as though I had interrupted a train of thought. 'Not certain. I think' – He frowned. 'It must have been 1947. I know he was seventy-four when he died and I seem to remember being told he was born in 1873, so I guess that's when the curse begins to operate.' He looked across at me, his eyes still blank, his brow furrowed. 'I was just wondering – about Tom, what's happened to him. You see, I found some sales agreements in his desk. They go back almost seven years. Clear fell agreements that provide for extraction and haulage down to a booming ground on the Halliday Arm. Also bills for towing. He was marketing the Cascades timber. Not High Stand, but the poorer, scrubbier stuff on the slopes above. That is, until the last of those agreements . . .' He shook his head. 'The amounts had been dwindling all the time, until this last one. It was for two hectares of western red cedar, and it gave the grid reference.' He paused there, looking straight at me, waiting for it to sink in. 'It may not sound all that important to you. Not very real, I mean, here in Sussex, in a solicitor's office. But out there, so much of the west raped of its best timber – do you know anything about trees?'

I shook my head.

'Let me just say one thing then: but for trees you and I wouldn't be alive.' He was leaning forward, a strange intensity in his manner and in his voice. 'It was the trees, through their infinite numbers of leaves and needles, that converted our atmosphere from deadly carbon dioxide into the oxygen we breathe. Does that help you to understand? The curse, I mean – and Tom's reaction to it when he realized what he'd done.'

'You're hinting at suicide, are you? You think your father might be dead.'

He shrugged. 'What do you think – now you know about that curse? Put yourself in his place. How would you feel, having negotiated the sale of two hectares, and knowing all the time that your own father had sworn a curse on anybody who felled even a single tree? And he did know. He didn't have to get the deeds out of the bank. The old man had told him, and hearing it direct like that, when he was little more than a kid himself – why do you think he told me about it if it wasn't there always at the back of his mind? And he'd just been over there. Only a few days back he'd been looking at those trees.' The intensity was back in his voice as he added, 'Trees are alive, you know. They have an aura, a very powerful feel about them. And a curse like that –'

'Yes, but I hardly think your father was the sort of man to take much note of a thing like that.' I thought he was letting his imagination run away with him somewhat. 'He was much too much of an extrovert, surely.'

'Tom?' He shook his head. 'Nobody who needs a drug, even if it's only drink or nicotine, can be totally extrovert. And just think of the effect on him as a youngster in his teens – he was the son of a late marriage so he must have been that sort of age at the time. And he wasn't unimaginative. Quite the contrary in some ways. Then years later, with the mining income gone and all the timber on the slopes felled and cashed, nothing much left except High Stand . . . And then, after he had sold those two hectares, at some moment when he was real high, remembering that curse – well, he'd be capable of anything then, wouldn't he? Or on the let-down maybe, in a fit of manic depression . . .' He gave a little shrug, a gesture of finality. 'Yes, I think he's dead. I think he's done what his father swore he'd cause any man to do who cut those trees.'

'The cutting was done presumably by a logging company.'

'But he signed the agreement. He caused it to be done.' And then he switched my mind back to the Yukon. 'I suppose the mine is finished?' And when I gave him the figures for the last three years, he nodded as though that was what he had expected. 'But you haven't checked the mine itself. You haven't had a mining consultant go over and have a look at it?'

I shook my head. 'What are you suggesting – that somebody has been creaming off the best of the gold?'

'Well, it's happened before.'

'You seem to forget your father had only just returned from the Yukon, a longer trip than usual, Miriam said.'

'He'd been to Canada, yes. But he didn't say anything about the Yukon or the mine. He could have been in BC organizing the sale of another two hectares of High Stand.' He gave a rather helpless little shrug. 'I've been down several gold mines, but all of them mines with ore bodies where you drill ahead and have a good idea what the reserves are. Ice Cold Creek is placer mining. You're just shifting tons of river silt, screening, washing – yes, I guess it could peter out like that, no warning.' The brown, remote eyes fixed on me again. 'Is that where Miriam's gone? Suddenly she wasn't there any more, the house locked up.'

'So how did you know about the silver?' I asked.

'I'm living there, aren't I? And you, I suppose you have a key, too?'

I nodded.

'And you're one of the executors?'

'Yes.'

He was back to the trees again. 'Have you any idea of the value of that stand? For just those two hectares he was getting over three thousand dollars – that's standing, no charges. Cash on the nail like Judas or any goddamned murderer. Anyway, that's the figure given in the sale agreement, so they were paying something around five or six dollars a cube. I don't know whether that's good or bad, bearing in mind the market at the time and the problems of getting it to the water and then the long tow down to Seattle, but with near on a thousand acres it values High Stand at about six hundred thousand dollars. There's men a lot less pressed than my father who'd do almost anything for a sum like that. I wonder . . .' He put his hands over his eyes, his head bowed in thought. 'I wonder,' he murmured, 'if that's why he left those trees to me.'

'Because you were pressing him for money?'

His head jerked up, his eyes suddenly blazing. 'No. Because he knew I'd never cut them. Because the curse was on him and I belonged to the Men of the Trees. He knew that. He knew I wouldn't sell them. Not now. Not ever.' And then, his voice suddenly anxious, 'He did leave them to me, you're sure about that?'

'Of course,' I said. 'I drew up the codicil myself and he signed it that day he was here in this office, sitting where you're sitting now.'

'But the executors, they can still sell them to pay bills, if the estate's in debt, I mean. That right?' He didn't wait for a reply. 'You're one of them, and Miriam, she's an executor, too, I suppose. Who else?'

'His accountant in London,' I said. 'Trevor Richardson.'

'Not Martin. Not me. Just the three of you.' I nodded and he got suddenly to his feet. 'Okay. Well, just remember this – that curse, it's real. And it applies to you, to anyone – you let them put a chainsaw into a single tree without there's a silvicultural reason' – his voice had risen, his dark eyes staring straight into mine – 'and it doesn't have to be the man who operates the saw, it's whoever's responsible . . . You sell High Stand to a saw mill company – ' He leaned further forward, almost a crouch, the eyes strangely alight. 'Do that and if it's the only way to stop you I'll kill you myself.'

He stared at me a moment, quite wildly and in absolute silence. Then abruptly he turned and left my office without another word.

I sat there thinking about him for some time, his Indian background, how dangerous he might be. Then, almost unconsciously, I picked up the deed and read again those words of Joshua Francis Halliday written all those years ago.

And then my secretary put the file back in the strong room and I went off to Brighton, only just making the court in time. Looking back on it, I suppose I should have made more of an effort. But there was an undercurrent of hostility between us, and though there are things he could have told me about his father if I had taken the time and the trouble to ask the right questions, it never occurred to me I would not have another opportunity until it was almost too late.

The week passed in a flash, a hectic rush of work, and still no news of Tom Halliday. The police had received negative reports from the RCMP in Canada. There was no indication that he had visited either the Yukon or British Columbia, and the emigration people had no record of his either leaving Britain or entering Canada. The only hope seemed to be that Miriam would pick up some information in Vancouver where presumably he had friends. My partner was still on holiday and when my secretary came in with the mail on Friday morning I was leaning back in my chair staring up at the clouds scudding low over the downs and thinking what it would be like that night in the Channel. I had planned to sail over to the French coast and it looked now as though I would have a fast passage. 'I thought you'd like to see this straight away – it looks a little personal.' She put the flimsy sheets on the desk in front of me, her face deadpan, not a flicker of a smile as she added that my first appointment was already waiting for me.

I stared down at it, too surprised to say anything. It was on the notepaper of a hotel named the Sheffield, the address Whitehorse, Yukon: *My dear Philip – I feel suddenly very lonely here and turn to you for reasons I'm not quite sure about, only that I know writing to you will somehow help. Silly, isn't it – I don't know your home address, or if you told me I've forgotten it, so I'll send it to your office. But please don't charge for the time it takes to read it! There's no money. That was a shock – first Tom disappearing, then the bank phoning to say I couldn't cash any cheques. It was a joint account, as you know. Tom was good that way. He always trusted me. God! What a mess! . . .*

There were five pages of it, on thin airmail paper, the ink tending to run and her scrawl not easy to read. I folded it carefully and slipped it back into its envelope. If she had discovered anything new it would surely have been referred to in that first paragraph. I stuffed it in my pocket to read later and told my secretary to show the man in.

That evening I slipped my moorings and headed out through the harbour entrance as the sun set and the downs darkened to merge with a line of cloud coming in from the north-west. It was a downhill sail, no engine and everything very quiet as I slipped south at about 5 knots, the little boat rolling gently to the long swell coming in from the west. By dawn, if the wind held, I would be in France.

It was past midnight before I was across the westbound shipping lane and content to leave it to the windvane steering and go below. It was then, in the lamplit warmth of the saloon, with my pipe and a malt whisky, that I read the rest of Miriam's letter. It was an unusual letter because it was full of description, and what she was describing was a very strange part of the world. *And I'm being followed.* That was on page 2, the words leaping out at me. *You'll think I'm crazy, but it's true. Every time I leave the hotel, he's there, dogging my footsteps. And it's not my imagination. I've checked, by doubling back through the hotel. It has two entrances, the front on Wood Street, and the back down a long corridor, past a shop full of lovely Arctic prints and out onto Steele Street, which is where the travel agents all seem to hang out. He's a very small man with a lined, craggy face, high cheekbones and puffed eyelids, very black, straight hair – not unlike some of the Indians that hang about the streets here. Perhaps it's just that a woman walking around this northern frontier town on her own is a bit of an oddity. Talking of Steele Street, wasn't Steele the Mountie Tom used to talk about, the man who ran the North virtually singlehanded back in '98?*

And then she was describing Whitehorse, the frontier atmosphere of it, the grid pattern of dirt-impacted streets, the fine government building down by the Yukon River *within sight of the old white wooden steamboat that lies like a stranded whale on the far side of the bridge*, the mixture of gold rush and modern buildings, the bellow of the train coming in from Skagway in Alaska. *It's all so strange, so exciting . . . I'm sleepy now. It's the dry air. Tomorrow I have a hire car and will be driving the Alaska Highway to Haines Junction, then down the Haines Highway to Lakeside Lodge, which is beside a lake called Dezadeash. After that I'm told I'll need a four-by-four, which is what they call a four-wheel-drive truck. Looks like I'll have to see if I can charm one of the locals. Bumming a ride from Dalton's Post up to Ice Cold will be quite something. It's right on the edge of the Kluane, which according to my lodge brochure is an ice wonderland of 8500 sq. miles that includes the highest mountain range in North America, icefields that are the largest anywhere in the world outside of polar regions, masses of glaciers and one that 'gallops'. Half the men around here seem to be Indians and the whites wear braces and coloured shirts and wide-brimmed sweat-stained hats. Getting one of them to drive me into the Noisy Range area should exercise my talents! Anyway, you can imagine how excited I am about tomorrow. I'll be right under the 'Front Ranges' of the Kluane (they pronounce it Klewarny) . . .* Then she had scribbled: *I've got the car, I'm on my way. I'll leave this at the desk. If you don't hear from me you'll know I'm lost in the Kluane. I can see my 'follower' watching from across the road. Do you think he'll jump into a pick-up and follow me when I drive off down the Alaska Highway in my little Ford? Love. M.*

I didn't give much thought to her claim that she was being followed. Her description of Whitehorse, stuck out there in a dark wilderness of spruce with the Yukon flowing deep and fast alongside the railroad track, would presumably make any visitor an object of curiosity, particularly a lone woman. In any case, Miriam was not above a little sex play, even in present circumstances. What interested me far more was the fact that she had written to me – and the effect it had on me, which my secretary had noticed. I had seen her recognition of it reflected in her eyes, and now, still in my oilskins, slumped on my bunk, the sound of water moving along the skin of the hull and the lift and fall of the westerly swell making me sleepy, I could see her face so clearly, the casual way she tied the scarf at her throat, the hair glinting with that Titian warmth in the sunlight of my office, the large, almost greenish-blue eyes . . .

I stuffed the letter back into the old briefcase I had propped at the rear of the fold-down shelf that was both eating surface and chart table and poked my head up into the plastic observation dome. A cluster of lights on the port bow, probably fishing vessels trawling one of the banks, the lighthouse on Dungeness blinking clear and bright to the east, and my mind still on Miriam driving the Alaska Highway, enticing some wild stranger to take her up the track from Dalton's Post to the mine on the upper reaches of Ice Cold Creek.

She was with me all that night, which was a very broken one, the alarm waking me every twenty minutes. There is too much traffic in the Channel for a lone sailor to risk much in the way of sleep and the thought of Miriam, going up into the arctic north of Canada on her own to find out what the hell had happened to that mine . . . to go off like that, pinching the silver to pay for the trip, and here was I, bumbling across to Fécamp, never having been further afield than Europe in my life. Quite a girl, I thought, knowing that I was half in love with her and that if I let it take hold I'd be in trouble.

Miriam was too hot a property for me to handle. I was smiling to myself, a sort of fixed grin – I could feel the muscles of my mouth creased up as I savoured the word 'property', thinking of that night on the downs, the urgency of her. It was just past three, the eastern sky paling to the first breath of dawn, and I was tired.

When the sun rose I could see the coast of France, and by midday my little boat was lying snug in Fécamp and I was sitting alone at a café eating a croissant and drinking a cognac with my coffee, the first single-handed sail in my own boat completed. I should have felt excited, filled with a sense of achievement, but in fact I felt nothing. If I had had somebody to share it with . . .

I went back on board and lay on my bunk, too tired, and my nerves still too tense, for sleep, my mind groping with a feeling of emptiness – a house, an office, clients, and now a boat. It was quite an achievement, starting from nothing, and yet it seemed so hollow, lying there alone on my bunk, the sound of French voices all around me, families arguing and the laughter of youngsters. Was that what life was about, the shared happiness of the smallest and most basic of tribal units? And I dealt in death and family disaster, sordid squabbles over money.

I had a night in Fécamp, with a lonely meal in a restaurant and then a round of portside bistros getting gradually a little tight on Armagnac, and early on the Sunday morning I sailed out with the wind south-west force 6 and a rising sea that was soon breaking quite viciously. I wasn't thinking of Miriam then. It was raining and visibility poor, but at least I had a fast passage and the next morning I was in court arguing a paternity case.

My young partner was back and life was suddenly easier, my own holiday only two weeks away. The following morning I heard from Miriam again, just a postcard showing timbered cabins dark against a brilliant sunrise reflected in the pewter surface of a lake, and across the middle of it, in bold black type:

LAKESIDE LODGE
DEZADEASH
Mile 123 Haines Highway

On the back she had scribbled:

I'm in luck. An Italian from Medicine Hat – what a name for a birthplace! – a real nice guy with a 4 ↔ 4 who spends the summer working a claim on the Squaw. Our creek runs into it, he knows the way and we leave in the morning. It really is very exciting, everybody so kind, but the word is that I.C. is cleaned out. Will write you again when I get back to Whitehorse. How's the boat – happy sailing! M.

That was the last I heard from her. She never wrote from Whitehorse, or from anywhere else. I couldn't blame her. It was nice of her to think of me, but I was under no illusions. She had been alone in Whitehorse and I suppose I was uppermost in her mind at the time, so closely connected with what had happened, but once she had got used to the country and begun to make new friends her need of any contact at home would have receded. Indeed, England would probably seem as remote as the Yukon did to me and she had already indicated that the mine was finished. She probably felt there was nothing more to say, but it irked me all the same, and though I was very busy running in my new partner and getting to grips with the boat, I still found it difficult to get her out of my mind. Once I drove over to Bullswood House to see that everything was all right. The staff were provided for – I had checked that already. Miriam had sent them a quarter's wages in advance before leaving for Canada. Mrs Steading, the house-keeper, opened the door to me. 'Mr Brian still here?' I asked her.

She shook her head.

'Did he leave an address?'

Again the negative shake of the head. She was a small, very quiet woman, born locally and still living in the village. 'Never said a word. One day he was here, the next he was gone.' I already knew that she didn't approve of him.

'Anything missing?' I asked. I had had to find out about the silver myself, but now she didn't hesitate. 'Two pictures,' she said, and she took me into Tom Hal-liday's study, pointing to where they had hung, one on either side of the sad-looking moose that dominated the fireplace. I remembered them vaguely, two small ship pictures, very Dutch. 'Mr Halliday thought a lot of them.' I wondered who they were by, how much his son

57

had got for them, whether he had flogged them to a picture dealer in the Lanes in Brighton or taken them up to London, to the Portobello Road, something like that, where they'd never be traced. 'Have you mentioned it to anybody else?' I asked her.

She shook her head. 'None of my business, but since you asked I've told you.'

'Very proper of you, Mrs Steading,' I said, wondering what the hell to do about it now she'd told me. I couldn't really blame either of them, Miriam using the money to take a look at the mine, and Brian – where had he gone, back to India and his Himalayan guru? Or had he gone to stand guard over those Cascades trees? I sat down for a moment at Tom Halliday's desk, my eyes going involuntarily to that extraordinary photograph of his father dancing and shouting for joy there by the wooden sluice box, his teeth gleaming and his hand with the pan in it held out, the snow on the mountain behind him yellowish-white and speckled with damp marks.

The housekeeper had left me. I could hear her moving about upstairs. I went through the drawers quickly, none of them locked and all of them full of the usual backlog of papers, bank statements, old cheque stubs, and in the top right-hand drawer the timber sale agreements. As his son had said, the sale agreements and related correspondence, including felling and towing contracts and forestry reports from a consultant in Campbell River, Vancouver Island, went back seven years with new agreements every six months and the payments steadily declining. All the agreements were with Canadian companies, except the last, which was with SVL Timber and Milling Coy. Inc. of Seattle, and with this contract there were no felling and towing contracts, only a letter from the forestry consultant advising that the American company was more cost-effective in its felling and towing arrangements and was therefore offering a better price, having also outlets in the midwest of America, particularly Chicago.

I made a note of the dates of those agreements, also the address of the Vancouver solicitors who had drawn them up. Then I was sitting back, looking up again at the wall above the desk, thinking of Tom – and of Miriam, the life they had shared together in this house. By now she would have been where the sluice box in that photograph had stood, where young Josh Halliday with the ridiculous drooping moustache and the battered hat had proved a dud mine so full of gold that it had given him and his son a steady flow of wealth for the better part of a century. Was there anything here she would want to keep if he didn't turn up, anything personal – of Tom or the mine? Idly I began opening the drawers of the desk, not looking for anything specific, just thinking how odd it was to be sitting there in Tom's study, everything just as it was when I had last been to dinner, and soon perhaps it would belong to somebody else who would probably change it all round, throw out that photograph and the moose head and the bits and pieces of mine equipment that hung on the walls and lay scattered about the hearth. I was surprised Brian hadn't taken the photograph, a reminder of the man who had planted High Stand all those years ago.

The desk was an old one, Queen Anne by the look of it, a lovely silky walnut, the top slightly stained with ink, a let-down flap and little drawers and pigeonholes full of note-paper, envelopes and postcards. I had seen one rather like it in the home of a retired oil man and I moved my hands gently across the flat wood below the pigeonholes, feeling for movement. That's how I found it, a secret well with a sliding top, the space beneath broad and shallow, and in it a gold Hunter with a flip-up top and a tinkling chime, a gold chain with a nugget of rough gold about the size of a lump of sugar, and beside it a slim book, rather like a ledger, the ink faded to a dull brown.

It was Joshua Halliday's diary. It began on 20 July 1898:

My birthday, and everything I own now aboard this ship. A great number of people too, many, like me, with stores, also horses, some bullocks, several big cast-iron stoves, and the SF water-front crowded, the hubbub of excitement swelling all the time, thrilling me through and through. So much hope, every man I speak with sure he will strike gold and come back a millionaire.

I turned the pages. Shipboard life. Seattle. Vancouver.

5 September: This day we reached Skagway, Great excitement, but also chaos. So many people ashore, tents and makeshift huts, the

*squalor and the stench – and rising above this
wretched encampment the mountains we have to
cross.*

After that entry the writing became less copperplate,
in places quite shaky, the ink often giving way to pencil
scribblings that were so faint the words were difficult to
decipher. But it was all there – how he'd cut across the
frozen expanse of a lake called Bennett and made it to
Dawson in the depth of winter and then to the Dalton
Trail and the Squaw. *I was about done when I started
up the Ice Cold, my breath freezing on my beard, the
range all white, and next day the wind came westerly,
thick mist and the snow melting to slush on the surface,
like ice underneath.* That was the first day of April and
next morning he had reached the claim.

I sat back, staring up at that photograph. Was this
how Tom had first read the diary, sitting at his desk with
that faded photograph hanging on the wall in front of
him, or had he gone out to Vancouver Island on his
father's death and read it there? Whichever way it was,
he had certainly had it here at this desk. I picked up the
watch with its chain and nugget and slipped it into my
pocket, certain Miriam would prefer to have it kept safe
in a strong room, particularly now she had been out to
the mine.

I glanced at the other relics, the battered metal pan
on the wall behind me, the bits and pieces of iron and
wood by the hearth. I wasn't sure whether the pan was
the one with which he had made the first find. There
was a bit of a shovel, all rusted into holes and carefully

blackleaded, a cartridge bandolier, a military-type water bottle, two rusted tins of corned beef and, slung above the mantelpiece below the moose head, a long-barrelled rifle with the wood of the butt half rotted away, barrel and stock pitted with rust. They were the sort of things you would expect to find discarded round an old camp site, rotting in the damp air.

I closed the diary, tucked it under my arm and got to my feet. I took the photograph too. I told Mrs Steading, of course, but not about the diary and the watch, and when I got back to the office, I put them away in the Halliday deed box, and that was that, my mind switching to other things, the oil man dying of cancer and all his affairs to cope with in a rush.

The last days of August had slipped away in a blaze of summer heat and now we were well into September and it was raining, my first real holiday less than a week away. I took the boat down to Bembridge. No word from Miriam, and her husband still missing. The following day I set off for Brittany with a girl I had met only once, at a party given by a client, and it didn't work out. It was a beat all the way, quite rough at times, and she was seasick. She left me at Paimpol, and it was after that, when I was on my own, starting to rock-hop westward along the coast, that I began thinking of Miriam again and how it would have been if I had had her on board, wondering what she was up to, who she was with – why, after that postcard and her visit to the mine, she hadn't bothered to write.

I was becalmed for a whole day by Les Sept Iles with nothing to do but listen to the radio. That was when I started to worry about her. It was two weeks now, a little more. After Whitehorse she would probably have gone down to Vancouver, or Victoria, where Tom at any rate would have had friends but, however hectic the social life, it seemed strange she had not written to me again, if only to make certain that I was keeping an eye on the house.

It was there, in the solitary confinement of my little boat, with the moon coming up and the sails slatting, not a breath of wind, that I made up my mind. It wouldn't take more than a week at the outside, and even if she had forgotten all about me, and her promise to write after she'd been up to the mine, it would at least settle the nagging thought that something had happened to her. And at the same time I could check for myself whether the mine was really exhausted, possibly see the BC property and that stand of timber in the Cascades valley.

In the early hours of the morning, just as dawn was breaking, the wind came in from the west again and it began to cloud over. I turned the boat about and headed for home. And when I got there my partner told me over the phone that we had received a reply to the letter I had sent to the solicitors in Vancouver before I had started on my holiday. It stated unequivocally that the previous year's September timber sale agreement was the last they had drawn up for Mr Halliday. But he had been into their office on Thursday the fifteenth of last month to enquire about the possibility of selling the whole Cascades property through a nominee, or perhaps forming a special trust to handle the sale. They had not seen him since, only Mrs Halliday who had been in to see them on 9 September, which was the day I had received her postcard. His manner at that meeting in August was described as 'quite normal, but not relaxed'. And the letter concluded with the words – 'we have no reason to suppose our client was ill, nor did he show any indication of being on the verge of a nervous breakdown or any other disturbance that would account for his disappearance'. It was signed McLaren & Partners.

Two days later I was on a Wardair flight out of Gatwick bound for Vancouver across the top of the world.

PART TWO

ICE COLD CREEK

CHAPTER ONE

It's an odd feeling sitting with earphones on and a drink in one's hand listening to a symphony concert and looking down through drifting cloud to a scattering of growlers so far below that the sea appears dusted with salt, the pack-ice beyond and an occasional berg. Tim Severin would have been glad of this aerial view when his leather hide boat was caught in the ice, for it showed St Brendan was right. Even now, almost fifteen hundred years after that Irish saint recorded the details of his voyage to North America, there was still the ice-clear gap between the pack and the coast of Greenland. It showed quite clearly from where I sat, 37,000 feet above sea level, a dark lane of water, and beyond it great rivers of snow and ice sweeping down between the black mouths of overlapping craters, and then the white blank-out of age-old, depthless snow as we whispered our way across the Greenland icecap. Baffin Island for lunch, the sun standing still as we flew almost as fast as the earth was spinning with bergs like ships between dark-coloured outbreaks of land. Black, black mountains, sheer cliffs, everything brittle-bright, the clarity of the air unbelievable.

The man next to me leaned across. 'Don't want to drop into that lot, eh?' It was the first time he had said a word. 'Guess we must be just about over the spot where Franklin and all those others wintered and died.' He looked at me hard, steel-grey eyes and a baldish head. 'First time you bin on this run?'

I nodded.

'Thought so. I do it three, four times a year. Always Wardair.' He nodded emphatically. 'I got contracts to supply you people with fruit, apples mainly.' He smiled a hard, tight-lipped smile. 'You wouldn't believe it, but we grow them right in the middle of the Rockies. Grapes, too. You should take a trip up and see for yourself. And this is the right time, Indian summer weather, real warm.' He reached into his jacket pocket, produced a business card and placed it on my meal tray. 'Be happy to show you around.' He nodded, pushed his earphones back in place and was lost to the world again.

We crossed Slave Lake, the Rockies looming ahead, the murmur of the engines barely audible as we began to slide down the sky towards a world of jagged peaks and the dirty yellow of snow that had lain exposed all summer. On and off I had been thinking of Miriam. Almost a month ago she had come this way, maybe in this very seat since she, too, had flown Wardair. Had the sky been as clear as it was now? Had she sat there looking down on the barren, ice-scarred land below, thinking of her destination, knowing the Yukon border was only a few hundred miles away to starb'd? And not a word since that postcard.

It had seemed strange enough back in England, but now that the wild bleakness of northern Canada was spread out below me, the vastness of it and the loneliness, it seemed stranger still. To have reached out to somebody as she had – never mind the reason – and then to cut the contact as though it didn't matter any more. All that space, a wilderness of mountain, lake and scrub just beginning to take on an autumn blaze on the heights below the snow line, and in the Yukon on the ground, it would still be a vastness of space full of rock and trees, the humans few and strange. Surely in the remoteness of that glacial national park, having penetrated to Ice Cold Creek, she would have come back urgent to tell me about it, about the mine, about what she had found. It didn't seem natural that she should suddenly have gone silent on me, not now that I, too, was conscious of the vastness, experiencing that sense of smallness and loneliness that she must have felt.

There was a marvellous view of Vancouver sitting like a miniature Manhattan surrounded by vast expanses of sun-bright water as we came in to land. Ships, and tugs with long trains of barges, some with log rafts, the Strait of Juan de Fuca reaching out to the American mainland and the distant shapes of snow-clad mountains. It was for this, and the sight of the Arctic Ocean, that I had flown the northern route instead of the more prosaic and slightly cheaper route via Edmonton. As soon as I had settled into my hotel, which was in the rather congested eastern part of Vancouver known as Gas Town, I took a taxi across town to the Bayshore Hotel. It was right on the water, close against the old wharfs and boatyards of Coal Harbour.

At reception I was able to confirm that Miriam had in fact spent three nights at the hotel the previous month, but she had left no forwarding address and had not booked in again. Presumably while staying at the Bayshore she had made contact with friends, or people her husband had known, and had been invited to stay on with them on her return from Whitehorse. It was something I had expected, but it still came as a disappointment. At the back of my mind, I suppose, I had been hoping to have her company for the evening. Instead, I walked through Stanley Park as far as the light on Brockton Point with its view of the First Narrows and the Lions Gate Bridge, then dined at a restaurant in Coal Harbour.

This half-derelict area between the Canadian Pacific railway tracks and the waterfront is almost the last remaining relic of the old part of Vancouver, and after my meal I wandered round the whole complex of crumbling boatyards, half-collapsed wharfs and charter boat offices. The air was very still, a warm, balmy night, the water dead calm and the only sound the slap of wavelets against the wooden piers as the wash of the occasional yacht or motor cruiser reached the shore. It was a late night tour of one of the most atmospheric parts of the city that was later to save my life. But I didn't know that at the time, of course, and spent several minutes at the end of a tumbledown jetty looking enviously across the water to that extraordinary marina of timber housings over towards Deadman's Island that shelters the Royal Vancouver Yacht Club's motor cruiser fleet. I would dearly have liked to 'borrow' one of those craft to explore the waters between Vancouver Island and the mainland. At least it would be nice to be staying here at the Bayshore with that magnificent view across to the lights of the North Shore with the Rockies beyond. So much to see, so much of grandeur and beauty, and neither the time nor the money.

Next morning the sun shone out of a clear blue sky and I strolled up Cordova Street, Granville and Dunsmuir and south down Burrard as far as Robson's Square. It was on Robson Street that the solicitors who had drawn up the timber agreements had their offices, on the twenty-first floor of a tall glass building with a view past the green copper summit of the Hotel Vancouver to the BC Ferries' jetty and the CPR tracks running towards Coal Harbour. By comparison with my small set-up at Ditchling their premises were palatial. I had no appointment and was quite prepared to arrange for a meeting either the following morning before my plane left for Whitehorse or on my return. However, the partner who had looked after Halliday's Canadian affairs was available and after only a short wait I was shown into his office. His name was Roy McLaren, a paunchy, heavily built man of about fifty with thick gold-rimmed glasses which gave his round, rather boyish face a look of enquiring wonder. Yes, Mrs Halliday had been in to see him – he reached for his diary, turning back the pages – 'I think I gave you the date in my letter.'

I nodded. 'And you haven't seen her since?'

'That also I said in my letter. Neither her nor her husband.' He looked across at me from behind his glasses. 'Did you know Tom well?'

I had to explain then that I had only acted for him in the matter of his Will and had known him for no more than three years. 'Ah well,' he said, 'we've been acting for him since his father died. And the firm, of course, acted for his father before then. I'm afraid I never knew Josh Halliday. A great character by all accounts. My uncle was the one who dealt with him.' He put his hands together, the fingers forming a steeple, pressing them hard as he stared at me enquiringly, an expression of large-eyed innocence. 'When Tom inherited my uncle handed him over to my father. This is a very inbred firm, you see. Even my eldest sister is a partner. Damn good lawyer, too.' He relaxed his fingers, smiling. 'I took over Tom's affairs here when my father retired about six years ago.'

'About the time the output from the Yukon mine was beginning to decline.'

'I didn't know anything about that. There was some talk about it later, of course, but at the time all I was concerned with was drawing up the agreements for the sale of timber on that property of his up north along the coast. He was acting on the advice of a forestry man named Hugh Ringstrop over by Campbell River.'

'Did Ringstrop negotiate the price?'

He nodded. 'Yes. And he marked out the areas. He was Tom's forestry adviser.'

'And that last sale agreement?' I asked. 'Did he negotiate the price for that too?'

The fingers pressed tight again. 'Not sure, but I think so. I remember he said it would be difficult to get an export licence, and anyway the stand was really too young. "Hadn't reached maturity" was one way he put it.'

'But you still drew up the agreement.'

'Yes.'

'Knowing about the curse.'

'Ah!' The fingers pressed very tight, the eyes wide and innocent behind the thick glasses. 'Yes, of course – we sent the deeds over to his bank in London above five years ago. That was after the divorce had gone through and he remarried.' He smiled. 'You never met his first wife, of course.' The hands fell suddenly flat on the desk. 'A very beautiful, very terrible woman. I think he might have killed her if she hadn't gone off with another man. Martina. They had two sons. Which brings me to something else. There has been one small development since I replied to your original letter.' He pressed a bell on his desk and a very severe-looking woman in a bright pink cotton dress came in and handed him a folder. 'The younger of those two sons – do you know him?'

'Brian?'

He nodded. The woman went out, closing the door without a sound.

'Yes,' I said. 'You've seen him, have you?'

He was smiling again, the eyes slitted now and wrinkles showing. He opened the folder. It contained a single sheet of typing and some newspaper cuttings. 'He came to see me – week before last. His father has left him the Cascades, is that right?' And when I nodded, he went on, 'I didn't altogether approve of his manner, or his dress for that matter, so I taped the whole interview. It didn't last long. Five or six minutes, that's all. Then he was gone.'

'It was about the Cascades he came to see you, was it? An area of timber he calls High Stand.'

'That's it. Four hundred hectares of what Ringstrop describes as the finest plantation of western red cedar he has ever seen.' And he added, 'I've written to you, giving the gist of our conversation, but my letter probably arrived after you'd left. I was on holiday last week, fishing up the coast by Kelsey Bay.' He picked up the largest of the newspaper cuttings, unfolded it and passed it across the desk to me. 'This appeared while I was up the coast. Recognize anyone?'

It was a full page of the *Vancouver Sun*, half of it taken up with a picture of a huge barge under tow. The barge was piled high with the rounded trunks of large trees and below the steel hawsers of the towing bridle, riding the barge's bow wave, was a man in an inflatable holding aloft a banner. He wore a baseball hat and a T-shirt with Greenpeace on it, and the words on the banner were the same as the headline that flared across the page:

GREEN SOLDIERS AGAINST POLLUTION
Killed in Action

Below were three smaller pictures, one of a tree falling in a clear-felled section of forest land and under it a quote – *An unknown soldier of the forest*. The middle picture showed a close-up of the man holding the banner. The long face, prominent nose and high cheekbones, the black hair showing beneath the cap and the way the ears stood out, even the same T-shirt. The third showed the inflatable, one side collapsed, the man with the banner diving over the side, and above him a man leaning over the bows of the barge with a boathook in his hand.

I looked across at McLaren. 'Brian Halliday?'

He nodded. 'Taken last Wednesday. I'm told the silly fool nearly lost his life. But he had it all organized and was intent on causing the SVL Timber Company and the towing people as much hostile publicity as possible. There were film cameras out there and he deliberately let himself be run down. He dived overboard, as you see, just as the inflatable was trampled under by the bows of that tow. Damn lucky, if you ask me. He was picked up by a salmon fisher. By then he was half full of water, but uninjured except for a few bruises and abrasions. It was all on TV that same night. And the next day Greenpeace disowned him. Said it was nothing to do with them. They're concentrated on whaling again, not running a West Coast save-the-trees campaign. Without their backing the story had a quick death, but he certainly made an impact. I watched the TV film of it on a friend's boat and it was quite an action spectacular.'

'The logs were presumably from the Cascades property.'

He nodded. 'From the plantation he calls High Stand. It's all there in the caption story at the bottom of the page.' He rang the bell again and the woman in the pink dress appeared. 'Copy these cuttings for Mr Redfern, will you.' He handed her the file. 'Then you can look them through at your leisure. Not that they'll tell you anything you don't already know.' He glanced at his watch.

I apologized again for interrupting him and he smiled and shrugged and said, 'Not to worry, but it is Monday, and that's never a good day. Is there anything else I can do for you?'

'Just one thing,' I said. 'That sale agreement dated 20 September of last year. I take it that was the only one you drew up for Tom Halliday covering the western red cedar down by the river, the High Stand area?'

He nodded, smiling, his hands forming a steeple of his fingers again. 'I know what you're going to ask. I phoned the office the very next day and had my son get on the phone to SVL Timber in Seattle. He was informed that they were still working to the agreement covering the two hectares. The logs were of exceptional quality and because of that they would be kept clear of the water, no rafting or parking them in a booming ground the way they do pulp. Instead, they were bringing them down by barge and, again because of the quality, had spaced the delivery dates. Last week's tow was the second of three separate deliveries to be made to the mill.'

'And they won't be cutting any more trees?'

'Definitely not. Hugh Ringstrop made that quite clear to them – no trees could be felled, outside of the original two-hectare lot, until a new sale agreement had been negotiated and signed.' The fingers pressed hard together and he added, 'And, of course, nothing can be signed until Mr Halliday is found. That they understand and accept.'

I wasn't sure about that and I wondered how forcibly his son had made the point. But when I told him about Wolchak's offer, he nodded. 'They made similar approaches, first through Ringstrop, then direct to us. That was just after Tom was reported missing.'

'You didn't say anything about that in your letter to me.'

'No?' He hesitated. 'No, you're right. I thought about it, but it didn't seem relevant. Not then. If Tom Halliday was dead, then of course I would have let you know. But right now any sale of the property is legally out of the question.'

I had a few other queries, small points of law mainly concerned with Tom Halliday's position as a Canadian citizen and how the estate would stand from a tax point of view if that proved to be the basis on which we had to operate. Then I left him with the assurance that I would see him again before leaving for England if my visits to either the mine or the forestry area raised any further queries. To my surprise he had not been to either of the properties himself. 'Our business is very much centred on Vancouver, companies chiefly.' This as he rose to see me to the door. 'My father and my uncle had a great many personal clients, but most of them are dead now and times have changed. The sons have tended to move into companies. It's just the way we have expanded.'

I picked up the copies of the press cuttings from the pink dress, now looking even more severe with her glasses on the end of her nose and seated behind a word processor.

I lunched later that morning at a fish restaurant virtually under the high span of Granville Bridge, reading carefully through the press cuttings as I ate.

One of the cuttings had given the names of the towing company as Angeles Georgia Towing of Port Angeles, which my map showed to be just across the Strait of Juan de Fuca from Victoria and the south end of Vancouver Island, an ideal position for a tugboat company. I phoned them as soon as I got back to my hotel and when I said I had a query about the Cascades I was put straight through to Mr Stutz who sounded gruff and very Scandinavian. What I wanted to confirm, of course, was whether this was the second of three barge-loads and that there had not been any further felling of timber. 'Ja,' he answered immediately, 'I think you are informed correctly, there is vun more tow to make.'

'Only one?' I asked.

'Ja, vun only.'

'When will you be towing it down?'

'I dunno. No orders yet.'

'But there are definitely some more logs to bring down?'

He didn't answer that and when I asked him exactly how much timber was allowed for in the export licence, he said, 'Look, who are you? A newspaper man, no?'

'The owner's English solicitor,' I said and he closed

up on me, referring me to SVL Timber. 'Ve just tow. I know nothing about the ownership of timber, nothing about legislation. Okay?'

I had a thought then. 'How many tugs do you operate?' I asked him.

'What you say? – how many tugs I got? None of your business. You talk to SVL, okay?' And he put the phone down.

But when I got through to SVL Timber I found myself dealing with a Mr Barony who was as smooth as the towing company man had been gruff. There was one more load to be towed down under the existing agreement. It hadn't yet been decided when. 'I guess you've seen the reports of young Halliday putting himself under the barge. Well, we don't want a repetition of that, do we, whether he's a Greenpeace man or not, so you'll appreciate when we do decide on a date for the tow we won't be announcing it to the press.' And he gave a gentle, conspiratorial chuckle.

He was not quite so forthcoming, however, when I asked him whether they were negotiating a new sales agreement. 'We would like to, but as you will know, Mr Redfern, there are certain difficulties at the moment.' He was referring, of course, to Halliday's disappearance, and when I asked him how long it was since he had seen Mr Halliday he said, 'I have never seen him. All our business has been through Ringstrop, his forestry man, and McLarens, the solicitors. If you know where he is please tell me.' And when I said I didn't know and that was the reason I was in Canada, he sighed gently and said that was a pity. 'If you find him please contact us immediately.'

'Of course,' I said. 'Meantime, have I your assurance that no more than two hectares of High Stand has so far been felled?'

'The loggers cut only the area Mr Ringstrop marks out. That I promise. It is all being done through Mr Ringstrop, you understand.'

'And you've no plans to fell any additional area?'

'We would like to. That is why we need Mr Halliday – or perhaps you or his wife. If he is dead we are informed from London that you are the executors, not that son of his. Maybe soon we have to deal with you. Let me know, Mr Redfern. Let me know as soon as we can negotiate a purchase. Okay?'

'One final question,' I said. 'Mrs Halliday was in Vancouver some three weeks ago. You didn't see her?'

'No. No, I didn't see her.'

'And she didn't phone you?'

'No, Mr Redfern. No, she don't phone. So – I wait to hear from you, or from Mr McLaren, yes?'

That was that, and the rest of the afternoon I spent in Stanley Park, part of it watching the antics of the dolphins and the large black and white Orca and all-white beluga whales in their very restricted public display pool. While at the hotel I had, of course, phoned Ringstrop, but he was not in the office that day and the girl who answered the phone said he would be at the Crown Forest logging camp at Beaver Cove. I could ring him there. I had explained who I was and had asked her to tell him I would be visiting the Cascades in a few days' time and if there was anything he wanted to tell me to ring me that evening at my hotel, otherwise I would contact him on my return to Vancouver.

Back at my hotel, I went through the press cuttings again. One piece of information was new to me – the weight and size of the logs. From my pocket calculator I worked it out that each tree contained something like a cubic metre of timber, the logs measuring upwards of 36 metres with a butt diameter of about 15 centimetres. Maybe they had got it wrong. The *Sun* reporter had presumably been looking at the top layer of logs, measuring them by eye and probably exaggerating, but even allowing for that it suggested High Stand as a whole was worth more than Brian Halliday had indicated, or that his father had been paid less than the true value. I couldn't be sure of that since I was merely multiplying by the market value per cube for cedar that the girl at Campbell River had given me, and that was a figure she admitted was the going rate at waterside for Vancouver Island timber. As Brian had said, it was a long way from the Cascades to Seattle and the value depended very much on the price of the tow.

I walked down to the Canadian National Railway pier, watched a big rust-coloured bulk carrier come into Burrard Inlet from the Narrows, pick up its tugs and berth at the pier. Then I walked along Main to Hastings and strolled through the bright lights of Chinatown where I had an excellent meal in a little restaurant patronized by Chinese rather than tourists, mostly shopkeepers and local businessmen, I guessed by their appearance. I was reading a paperback history of the Yukon gold rush I had picked up at a nearby bookshop.

Next day I checked out of my hotel and caught the bus that runs across False Creek and south down Granville to the international airport stuck out on Sea Island, which is little more than a silt bank on the North Arm of the Fraser River delta. I had to wait there for the Whitehorse flight to come in from Victoria, and when we finally took off the sky was clouding over so that I only had a momentary view of Vancouver and the Fraser, with the treed humps of the Gulf Islands merging into the bulk of Vancouver Island as we banked, the Strait of Georgia running north-west between the islands and the mainland, the pewter calm of its waters criss-crossed with the wakes of ferries, coasters, fishing vessels and motor cruisers – also one or two yachts under power, their sails hanging limp. Then we were into cloud as we climbed across the Rockies to meet up with an Edmonton plane at Fort St John, and we stayed in cloud until we were dropping down into the province of Alberta, where in an instant the air cleared to reveal a brown and arid world with splashes of poplar green relieving the dark monotony of spruce, and the Peace River a snaking ribbon of water between clay-coloured banks.

The heat, when they opened the door, was tinder-dry, and in place of the pale-suited businessmen who had flown up to Fort St John, the passengers joining us from the Edmonton plane were from a different world – men in faded bush shirts, broad-brimmed cowboy hats and braces, girls with glistening black hair and dark, high-cheeked, slightly flattened faces, and full-blooded Indians moving as though nobody had told them about the force of gravity, the whole plane suddenly full of a frontier atmosphere.

We flew north-west now, cutting obliquely across a series of high, jagged ranges, clouds piling up to the west. The man in the seat next to me, who was dressed in a greenish uniform, proved to be one of the Kluane Park wardens. His name was Jim Edmundson, and without any prodding from me he began talking about the wildlife and describing the way the Indians had lived in the days when Mackenzie and the North-Westers had first opened up the country trapping beaver. 'Now we keep the Indians on a welfare state basis, the Eskimo, too, and the beaver are protected.' He had a slow, very Canadian voice, almost a drawl. 'But we dam' near killed them off one time, the beaver I mean.' The resulting decline in beaver dams had meant there was nothing to stop the run-off of rainwater from the mountains. 'Soon there was drought and Alberta became a dust-bowl.'

He was so easy and friendly I didn't resent it when he asked me straight out the purpose of my trip to Whitehorse. My briefcase, and the sort of questions I was asking, must have made it clear I wasn't just a tourist. He had never met Tom Halliday but he knew the history of the mine and was able to tell me a lot about the area. He talked about the gold rush, too. But it was the mountains, the whole environment, and the balance of nature that he talked about most, and also the forests. He had trained as a forester. He had even written a book about forestry developments on Vancouver Island and the Charlottes. A large man with battered features like a boxer who was wholly absorbed in his work.

The clouds had thickened below us, and soon after starting the approach run to Whitehorse, we were into them and flying blind in a grey, ghostly world.

'You headed straight for the Kluane?' he asked me, his pronunciation confirming Miriam's impression of it as *Klewarny*. 'I never bin to the mine, but the Noisy Range I know, and if it's near the Noisy . . .' He shook his head. 'I wouldn't advise going in behind the Front Ranges in this weather.'

'I'll probably stay the night in Whitehorse and leave in the morning,' I said.

'Who's meeting you?'

'Nobody,' I told him. 'But I've got the mine manager's address. Takhini Trailer Court. That's near Whitehorse, isn't it?'

He nodded. 'Bout a mile down the highway from the airport.'

'Any difficulty about hiring a car?' I asked him.

'Not this time of year. Tourist season's just about over. But if you're planning a trip out to that mine, you'll need a four-by-four, that's for sure.' He nodded to the grey swirl of cloud skimming past the wings. 'Be raining on the ground. Might even be sleeting in the mountains over towards Haines Junction. Looks like winter's starting early this year.'

We broke out of the cloud into driving rain, Whitehorse a rectangular grid of wide, blackly shining streets laid out flat in the elbow of a river. 'The Yukon,' he said. 'One of the few rivers that runs north then south.' I traced the course of it on the map spread out on my briefcase. It started in BC, almost reached the sea at White Pass above Skagway, ran north to Dawson City, then west almost to the Bering Strait before turning south and ending up after two thousand miles in Norton Sound.

I turned to the window again, the river below me, a broad brown ribbon of water running fast all along one side of the town, paralleling the railway line, and on the other side the airport spread out along the top of a brown escarpment. 'Depends how long it's been raining whether you get through to your mine, but in any case it'll be rough going . . .' He looked at me, frowning. 'Guess you wouldn't have much experience of four-wheel-drive trucks in the old country.'

'I'll manage,' I told him.

'Sure. But this is bad country to get bogged down in. Half my time is spent helping men get out of trouble they could have avoided if they'd had the sense to realize what they were up against. Tell you what, Philip' – right from the start he had been using my Christian name – 'I've got my truck parked at the airport. Why don't I run you out to Takhini? It won't take me five minutes and I've got to see the Parks man at the Government Building, also the Met. people. I'll be about an hour in town, then I'll pick you up and we'll drive to Haines Junction. That's where our HQ is, and it puts you almost a hundred miles on your way, right against the Front Ranges of the Kluane.'

I told him I wouldn't wish to put him to so much trouble, but I was into a country now where helping others was a part of living. A friend of his might even lend me his four-by-four if it was only for a couple of days, and there was a reasonably comfortable lodge just outside Haines Junction. 'Food's okay, too,' he said. 'And maybe in the morning the rain will have stopped.'

We landed in a downpour, spray flung up higher than the wings, the wheels skimming the surface water, and since he wouldn't take no for an answer, even saying if there was no room at the lodge his wife would make up a bed for me in what they called the nursery, I accepted his offer of a lift. The prospect of company on the drive to Haines Junction was too good to refuse.

We hurried across the wet concrete, flung our cases into the big Parks vehicle and piled in. The interior of the truck was damp and cold, the surrounding country lost in the driving rain and the flat rectangle of White-horse only just visible like a toy town below us. 'The Alaska Highway,' he said, as we swung north out of the airport, the asphalt road gleaming, the black of spruce closing in. Almost immediately we were into the settle-ment of Takhini and he turned right, down a dirt road that forced him into four-wheel drive. The surface was some sort of boulder clay. 'Slippery as hell soon as there's any rain.' Ahead of us the river expanded into a small lake. Spruce everywhere. White spruce, he said, though the forest it made was funeral black.

The trailer court was wet and sticky with mud, nobody about, so I had a miserable time finding some-one to direct me. The man I had come to see lived at the far end, a large home on wheels with the name Jonny Epinard painted on the door. A red Dodge pick-up stood beside it almost completely coated with a glistening layer of mud. Maybe it was the rain, or the fact that his wife was in hospital, but he was there, the door opening almost as soon as I banged on it. He was a wiry little man, rather Irish-looking, with a dark, screwed-up face. He hadn't shaved that morning, the stubble showing grey, though his hair was black, jet black and very straight. In his faded bush shirt, open at the neck, and mudstained jeans held up by braces as well as a thick leather belt, he had a wild, outlandish look.

His dark eyes switched from me to the Park warden, then back to me again. 'Who are you?' His grip on the door had tightened, his voice a little high. 'What d'you want?'

'Answers,' I said. 'To a few questions.' I could hear the suck of his breath as I told him who I was and got my briefcase from the truck. I think he would have liked to close the door on me then, but Jim Edmundson called, 'Back in about an hour, okay?' and without waiting for an answer drove off. The man had no alternative then: 'You'd better come in,' he said, his voice reluctant.

The rear of the trailer was fitted out as a sitting-room, chintz curtains, imitation-leather chairs, pale wood cupboards and shelves. He waved me to a seat, but then remained standing, staring at the floor as though he didn't know what to do about me. I let the silence run on until finally he said, 'Well?' The question hung in the air. He was nervous and I wondered why. 'You like a beer?'

I shook my head.

His eyes darted about the room as though seeking some way of escape. Then abruptly he sat down. 'You're Tom Halliday's lawyer, you say.' His eyes fastened on the briefcase. I opened it and showed him copies of several letters that gave my firm's address, but I could see he had already accepted my identity. 'What do you want to know?' His tongue flicked across his lips. 'Sure you won't have a beer?'

'No thanks,' I said. 'I had a drink on the plane.'

He nodded, then got suddenly to his feet again. 'Well, I think I will. Don't mind, do you?' He opened a cupboard, busying himself searching among the bottles and cans. 'You come all the way from England?'

'Yes,' I said.

'To see me? Or to see the mine? You going there?' He looked round at me. 'There's nothing to see. The mine's finished.' He had a can in his hand and he snapped the ring. 'It ran out years back. But you know that, don't you?'

'How many years back?'

He stared at me, his eyes probing as though he was trying to decide whether the question was some sort of a trap. 'Didn't he tell you?' I waited, and at last he sat down again, taking a swig direct from the can. 'It didn't happen all at once. The pay dirt just thinned out, yielding less and less each year.'

'When did you first realize the gold was petering out?'

'Hard to say exactly, but about seven years ago, I

guess. Why? What do you want to know for? Because Tom's broke, is that it?'

'Did Mrs Halliday tell you that?' I was thinking of her description of the man watching from across the road. 'You spoke to her in the end, did you?'

But he was still thinking of Tom. 'He's been a good guy to work for.' He was suddenly smiling. 'Used to come out about once a year. Wasn't much interested in mining, only the machinery – he liked that. What he really came for was the fishing. And camera stalking. Didn't want to shoot anything. But if he could get a close-up with his camera, moose in part'c'lar – he'd stalk moose all day down in the swampland below Nine Mile Falls.' He shook his head, still smiling – a slightly crooked, slightly uncertain smile.

'You kept the mine running.'

'That's right.'

'Why did you do that? It was losing money.'

'He wanted it kept running, that's why. Not flat out like it used to be, but ticking over.'

'Why?' I repeated.

He shrugged. 'Why does any man do anything if he's got the money? He liked it, liked the idea of being a mine owner, that's what he told me. It was in the blood, I guess, his father finding gold there when everyone told him he'd been sold a dud. Reck'n Tom didn't want anybody to know the gold had run out.'

'It must have cost him quite a bit.'

'Sure, but a rich man like him – ' He laughed. 'Wish I were rich enough to run a mine just for the hell of it, just to keep up appearances. That's what he was doing.

Keeping up appearances. And now what?' His eyes darted at me, anxious now and worried about the future. This was a young man's country and he was certainly the wrong side of fifty. He leaned forward. 'You're his lawyer. If it turns out he's dead, then what happens about the mine? There's only myself and a young half-breed Indian, Jack McDonald, now, but we need to know.'

I didn't answer him for a moment, wondering what line to take. 'You'll have to ask Mrs Halliday about that,' I said. 'In the event you speak of, the mine will belong to her.'

'Mrs Halliday?' He seemed suddenly confused.

'You saw her here in Whitehorse, didn't you? When she was staying at the Sheffield.' Or had it been the half-breed Indian who had followed her? It had to be one of them. 'She hired a car and drove down to a lake called Dezadeash.'

'Dezdeesh.' From the way he said it I knew his correction of my pronunciation was to give him time to think. 'She stayed at Kevin McKie's place – Lakeside.'

'You spoke to her just as she was driving off, is that it?'

'No.'

'But you were watching her from across the road.'

He didn't answer.

'She said she was being followed when she was staying at the hotel. Was that you?'

He stared at me blankly, his face gone sullen, and in that moment he looked part Indian himself.

'She wrote to me,' I said. 'Somebody was following her about, watching her. That was you, wasn't it?'

He nodded, slowly and reluctant.

'Why?'

He hesitated, shaking his head. And then suddenly he blurted out, 'I was scared, you see. I couldn't make up my mind.' And he went on, the words coming in a rush, 'Tom had talked of her like she was a princess. Not often, but sometimes – over the camp fire, when he was lonely. And the way he spoke of her . . .' He paused, his mind remembering. 'She never came out here with him, you see. I'd never met her, and when I saw her . . . well, I guess there was something about her – ' He leaned suddenly forward, both hands clasped tightly round the beer can. 'What would you have done? She looked so beautiful, and at the same time so remote – like ice, or a sunset seen across a frozen lake. I knew she must be here to find out about the mine – the same questions you bin asking. Was I to go right up to her and say What about my job – my wife's sick and I haven't had any money for over six months? Could I go right up to her and say that? Would you, if you were me?'

He was staring at me, his gaze urgent, his eyes almost pleading. It was obvious what he wanted, what any man would want who'd held an apparently safe job for years and now didn't know whether it would continue, or even if he'd get the money he was owed. And I couldn't help. Also, there was something that puzzled me. 'How did you know Mrs Halliday was staying at the Sheffield? You say she'd never been out here before, yet you were there waiting for her, following her about.'

He didn't say anything, and his eyes dropped, one hand under his arm abstractedly scratching himself.

'Did she write you she was coming?'

He shook his head, his eyes shifting to the window.

'But you knew she was coming.'

'Yes.' He finished his drink and got slowly to his feet, putting the empty can down and reaching into a drawer stuffed with papers. She hadn't written to him. She had cabled him. He handed me the flimsy. It was addressed to a box number in Whitehorse. It gave her date of arrival and flight number and asked him to meet her either at the airport or the Sheffield. PLEASE ARRANGE VISIT ICE COLD MINE. MIRIAM HALLIDAY. 'That's when I first saw her, at the airport.'

'But you didn't talk to her then.'

'No.'

'What about the visit to the mine – did you fix that?'

'Yep. She went in with a guy who works a claim on a neighbouring creek. I fixed that for her at the airport. Bit of luck, he was there to pick up some radio spares.'

'An Italian.'

He nodded. 'Tony Tarasconi. She was staying at Lakeside Lodge. He picked her up from there and took her in.'

'You fixed that for her, at the airport. But you didn't make yourself known to her, though you were there and she had asked you to meet her. What were you afraid of?'

'Nothing.' He said it quickly, his eyes darting. 'I told

you – I was worried about the future. I couldn't face it, not then.'

'So when did you finally talk with her?'

'Later. I spoke to her later.'

'After she'd been to the mine?'

'Yep.'

I handed back the cable slip, wondering what had made him change his mind. 'I'll be going up to the mine myself,' I said and an expression almost of hostility showed for an instant in his dark eyes.

'What for?' He stared at me. 'There's nobody there, nothing – only the equipment. Anything you want to know I can tell you right here. Any questions about production, how much it would cost to move the screening plant and have a try up the Stone Slide Gully.' It was clear he didn't want me there. But why? 'I tried to persuade Tom to have a go at Stone Slide, but he wouldn't. I guess he was finding things difficult by then. Financially, I mean. We've cut right back. Everything we can, so no point your going there.' And he added, 'It's bad going at any time, but after all the rain we've had – '

'It's not the rain,' I said. 'It's something else.'

He shook his head, his face taking on that sullen look, his hands clasped very tight as I told him I was determined to see the mine now that I was here. In the end he agreed to contact the Italian for me. He couldn't drive me in himself because of his wife. Just why he had been willing to talk to Miriam after she had been to the mine, when he wouldn't speak to her before, I couldn't discover. And after she had been to the mine Miriam had only stayed one night at the Sheffield, then in the morning she had taken the train down to Skagway in Alaska.

'And after that?' I asked. 'Where was she going after Skagway?'

He gave a little shrug and shook his head. 'Vancouver, I guess.' It wasn't for him to ask her where she was going, and he added that people who went down to Skagway on the old Yukon and White Pass Route railway were usually headed back to Vancouver by the sea route, in which case she would have been taking one of the American ships as far as Prince Rupert, then changing to the BC Ferries service. I suggested she might not have gone straight back to Vancouver. 'Did she give any indication she wanted to see the forest land her husband had inherited on the west coast of BC?'

He didn't say anything, a slight shake of the head, that was all.

I asked him then about Brian, whether he had ever met him. 'No,' he said. And then, after a pause: 'Tom wanted him to come out. He said so several times. But Brian never came. First he was in Peru, then India, I think.' The eagerness of his reply made it obvious he was glad my questioning had switched away from Miriam. 'Tom thought he'd be interested in the spruce forests here, but I got the impression that what his son was really interested in was people – people in trouble, I mean. Like the Peruvian Indians, or those being exterminated by the destruction of the Amazon rain forest.' He saw I was surprised and quick as a flash he said, 'You see, Mr Redfern, we're not ignorant of what goes on in the world even if we are just a handful of people on the edge of the North Polar Sea. There's plenty of magazines and we've all the time in the world to read – a good library, too.' He was smiling then and for a fleeting moment he seemed suddenly more relaxed as I asked him about Tom Halliday's interest in the forestry land. 'Did he talk about it?'

'He may have done.' And he added, 'I don't know. I can't remember.'

'Did he ever go down there? Before coming to see you at the mine, or after?'

'He may have done.' He gave a quick little laugh. 'Not much interested myself, you see. Trees are all right for shoring and sluicing, building a log cabin. But if you're a mining man like me you tend to think of them as something that's got to be cleared out of the way before you start shovelling the dirt.'

'You don't think he was paying for the continued operation of the mine out of the sale of timber?'

'I wouldn't know – about his business affairs, I mean.' He said it quickly, getting up and going to the cupboard for another beer. 'Sure you won't change your mind?'

I shook my head, watching him and wondering why he was suddenly nervous again.

He snapped the ring seal and took a pull at the can, standing in front of the window, his feet apart, one hand clasped on the bright red elastic of his braces, staring out at the rain. 'He was a rich man, wasn't he?' He looked at me then, his eyes brown and worried under the dark puckers of his brow. I realized then that he wanted confirmation of that. 'He was rich, wasn't he? I mean, when he came up here, he'd hire planes, anything he wanted, throwing money about . . .' His voice trailed away.

'He was broke,' I said, thinking it best to tell him the worst straight out. 'When he disappeared – ' I stopped. 'You do know that he's disappeared, don't you?'

He had sat down again, his hands clutching at the beer as though he desperately needed something to hold on to. 'Yes,' he muttered, his voice so muted I hardly heard his reply. But of course Miriam would have told him. And then he said, 'I heard it on the radio. Late one night. It was on television, too. Just the announcement that he'd gone missing. Didn't see it myself, but the radio said something about financial trouble. It was a hell of a shock, I can tell you, always thinking of him as being so rich – until these last few months, that is.'

'And it was on the media.' I hadn't expected the man's disappearance to be news up here in the far north.

'The mine, you see. Anything to do with mining is news here and he was quite a guy. You talk to the fellers up at the airport who fly the Kluane, they thought the world of him, so did Kevin McKie and some of the others around Dezadeash and the Lakeside Lodge.'

'Do you mean he impressed them, or was he a popular figure up here?'

'Oh, he was real popular – everyone he met, they liked him.'

'So if he'd come over here he would have been recognized instantly.'

He hesitated, the dark eyes suddenly wary. 'Sure. If

he'd flown in to Whitehorse, the buzz would have been half over town in no time. Most of them up at the airport knew him.'

So he wasn't here. I had vaguely hoped . . . but the RCMP would have known and they would have notified our local police. Perhaps his son was right and he was dead. 'Has Brian Halliday been in touch with you?' I asked, thinking that perhaps he hadn't headed for the Cascades, but had come up here, as Miriam had done, to see the mine for himself.

'No.'

'He's not in the Yukon?'

'Not that I know of.'

'And he hasn't written to you?'

'No.'

All the time I had been talking to him, from the moment I had knocked on the door of his trailer, I had been conscious of a block, a lack of openness. He hadn't volunteered anything. Maybe it was the north. I was used to a different kind of people. If he were part Indian, that might account for the secretiveness. But not the nervousness. Human nature couldn't be all that different up here, even allowing for a racial mix. The man was on edge. And yet he had been perfectly open about the mine. He'd answered my questions about that quite freely, but he hadn't wanted me to go there. Why? What had he got to hide? 'You mentioned a gully,' I said. 'Stone Slide.'

He nodded.

'You think there's gold there?'

'There's traces. That's all I know.' And then his eyes

suddenly brightened, his voice rising on a note of excitement as he said, 'But there's gold there, sure.' And he went on to explain how the bed of Ice Cold Creek swung away into a narrow valley with benched sides, and at the point where it swung away an old stream bed came in from the right that was all boulders, the mountain beyond gashed by a slide that had opened up a gully big as Hastings Street in the middle of Vancouver . . . 'I've panned there, in a silted pool after heavy rain brought water flooding through the gully. There's gold there all right. Now, if you could per- suade – ' He stopped there, a sudden wary look. 'That's the way we should have gone. The mountain above is heavily benched, the slide cutting right across the benches. Seven, eight years ago, that's when we reached the Stone Slide junction, but the consultant Tom called in said the prospect was too small. He advised continu- ing on up the main valley, so we kept to the Creek and in no time at all we were screening double the amount of rock and silt for the same yield.' He hesitated, staring past me to the window. 'We got most all of a million dollars' worth of equipment up there, just rotting its guts out. Now if you were to talk somebody into moving the screening plant back down to the junction with Stone Slide – Mrs Halliday, whoever it is that's got the necessary cash . . .'

He was still talking about his dream of taking a 'flyer', as he put it, at the gully area when Jim Edmund- son came back for me. He didn't get out of the cab, just wound down his window. 'Hey, Jonny,' he called, 'you got a caretaker up at that mine of yours?'

'Caretaker? How d'you mean?' He looked startled. 'Who says I got a caretaker up there?'

'Matt Lloyd. He was down at Dezadeash a few days back.'

'What for?'

'Two men from across the border. They spent a night at Lakeside Lodge. Hunters, they said, but Kevin didn't like the look of them, so he phoned the RCMP post at Haines Junction. Matt's report says they had game licences and one of our people went up the Ice Cold and Squaw Creeks to check they hadn't been hunting inside of Kluane National Park.'

'Ice Cold is just outside the Kluane boundary.'

'Sure. But he thought they might be shacked up there as a convenient stepping-off point for hunting expeditions into Park territory. In fact, as he drove past your screening plant he thought he saw somebody moving up by the hut where you have the table that does the final screening. Nobody answered his calls but there were fresh footprints in the mud by the latrine, and by the doorway of the bunk hut.'

'The huts are all locked,' Epinard said quickly.

'Yes, they were locked.'

'You say he thought he saw somebody. If he caught only a glimpse, then it could have been a trick of the light, a bird or a deer. We get deer up there.'

'That doesn't explain the footprints.'

'Could have been those hunters.'

Edmundson nodded. 'Could be.' He turned to me. 'You ready? As it is, it'll be just about dark before we get in.'

I suggested to Epinard that he get the Italian to take me up to the mine. He said he'd try, but he didn't sound very sure. 'If not, I'll drive in on my own,' I told him as I climbed into the Parks truck.

He stepped out into the rain then. 'I wouldn't do that. The track will be thick with mud, very tricky. Some nasty drops, and after all this rain . . .' His voice was lost in the roar of the engine. 'I'll be at the Lodge tomorrow night,' I yelled to him as we pulled away, leaving him standing there in the rain, his eyes wide, his mouth open as though shouting something.

A few miles and we were at the junction of the Klondike Highway where it follows the Yukon River north to Dawson. We headed west past the tiny settlement of Takhini Crossing. We were on dirt then, the tyres thrumming on the hard, impacted surface, the windscreen wipers flicking back and forth. Ahead of us, the Alaska Highway ran like a great swordthrust, the spruce a black wall on either side, the occasional log cabin surrounded by wheel tracks in a muddy clearing, a horse or two grazing on the broad road verge, that was all, the telegraph poles either fallen or leaning drunkenly without wires, the glimpse of reflector dishes at intervals marking the microwave technology that had superseded them, and the rain incessant.

Hardly a vehicle passed us, the clouds low and driving curtains of cloud mist blotting everything out except the endless black of the spruce on either side. The truck's cabinet was overheated and my eyes became heavy with staring into the void ahead, the white posts of the distance markers sliding past, the emptiness and the loneliness of the country taking hold. I began to have an odd feeling that Tom Halliday was with me, that we were in some way linked together. He would have come down this road, heading for Dezadeash and Dalton's Post, going up to the mine to fish the Creek or stalk moose in the flats.

He may have been a bit of a playboy, but he was still a part of this country. Epinard had made that clear, so now did Jim Edmundson: 'Most everybody around here knows about Josh Halliday and the Ice Cold mine.' And he had told me something then that Tom had never mentioned. A few years after his father had struck gold at Ice Cold Creek he had started taking it out through Dawson instead of Haines. This was when Silver City, the trading post at the head of Lake Kluane, was booming on the back of the placer gold fields of the Kluane Lake district. 'You can still see the log buildings,' he said, 'the old smithy, the lines of stabling, the road-house, and the barracks of the North West Mounted Police, which was what the Mounties were called then.' It was just north of Silver City that he'd run across Lucky Carlos Despera again. There'd been a fight and he had left him lying unconscious where the trail ran close above the lake. Later he had gone back with some friends and found Despera's body lying in the water.

'Dead?' I asked him.

'Yup. And the story is Despera had a daughter, by some Indian woman he'd been going with. She was born after his death and Josh Halliday sent the two of them down to Vancouver.' He looked at me then, a sideways glance – 'She married an Italian.' And he had added, very quickly, 'We got an awful mixture of races out here. There's Indians, of course, and Scots.' He laughed. 'BC was practically run by Scotsmen in the early days. When the Canadian Pacific and the National were pushed through the Rockies – Italians, Poles, Germans, Irish, all sorts of refugees helped to build those railways. Then the mines brought Cornishmen from England, Welsh miners, too.'

He had already told me that in the plane as we had been coming in to Whitehorse, but it hadn't meant very much to me then, my mind concentrated on how I was going to handle the mine manager and where I would find him. But now it added to the picture I had of Tom Halliday's father, so that Tom himself seemed to take on a new dimension.

I must have dozed off, for my eyes suddenly opened to the sound of Jim's voice saying something about Champagne. 'You want to stop for a beer or something? We're about half-way.'

'I don't mind. It's up to you,' I said. 'You're doing the driving.'

He nodded. 'Well, if it's all the same to you, I'd rather keep going. Be dark early tonight.'

Incredibly there really was a place called Champagne, a huddle of log huts corralled with some trucks in a sea of mud and entered by a timber archway with the name spelled out in large wooden letters. A generator must have been running for there were lights on in two of the huts. And then we were past it, the world empty again, and shortly after that the rain began to strike the windscreen in large blurred spots. It wasn't sleet and it wasn't snow, but the speed of our passage made the glass cold enough to freeze it for an instant.

A truck passed us going fast, four Indians in the back huddled under plastic bags. A sign with a camera design marked a bridge that was a viewpoint for visitors. The rain lifted for a moment, the shadowy shape of white-topped mountains away on either side, the highway running ahead into infinity, the black of the spruce and a solitary horse.

'Another month and this'd be all snow.'

I nodded, seeing it in my mind, a wilderness of white. 'Will it be snowing now up at the mine?' I asked.

'Could be. I don't know what height it is, but it's above the timber line, I know that.'

I tried to picture it deep in snow and myself handling a truck I'd never driven before. Was there really any point in my going up there? Just looking at the mine wouldn't make any difference to the problems that faced me dealing with Halliday's affairs.

'That Italian who works a claim on the Squaw, his name's Tony Tarasconi. Right?'

I nodded.

'You'll be going in with him, I gather.'

'If Epinard can fix it.'

'Something I learned in town this afternoon.' He hesitated. 'Maybe just coincidence, but Matt Lloyd thought there might be something in it. He'd been reading up an old police file.' He glanced at me, then went on, 'Remember I told you Lucky Carlos Despera's daughter married an Italian? Well, his name was Tarasconi.' And he added quickly, 'Like I say, it may be just coincidence . . .' He left it at that, and shortly afterwards we ran into Haines Junction. Seen in the rain and gathering dusk, with the lights glimmering on pools of water, it looked at first glance a dilapidated frontier settlement of wooden shacks and gas stations. But then we turned right, off the highway, and were into the Parks area, a neatly laid-out estate of residential and office buildings.

'Won't be a jiffy,' he said as he stopped at one of the houses and jumped out, leaving the engine running. Through the clicking wipers I could see the outline of Parks HQ, a very modern complex with an almost solid glass rotunda that had clearly been built to give a view of the mountain ranges fronting the Park. I wondered what it would look like in the morning, what the trail would be like up to the mine. I might be on my own then, the trail impassable . . . I suddenly felt very inadequate, sitting there in that warm cab staring out at the grey-black void that masked the mountain slopes. Time passed, the emptiness beyond the last gleam of light accentuated as the black of night descended on the land.

It was probably only about ten minutes before Jim came hurrying back through the rain, but it seemed longer. 'Well, that's all fixed,' he said as he jumped in. 'I'll pick you up in the morning about nine. You can then have a look at the Park museum, see the film show – you ought to see that while you're here, it's something quite special – then about ten my wife will come for you and drive you to Lakeside.' We were out on the Highway again, turning away from the Haines road and heading north. 'The forecast's good, by the way. At least for tomorrow.' And he added, 'I phoned the Lodge, but the Italian hasn't been in for a couple of days. They expect him any time now, but if he doesn't turn up they've got a four-by-four you can borrow, that's if the mine road's driveable. Okay?'

I thanked him, still surprised that he should be taking so much trouble over a perfect stranger, and a moment later we swung right onto the gravel forecourt of a filling station, lights shining dimly on a ribbed and riveted battle-wagon of a coach nose-on to a wooden building that said it was a restaurant. 'That's the Greyhound bus in. This is their meal stop-over.' He parked beside it and I saw the words Anchorage-Whitehorse.

The passengers were just starting to return to their seats as we pushed our way into the entrance, which was part shop selling souvenirs and paperbacks. They had a room spare and as soon as I was booked in Jim left me. He had two kids and he was in a hurry to get back to them. 'See you in the morning,' he called, and I stood there on the wooden steps, watching his tail lights disappear in the rain, American voices all around me, Anchorage just a bus ride away.

I picked up my case and hurried across to the accommodation unit. The room I had been given had the heating turned full on. The window looked out onto the gravel forecourt and the parked cars and trucks of other guests. Right below me was a truck with what looked like a snow vehicle in the back, the word SKI-DOO just visible. It also had something roped to the left front mudguard and largely hidden under a plastic sheet, only its legs showing like stiff sticks. It was the carcass of a deer, its dainty little hoofs shining blackly in the forecourt lights.

The Greyhound bus left and I had a quick shower before running back through the rain to the restaurant, where I had my meal in the company of what seemed an inordinate number of stuffed animals and head trophies. As usual when feeding out on my own I had a book with me, so that it wasn't until a man jogged my elbow as he pushed past on his way to the toilet that I took any notice of the two seated under an elk head in the far corner. He was a small dark man in an ex-army camouflage anorak and a peaked cap. He didn't apologize, which is perhaps why I watched for him to come out. He had the walk of a man who thought he owned any piece of ground his feet were treading on, the arrogance of his movements reflected in the hardness of his features, the unyielding set of his jaw. His eyes met mine, very briefly, then darted away to take in the whole room so that I had the impression he was constantly on the alert. His companion was bigger, burlier, his beard and moustache streaked with grey, the nose broad and flat, almost negroid, except that his colouring was lighter. He had the build, the bullet head and thick neck, and the ears of a heavy-weight boxer, and he, too, wore a camouflage anorak, but his hat was of fur with a bit of a tail. It lay on the table beside his coffee cup and his partially bald head shone in the fluorescent light.

They had already finished their meal and they left shortly afterwards. I watched them through the window as they walked across to the truck with the dead deer roped to its bonnet, got in and drove away towards

Haines Junction. I finished my meal, and when I went back to my room the rain had stopped and a star or two was visible over the black outline of the mountains. Being on my own I had drunk too much coffee, so that for a long time I couldn't get to sleep. Perhaps it wasn't so much the coffee as the thought that I was very near now to the object of my journey. Tomorrow I would be at the Lodge where Miriam had stayed, where she had written that postcard, and the next day I'd probably be at the mine. I thought a lot about Miriam. Every now and then the headlights of a vehicle coming from Haines Junction swept across the curtained windows. For some strange reason I couldn't get those two men out of my mind. One short and treading daintily, the other large, with a bullet head and a slow, deliberate walk, both of them sallow-skinned, almost dark, with a watchfulness that made them somehow different from any of the Canadians I had seen since arriving at Vancouver Airport.

It must have been well after midnight that the head-lights of a vehicle beamed onto my window, growing so bright that the whole room was illuminated as the scrunch of tyres on gravel and the noise of an engine approached. It stopped, the engine was cut and suddenly the room was black again. The slam of doors, the sound of men's voices gradually fading, and a moment later footsteps in the passageway outside, the fumbling of a key in a lock. They were in the room next to mine and I could hear their voices. They were blurred, of course, by the wooden partition wall, but still quite audible, and yet I couldn't make out a word they were saying. I must have been listening to them for several minutes before I realized they weren't speaking English, but some language that was foreign to me.

Curiosity, and the need to relieve myself, got me out of bed. I went to the window and pulled back the curtain. The truck with the dead deer was back, parked right below me, the stiff sticks with hoofs on the end looking macabre in the light of a young moon. Beyond the highway the mountains of the Front Ranges were a black wall blotting out half the sky, and high up the blackness changed abruptly to a brilliant mantle of white. I went into the toilet and shower cubicle, the voices lower now, hardly more than a murmur. And when I had flushed they ceased altogether.

The truck was gone in the morning and the sun shone out of a blue sky. I was packed and coping with a greasy plateful of bacon and eggs when Jim Edmundson arrived. 'You got a nice day for your trip to Dezadeash Lake,' he said. 'Jean's looking forward to it herself. And if the weather holds over tomorrow the track up to the mine should be okay.' Later, as we drove into Parks HQ, he said, 'Those hunters, by the way, they're booked in again at Lakeside Lodge. I checked with Kevin while you were getting your bag. So just be careful. Some of them are a bit trigger-happy, shoot at anything that moves. Last year we had a guy from Toronto come through, two guns, all the right permits, and the bugger goes and shoots a pony, says he thought it was a bear coming at him out of the bush. Can you beat it?' He didn't like hunters. 'If I had my way I'd ban shooting altogether. But up here game is about all we got to attract the visitors and keep the money rolling in. Still, if you'd come into the Yukon with a gun, I wouldn't be giving you a lift, that's for sure.'

He left me in the Exhibition Centre. 'I got work to do.' And he added, 'I laid on the film presentation. The man who runs it will be with you at nine-thirty. It lasts twenty-seven minutes and by the time it's over Jean will have the car waiting for you outside. Okay?'

That morning, with the sun shining and in the dazzling white of fresh snow spread over the tops of the mountains like sugar icing, the view from the Centre's big windows was breathtaking. So, too, was the film show. There were perhaps a dozen tourists seeing it with me, but for the half-hour I was in that darkened room I wasn't aware of them. The slides thrown on the wall-screen by six projectors took me into a world as remote as that which I had looked down on during the flight across the top of the North American continent. Ice and snow and glaciers, the thaw and running water, rare flowers opening with the sun, small animals rearing young, the aurora and the winter's grip on frozen peaks – I sat transfixed by a glimpse into something so primeval, so terrible in its cold beauty, that the human race and all its problems, the reason for my own presence here at an intersection of the Alaska Highway, everything seemed of no account, as though I were at the birth pangs of the world, living the Creation.

Then suddenly it was over and the lights came on. I was back in the Parks Headquarters, the real world breaking in on me with the appearance of a small, plump woman with a smiling face. 'You're Philip Redfern, aren't you?'

I nodded, my mind still dazed by the wild remoteness of what I had just been shown.

'I'm Jean – Jean Edmundson. I'm taking you to Dezadeash, that's right, isn't it? Jim said to take you to the Lodge there and introduce you to Kevin McKie. He owns the place.' And she went bubbling on about Jim having to go over to Destruction Bay, the Mounties having had a report of somebody with a gun stalking Dall sheep up on the mountains above Lake Kluane. She pushed open the doors and led me out to where her car was parked. 'I'd have been here earlier only I have to take my little boy to school, he's too young to go on his own yet, and then there's the usual household chores. It's nice to have an excuse to drive over to Dezadeash. It's a lovely run, all along the Front Ranges.' She flung open the car door. 'And such a beautiful morning, too, after all that rain, and the snow on the mountains. Jim says the winter will be early this year. Jim's usually right about the weather. Six years he's been a warden here. Six years next March. Before that we were with the Forestry Service. We had a lovely little doll's house of a place just out of Port Hardy on the Beaver Harbour road. Jim's done all sorts of things, but this is the job he likes best. I guess he'll stay with the Kluane Parks now, and I don't mind it – as long as he's happy . . .' She prattled on as she drove out to the Highway and turned left where a sign showed the Haines Highway breaking off from Alaska Highway No. 1, which was the road to Anchorage.

We passed a police post and a Met. station, a few other buildings, and then there was nothing but the road stretching ahead through spruce and scrub with the Front Ranges a towering 8000-foot rampart to our right, the autumn colouring of the upper slopes gold and red in the sunlight, changing to the crystal white of new snow on the tops. I wondered what it had been like when Miriam had driven to Lakeside Lodge along this same highway – had she felt any sense of unease? I wished the woman would stop talking. I would have liked to consider whether there was any real justification for the tension that was growing in me – or was it just my imagination? Why should that slide show have affected me so? It was as though I had been given a glimpse into the cold realities of the world beyond, the things I couldn't quite grasp – dust-to-dust, city lights and offices all transmuted into the glacial cold of life after death, a nuclear winter . . .

Perhaps I was tired. Perhaps it was the jet-lag that some people talk about, or was it the spirit of this far northern country entering my soul – or was it pre-monition?

'Jim said to be sure and show you our rock glacier. You ever seen a rock glacier, Philip?' The car slowed and we turned right into a parking area. 'You can just see it above the spruce there.' She pointed to a long brown gash in the scrub-covered slopes that looked like scree, except that it was heavier stuff, all boulder and rock. 'Come on, I'll show you.' She was bouncy and full of energy, her eyes alight with a girlish enjoyment of life, the whites bright with the health that radiated from her.

'Come on, this way.' She plunged into a forest of spruce on a beaten path that became a boardwalk where it crossed an area of swampland. Then we were climbing sharply up until we reached the edge of the slide, which towered above us like the decayed remains of a gigantic stone fortress. 'It moves just like a glacier, very slowly, but never really stopping. I don't understand the mechanics – boulder on an ice-polished rock surface underneath, I suppose. You must ask Jim. He'll explain.'

The boulder and rubble ran in a long sweep high above me. 'Is this anything like a placer mine after they've got the gold out?' I asked her.

'I don't know,' she said. 'I've been here six years, but all the Kluane mines are closed now. They're not allowed to mine gold or anything else, not in the Park area.'

Feet had worn a path in the rock to a viewpoint. When I reached it I could see the road stretching away to the south-east and in the distance the gleam of water. 'That's Dezadeash Lake,' she said.

Less than an hour later we were at the Lodge and Kevin McKie was telling me there was no way I could get up to the mine. 'There's been a slide and the track's impassable.' He advised me to return with Jean Edmundson to Haines Junction and forget all about Ice Cold Creek. 'It's finished. Tom knew that, so what's the point?'

'I just wanted to be sure,' I said, watching his hands. We were in the restaurant and they were gripped tight on the edge of the long counter.

'It surely don't need a lawyer visiting the mine to

confirm the gold's run out. How would you know anyway? Besides,' he added, 'everyone from here to Whitehorse, all the way down to Haines I guess, knows Jonny hasn't been running anything but a token mine for years.'

'Then I'll stay and talk to some of them.' He didn't want me there, and I wondered why. 'Jim Edmundson said he'd fixed a room for me.' He couldn't refuse, for he still had his Vacancy sign out on the edge of the highway. 'And if somebody would lend me a pair of boots, then drive me as far as the slide, I could walk the rest.'

He shook his head. 'Not on your own. Too risky. Suppose you met a moose or a grizzly ... Anyway, my truck's out of action.' He said it was probably a half-shaft gone, but I didn't believe him.

'Then I'll wait for Tony Tarasconi to come in.'

He didn't like that. 'He has his own axe to grind.'

'I haven't come all this way,' I told him, 'to be turned back now.'

He hesitated, then shrugged. 'As you please.' He signed me in then and the book showed that Tarasconi was already at the Lodge. He had cabin No. 3 and had presumably arrived that morning. Two other names had also been entered for the same date – Camargo and Lopez. 'Spanish?' I asked. 'No, South American,' he replied. 'We have quite a number of South American gentlemen come to the Yukon for the hunting.'

CHAPTER TWO

Because a lawyer spends so much of his time dealing with the vagaries of human nature, I suppose the suspicious element that is in all of us becomes highly developed. It is an exaggeration, of course, to say that McKie's reception of me was hostile, but that is how I felt about it at the time. I had the impression he was trying to conceal something from me, and if I could only get hold of a vehicle I would find no slide and the road to the mine open.

I didn't have a chance to think about it then. Jean Edmundson stayed to lunch and throughout the meal her chatter was a distraction, which, oddly enough, I missed as soon as she had gone, for she had talked about ordinary things and her vitality had been infectious. I felt suddenly at a loss then, for I was on my own with no vehicle, and in the Yukon without a vehicle is about the same as being a knight without a horse.

I walked down to the lake where planks led out to a little boat stage. A heron rose, evacuating a white jet as it struggled to gain height. The sun was warm, the ground still frosted in the shadows. Back at the Lodge I wandered round the sheds at the side. There was a truck there with a jack under the back wheel, but nobody working on it. In the generator housing I found a blond-bearded giant of a man in an elaborate Indian jacket pumping diesel fuel from a drum into a tank. I asked him about the truck, but all he said was, 'Kevin's the mechanic. Better talk to him about it. I'm just barman and general handyman around here.' His name was Eddie and when I started questioning him about the track up to the mine, he shook his head. 'Sorry, feller, I don't belong here. I only took this job a couple of weeks back.'

I went to my cabin then, which was last in the line. They were all built of wood with shingle roofs and antlers on the gable ends above a verandah. I lay on my bed and tried to think, haunted by that postcard from Miriam – *Will write you again when I get back to Whitehorse.* Why the hell hadn't she? And why had she been able to get up to the mine and not me? I felt confined and frustrated, too restless to stay in the cabin. My time here was precious and I knew I ought to be doing something. But what?

In the end I went out again, taking an old sailing anorak I had with me and the Breton cap I had bought in France. The sun was dropping now towards the mountains, the shadows lengthening as I took a track up the valley behind the Lodge, walking fast. It ran through thickets of aspen and balsam poplar and was signposted to Alder Creek and Mush Lake. I made it to the creek before turning back, and quite why I went that far I don't know, except that walking helped me to think and I had an instinctive urge to acclimatize myself to the country.

Long before I got back the sun had dropped below the ranges, the track darkening in the shadow of the trees. I heard the generator before I came in sight of the Lodge. The lights were on, several trucks now parked outside the cabins. One of them I recognized, though the dead deer was no longer roped to the mud-guard. The Alaskan registration and the ski-doo in the back indicated that they were not locals; they were definitely the same two hunters and it looked as though they would be with me for the evening meal.

They were seated at one of the windows, the big man bent over his plate, his baldish head gleaming in the lamplight, the jaws moving. His eyes lifted at my entrance and he said something, his companion turning on the instant, so that I was conscious of the two of them watching as I crossed to an empty table. By the time I was seated they were bent in silent concentration over their food again, both of them dressed in the clothes they had worn the night before, but now their calf-length boots were muddied to the tucked-in denim of their jeans. The only sounds were the murmur of the generator and the strum of a guitar from a back room. The hunters didn't talk even over their coffee, the smaller one facing me and smoking a cheroot in complete silence. They left before I had finished the main course, which was venison pie.

It was after the meal that I met Tony Tarasconi, in

the back room. It had a bar counter and a big log fire; McKie and several others were sitting at a table drinking. The Italian, wearing a bearskin poncho, was balanced on the wooden back of a chair, a guitar slung around his neck. He was drinking beer from a can while he strummed, his feet beating out the time in a worn pair of carpet slippers. At the mention of my name he stopped, his dark eyes staring, the glow of the fire reflected in his glasses. 'You the guy wanting a lift up to Ice Cold?' His voice was a little slurred, the perspiration beading his high-boned features.

'You keep out of it, Tony.' McKie's voice was quiet, but firm. 'Your claim is down on the Squaw.'

'Okay, okay, but if he's Tom's lawyer . . .'

'Just get on with the music, Maestro, and stop worrying about the Gully.' McKie said it jokingly, but I caught an undercurrent of command in his voice. And when I told the Italian I'd been given to understand it was all fixed for him to take me in, he shook his head. 'I don't go up there. Not any more.'

I asked him why, but he didn't answer, his eyes on McKie.

'You took Mrs Halliday,' I said.

There was a long silence. 'That was quite a while back. Nice lady.'

'Was Epinard there?'

'Jonny? No, he wasn't there.'

'You mean it was deserted?'

'Except for Jack-Mac.'

'Who?'

'Mac. The Indian who helps Jonny.'

'Do you remember what they talked about?'

'Course not. I had things to do, didn't I? I just left her there with him, then came back for her later.'

'How much later? How long was she up there?'

'Couple of hours. Three maybe. Hell!' he said. 'You want to know what she had for lunch, why she came visiting, where she was going next? I can tell you that. She was going back to Whitehorse to see Jonny, then taking the ferry out to Vancouver.' And he added, 'What's a bloody lawyer doing up here, anyway? You going to sell the claims?' His eyes were suddenly bright like a bird's. 'Is that it?'

I didn't answer that, but I did indicate that I was trying to find out what value should be put on the mine.

'Jonny is the man to tell you that,' McKie said quickly. And he made the point once again that the mine hadn't produced anything much in the way of gold for a long time. 'Jonny ran it at a loss. Ask anybody here.' He looked round at the others, most of them local men with woollen shirts and muddied boots. They nodded, and one of them said that whether Tom Halliday was alive or dead didn't make any difference to the mine because it wasn't worth a cent anyway. 'The claim's worked out, and Jonny knows it, poor bastard.'

A hand touched my shoulder. Eddie had come from behind the bar. 'On the house,' he said, thrusting a drink into my hand. It was a large Scotch and I looked across at McKie, who nodded and raised his glass. The log fire, a moose head above it with a huge spread of plate-like antlers, the weathered faces and the outlandish clothes – I was very much the stranger from outer space. And

Tony Tarasconi, a bright red scarf tied in a knot round his neck, his hair very black, not straight like an Indian's, but running back across his narrow head in waves, his eyes bright, his appearance birdlike. He began playing again, softly now and crooning to himself. Several times he glanced at me curiously as though trying to make up his mind about something. I had the feeling he would have talked if we had been on our own.

I bought a round of drinks and shortly afterwards I went to bed. Half dozing I heard voices, the slam of car doors, then the sound of engines fading into the night. The murmur of the generator ceased abruptly and the verandah lights went out. A moment later there was a knock at my door, and when I opened it I found Tony Tarasconi standing there. He was swaying slightly, a dim shadow only recognizable because of the guitar still slung from his neck.

'You still want to go to Ice Cold Creek?' His voice was little more than a whisper. 'I'm going back in to my claim tomorrow. I can take you up – if you like.' He sounded uncertain.

It was freezing cold standing there in my pyjamas, but he wouldn't come in, his eyes on the restaurant entrance. 'What time?' I asked.

'Ten, or a little later perhaps.'

'What about the slide?'

'I don't know. You may have to walk a bit. We'll see. But you be ready by ten, okay?' He wanted me to set off walking towards Haines and he'd pick me up. 'That way Kevin won't know I'm giving you a lift, see. Nobody will know.'

I asked him why it had to be done so secretly, but he shook his head, giving me a perfunctory goodnight and staggering off to his cabin.

I was shivering with cold by then so I didn't try to stop him. I was now so convinced that it was the Gully and the gold that might lie hidden in the ground there that motivated them all that I hardly gave it another thought. Tomorrow I would take a look at Stone Slide Gully and the Italian would doubtless make some sort of offer that would trigger off a bid from McKie and the others. Perhaps I wouldn't need to do anything about the trees Tom's father had planted. A few moments and I was asleep, and when I woke the sun was coming up over the lake in a great red ball of fire that had the whole vast expanse of water lying like molten lava against the black outline of the distant mountains over towards Whitehorse.

I dressed quickly and went out. The sky was clear, the sun bright and my breath smoking in air that had a tang of frost in it, not a breath of wind. A few hours now and I should know why they didn't want me to go up to the mine. Was there gold there that Tom hadn't known about? A workable mine? But then Miriam would have written. And if there was nothing – nothing of value . . . but the question seemed burned into my mind – why hadn't she written? It rankled. I suppose that was it. A blow to my manhood, though God knows the frosty air hadn't done it any good either, and the chill remoteness of that flat calm lake had the effect of making me seem very small, the long high rampart of the Front Ranges stretching into the distance, the autumn colours flaring lemon in the sun, and along the tops the new snow shining crystal white. It was a fairy scene, so brilliant and so beautiful that on the instant I knew why sensible urban businessmen would give up commuting for the hard life of a northern settler. I reached the lake, the heron watching me from a bed of reeds, still as a sentinel expecting snipers.

When I got back to the lodge Tony and another man were unloading a mud-spattered pick-up truck. He glanced in my direction, then deliberately turned away. The hunters' truck had gone. I went into the restaurant. No sign of McKie, but Eddie was there, and a girl who mixed cleaning with serving. I bought a couple of post-cards of Dezadeash Lake and wrote them while waiting for my coffee and a great plateful of bacon and egg and sausage. The postcards, the brightness of the day, the prospect of a drive deep into the Ranges under whose shadow I seemed to have been for so long gave me the feeling of being on holiday. I sent one postcard to my mother, the other to that tiresome little bitch I had taken with me to Brittany – why I can't think, except as a sort of flourish, like sticking a pin in the North Pole and saying That's where I am now, aren't you impressed? God, how simple, how obvious the needs of one's psyche!

There was movement on the Highway now, several trucks headed for Haines, a car in for gas, another spilling an American family homeward bound and wanting breakfast, some foresters. I sat over my coffee, watching them all, relaxed and enjoying the strangeness of it. A truck with two Indians, then more Americans, elderly and in a tetchy mood, taking their mobile home down to catch the ferry to Prince Rupert. 'There's a ride back to Whitehorse if you want it.' Kevin McKie was at my elbow, nodding towards a big estate car crowded with children that was just pulling in from the gas pumps. 'They say one more won't make any difference.'

I shook my head. 'It's too lovely a day,' I said. 'I'll take a walk and stretch my legs.'

'Okay. But I warn you, there's not too much going to Whitehorse. The visitors are pulling out of the Yukon, so most of the traffic is going the other way.' He hesitated, looking down at me. 'And don't think you can just head into the Kluane on your own. The law says you got to notify the Park authorities.'

'Ice Cold is not in the Kluane National Park,' I said.

His eyes narrowed, his voice hardening. 'Sure it isn't, but it's damn close and you could easily get lost or snowed in or treed by a grizzly, and there's hunters around, too. We don't like being called out in the middle of the night to go looking for people.'

'I'll be careful,' I told him.

He nodded. 'Okay, but you remember, we're on the edge of a lot of mountain and ice here, on the brink of winter, too. The weather can change very fast.' One of the foresters called to him, a big barrel-bellied man, braces over bright red bush shirt and a hat with a feather in it rammed tight on a round bullet head. 'Be with you in a moment, Rod.' His hand gripped my shoulder. 'If you got some idea of walking in to the mine, forget it. It's twenty-two miles down to the turn-off to Dalton's Post, and when you reach the Post it's another twenty-odd to the mine. There's two fords to cross, several thousand feet to climb and that's hard going even for a fit man. And I don't have room for you after tonight. It's the start of the weekend and we're fully booked.'

I thought for a moment he was going to press me to change my mind about the lift, but instead he smiled as he let go of my shoulder. 'If the worst comes to the worst I guess I can always ring Jean. Haines Junction you'd be all right. Have a nice day,' he added as he walked away. 'And if you want a packed lunch tell Eddie or Sue, whoever's around.'

Through the window I watched Tony Tarasconi and his partner finish the off-loading of their four-by-four truck. When it was empty, and everything neatly stacked with a tarpaulin roped over it they came in for breakfast, Tony glancing up at me as he passed beneath the window and nodding in the direction of the Highway. Considering the amount he must have drunk the night before, that he had been playing his guitar for at least three hours and had just unloaded a full truck, he looked almost effervescent with health and vigour as he came hurrying in like a bantam cock half-hidden under his poncho. 'Morning all. Is-a good morning, no?' He was grinning, teeth showing white in his wind-brown face, the exaggeration of his Italian accent, his bubbling, good humour giving an instant lift to the faces around the room. '*Fame fame* – *Io* bloody hungry. Sue! *Mio amore* – ' the girl virtually fell into his arms as he embraced her. '*Mio amore, eh*? *Due* breakfasts *gigantici. Subito, subito.* That means bloody quick and lots of it.'

He and his partner pulled up chairs to join the foresters, the noise of their talk rising perceptibly.

Breakfast was a meal that apparently went on from dawn till lunchtime. About ten I left my postcards at the counter and picked up the lunch I had ordered. Eddie produced a knapsack for me. 'When you've eaten your lunch you can stuff your parka in it. Could be quite warm by then.' He offered me the loan of a pair of boots, but his feet were a lot bigger than mine and anyway I had had the sense to wear a stout pair of walking shoes when joining the plane at Gatwick.

It was just after ten-fifteen when I left my cabin and walked on to the highway, turning right and heading towards Haines. I had my camera with me and if McKie wanted to know where I had been I could always say I had hitched a ride and walked the Dalton Trail as far as the old Post. It was the obvious thing for a visitor to do, for Dalton had established his trail as early as 1898 and the previous evening McKie had told me the Post had bunkhouse and stabling, even a two-holer toilet, all built of logs 'and still in good condition, like the old staging post of Silver City at Lake Kluane'.

A car slowed, going towards Haines, but I waved it on, happy in the freedom of walking the hard dirt of the highway, enjoying the bite in the air, the warmth of the sun. Within the space of five minutes two more vehicles had stopped to offer me a lift, and when I looked round again at the sound of an engine, expecting it to be Tony and once again finding a stranger slowing to pick me up, I thought, What the hell! If he were delayed, or McKie stopped him, I would still have time to walk the twenty-odd miles to Ice Cold and back.

The vehicle was one of those big American campers about the size of a Greyhound bus, a craggy Californian driving it, his wife in the galley brewing coffee, the smell of it filling the cab. 'Where yah going?' When I said Dalton's Post, he nodded. 'We bin in one of the camping lots close by Silver City looking for Dall sheep on the mountain there. Got some good pictures. Guess we seen quite a bit of that old Trail.' He relit the thin cigar he was chewing and started the big machine rolling again. 'You're from England, are you? Then you probably wouldn't have driven one of these – ' He patted the steering wheel. 'First time May and I have – great way to see the country. Only way, I guess. You know if the Million Dollar Fall campground is still open? That's at Mile 102.'

'Sorry,' I said. 'It's all new to me.'

'You just visiting then?' He nodded, slowing for a bend as we began a steady downhill run, his voice droning on, telling me about his family, his house, the car he had just bought and his business, which was electronics.

They were kindly people, but it was a relief when we came to the sign for Dalton's Post and I was on my own again, the sun warm on my back. I crossed the road to the well-worn dirt track leading to the mountains and in minutes the highway was gone, the bush closing in, no sound of vehicles, just complete and utter silence except for the faint murmur of water far away and the rustle of a small breeze shaking the leaves of the aspens.

The water, when I came to it, was immensely wide

for something that was called a creek; more like a river, its bed full of low banks of stone and boulder. A track had been worn to the bank, dipping down into the water, tyre marks visible on the first grey bank of shingle and coarse sand. This was the first ford and no way I could cross it without getting soaked. Ahead of me the Dalton Trail track finished in a clearing of flat grassland where the scattered remains of log huts still stood, sod-roofed and the window openings without glass. The creek swung in to run quite fast along the bank where more tyre marks led down into the water. Standing in the long grass at the edge of the swirling water I tried to visualize the Post as it had been when it was full of men and horses and wagons, and the hot fever of the gold rush. Clouds hung over the mountains ahead, but here the sun was still bright, its warmth cooled by a small breeze coming down the creek.

A horn blared and I turned to find a truck almost upon me, the sound of its engine overlaid by the murmur of the water at my feet. 'Hi!' It drew up beside me, Tony Tarasconi leaning out of the cab window. 'Somebody gave you a ride, eh? I got held up. Didn't reckon you'd have got this far.'

I took a picture of Dalton's Post, another of the fording place, then climbed into the truck. 'That's our road, over there.' Tarasconi nodded to the further bank, swinging round and heading back to where the first set of tyre marks led down to the water. He rammed the gear lever into first as the yellow snout of the truck with its radiator guard dipped down into the creek and we began crunching our way across from one grey shingle bank to another until at last we came out on the far side dripping water, the track ahead climbing steadily. 'It's all right here. To my claim is only about ten miles, pretty good going all the way. But the claim . . .' He shrugged. 'My claim not so good, lot of work, not much gold. Is placer mining, of course. (He pronounced it "plasser".) Reckon the boys who worked it before got the best of it. Anyway, I pay too much royalty. Thirty per cent is too much.' He grinned at me, his teeth showing white under the hooked nose. 'Higher up is different. Up above the timber line they got a real "plasser" mine, the benches clearly defined, like raised beaches, a good yield of pay dirt, and down near the bedrock gold that you can see.'

We were doing a steady 30 kph on the clock, the truck bucking and rearing as we climbed towards a hump of land that was like a small pass. 'Why do you do it if it doesn't pay?' I asked, and he laughed: 'Is a good question. Why do I do it, eh? You ever been a plumber?' He saw the look on my face and laughed again, beating the side of his door with his hand. 'Six months' plumbing, flushing out other people's shit – you need a breath of clean fresh air then, so six months' mining. You know Medicine Hat? No? It's down in the prairie country, Alberta, an old CPR town. Plumbing six months in Medicine Hat is enough. Okay? So now you know why I come here. Some day – ' his eyes were shining again – 'some day I strike it rich. Not on the claim I work now, but somewhere . . . Stone Slide maybe – ' He gave me a quick, sidelong glance, and then we were over the hump and dropping sharply. 'The gorge is down there.' He jerked his head to the right and a moment later he was thrusting the truck round a bend, slithering on the slime of frozen mud just surface-thawed by the sun. A side track dropped away to the right and he swung onto it, and in an instant we were bumping our way down a steep hill that looked as though in heavy rain, or when the snows melted, it became the bed of a torrent. 'Now you see the difference,' he yelled at me. 'We're on the Ice Cold track. Is bad, this one. Nobody do nothing to it for many years now. No gold, no money – that's the way it is in this goddamned country.'

He was fighting the wheel all the time, his lips drawn back in a grimace of concentration. 'Soon we get to the Squaw. Once we are back on the north side of the creek, then you see how bad a track can get without any maintenance.'

We had reached the bottom and we were in mud, the track deep-rutted. He picked a patch of hard standing and stopped. 'Guess it's time we went into four-wheel drive. Anyway I need a leak.' It was an old Ford and to put it into four-wheel drive necessitated his getting out and turning the hubs on the front wheels with a special spanner. He had switched the engine off and in the silence I could hear the faint murmur of water pouring through the gorge. We were in thick bush now, nothing visible except the green and black of balsam, aspen and spruce, the gleam of mud and water.

Less than a mile after we started again the gold of the frosted aspen leaves began to shimmer and shake to a wind we could not hear above the solid grinding noise of the engine. Suddenly there was water glimmering beyond them, a miasma of brightness. The trees fell back. We were driving along the creekside then, water rushing past, and ahead the country opened out, the creek widening till we were onto the bed of it, growling our way over rock ledges and boulders to the far side where the track was again the bed of a torrent as it climbed steeply up a shoulder of the mountain.

The crest, when we reached it, came very suddenly, the ground falling abruptly away from the reared-up bonnet of the truck, and there, across frost-sered miles of aspen and balsam, with glimpses of water in the swampland meadows, was a great gleaming barricade of high mountains. 'There you are – the Noisy Range.'

I reckoned, if the Front Ranges were 8000 feet, this mountain range that blocked the whole view to the west must be at least 16000. From foot to summit, along the whole great massive bulwark, it was a wall of brand new, whiter-than-white snow – a fairy range of infinite beauty in the hard brightness of the sunlight and against the blue of the sky.

'Summer time it goes growling and banging away any hour of the day or night.' He had stopped to lift the gear lever into normal drive. 'Now it's going silent again as the ice gets hold.' He nodded away to the left where the rounded shape of another of the Front Range mountains showed a white crest fanged with the grey-black stumps of ice-split rocks. 'We go round that till we get the other side, then through a bit of a gut and we're at the headwaters of Ice Cold Creek. So this is about the nearest we get to the Noisy.'

'Where does Ice Cold join the Squaw?' I asked.

He leaned forward, pointing across my left shoulder. 'Right down there, about a coupla miles above where we've just forded it.' He let in the clutch and we began slithering and sliding on a track that would have been good going but for the fact that we were above the treeline, nothing but small shrubs, a sort of arctic maquis, and the sun shining full on the track had melted the surface to form a viscous film of mud. 'We're swinging southerly now. Then we start climbing again and another ten minutes we'll be round that mountain and way above the timber line.'

I asked what height we would be then, but he didn't know. 'Four thousand, maybe five. We'll be into BC then and none of the Park or Reserve laws apply. You can hunt, mine, do pretty near any dam' thing. Indian country.' He laughed, his eyes gleaming as he glanced at me speculatively. 'I wouldn't mind a claim in BC.' And he added, 'You really are Tom Halliday's lawyer, aren't you?'

'Yes.'

'And Mrs Halliday's too?'

I nodded. He suddenly stopped the truck, leaning on the steering wheel, staring at me. 'And they're short of money, right?'

I didn't say anything. Here it was, the proposition I had been expecting, the reason doubtless that he'd offered to drive me up here. 'Okay, so what are you going to do about the Gully? It isn't worth a lot – I mean is very speculative. You talked to Jonny, did you?'

'Yes,' I said. 'And if you're thinking of bidding for

the Stone Slide Gully claim, then I must warn you he's interested in it, too.'

'Sure.' He nodded, still bent close over the steering wheel. 'Jonny would like to mine the Gully. But he's got no money. I have.' His teeth showed white in a quick grin. 'There's nobody else up here fool enough . . .' He let it go at that, waiting for me to react.

'Did you know Tom well?' I asked him.

'Not really. I don't think anyone could know him well.'

'Did he ever talk to you about his father?'

He looked at me hard. 'So – you know, do you?' And he rammed the truck into gear, hands clenched on the wheel as we slithered on the thawed-frost surface towards a hundred-foot drop to a little ravine where the rocks in shadow showed patches of virgin snow.

'I know he was the cause of Carlos Despera's death,' I said.

'Okay, so you know. But it didn't make any difference. It didn't affect Tom and me. He was not a very nice man, Lucky Carlos Despera. And by all accounts it was his own fault.'

'You never felt any resentment?'

'About the mine?'

I nodded.

'The luck of the game, isn't it? Lucky Carlos sold Tom's father a claim he figured was a dud. Too bad! He was wrong. The fact that he drank and gambled away the cash was all a part of the man. He salted the mine. He admitted it. That's what my mama told me – admitted it in one of his fits of drunkenness. She was only seven and her own mother dying. That's why she remembered it.'

'And Josh Halliday looked after her from then on?'

He nodded. 'Until she married my father, who was the son of one of the cable drillers that followed the line of the CPR when it was building. They were drilling for water. At Medicine Hat they found oil, not water – ' His teeth flashed. 'Daft, isn't it, but who wanted oil when the engines were fired with coal and needed water to keep the steam up? Drilling and plumbing, not much difference, eh? So he picks a settler's daughter, marries her and settles down to look after pipes and drains, what they now call infrastructure.'

I asked him again how well he'd known Tom Halliday and he glanced at me, a quick sideways glance, trying to guess from my expression what would serve his interests best. It was an oddly sly glance, as though suddenly he were a different person – or rather I was seeing the obverse of his personality. 'Did I know Tom well?' he repeated to himself. He was silent for a moment, thinking about it. 'Depends what you call well, don't it? I mean, how well does one ever know somebody else?' He paused, his grip on the wheel tightening. 'Is hard enough to know oneself, right? He was good company, I know that.' And after a moment he went on, 'Often he'd spend the day fishing the Squaw, then he'd drive up to my camp, and if he'd caught some trout, or a salmon, then we'd cook it while we had a drink. He always had beer in his truck. And after the meal we'd sing. He hadn't a bad voice. That's how much I knew him. We'd drink and sing together. But he'd never talk,

not about anything serious – he was a sort of lep . . .
what's the word for somebody you can never reach?'

'Leprechaun?'

'That's it – leprechaun. He was like a leprechaun.
So, no, I never knew him well.' He was silent then, the
mountain ahead growing larger, the track a raw line
running up the shoulder of it and swinging out of sight
on the skyline so that the nick made by the bulldozer
blade showed sharp against the blue of the sky. He
began humming to himself, a sort of protection, I
thought, against further questioning. A few minutes and
we were climbing again, the track worsening, a nasty
drop to the right. We reached the point where it began
to curve round the mountain. It was here that stone had
been quarried to pave the track in the days when it
had been properly maintained.

He pulled up. 'Don't know about you, but I need
another leak. I guess it's the cold. Coffee and cold don't
go together.' He grinned, jumping out and standing
close beside the cab. 'We could turn here,' he said to me,
looking hopefully over his shoulder. 'You agree to my
trying my luck in the Gully and we could turn right
round and be in Whitehorse tonight. There's a lawyer
there – Williams. Tomorrow it could all be signed and
sealed – lease or purchase, whatever you like.'

He zipped himself up, leaning in at the open door,
his eyes pleading. 'I want to try and do what old Josh
Halliday did, take a no-good claim, a mine that's
washed out, and before I'm too old . . .' He smiled and
shrugged, his eyes very bright, a gleam of tense
excitement. 'Maybe there's nothing there, but it's worth

a try. And that's my dream. That's always been my dream. To strike it lucky.' He waited then for me to say something, and when I didn't he climbed slowly in. 'Well, what do you say? I got money saved. It's as good an offer as you'll get. Jonny's about broke and his wife's sick. He can't buy it. And nobody else is looking for a washed-out claim. You'll soon discover that. Well?'

'We'll talk about it,' I said, 'after I've seen the mine. Maybe in a day or two, after I've talked to Epinard again.'

'That'll be too late.' He said it quickly, then pressed the starter. 'Tomorrow evening I go to Haines, catch the boat. Back to the plumbing business.' He paused there, staring at me, the pleading look back in his eyes. 'Well?'

'How far to the mine?' I asked.

'Some way yet.' He was still staring at me as though trying to make up his mind about something. 'Okay then.' He slammed the truck into gear. 'You look at the Gully, then make up your mind.'

He didn't talk after that. It was as though the matter of the Gully loomed so large in his mind now that it was out in the open between us that he could think of nothing else. He was driving fast, leaning forward over the wheel, urging the truck up the track and fighting it through the thawed-frost patches where the fine dust of usage was coagulated into a mucilage that was as slippery as ice. Twice I tried to get him to talk about his mother. 'At the time of his death,' I said, 'was Josh Halliday still supporting her?'

He shrugged and shook his head. 'I wasn't around then, was I?'

'But you must have talked to her about it?' He didn't answer. 'Was she married then?'

'I don't know. What's it matter, anyway?' And when I asked him when his mother and father had got married, he said, 'It's none of your business, is it?'

'No. But if I'm going to advise the Hallidays to lease that claim to you I need to know a little more about you than I do at the moment.'

He thought this over for a moment, frowning in concentration. 'Okay,' he said finally. 'I suppose what you mean is, how much am I my father's son, and how much have I inherited of my mother's background.' He glanced at me quickly out of the corners of his eyes, the front wheel sliding on surface slime. 'Fair enough.' He nodded. 'But I'm not sure I know the answer. Sometimes I think I'm part Indian. Sometimes I find myself thinking like an Indian, or rather the way I imagine Indians think, since I can't be certain, can I, how in any given situation my grandmother would have behaved. You know about that, eh?' Again that quick sideways glance. 'When Josh Halliday killed Lucky Carlos – ' He must have seen the expression on my face, for he added quickly, 'All right, caused Carlos to go off and get himself drowned . . . When he died, he had an Indian woman in tow. She was with him in Silver City, a young girl really, and pregnant. She was my grandmother. And when my mother was born Josh Halliday at least had the decency to send the two of them down to Vancouver, to a friend of his who worked on the CPR. They finished up at Nelson in the Rockies, my grandmother working for one of the regional track engineers. She died of TB, something that was very common amongst the Indians – the camp life, the crowded, unhygienic conditions. After that my mama went to work for a farmer's family just outside Medicine Hat. It was the Depression then, and in 1932 she goes and marries an impecunious plumber's mate.'

'How old was she then?'

I thought he was going to tell me to mind my own business. We were crossing an old trestle bridge, a rock canyon below and the tyres thudding on heavy timbers that were loose and greasy with age. He concentrated on driving until we were across, then he said, 'Twenty-three, maybe twenty-four.'

'And you were born – when?'

'Early days of the war.'

So he was older than he looked; too old, in fact, to go on playing at mining in the Yukon much longer, not if he were doing the labouring himself. 'You're married, I take it.'

'Yup, married with two lovely girls – one's twenty-two, she's married to an insurance salesman and lives in Winnipeg, the other's only just left school.' We were climbing steeply and he suddenly pointed to a white-capped peak glimpsed through a gap in the mountains away to the right. 'That's when we know we're across the border into BC. Soon as we get a view of Mount Armour.'

'We're in BC now?'

He nodded. 'That's right. The Yukon's behind us. The Pacific's straight ahead – that is if this old crate of mine had wings.' And he suddenly began to sing something about the wings of a dove. 'You like hymns, religious stuff?'

'Some,' I said.

'Me, too. Like *Jerusalem*. But that ain't really a hymn, is it?'

'No, it's a poem,' I agreed.

He nodded and laughed. 'Po'ms – that's what I like, real po'try provided it's got a swing to it.' And suddenly he was singing *Jerusalem* at the top of his voice, banging his hand against his door panel to keep the rhythm – '*Bring me my bow of burn-i-ing gold, Bring me my arrows of desire, Bring me my spear* – ' He stopped there, his hand pointing. 'The Gully. Stone Slide Gully.' Then he slammed on the brakes so hard I almost hit the windshield.

We had been coming round a bend on the shoulder of the mountain, the side of the track dropping away to a rocky streambed on our right with the V of the Gully beyond, and rising almost sheer to our left where it had been blasted out of the rock. The sun was shining straight in our faces, and suddenly the track wasn't there any more, the surface of it obliterated by a mass of stone.

The truck stopped with its bonnet right against the first big segment of rock, raw-edged and clean-sided where it had broken away from the piled-up side of the mountain. So there *was* a spill across the track, and this was it. And at the head of the valley to our right, black against the blinding sunlight, the streambed narrowed to a huge rock V out of which the water had forced a spill of jumbled rock and boulder that reminded me of the rock glacier Jean Edmundson had shown me the previous day. 'The Gully,' he said again, sitting there, staring at it.

'When did this happen?' I asked, nodding to the massive pile of detritus that blocked the track.

'Don't know.' He cut the engine and jumped out of the cab. I followed. 'Kevin or Jonny, somebody's hammered a vehicle over this lot.' He was shading his eyes against the glare, pointing to the parallel line of tyre marks climbing across the rubble to where the track showed clear again on the far side. 'Could be Jonny, or Mac maybe, that Indian of his, Jack McDonald. Looks like they been running their shovel over it. Can't tell for sure. The tyre tracks have got widened out with all the to-ing and fro-ing. And they've been down into the Gully, too. Look at those track marks.'

He thought they'd probably been getting supplies and equipment out before the onset of winter. 'First time I seen this rock fall.' He turned his head, staring up at the sheer rock wall above us. Beyond it the shoulder of the mountain opened out into a sort of amphitheatre with broad terraces faintly visible like the mealie patches of some ancient Indian civilization.

'Is that the mine up there?' I asked him. There was snow everywhere, blinding white, so that the shape of things was difficult to identify, but I could just make out what looked like the tin roof of a hut, and behind it a sort of watch tower, a gaunt skeleton of timber rimmed with frozen snow.

'Yup. That's the bunkhouse, and the spruce scaffold is where they hang their meat, up the top, clear of coyotes and bears. The mine itself, the screening plant and all the rest of it, that's just out of sight, right in the bed of the creek's headwaters.' He shook his head, his gaze swinging to the Gully, his eyes bright again, his hands literally trembling as though he were in a fever, which is exactly what I think it was – gold fever. He hadn't been up here for a long while, he said.

'But you brought Mrs Halliday up here,' I reminded him.

He shook his head. 'Not up here. They wouldn't let me come up here. Mac met me with the little tractor shovel down at the ford and she went up on that. The best way. There'd been heavy rain and the track was bad.'

'How long was she up here?' I asked.

'Four hours maybe. No, less. She couldn't have had more than two and a half hours actually up here because I picked her up at the ford again about four in the afternoon.'

'And she was going down to Vancouver?'

'That's what she said. Back to Whitehorse to see Jonny, then down on the train to Skagway. She was taking the ferry.'

'Did she say why she was going to Vancouver?'

'No. Why should she?' And he turned away, his eyes on the great V of the Gully etched black against the sun on the far side of the streambed.

'After she had seen the mine,' I said, 'was there any difference in her mood? When you picked her up again down there at the ford . . .'

'I don't know.' He was looking up at the rock fall

now, his mind on something else. 'I didn't notice,' he said and moved out onto the rubble that blocked our way. And when I pressed him, asking what she had talked about, he answered quickly, 'I don't remember – not very much, I think. She was a little cold, a little tired, I guess. She don't talk hardly at all the whole way back to the Lodge.' Then he turned away again, bending down and looking at the track marks across the fall. 'Always was trouble here,' he said over his shoulder. And then quickly, as though to block any more questions from me: 'They sure had problems here when they started getting in the new machinery. The plant itself, just the screening plant, cost over half a million dollars. You'll understand why when you see it. It's big, and it's heavy, a lot of steel. Two months, that's what it took them to drag it up here – up this track.' He looked back at me, emphasizing his point with an emphatic nod – 'That's right. Two solid months to drag it up, piece by piece, from the highway to Ice Cold. That's when they blasted this section of the track. They had to, it wasn't wide enough. They got the heaviest parts as far as that turning or loading bay we passed a couple of hundred metres back, then they stuck; they couldn't get it round the shoulder of the mountain here, so they blasted a new road, and right after that they got a scree slide from up the top – ' He nodded to the scree and rubble half choking the streambed below us. 'Two weeks it took to clear it and there's been trouble here ever since, always something falling from above when the frost cracks the rocks and a thaw sets in. It's hellish cold up here in winter.'

He was bending down, examining the sharp edge of

the rock that was almost against the front guard of the truck. 'Is newly split, this big 'un.' He shook his head, running his hand over the exposed side of it. 'Never known anything as big as this come from the top. Is like I say, the frost cracks it up, so it's mostly small stuff that blocks the road here, rubble that's half a day's work with a 'dozer to clear. This lot would take a week or more, and some of it's big, like this feller.' He straightened up, gazing across to the Gully again, not saying anything more, just standing there, drinking it in. And the sun was almost warm, though the breeze from the west had a bite to it, a damp bite, and there was a suggestion of haze building up, for this was a Pacific airstream that had come over mountains and glaciers that were almost 20,000 feet high.

'Guess you'll have to walk in from here.' He got my haversack from the cab and dumped it at my feet. 'You got some food in it?'

I nodded.

'Good. 'Cos I got things to do, back at my place on the Squaw. I'll be a little while. Okay?'

I hadn't expected this, I don't know why. I suppose I hadn't stopped to think that he wouldn't come all this way into the mountains just to give me a lift. Obviously the trip had to answer a purpose. 'I'll be all right,' I said.

'Grizzlies is all you got to worry about, but they won't bother you, not in the daytime – so long as you make plenty of noise. Just don't go wandering down the Ice Cold into the bush below the timber line. It's pretty dense down there.' He was climbing into the driving seat and I asked him when he'd be back to pick me up.

He glanced at the dashboard clock. 'Meet me here, say about three-thirty. It won't be earlier than that. I've got to drive back down, ford the Squaw, and my place is ten miles after that. Altogether about forty miles there and back, all slow going, and I got to load up and have some food the other end. Make it four o'clock, then if I'm early and you're not here I can put my feet up for a moment and have a rest.' His lips flickered in a smile, but it was a nervous smile, his eyes on the Gully, watchful now as though expecting the ghost of some long-dead miner to materialize out of the rocks. Abruptly he turned the ignition key and started the engine. 'Okay,' he said, and managed a wave of his hand and a cheerful grin as he slipped the gear lever into reverse.

But then, as the truck began to move back from the slide, he jammed his foot on the brake and leaned out of the window, looking down at me. 'A word of warning,' he said, his voice on a high note. 'There's hunters around, remember. And in Canada it's not just the deer that need to watch out for hunters. It's humans, too. Hunters get a good bag of humans by the end of the season, and there's no licence required for shooting your own kind!' He laughed and the echo of it sounded hollow among the rocks. Then he put his hand on the horn, a long blast that went reeling across the streambed and into the Gully, to come beating back at us when he stopped. He did that three times, then nodded at me. 'That should warn anyone there's somebody here. Okay. Be seeing you.'

He turned his head then and began backing the truck down the track, while I stood there watching its battered, mud-stained snout slowly disappear round the bend. Then suddenly it was gone and I was left with nothing but the sound of the engine, which rose and fell as he manoeuvred in the turning bay, then gradually faded until I couldn't hear it any more.

That was when I became conscious of the silence. It was suddenly intensely silent, only the murmur of water in the rocks below and the breeze flapping the collar of my anorak. God! It was quiet. Twenty miles down to Dalton's Post, and all around me nothing but mountains, and the ghosts of men who had worked up here at Ice Cold Creek since the turn of the century. I felt suddenly chill and very small, alone there in the vastness of the border mountains between BC and the Yukon. I shook myself, taking a grip. Don't think about the loneliness, or what happens if Tony's truck breaks down and he doesn't come back. Concentrate on assessing the potential of the mine, the value of the equipment, and on the fact that for almost a hundred years now men have been living and working up here throughout the summer months. And anyway, there was always the track out. A walk of twenty-odd miles back to the highway would do me more good than being bounced around in the cab of a truck, so what the hell did it matter if Tarasconi was late, or even if he failed to come back for me at all?

CHAPTER THREE

It must have been shortly after midday that I scrambled across the rock fall to the track on the far side and began following it round the mountain, climbing all the time, more and more of the Ice Cold mine coming gradually into view. The camp showed up first, being further ahead and higher up the mountain, two or three buildings clinging to the edge of a snow-covered bench at the head of a valley that narrowed to a ravine. To my right Stone Slide Gully was no longer a clearly etched V. Indeed, it was almost behind me now, the cleft visible only as an ugly spill of torrent-scattered boulders coming out of the cliffside, the grey of it shot through with fast-moving runnels of white water, and a rough track hugging the cliff and turning into the Gully.

That track merged with the streambed below me, climbing steadily until it joined the main track on which I was walking. At this point the valley opened out into a bare plateau of grey silt and rubble with here and there the remains of old tailing dumps scattered like the tumuli of some Stone Age mountain tribe. The going was easier when I had reached the first dump, the surface of the track packed tight and smooth with small stones and silt, everything very grey and the barren moonscape sloping gradually downwards.

I could see the screening plant then, about half a mile ahead and slightly below me, a black skeleton of steel, like some prehistoric monster all rimed in snow, a heavy tracked bulldozer parked beside it, and everywhere banks and piled-up dumps of stone, the tailings much higher down there and the thin waters of Ice Cold Creek running through them, threads of silver flickering in sunlight. That was when I stopped and took my first picture, then looked at my watch. The time was 12.23, and the thing that struck me most forcibly was how abandoned it all looked, everything so silent and still, nobody about, nothing moving, the whole scene one of frozen immobility, with the camp in the background and the Ice Cold Creek cutting down from the mountain top in a broadening ravine.

I think it was then that the first chill ran through me, the first sense of unease. It seemed unnatural, the mountains round watchful and white, an alien world from which all life had been expunged by the onset of winter. The sun had a faint halo round it, the air getting colder, and I started walking fast, up over the divide separating the Stone Slide waters from Ice Cold, the track no longer curving but running direct to the screening plant, and on the mountainside to my left occasional stunted bushes clinging precariously to life. The track reached down to the bed of the creek, the surface of it becoming very rocky, trickles of water moving frostily and the skeleton shape of the plant getting bigger until, breathless, I stood within a few metres of it and could see how the paint had peeled, the steel rusting with age. But the working parts were all right. They had been heavily greased.

It was the same with the bulldozer, the hydraulically operated pistons for raising and lowering the blade carefully protected with a dirty yellow coating of grease. Sheets of tin lay rotting on a dump of stone and nearby was a bucket and dredge attachment for the bulldozer. A little higher up the creek a crawler tractor lay abandoned and rotting, flaked holes of rust appearing in the metalwork of the cab. More machinery, cogs and wheels, a long, twisted snake of wire hawser, all dumped there and disintegrating in the cold and the wind and the snow. The whole scene was one of desolation, a shocking picture of dereliction in that lost amphitheatre in the mountains, nothing but snow-whitened rock and rusting machinery.

Obviously I had no way of checking whether the mine was really worked out or not, but I took some pictures of it just in case, and some close-ups of the screening plant, which should be worth something if it could be dismantled and got down to the Haines Highway. Then I went on up the track to where the pale wood of the pre-fabs with their tin roofs stood in silhouette above me, the track climbing very steeply here and the buildings seemingly poised on the edge of what was becoming a very steep-sided valley, poised like that teetering hut in the Chaplin *Gold Rush* film. There were five buildings in all, plus a little box of a one-holer loo. The first of the buildings was quite large, surrounded by a dump of old spare parts, bits of an engine, cooking pots, the remains of an old fridge that had virtually disintegrated, a cooking stove that looked as though it was a woodburner. The hut was locked, of course, but through the fly-blown window I could see a big engine that looked like a generator, and there was a table, sloping and ridged, with a layer of fine silt at the lower end. A panning dish lay on the table, and there was also a bucket half full of sludge. There was a small engine with a belt-drive to the table so that it looked as though this was where the final gold-sifting process had been carried out.

The rest of the buildings were about fifty metres away, all on the edge of the ravine looking down towards the screening plant. There was a cookhouse with a table and two benches, a stove, shelves and a sink that emptied straight out into a small stone channel running over the ravine edge. Close by was a caravan, chocked up with its wheels rusting off and holes in its side. Presumably it had been an early accommodation unit brought in to replace the original log cabins. I had passed the remains of three of these coming up from the rockspill. Finally there were two pre-fab accommodation units, one much older than the other, and the loo. The older of the two bunkhouses was not locked, nor was the toilet, which I was glad to see had a half-used roll of toilet paper hanging damply on the door. It was by the loo that I found the clear imprint of boots.

I don't know why it came as a shock to me when I

had already been told there was an Indian still up here looking after things. I suppose it was because all the machinery, everything about the mine, cried aloud the fact that it had been abandoned. There was new snow, fallen within the last twenty-four hours, so the imprints of those boots had been made as recently as that morning, the snow round the bunk-house all scuffed up where the sun had turned it to slush. There was a yellow mark where somebody had urinated, and a path had been trampled to the cookhouse door.

All my senses were suddenly alert as I searched the camp area, looking for tracks heading up to the mountain above or even some indication of the direction from which the owner of the boots had come. But all I could find was the marks where something big and heavy had gone down to the streambed in great leaps and bounds to be lost in the first thin trickle of water running down the valley.

The older bunkhouse had been slept in. I could smell it as soon as I pushed open the door, a fustiness lingering in the damp air. The windows had been boarded up, but the light from the open door was sufficient to show that one of the bunks had been occupied. Presumably this was where Jack McDonald slept and the other, newer accommodation unit, which was locked, had been occupied by the mine manager. There was, of course, another possibility, particularly since Epinard hadn't been paid for several months. The camp could have been hired out to a succession of hunting parties, the whole thing organized by Kevin McKie down at Lakeside. It would explain McKie's behaviour and Epinard's nervousness, and it wasn't unreasonable since it would bring in a little money and at the same time mean that the mine wasn't left entirely deserted. It would also explain Tony Tarasconi's initial reluctance to drive me up here and his warning about hunters, the three blasts on the horn. It would all be so simple for McKie to organize, an added attraction for a party visiting his lodge at Dezadeash, all those involved making a few dollars on the side.

I had my lunch sitting in the sunshine at the open bunkhouse doorway with a view straight down the boulder-strewn valley to the mammoth skeleton of the screening plant and the distant view of mountain ranges white against a milky blue sky. When I had finished I lit my pipe, the first smoke I had had since breakfast, time slipping by as I roughed in the layout of the mine in the back of my diary, the sun quite warm where I sat sheltered from the breeze. And the view was magnificent, for I was looking back into the Yukon, and across the tops of the Front Ranges it was all white, a vista of sparkling peaks and distant snowfields.

It was just after two that I took one final picture of the mine and started back down the track, headed now for Stone Slide Gully. This meant that, after crossing the divide, I had to diverge onto the track that followed the course of the little stream that flowed away from the Ice Cold watercourse. The odd thing was, I had some difficulty in finding it, so that for the first part I was literally walking the streambed, water over my shoes at times, my feet soaked. The ravine steepened, dropping sharply as it curved round the shoulder of the mountain. At last I could see the rock slide spilling out of the cliff ahead and the track clearly visible where it hugged the overhang and turned into the Gully.

There was no way, of course, I could assess the mining potential of the Gully, but once I had seen it I should at least have a visual impression and some idea of the physical problem of dealing with what looked like a heavy overburden of fallen rock. This would enable me to handle my leasing negotiations with some degree of confidence. And if it came to that, then I hoped Miriam would also have had a look at it on her way up to visit Ice Cold. If she hadn't, then I could produce some pictures to show her what the problems were.

There were problems, no doubt of that. Extraction for one. And the danger of working with the threat of another slide hanging over the place. I was under the overhang now, the cliffs bulging above the makeshift track, and all to the right of me, filling the whole cleft, a great mass of jagged rocks, some of them as big as the bunkhouse I had just left, and through the middle of it, already cutting and smoothing a way for itself, the white foaming waters of a small torrent that showed the cold green of melted snow where it lay calm in pools among the rocks. The noise of it, the dark cliffs looming – the place was so much starker than Ice Cold, the feeling of emptiness so much greater, the sun lost behind the mountains, everything in shadow, the endless rushing sound of water, a sound that seemed to grow in volume as I followed the track round into the Gully itself.

Once into this cavernous gut the full extent of the slide became apparent. The whole side of a mountain, benches and all, had fallen away, spilling over most of a great bowl that was like a crater with snow sloped all round it. Here the track cut diagonally across the body of the slide, the marks of the bulldozer blade quite clear in places. The sound of the torrent gradually lessened as I moved onto the floor of the bowl, fingers of water now coming in from all directions to meet in the centre, tumbling down through bare, ice-scarred rock to go rushing out through the rift of the Gully in one single stream.

The floor of the bowl was not flat, great outcrops of bare rock partitioning it off, the track weaving its way round massive rock features, some as big as a Norman castle. In this gloomy and sunless place there was an extraordinary sense of geological power.

After crossing one or two of the tributary streams coming down from the snow slopes above I was far enough into the centre of the bowl to take a picture looking back at the Gully, its V shape blackened by shadow, the problem of mineral extraction very obvious, all the foreground a wild jumble of rocks. Ahead of me now was the first of the big outcrops and as I picked my way towards it over the boulder-strewn surface of the track I stopped several times searching for a way to the top of it. But the rock was quite vertical and very smooth at the base, ice-worn probably; in the spring, when all the mountains round dripped melted snow, the volume of water rushing into the bowl and out through the Gully would be very considerable.

I don't know when I heard it first, for the sound of it only gradually reached my consciousness. It was like the roar of a distant waterfall or another torrent beyond the second sprawling outcrop of rock that was just coming into view as I followed the track round the base of the first. I was on bare, ice-worn rock then, water flowing across it.

Between that first outcrop and the next the water deepened in places. I splashed through it, having long since stopped worrying about getting my feet wet. Halfway between the two outcrops I stopped to take another picture; then I stood there for a moment looking around me. *Where all life dies, death lives, and nature breathes, Perverse, all monstrous, all prodigious things* . . . Those lines of Milton flashed into my mind as I wondered how on earth Tony Tarasconi, or anybody else for that matter, thought he could mine for gold here in this desolation of rock and snow, the whole place frozen solid for six months of the year, a raging fury of ice-cold water for perhaps a third of the remainder. That would leave four months, just four months out of the twelve, and the track to be recreated annually. It was a hopeless proposition and my advice to Miriam would unquestionably be to lease it out to anyone fool enough to attempt the impossible, but on a sharing or royalty basis, so that if the lessee did uncover a pocket of nugget gold she would get a share of it.

I would have turned back then, I think, but looking at the big outcrop ahead I thought I saw a way I could climb to the top of it. Its height wasn't more than fifty feet or so, and it was flat-topped, so that the long run of it should enable me to get shots covering the whole basin. The roar of the water ahead seemed to have stopped now as though the source of it had been suddenly cut off. I guessed it was some trick of the topo-graphy, the sound blanketed by the massive extent of the outcrop I was approaching.

The way up looked quite easy, except for the first few feet. This again was vertical and smooth. I picked my way slowly along the length of it, searching for a foothold, and at the far end found a sloping fault with a crack for my fingers above. I was just hoisting myself up when I heard the clink of metal on metal, and a voice said, 'Wot you do here, feller?'

I turned, my heart in my mouth. Where the outcrop ended a man stood, a rifle in his hand. He wore a broad-brimmed hat, his hair, black and straight, hanging almost to his neck, his face broad and flat, his eyes slitted and slightly puffed, the skin dark. 'Wot you do?' he repeated with a jerk of the rifle in my direction, all the fringes on his Indian jacket of soft skin dancing as he moved his hands. He was a short man, his denims tucked into calf-length leather boots stained with mud except where water had washed the uppers clean. All this I took in in a flash, his presence so unexpected I almost let go my hold on the rock. 'You must be Jack McDonald,' I said. He was obviously Indian.

'Jack-Mac.' He nodded. 'Wot your name?' And when I told him, he said, 'You got business here?'

I dropped to the ground and tried to explain, but the business of a lawyer seemed beyond his comprehension. He stared at me woodenly, and continued to stare when I asked him what he was doing down here in the Gully. 'Are you hunting?' I asked.

He didn't reply, his brown eyes fixed on mine, his

broad forehead creased in concentration. The only sound in the cold shade of the amphitheatre was the murmur of water flowing endlessly down the sloping floor of rock and silt. 'You remember Mrs Halliday visiting the mine?' I asked. 'About three weeks ago.'

'Mrs Halliday. Yes.' He nodded, his eyes watchful.

'Did she come down here?' And when he didn't answer, I asked him who else had visited Ice Cold recently. 'Tarasconi? McKie? Who?'

He shook his head, his face impassive, totally blank. I started to move round him, but he blocked my way, the gun pointing and his hand on the trigger. 'You go back plees.' And when I started to argue, he said, 'Come. I show you Ice Cold mine. Here nothing. See nothing here.' And he started to push me back the way I had come.

I think I would probably have done as he said, for I had been standing still now for several minutes and I was feeling cold, particularly my feet which were in a rivulet of water that was rimmed in ice, but at that moment I heard it again, the sound of water cascading down. Or was it? The sound had started so suddenly. The flow of a waterfall doesn't stop and start, it goes on and on. And he had moved to block my way.

A machine! 'You're mining here,' I said. 'Somebody's mining here.' And I pushed past him, ignoring the gun, moving fast so that I was round the end of the rock outcrop before he caught up with me. He grabbed hold of my shoulder, but by then I had stopped of my own accord. Barely two hundred yards away, close against the mountainside, a small wheeled tractor with a shovel attached to the hydraulic lifting gear was digging down into an old streambed and dumping the rock and silt it scooped up into what looked like a line of wooden shuttering. The man driving it was hidden by the cab. 'Who's that?' I asked. 'Is it Mr Epinard?'

'Jonny? No.'

The shuttering led from the base of a cascading torrent. I could see the water frothing in it as it rushed down the sloped wooden channel to spill out into a great box-like contraption that I recognized from old gold rush pictures I had seen. It was a sluice box, a large, old-fashioned working sluice box. No wonder they hadn't wanted me to come up here. 'Who's doing this?' I had rounded on the Indian angrily. 'Come on, you tell me. You're mining and I want to know who's behind it.'

He shook his head slowly, his face still wooden, but a slightly bewildered look in his eyes.

'Well, who?' And once again I explained that I was a solicitor and acting for the owner.

He shook his head. I don't think he understood about the legality of it any more than he knew about solicitors, but he had got the message that I was trouble, his eyes shifting to the distant tractor, then back to me as he said, 'Okay. Stay here.' His grip on my shoulder tightened and he spun me round, giving me a push that flung me against the rock of the outcrop. 'You stay. Okay?' He left me then and went loping across the wet grey detritus to where the tractor was still shovelling dirt. It stopped as he reached it, shovel poised, and a man's head and shoulders leaned out of the cab. They talked for a moment, the tractor ticking over and the driver with his head twisted round so that he was looking back at me. Finally he nodded and withdrew, the tractor engine roaring again as he dumped its load, then backed it down to the sluice box, swinging it round and manoeuvring it close against the lower end.

McDonald had moved down with the tractor and now the two of them rigged a broad loop of belting from the tractor's power drive to the big wheel on the side of the sluice. As soon as it was adjusted correctly and the power drive engaged, the sluice began to rock back and forth. Only then did the driver turn and begin walking towards me. There was something about the way he moved, the jerk of his head as he talked, but even then I didn't guess. It was not, in fact, until he was within a few yards of me, was actually speaking to me, that I realized who he was.

Even then I could hardly believe it, he was so changed. For one thing he had lost a lot of weight. All the flab of good living had gone, his body so thin he looked like a famine relief figure. And his face was changed, too, much thinner and the bones of the skull showing through, so that he looked almost gaunt, his once-black hair turned grey and so long it covered his ears. But it was the moustache that changed him most. He had shaved it off and the absence of it seemed to alter his whole face.

For a moment I was so shocked I couldn't say anything. He, too, seemed stunned. At the moment of recognition his mouth had opened, and then he just stood gaping at me, both of us standing there, saying nothing. At last he found his voice. 'Kevin should have warned me,' he murmured to himself. Then to me – 'How did you get here? Who brought you up?'

'Tarasconi,' I said.

He nodded as though he had expected that. 'So you've caught up with me. What now?'

I still found it difficult to believe it was true, and when I had recovered sufficiently to question him it was to ask him if he'd seen Miriam. 'She wrote me she was going up to Ice Cold. Did you meet her, did you talk?'

'What's it to do with you?'

'She said she'd write again. That's three weeks ago and she hasn't.' There was sudden hostility in his eyes. 'And you – disappearing like that. Why?' I knew why, of course, but that's how it came out. I was so shocked by his appearance, his face so gaunt, his eyes sunk in their sockets and his body thin as a rake as though he were suffering from some wasting disease. 'You can't hope to recover your fortunes slaving up here on your own.'

'Why not?' My words had got under his skin and he was suddenly bristling. 'There's gold up here. Why shouldn't I strike lucky like my father did? He worked up here on his own.'

'This isn't the same as the Ice Cold Creek mine,' I said.

'Why not? What's the difference?'

'Just look at it.' I made a vague, all-embracing gesture with my arm. 'The situation, the logistics, everything – it's all so much more difficult.'

'Okay, but if there's gold – ' His eyes had taken on that feverish glint that I had seen in Tarasconi's. 'And there is gold. Real good solid stuff. Nuggets. Look!' And he pulled at a piece of orange agricultural twine round his neck, yanking out a small white cotton bag tied to the end of it. 'Look at these!' He squatted down on a boulder, his thighs pressed hard together to form a safety net as he emptied the contents out into the calloused palm of his hand. 'Found these f-five days ago.' That was when I first became conscious of the slight hesitation in his voice, the near stutter Miriam had referred to. He held out his hand. 'They were all together, a little pocket in the bedrock.' They were a darkish gold and there must have been more than a dozen of them, about the size of a pea, some a little bigger, some smaller. 'And we're getting dust, of course. We're getting dust all the time.' He put the nuggets back in the little cotton bag, slowly running them off his palm as though reluctant to see them pass out of his sight.

The bag back under his bush shirt, he got to his feet. 'You haven't told me why you're here. Whitehorse isn't exactly the centre of the universe and to get up here isn't easy. You must have had a reason. And how did you know? – I suppose Miriam . . .'

'So you saw Miriam?'

'Oh, yes. But she swore she wouldn't tell anyone, and I believed her.' He said it resignedly. 'I always believed whatever she told me. It was probably a mistake.' He stared at me as though he hated my guts. That was when I realized he knew, had known all along, and I was sorry for him.

'Where is she now?' I asked.

'Vancouver. She should be in Vancouver now, or back home.' And he added with a wintry little glimmer of a smile, 'So she didn't write to you again.'

'No.'

'And you've come rushing out here to discover why? Oh, my dear fellow. This heart of mine bleeds for you.' He tapped his chest, the smile broader now. 'Come on.' He got to his feet. 'We'll go up to Ice Cold and have a brew of tea. Not much sun gets into this place and it's cold. Jack-Mac here doesn't mind. None of the Indians worry much about the cold. But I do. Used not to, but now . . .' He laughed, shrugging his shoulders as he added, 'Getting old, I suppose.' And we started back across the sloping floor of the amphitheatre, over the great rock slide and through the Gully with its beetling cliffs, and all the time he was talking, the words pouring out of him as though he couldn't help himself. He was a gregarious man who had probably been very little on his own. Now, after a month or more up here, most of the time with only an Indian for company, it was hardly surprising he was desperate for somebody to talk to.

I didn't really take in what he was saying, except that it was about the way he and Jonny and the Indian had set about trying to get at the gold they had convinced themselves lay under that massive overburden of rock in the Gully. It was talk for the sake of talking and I was only partly listening, my mind concentrated on trying to understand what was behind his extraordinary behaviour. To walk out without telling a soul . . . not even Miriam, or his son, though he was living in the house. 'If only we'd drilled, test-drilled right here when I had the money.' We were under the cliffs then, in the Gully itself. 'If there's a f-fortune, it'll be right here, deep under the slide. As it is, all I can do with the puny implement I've got is dig away at the upper end. That's the wrong end. Always work upwards, boy. That's what my father told me. And it was he who told me he'd acquired the claims over the other side of the watershed so that there'd always be Stone Slide to fall back on.' And he added slowly, his voice sounding weary, 'He knew. He had a nose for gold. He was sure there was another fortune here in the Gully. But by then he was only interested in his trees. He'd got all the money he wanted and he didn't care. And I go and listen to that fucking mine consultant.' He snorted, a little neigh of a laugh. 'And now, the best I can hope for is to do a little better than break even and pray to God I'll uncover a real deep fault in the bedrock that's jam-packed with nuggets.' He glanced at his watch. 'Tony coming back for you?'

'About four,' I said.

'Okay, you got just over an hour. He'll wait, will he?' And when I nodded, he said, 'Good. But you'd better get down there in time. I don't want him walking in looking for you. I don't want to see the bastard.'

'Because he brought Miriam in?'

'That and other things. Bringing you.'

'He knows you're here, does he?'

'I don't think he knows. But Kevin says he suspects. He's a scheming little shit, that man. You know he's descended from Lucky Carlos Despera on his mother's side.'

'Yes.'

'A chip off the old block.' He laughed, but without humour. 'He can't forget that his grandfather had a fortune in his pocket and threw it away. He wants to get his hands on the Gully, and if he did Kevin says he's got friends, South American he thinks, who'd give him the backing.'

'They'd finance him?' There was no doubt about it, they all believed there was gold there, but looking back at the sheer weight of rock that had been sliced off the mountain by that slide I thought financing it would be taking a hell of a chance. 'It would cost a great deal,' I murmured.

'Sure. But in this sort of situation, the Gully being like the neck of a bottle, the rocks of the slide the cork . . .' He paused, his voice almost choked. 'It could be another B-Bonanza.'

'It could equally be nothing at all,' I said sharply, trying to bring him back to reality.

'Oh, yes.' He nodded. 'Life's like that, isn't it? Everything a gamble. One man smokes and drinks all his life and lives to a hundred; another doesn't smoke and gets cancer at fifty; or a fellow doesn't drink and dies of a liver complaint. I was at school with a boy who died at sixteen. Just a gamble.' He stopped then. 'Like this thing was when Josh arrived and dam' near killed himself trying to prove what everyone told him was impossible. When they told him that, he'd point to the benches that terrace so many of the mountain slopes here and get on with shovelling dirt. And he did it with pick and shovel and his own sweat, not like me, having it easy with a machine.' We had reached the watershed then and were looking down towards Ice Cold and the skeletal shape of the screening plant.

I didn't say anything and he added, pointing away to the right, towards the headwaters of the Ice Cold Creek, 'All those benches you see up there above the camp on the shoulder of that mountain ... There's bigger benches on the mountain slopes that ring the basin inside the Gully and a hell of a lot of them came down in that slide. Christ! I'd like to wring that bloody little consultant's neck. But I hadn't read up on the geological background of placer gold deposits then. Hadn't any need to.' He laughed, that same mirthless, neighing laugh, and after that we walked on in silence until we came to the camp. 'What'll it be – tea? Or would you like something stronger? I've a bottle of malt I keep for special visitors.' He smiled thinly.

'Tea,' I said. There was a cold wind blowing up here and it was such a comforting thought I could almost feel the warmth of it in my mouth.

He took a bunch of keys from the pocket of his old corduroy trousers and opened the door of the cookhouse. It was well stocked, shelves full of canned food, a sink and draining board, a fridge, a stove with an oven below, and at the other end of it a bare spruce table and two benches. 'Pretty basic,' he said, 'but once you get used to it . . .' He filled the kettle from a tank clamped to the wall. 'You've heard from Miriam, you say. When?'

'About a month ago,' I said. 'A letter from the Sheffield House Hotel in Whitehorse, then a postcard from Lakeside Lodge.'

'But nothing since.'

'No.'

He sighed, striking a match. 'For a moment – just for a moment I hoped . . .' The stove, like the fridge, was run from a large butane gas cylinder, and when he'd lit it and put the kettle on, he nodded to the table. 'Sit down. Since you're here there's some questions . . .'

I sat down, watching him as he got the tea things ready. It was extraordinary how changed he looked without the moustache, and the hair long and grey. I made some comment about it and he said, 'You must have known I dyed my hair. If you're married to a woman much younger than yourself, then you try to keep up appearances, don't you?' He said it sadly, fumbling in his pocket. 'You got a cigarette?'

I reached for my haversack, found a packet and passed it to him. I also found my pipe and began to fill it. 'You wouldn't know about keeping up appearances – yet,' he went on. 'You're young and you just move in, like a young stag when the rutting season's on. I had a feeling –'

'It was only once,' I said quickly.

He laughed, showing his teeth in what was almost a grimace. 'But you'd made your mark, eh? She wrote to you.' He was silent then, standing there staring at the flame under the kettle, his thoughts seeming to drift. 'Why didn't you stop her?' he asked suddenly.

'Stop her?' I repeated, wondering what he meant.

'Yes,' he said, quite angrily. 'Stop her from coming out here. I'm in enough trouble – '

'Why should I?'

He cocked his head on one side, listening. 'Did you hear anything?'

'No,' I said.

'I thought I heard something.' He moved to the open door, leaning against the jamb of it, his body very still.

I couldn't hear anything, only the gentle murmur of the stream below. 'For God's sake shut it,' I said. The place was getting like an ice-house. 'How did you leave England?' I asked. 'By boat?'

'By boat, yes. The ferry from Felixstowe across to Rotterdam, then a flight to Toronto out of Schiphol.' He held up his hand. 'There! Did you hear it?'

'What?'

'The clink of a stone.'

'It's the stream,' I said.

He listened a moment longer, then nodded. 'Yes, the stream – you're right. Living virtually alone in a place like this, it gets on your nerves in the end.' He started to shut the door, but then he said, 'I'm going to get myself a woolly.' He was shivering with cold. 'I build up quite a sweat operating that shovel. Do you want to borrow one?'

'No, I'm all right.'

He went out, shutting the door behind him, and I sat there, wondering about him and about what advice I was going to give him now that I'd stumbled on his hideout. I had been cold standing in the Gully, but I had my anorak on and the walk up to the camp had warmed me. With the door shut the cookhouse was already beginning to get the chill off it as the gas flared under the kettle.

He was gone longer than I had expected and the kettle was just beginning to whistle when the door burst open and he came in, a paper in his hand, his face quite white, his eyes staring. 'Did you leave this? I found it under the door. Did you slip it there?'

I stared at him, wondering what the hell he was talking about, why he was so upset. 'Of course I didn't.'

'Who then? Tony? Where would he have got it?'

'What's the trouble?' I asked.

'Miriam.' He slammed the door shut, coming across to the table, leaning over me. 'You sure you didn't s-slip it under the door?' He held an envelope out to me. 'That's her writing, isn't it?'

It was addressed: Tom Halliday, Ice Cold Mine, via Haines Junction, Yukon, Canada. 'You know her writing better than I do,' I muttered, knowing it was hers and wondering how it had got there. 'Tony couldn't have put it there,' I said. 'I'd have seen him.' And I told him my movements.

'Who then?' His voice trembled, a note of panic almost.

'Where is she?' I asked.

He hesitated. Then suddenly he thrust it at me. 'They've got her, the bloody scheming bastards. They've got her hidden up somewhere, and now . . .' His voice was breaking, his face screwed up, on the edge of tears. 'Read it,' he cried. 'You read it. Then tell me what I ought to do. My God! I never thought . . .' And he suddenly collapsed on to the bench beside me and buried his face in his hands.

The kettle had been whistling urgently and he got up again, slowly. 'If it wasn't you slipped it under the door, and it wasn't Tony – who? Do you think that sound I heard . . .?' But he shook his head. 'I'd have seen anybody – anybody as close as that.' I don't think he expected me to answer; he was really asking himself the questions as he reached for the tea tin, turned off the gas and poured water into the pot, his movements those of a man in a daze. 'Sugar?'

I shook my head, staring down at the envelope, the letter underneath it a scribbled scrawl in a neat sloped hand. It was Miriam's writing all right:

Darling – I was picked up in Vancouver and brought here by boat almost a fortnight ago, just as I thought I had found you a backer for your Stone Slide project. Enclosed is my wedding ring as proof I am held here, surety apparently that you will carry out instructions already given you. 'More personal reminders' of my presence here could follow if they don't hear from you soon. I don't know who these people are or what their purpose is, but for God's sake do what it is they want and get me out of here. You are mixed up in something you didn't tell me about and I am very, very frightened. Love – M.

A steaming mug of tea had appeared at my elbow and I drank it gratefully, the scalding liquid almost burning my mouth as I read that wretched little note through again, still finding it almost unbelievable. And it didn't sound like Miriam. 'Where's the ring? She says she enclosed a ring.' He held it out to me, a platinum circle that gleamed dully in the light from the dirty window, the pattern so worn it was almost smooth. Probably it had been dictated to her, the last part anyway. 'Is she right?' I asked. 'About you being mixed up in something? You said something about being in trouble.'

'Did I?' He had sat himself down beside me. 'What do I do now? What the hell do I do?' He was talking to himself again.

'You'd better tell me what it's all about,' I said, still staring down at the letter, wondering how it had got here, where it had come from. Where had she written it? They'd taken her there by boat, she said. But almost anywhere on the Canadian coast could be a boat journey. And who were they? 'Well?' I asked.

He shook his head, not saying anything.

'You're in trouble and you don't know what to do. How the hell can I help you if I don't know what the trouble is?' His hands were trembling, his eyes wide and staring blankly. He had put on a thick polo-necked sweater, but he was still shivering, his body seemingly stricken with ague, his mind gone into some sort of limbo of its own.

I put my hand on his arm, gripping it hard. 'Somebody is holding your wife hostage – who? Do you know?' I had to shout the question at him again before my words registered, and all he did was shake his head.

'Why?' I shouted at him. 'What do they want you to do?'

He shook his head again, not answering.

'You said you were in trouble – what trouble?'

He rounded on me then, his face distorted. 'Shut up and let me think, can't you? I got to think. I got to think – what to do.' And suddenly he was crying, his nerves all gone to hell and his shoulders heaving to the sobs that shook his whole body.

I picked up the letter, thrusting it under his nose. 'Read it,' I said. 'Read it again. It's your wife, and she's in danger. Have you got yourself mixed up in something political – extremists?'

'Political extremists?' He looked at me, staring wildly and neighing that silly laugh of his.

'Terrorists then?'

He just stared at me. 'You d-don't understand,' he breathed.

'It's you that don't seem able to understand,' I told him, waving the letter at him. 'This is Miriam – your wife. She's in danger, and she's asking you for help.'

'Later,' he mumbled. 'We'll talk about it later.'

'I won't be here later.'

'Yes you will – I need you.' He was still mumbling, but his voice had taken on a higher pitch. 'And M-Miriam – she'll be all right.'

'Will she? How do you know?' And once more I asked him what it was they wanted.

He shook his head, and when I tried to insist, he turned on me, his voice suddenly losing all control as he screamed, 'You stupid little fornicating bastard, do you think I don't care? I'm worried sick, so shut up. Shut up, d'you hear, and let me think. Miriam will be all right. I'll see to that – somehow.' He said that slowly, getting to his feet and pouring more tea.

I looked at my watch. It was almost three-thirty. But when I said it was time I started back, he insisted I stayed the night. 'There's spare bunks, plenty of food, and I need you, Philip.' He was pleading now. 'I really do. I need you. There's legal matters . . .' His voice trailed away as he finished his tea, gulping it down as though he was half dead of thirst. 'It's the Cascades, you see. The BC property. That's what they want.'

'Wolchak?' I asked.

'Wolchak?' He shook his head. 'I don't know who it is.'

'He mentioned a man named Mandola.'

'You saw Wolchak, did you?'

I nodded.

'And that's how you know about Mandola?'

'Yes.'

'Mandola's one of them – but whether he's the boss man . . .' He gave a little shrug. 'More tea?'

I shook my head.

He got up, taking the mugs to the sink. 'I'll tell Mac to get across to the main track right away. Tony can let Kevin know you'll be down tomorrow.' He had reached up to a line of wall hooks hung with old anoraks and mud-stained overalls and oilskins, taking down a hand transmitter and moving to the door. 'Won't be long,' he said. 'Works better a few hundred yards away on the trail to the Squaw. We're a bit blocked here for short-wave transmission into the Gully.' He shut the door and I was left on my own, wondering whether to stay on with him or go down with Tarasconi. There was still time if I went now. I could be back at the Lodge and phoning the police by six at the latest.

But would that help Miriam? I picked up that note and read it again, seeing her shut up in some little hut somewhere on the coast of BC, or it could be in America, across the Strait of Juan de Fuca in the State of Washington. If only she had been able to tell us what sort of a boat, how long the passage. As it was, I had nothing to tell the police. Her note would merely alert them to Tom's presence in the Yukon, and it wasn't for me, his solicitor, to do that when I knew he was in trouble.

I got up and went to the door to knock out my pipe. The wind had dropped and it was less cold. I could see him standing in silhouette against a westering gleam of sun where a bench end slipped over the shoulder of the mountain, the walkie-talkie close against his face, the aerial antenna standing like a stalk growing out of his head.

I refilled my pipe, still uncertain what to do, knowing only that it was Miriam I had to consider, but quite unable to think of anything I could do, except contact the authorities. I saw Tom push the aerial down into the body of the transmitter and start back along the track towards me, and I think at that moment I had almost decided to keep my rendezvous with Tony and get back to the Lodge and a telephone as soon as possible. But then he reached me, his gaunt face drained of colour, a scared look in his eyes. 'Two men,' he said. 'Both with rifles. Mac saw them going down the main track.'

Two! 'What did they look like?' I asked.

'One big, one small. That's what he said.'

'But you can't see the main track from your sluice box.'

'He was in the mouth of the Gully checking on a small rock fall. Happens all the time. He saw them quite clearly.'

'Did they see him?'

'No, he's quite sure they didn't. They were in a hurry, walking fast.'

I told him then about the two hunters staying at Lakeside. But when I asked him whether the names Camargo and Lopez meant anything to him he shook his head. 'Mac's coming up here now, just as soon as he's had a word with Tony.' He said it slowly, almost hesitantly. 'You can't be sure,' he murmured. 'But if Tony brought them up here . . .' And then suddenly he asked me the nationality of the two men staying at the Lodge.

'South American,' I said.

We were back in the relative warmth of the cook-house then and he turned in the act of closing the door, staring at me. 'How do you know?' He put the question so reluctantly I had the impression a South American connection was something he didn't wish to know about.

'Kevin McKie,' I said. And then I asked him where else he had been in South America besides Peru.

He shook his head, looking strangely bewildered, so

that I had to repeat the question. 'All over,' he said. 'Martina and I, after we were married . . . You know about Martina, do you?'

'Miriam told me.'

He nodded. 'Of course.'

'She told me after you had disappeared,' I said.

'So the two of you – ' he shrugged. 'Oh well, I suppose it doesn't matter now.' He turned away, shaking his head and moving towards the table where the letter and its envelope still lay. 'But to answer your question, we sort of did South America – Ecuador, Colombia, Venezuela, the old Guianas, Brazil and back through the Argentine, Chile and Bolivia. Quite a trip!' He was standing there, talking to himself, his mind in a daze and trying to lose himself in the past. 'She was a bitch, of course. Miriam will have told you that. But, oh boy!' He gave that neighing laugh. 'If the devil came to tempt me with a wish, that's what I'd want – that trip all over again . . . riding, surfing, all those Indian ruins, up the Urubamba, and the hot nights . . . Jeez! That woman knew how to do it. But yes, she was a bitch, God rot her!'

I didn't press the matter further, knowing I had all evening to question him. But when Mac arrived, and by his description confirmed the identity of the two men, I began to regret my decision to stay. It was too late then, of course. He had found Tony waiting in the quarry below the rock fall and had told him I wouldn't be going back to Lakeside that night. He had also asked him whether he had seen the hunters or had seen any truck on his way up from the ford. 'Tony not liking my question, tell me bugger off. Then he drive away.' All this said with a smile, though his face was otherwise without expression, the tone of his voice quite impassive.

I have tried several times, while writing this account of what is quite the strangest period of my life, to assess my reactions and behaviour. But all I can say is that it was like being dealt a hand of cards, never knowing what would turn up, only that the joker had to be Miriam. Without her involvement I am quite certain my own actions would have been simple and straight-forward. As it was, they appear to have been about as unpredictable as Tom Halliday's. A legal training had not equipped me to handle matters that did not have a precedent in law. Terrorism, or something akin to it, was quite outside my experience and beyond my ability to handle. I was over six thousand miles from my home base, in a strange country with no real knowledge of either gold or trees. The only thing I think I knew at the time was that Miriam meant more to me than anything else.

I can't explain it. I was up there in the Yukon, on what for desolation might be described as the roof of the world, alone with her husband and a North American Indian. I hadn't had an affair with her. Just that one brief sexual encounter, a few casual meetings, mainly social, a dinner party at their house, that interview in my office, then one letter and one postcard. And yet . . . all that evening I could see her as clearly as if she were sitting there with us, her glinting Titian hair, the wide eyes that were almost turquoise, the cheekbones and the nose, that mouth – lips that I could still feel.

And her husband moving constantly, unable to settle, his nerves taut, his face even more haggard and exhausted than when I had first seen him down there in that bowl beyond the Gully. He wouldn't tell me what he'd got himself mixed up in. He wouldn't talk about his troubles. He didn't trust me. I think that was it. There were legal matters, connected he said with the BC property . . . He needed my advice, but he wouldn't confide in me. And time was passing.

We had a meal – bacon, eggs, some tinned beans, a sort of bannock of flour and honey, more mugs of tea. It was after this, after he'd been across to the bunkhouse to 'freshen up', that his manner changed, the moroseness seeming to fall away from him. He suddenly became very talkative, his face slightly flushed, his eyes much brighter. I thought perhaps he was a secret drinker, but then he suddenly jumped to his feet, reached into the cupboard above the sink where Mac was doing the washing up and produced a bottle. 'It's malt. That's all I got. I keep it for Kevin. He likes it. I hope you do.'

'What about you?' I asked.

'Me?' He smiled at me crookedly. 'I have my own poison. Didn't Miriam tell you?' He picked up an undried mug from the draining board, slopped some whisky into it and handed it to me. 'Glad you came. The girl's in trouble – my fault. I gave her the names of a few people I know in Vancouver and Victoria, men with money I thought might like a bit of a gold gamble.' His eyes gleamed almost wickedly. 'That shock you? Women are sometimes better at that sort of thing . . . I've seen it so often, all over the world, even Muslim women.' And he added, 'They must have been keeping tabs on her. On you, too. Wolchak probably. And when he told them you were on your way out here – a lawyer . . . Reckon that's what got them worried.'

His words had been strangely disjointed. But not his thoughts. They were quite logical and clear, and they were centred on Tony Tarasconi. 'I should have known what the little bastard was up to. But I didn't, did I? I didn't know he was mixed up in that sort of world, had contacts . . .' His mouth clamped shut. 'God! I've been so blind. But how could I guess? I don't know the man really. He was half the year away in Medicine Hat or wherever, and I was only here occasionally. How would I know who his friends were? There's South American finance here and there in mines all over the Yukon, Brazilian mainly. When Kevin told me he might have backing it never occurred to me . . .'

He sat down suddenly, facing me across the table, talking of an old trail that ran down the east side of Ice Cold to a ford across the Squaw just above the point where the two creeks met. Tarasconi's claim was on the far side of the Squaw, a little downstream of the ford. If the two South Americans were at his camp, then we could question them there; otherwise we'd borrow Tarasconi's pick-up and catch up with them at Lakeside. 'Then we'll drive over to Whitehorse – maybe Jonny will have heard something, otherwise we take the ferry south and fly into the Cascades.' He had friends, he said, among the floatplane pilots. 'I'll scrounge a flight, and when we've talked to Thor Olsen . . . Well, we'll see. He's half Finn, half Lap. He looks after the logging camp, a sort of caretaker. His grandfather came over with the reindeer they drove up the Dalton Trail to Dawson in an effort to relieve the famine. That was the first year of the gold rush. He'll know if anything odd has been happening down around the Halliday Arm. That's the inlet leads up to the Cascades.'

By then he had convinced himself that Miriam was being held either at the logging camp or at one of the outlying float-houses. 'They're built on logs and towed around,' he said. 'Sort of water caravans, but all solid fir and cedar logs.' He wouldn't tell me why he thought she might be there. Every time I broached the subject he would fall silent, a sudden moroseness coming over him, as though a curtain had been clamped down blanking out his mind.

We turned in shortly after nine with an alarm clock set for three in the morning. He had produced an old sleeping bag for me, but I still kept my clothes on, for the blankets on the bunk opposite his were damp, the air in the accommodation unit little above freezing. But it wasn't the bitter cold that kept me from sleeping. It was the knowledge that I was involved in something I didn't understand and going along with a man who not only refused to take me into his confidence, but seemed frightened half out of his wits. I was thinking over the sequence of events since I had caught the CP Air flight to Whitehorse, that note from Miriam running round and round in my head, and then I was woken with the light of a torch in my face and his voice saying, 'Wake up! The alarm's just gone.'

Tea and biscuits, and then we were off. It was cold

and very still, the sky clear and the stars diamond bright, the trail quite visible as soon as our eyes became accustomed to the night. It followed the contour line of the mountain, running above the placer plant, then dipping quite sharply. Soon we were below the timber line, small sticks at first, but the scrub becoming gradually taller and thicker. Tom was leading, a rifle slung over his back. 'Just in case we meet a grizzly.' And he had grinned at me, his eyes gleaming and his teeth white in the starlight. Later, as the timber became taller and the vegetation more dense, we had to use our torches. He had said it was about six miles and shouldn't take us more than two hours. In fact, we reached the Squaw just after five, the water quite shallow where we forded it, and ten minutes later we were approaching the Tarasconi claim along a well-developed track.

It was the fire we saw first. We turned a bend and the darkness ahead glowed with the orange flicker of flames. The camp was beside the grey shingle bed of a tributary stream. There was a battered-looking caravan jacked up on boulders, a log store shed, an old tent with a small bucket tractor close by, and two pick-up trucks side by side and facing downstream. The camp was virtually dismantled for the winter and they were sleeping in the open. We could see their figures, three of them rolled tight in their sleeping bags close beside the fire.

Tom stopped. 'So he did bring them here.' Again that hesitancy and his voice trembling. His hands searched his pocket. 'You got any paper on you? A dollar note – anything?' He had pulled me back into the shelter of some small spruce, his tone urgent.

I was shivering then, my feet wet from fording the Squaw and very cold. A niggling little breeze breathed icily from off the heights. I felt in my hip pocket and pulled out the wad of Canadian currency I had obtained in Vancouver, wondering what the hell he wanted money for. 'How much?' I held it out to him.

'Anything – doesn't matter.' He seized a ten-dollar bill, his fingers trembling; then he was gone, into the bushes. I saw the flash of his torch, and after a while I heard him sniffing. It was more like a snort really, then silence. A moment later he emerged. He didn't say anything, just handed the note back. It was curled up now as though it had been rolled into a tight tube.

It dawned on me then – 'Cocaine?' I asked him.

He gave what sounded like a giggle. 'A three-and-three, that's all, and it's well cut. You want some? I've still got a little left.'

'No,' I said. 'No, of course not.'

'You missed something. Better than alcohol if you're properly supplied and do it right.' This in a low whisper, the words running together.

'You trying to get high?' I asked.

'Of course.' He gave that little giggle again. 'What do you expect? Weeks of solitude, then you – and right on your heels those two bastards. And now . . . I've never done anything like this before.'

'Keep your voice down,' I whispered. It had become

slurred and very excited. 'What haven't you done before?'

'Never mind. Just do as I say.' His teeth showed and I sensed a wildness in him, his breath smoking in the raw air. 'Come on now. Let's get it over with.' His hand had fastened on my arm, his grip convulsive as he dragged me forward.

'What are you going to do?' I was scared of him now.

'Talk to them. I've got to talk to them.' And suddenly he had moved out into the open, a crouched run that took him across the banked-up debris of the old streambed. He had almost reached the fire, and I was following him, when one of the recumbent figures stirred, sat up, then began struggling to free his arms from his sleeping bag. It was the smaller of the two South Americans, the man named Lopez, and he was reaching inside his anorak when Tom yelled, 'Don't move!', repeating it in Spanish – '*No se mueva!*'

I stopped then, seeing the scene like a film in slow motion, the three figures lit by the red glow of the embers and all of them in movement, Lopez with his hand coming clear of his anorak, the dull gun metal glinting redly, the big man's bald head like polished ivory as his hand closed on the rifle beside him, and Tony Tarasconi, his eyes wide and his mouth open. And then the sharp crack of a gun, the smack of a bullet striking sparks on a rock and the whine of its ricochet, all the figures suddenly frozen into stillness and Tom's voice shouting wildly, 'Drop it! *Suéltelo!*' And then to me, sharply over his shoulder – 'Get their guns. Quick. And don't get in the way.'

He was round the fire then, and while I was retrieving the gun Lopez had dropped, he prodded the big man in the belly, demanding to know who had sent them. 'Did you bring this?' He pulled Miriam's note from the pocket of his anorak, thrusting it under the man's nose. 'Well, did you? It was left at Ice Cold, pushed under the bunkhouse door some time yesterday.'

It was then that the little man jumped to his feet with the speed of a cat, hands clawing and gripping hold of my arm. The next thing I knew his shoulder thudded into my ribs and I was flung to the ground. I looked up and he was standing over me, reaching down for the gun I had dropped, the big man stepping back and Tom turning. I saw it all as an instant flash, the three of them all caught in violent motion, their faces lit by the fire. Tom let out a yell, something in Spanish, the barrel of his rifle slamming home, his knee coming up as the big man bent double with a gasp. There was a gurgling cry, the body writhing on the ground an arm's length from me, the dark, bearded face contorted with pain, the bald head running with sweat. 'Hold it! Don't move!' The rifle was pointed at the man's belly, Tom's hand on the trigger, and the man above me frozen into stillness as the words were repeated in Spanish. 'Get his gun.' And when I didn't move, Tom yelled at me, 'Get it, d'you hear!'

I scrambled to my feet then and grabbed at the man's arm, wrenching it from his grasp, a nasty little black-metalled automatic. As I slipped it into my pocket Tom bent down, his rifle still jabbed into the big man's belly; he zipped open the man's parka, reaching down for the automatic in its armpit holder. I felt suddenly dazed, conscious of Tony Tarasconi, lit by a flicker of flame, standing frozen into stillness halfway to the trucks. And all the time Tom talking, questions in Spanish, the barrel of his rifle thrust into the body at his feet, the man mouthing replies.

Finally he stood back. 'You know about knots. Tie them up,' he told me and called to Tarasconi to get some rope. He hadn't got the answers he wanted and he was high on coke, his mood dangerous. But there seemed no alternative so I did what he asked, Tony handing me the ropes, his hands trembling and his eyes so large with fear they seemed to be starting out of his head. As soon as they were roped, Tom turned the big man over on his side, and with that crumpled paper in his hand, began yanking on the rope linking wrists to ankles, repeating over and over again – '*De dónde lo consiguió usted? Quién les mandó? Camargo – Digame dónde – dónde – quién les mandó?*' Finally he turned his attention to the other man. 'Your name Lopez?'

The little man nodded and began to squirm away.

'*Ese mensaje. De dónde lo consiguió? Quién les mandó?*' He repeated the question several times. Then suddenly he went over to the fire, selected a half-burned length of wood and turned back to Lopez, who screamed, '*No. No. No lo haga usted.*'

'You can't do it.' My voice sounded hoarse.

He rounded on me then, his eyes blazing – 'So her life doesn't rate against this little rat. You don't care –'

I started to protest, but he interrupted, speaking very quickly – 'All right then. Let's see you do it.' And he held the glowing brand out to me. 'Better still, pick the little shit up and dump him in the fire. Well?' He laughed, watching me. 'So you don't care where she is. Well, I do – ' And he turned, thrusting the ember down towards the man's face.

'No lo sé, no lo sé.' Lopez was suddenly pouring out an incomprehensible spate of words. He had rolled over and was facing Camargo. Tom joined in, a babble of voices, the three of them all talking at once, their faces lit by the glow of that ember, and I just stood there. I wasn't thinking of the two men lying on the ground. I was thinking of Tom, what he had been through to bring him to this pitch of desperation . . . And Miriam. What the hell had he got himself mixed up in, that two gunmen had come north to the Yukon looking for him, bringing him that note from his wife. Bogotá . . . There was Lopez mentioning it again, the big man answering him. Bogotá was Colombia, and Colombia was the land of Raleigh's Eldorado. 'What are they saying? Where is she?'

Tom shook his head, turning away in disgust. 'He doesn't know.' He tossed the ember back into the fire. 'Neither of them know.' His voice sounded bitter and despondent. 'Let's get going. You got the key of their truck?'

'No.'

He bent over Camargo, searching his pockets. Tony began to slip away into the shadows, but he stopped him. 'The keys of your truck, too.' He took them and stood for a moment staring down at the two Colombians. 'They were hired in Bogotá and flew up to San Francisco. That's where they were given Miriam's note. In a bar down by Fisherman's Wharf. A man they'd never seen before and he didn't give his name. Handed them the note and gave them verbal instructions, details of an account they could draw on at the Bank of Canada office in Vancouver, and that's about all they can tell us, except that they were to report my movements; yours, too, if you came up here.' He turned to Tony. 'You're coming with us. A nice long walk, and while you're walking, and those two hoodlums are chewing on their ropes, you can be thinking about the Gully and how it's got you into dangerous company, eh?' He was laughing.

'Who do they report to?' I asked.

'Just a telephone number.' He repeated it and I wrote it down, a Bella Coola number.

'No name?'

'No.'

'And the people who hired them didn't say why they were being sent up here?'

He shook his head. 'They don't know anything.' He was standing there, looking dazed. And yet it seemed obvious. 'It's the Gully they want. Isn't that right?' I asked. 'That second claim your father acquired.' But it was beyond belief that he should have become mentally unbalanced and disappeared, all because the mine he'd lived on all his life had run out of gold, when he had a second mine still undeveloped.

'Gold?' He stared at me as though he couldn't

believe it. Then he was laughing again, quite uncontrollably, the sound of it echoing back from the rocks above, and his voice, half-merged with the murmur of water in the creek bed, saying, 'So it's true – Miriam didn't write to you from Vancouver; you really don't know.'

PART THREE

BELLA BELLA

CHAPTER ONE

That drive down the Ice Cold track was in keeping with all the rest of the night, a nightmare ride that in the final stages required all my powers of concentration to stay awake and keep driving. Tom led the way in Tarasconi's old Ford. For the first ten miles or so I can't remember anything very much other than the track and the rear lights of the truck ahead bucking and swerving, and myself fighting the gears of the big Chevrolet I had been landed with, bouncing up and down, the front wheels slithering wildly in the ruts, juddering and grinding against the mudguards in the rough stony sections. I was dimly aware that Tom was driving hellishly fast; conscious, too, of the heat in the cab and myself sweating with the effort of keeping up with him in a strange vehicle, but it didn't occur to me that there was anything odd about it. I just put his speed down to the fact that he was a very accomplished driver.

But then, after he had dropped Tarasconi off, telling him he could either walk back up to Ice Cold and set the two gunmen free or walk out to the highway and thumb a ride up to the Lodge – 'I advise the Lodge. You'll find your truck there and you can get some food and think out what you're going to do about your friends at the mine.' This was shouted at Tarasconi. 'But I tell you this, you'll never get the Gully. Not now.' And he slammed the truck into gear and went careering off down the track.

I remember Tarasconi's face, caught in the glare of my headlights, a look of confusion, fear, and hate – yes, hate. It was there in his eyes, glimpsed for a moment. He yelled something as I passed him, and then he was gone, a lonely, pathetic-looking figure swallowed by the night.

It was after that I began to notice the erratic behaviour of the truck ahead. By then I think I was becoming accustomed to the vehicle I was driving so could spare a thought for what was happening in front of me; also, of course, Tom was now on his own. The track became steeper. It was the section where it looked like the bed of a stream, all stone with a drop to the left that was covered with scrub. I had closed up and my headlights showed the whole rear of the pick-up, so that I could follow its course as it meandered from side to side. Tom's driving was like that of a man half-asleep. My own eyes had felt heavy-lidded, but now I was wide awake. Stones and boulders gave way to mud, my wheels locking as I braked. I changed down quickly and an instant later I saw the truck ahead slithering almost sideways. He got it under control, but then it happened again, and he didn't correct in time. The left front wheel mounted the edge of the track, careered along it for a moment, then slipped over onto the slope, the cab tilting, the chassis bellying down, tipping slowly over onto its side.

I had stopped by then and I sat watching it slide and crash down into some stunted aspen, snapping the thin boles until finally it came to rest, hanging there.

It didn't catch fire, and after a moment Tom clambered out, apparently unhurt. He called to me, but the sound of my engine drowned his words. He staggered around for a moment like a man drunk, then he stood still, staring up at me, his face pale and his hair, almost white, standing up in a thick brush. Finally he clambered up onto the side of the cab, yanked open the door again and reached in for his things.

It was some time before I realized he was suffering from shock as well as the after-effects of drugs. Fatigue probably came into it as well. He had been so hipped-up and excited when confronting those men, no wonder his driving had been erratic. I had to help him up the slope, he was so weak. And when I had got him into the cab of my vehicle, he went out like a light, his face so pale I thought at first he had fainted.

In fact, he was asleep, and he didn't wake up until we reached the lower ford across the Squaw. Dawn was showing a faint glimmer above Dalton's Post, the trees black in silhouette beyond the creek, the water and the banks of stone and silt no more than a grey blur. I had to shake him really hard before he was conscious enough to guide me across the fording place, and he was asleep again before I had reached the further bank, his head rolling and nodding like some broken doll as my wheels ground their way over the rocks and boulders of the river bed and the water swirled up to the bonnet, seeping under the door and sloshing around the floor of the cab.

He didn't wake again until I had made the highway and we were several miles on our way to the Lodge. In fact, I didn't realize he was awake until I heard an odd snuffling and saw he was sitting slumped forward with his head in his hands.

'What's the matter?' I asked. 'You all right?'

He nodded slowly.

'You're not hurt?'

'No.' He sat back, feeling in the pockets of his anorak. It was only then I realized he was crying. He produced a dirty-looking handkerchief and wiped his face. 'I have to thank you,' he murmured. And then, after a while, he said, 'Everything's gone wrong.' He seemed to pull himself together. 'I've had a marvellous life – then suddenly . . .' Silence again. I didn't say anything, thinking he was running back over his life, but then he leaned forward and gripped my arm, his mouth trembling. 'You saw the deeds, did you? That plantation – my father's trees. You saw what he wrote?'

'Yes,' I said, preparing myself for what he would ask next.

'The mine I could stand. I could live with that. But now . . . now I wish to God I were dead.' He gave a sort of laugh, self-mocking. 'But I couldn't do it. When it came to the point – well, it was just a sham. I couldn't do it, not properly.' His grip on my arm tightened. 'Do you believe a man's spirit can come out of his grave to defend something he created when he was alive? Do you believe that?'

'It's more a question whether you believe it,' I answered him, and he nodded.

'It was only when I had signed that agreement and I went up there and saw them felling – it was only then . . . Odd, isn't it?' He took his hand away. 'Damn frightening.' He had his handkerchief to his face then and he was crying again, a soft, gurgling sound.

'Did Miriam know?'

'What – the deeds?'

'That, and about your selling those two hectares.'

'No. She didn't know anything. The only people who knew the mine was finished were here, people like Jonny and Kevin – Tony, too.'

'What about Stone Slide?'

'The Gully? Yes, I could have sold the Gully. Or leased the claim. But not for much, and it would have been only a drop in the ocean of what I was beginning to owe.' And he added, 'But it's been a good life. Trouble is, that doesn't solve the problem of today, let alone the future, and looking back . . . I never was one for looking back.' He was silent then, not crying, just deadly silent as dawn broke, the grey slash of the highway between walls of spruce becoming clearer every minute, my headlights fainter.

I thought he was asleep again, his head back against the rear of the seat, his eyes closed. His face looked lined and tired, his mouth beneath the thick flared nostrils a tight gap that bared his teeth in a grimace. He had always looked so young, but he seemed to have aged in the last few months. I knew his age, of course – he was fifty-seven. But now he looked a lot older.

I was thinking about his father then, about that curse he had written into the deeds. Obviously he had seen his son for the sort of man he would grow up to be and had done his best to prevent him taking the easy way out of any financial difficulty. He may even have known the mine would run out of gold in a few years. At least he had anticipated it. And now Tom had done what old Josh Halliday had feared, he had started cutting into High Stand. But I couldn't see that cutting those trees could be the cause of his wife being seized and South American gunmen hired to keep watch over his movements. But perhaps he had sold the whole lot on a word of mouth deal and then refused to deliver the deeds? Or more likely, far more likely, it concerned Ice Cold, or maybe the Gully – it had to be gold surely.

I was still thinking about that when he suddenly sat up, his eyes wide open. 'Where are we?'

'The Haines Road,' I said.

'I know, I know – but how far have we come? Have we passed Million Dollar Falls, the campground?' He shook his head, looking suddenly confused. 'No, of course, that's back towards Haines.' He was leaning forward, watching for the next distance marker. It came up, a white post with the figures on it in black – 172. 'Thirty kilometres to Lakeside. We'll stop at Kevin's for breakfast. You've got a cabin there, I take it . . .? Good. We can have breakfast in your room then.' And he added, 'Kevin's been a good friend to me. I'll tell him what's happened. Then afterwards, if you drive as far as Kathleen Lake, I'll take over for the long haul to Whitehorse. I'll be okay by then. Right now I don't feel so good.' He leaned back, closing his eyes again. 'It takes me like this sometimes now. Old age creeping on, I guess. I'll have a little nap . . . Be all right by the time we get to Lakeside. Wake me – when we get there . . .' His voice faded, sleep closing in, leaving me alone with my thoughts and the grey curved hump of the road stretching ahead.

It was 07.37 when we rolled into Lakeside Lodge, a mist on the water and the sun just risen above the black rim of the eastern mountains. I remember the time because, after I had stopped the truck, I just sat there, too tired to move, and there was somebody's watch on the top of the fascia board straight in front of me. Tom didn't stir either. He was slumped in his corner fast asleep. We stayed like that for several minutes, my mind trying to assemble things in some semblance of order so that I could get my priorities right.

I could, of course, have packed it in right then, phoned Jean Edmundson and asked her to drive over and fetch me. I suppose the reason it crossed my mind to phone her, rather than try to hitch a ride, was that she represented ordinary Canadian life and her humdrum sanity was just what I needed to counteract the crazy world in which I had suddenly become involved. A local Sussex solicitor specializing in testaments and executor estates, and here I was in the Yukon within an ace of getting myself gunned down by hoodlums from Bogotá, stealing trucks . . . I was looking across at Tom then, his

chin sunk on his chest, the heavy nostrils trembling to
the sibilant sound of his snores. God! He looked at least
ten years older than he was, and I remembered how
Miriam had talked about him that Sunday when we had
lunched together after I had seen that newspaper story.
He didn't look in the least like a real life Peter Pan now.
And remembering her, the animation of her face, the
way her eyes had shone as she described the excitement
and fascination this man had had for the inexperienced
daughter of an archaeologist, I felt a longing and a fear
for her . . . It was so ridiculous, getting excited and full
of a passionate desire, sitting there in the cab of a truck
by a log-cabin motel on the edge of a lake in the Yukon
with her husband snoring beside me. It didn't make
sense. Nothing made sense. Only that I couldn't go
home, not till I knew what had happened to her.

As though my thoughts had somehow communicated themselves to him, he stirred, his eyes slitted
against the sun. 'Where are we?'

'At the Lodge.'

He sat up then, very abruptly, his eyes wide open.
'Breakfast,' he said, his voice sounding wide awake and
full of vigour. 'Which is your cabin unit?' I pointed to
the last in the line. 'Okay. You get the key and ask Kevin
to come and see us there. Tell him to bring the case I left
with him. And order us some breakfast.' I asked him
what he would like and he laughed. 'Anything, so long
as there's a lot of it – bacon, eggs, sausages, toast, and
coffee, plenty of coffee. Jeez, I'm hungry.'

'Hadn't you better tell me what this is all about?'

'Later,' he said. 'Later. We got to get moving.'

We were there at the Lodge for less than an hour, and in that time we had the truck filled with gas, ate a huge breakfast, and Kevin lent us some money. Tom didn't have to ask for it. Kevin simply assumed he would be short of cash, said there was something around a thousand dollars in the office strong box and if that was any help we were welcome to it. He didn't ask for any security, not even a chit. He simply went and got it, dumping the wad of notes on the breakfast tray.

I don't know how much Kevin knew. I got the impression he thought Tom had got himself deep in debt with some very dangerous people and was hiding out from them, pretending to be dead. It was as good an explanation as any and Kevin's generosity, his involvement in Tom's affairs, could be motivated by hope of another gold strike in the Ice Cold area. The only question he asked, at least in my presence, was about Tony and the two men left up at the Squaw Creek camp. 'Do you want me to go up there and truck them down? I could drive them to the US border. It's only fifty miles from the Dalton's Post turn-off.'

'You think they'd cross?'

'They might.'

Tom shook his head. 'I doubt it. And anyway you've done enough to help me already. Some time this morning either that little bastard Tarasconi will walk back to his claim and release them, or they'll manage to release themselves. If they turn up here asking about their truck, tell them I'll be dumping it in Whitehorse, probably in the airport parking lot.'

'And where will you be?'

Tom shook his head. 'It's best I keep that to myself.'

Kevin nodded. 'I guess you're right.' He hesitated, then got up from his seat on the bed. 'Well, I'll leave you now. I got work to do anyway.' He held out his hand. 'Good luck, Tom.'

'Thanks.' He was on his feet, seizing Kevin's hand in both of his. 'I don't know how I can ever repay you.' He looked across at me and grinned. 'I'll give instructions to my lawyer, of course. But a hell of a lot of good that will be – in the circumstances.' The grin faded as he said that. 'If I were to tell you . . .' But he shook his head. 'You wouldn't believe me. Nobody would believe me.' He wasn't speaking to Kevin then. He wasn't speaking to anyone, only himself.

We left shortly afterwards. I drove as far as Kathleen Lodge, where we had some more coffee, then Tom took over. He had had a good sleep and looked a lot better. But he wouldn't answer my questions. 'You wouldn't believe it.' He said that several times, a sort of refrain, but he wouldn't say what it was I wouldn't believe. In the end I dozed off. I remember Haines Junction, the RCMP post and then turning east, away from the Front Ranges and the great white wall of the mountains. After that I slept most of the ninety-eight miles to Whitehorse.

He drove straight to the airport, where he parked between another pick-up and an empty mobile home so that we were screened as we collected our things. We got a taxi at the terminal and drove down Two Mile Hill, past the shopping mall and a gaggle of gas stations to Fourth Avenue and Wood Street where we booked into the Sheffield House for the night. There was a letter waiting for me, an airmail letter with a typewritten address and postmarked Worthing. It was from my partner, who hoped it would reach me in time and that I was enjoying the trip. He enclosed a letter from Brian Halliday – *I thought it important you should have this as you may wish to contact him or see for yourself what is going on at the Halliday forest property in B C.*

Brian Halliday had written from a place called Bella Coola in B C, a brief scrawl on a Canadian airmail letter card to inform me that there were several men at the old logging camp up the Halliday Arm, two of them cutting into High Stand using big high-powered chainsaws. He thought they had already felled more than the two hectares allowed for in the sale agreement, but he couldn't be sure as he had not been allowed to check the clear-felled area. In fact, as soon as he had challenged their right to continue felling they had called up a man named Lorient, who claimed to be the manager but looked more like a security guard. *He told me the property was licensed for felling by an American timber company and would I please get the hell out.*

The American company was, of course, S V L Timber. He had asked for Thor Olsen, his father's manager, but Lorient had told him there was no caretaker, that the camp had been deserted when they had arrived.

The letter ended with a request that I cable the police to check the whereabouts of Thor Olsen, and the final paragraph asked two questions: *What is my legal position? Can I have the law throw them off my land? Please advise. Also confirm that any felling additional to the two hectares covered by the sale agreement signed by my father is illegal. Kindly cable your reply to these questions soonest possible.* And he gave a post office box number at Bella Coola.

The letter was dated 20 September, two days after he had let the barge load of logs be towed over his inflatable for the benefit of the TV cameras. It seemed odd that he should write to me for legal advice when he was on the BC coast and could have obtained much better advice from his father's Canadian solicitors. And why hadn't he contacted the RCMP himself about Olsen? Also, the information about felling activity in the Cascades was in direct conflict with the assurances given me over the phone by Barony of SVL Timber.

I took the letter to Tom in his room down the corridor. He was having a shower and he read it with the water pouring down his back and his naked body dripping in a haze of steam. His eyes seemed slightly dilated. 'Always the same with that boy.' He handed the limp scrawl back to me. 'Why the hell can't he leave things alone?'

'Is it true?' I asked.

'What's that?' He stepped out of the shower and began towelling himself down. 'Is what true?'

'That they're still cutting those trees? Did you sign anything – apart from the sale agreement with SVL Timber covering those two hectares?'

He stopped towelling, standing there stark naked, the towel across his shoulders. 'You know about that?'

'The agreement was in your desk.'

'I see.'

'Have you signed any other agreement?'

'No, of course not.' And he added, 'You've seen the deeds, I suppose? You've read what the Old Man wrote. Nobody in their right mind . . .' He dropped the towel, turning away and reaching for his pants.

'What about Miriam? Did you give her power of attorney, anything like that?'

'No.' He pulled on his pants, then swung back towards me. 'If Miriam's signed anything . . .' He smiled at me. 'It's your problem. You look after it.' He was staring at me, his body hard and brown with high-altitude labour in the wind and the sun. 'If Miriam has signed anything – even if she claimed she was acting as executor . . . it wouldn't count, would it?'

'No.'

He was trembling slightly. 'If I'm dead the forest belongs to Brian. That's right, isn't it? That's what the Will says.' He waited until I had nodded my agreement, and then he added, 'And if I'm not dead, it still belongs to me.'

'And you've signed nothing?'

'No, I refused. That's what it's all about.' He was still staring at me, his eyes wide, a frightened look on his face. 'I wouldn't sign.' Then abruptly he seemed to pull himself together. 'Forget it. That's why I willed it to Brian. Let him cope with the bastards. It's Miriam I'm worried about.' He went to his case and rummaged for a clean shirt. 'More than a month's dirt and sweat I've just run down that plug'ole and not a dam' thing to show for it. Nothing changed – only Miriam, she was on the verge of clinching a deal that would have got me the gear I needed to prove the Gully.' He shrugged. 'Oh well – you cable Brian. Tell him we'll be at Bella Bella in three days' time. Well, three and a half. That'll be Tuesday. If he can meet us there . . .' He crossed to the bed where his clothes lay in a heap. 'As soon as I'm dressed I'll arrange train and ferry bookings, then I'll have a word with Jonny and after that we'll go out on the town for the evening, eh? Do us both good.' He said it with sudden cheerfulness – a determined cheerfulness that he managed to sustain throughout the evening.

The place he chose was what looked to me like the most expensive restaurant in Whitehorse, a red plush copy of the rich sourdough establishments of the Edwardian era, full of engraved glass mirrors with pictures of Diamond Lil and all the other gold rush characters staring at us from the walls, and we ate lobster claws and Alaska giant crabs and drank a great deal of wine and quite a lot of whisky. God knows what the bill came to, but somehow I didn't care. Everything had become so mad that all my training as a solicitor, all my natural caution seemed to have disappeared, Tom Halliday talking and talking – about odd places he had been, odd scrapes he had been in, small planes and forced landings, guerrillas on the border of Peru and Ecuador, the Le Mans and before that stock racing as a kid in old bangers, the crashes he had had. It was as though he needed to run through his whole life in that one evening – almost as though he were trying to justify it; to me, to himself, I am not certain which.

He was high, of course. God knows where he had got the stuff. Presumably there were drug pushers in Whitehorse same as in other towns, or maybe he had kept a little in reserve at Lakeside and had got it from Kevin. He just couldn't stop talking. Except towards the end. Towards the end, drinking Scotch, his mood had changed.

Afterwards, lying in my bed in the overheated room with its plain wood walls, my impression of him was of a man cast in the mould of the prodigal son. It didn't matter that he'd borrowed a thousand dollars and that he'd probably never be able to repay it, he had money in his pocket and money was for spending. And in the setting of that 1900s restaurant he had seemed so like the men of the period, the money easily got out of a good claim and easily spent in the honky-tonks of Dawson City, the main street of which was reproduced almost everywhere in Whitehorse.

There were bits and pieces of the gold rush still visible in the town. We had walked back, the night full of stars and our breath smoking, ice skimming the puddles. He had taken me along Fourth Avenue, past the old log church and the wooden skyscraper building on Third, then out to the solid mass of the Territorial Government Building and across the railway track to the road bridge over the Yukon where the SS *Klondike* lay with her keel on the grass of the bank, her wooden hull and towering superstructure glimmering white like a ghost ship.

He had leaned on the parapet of the bridge, staring down into the dark gurgling current of the river. 'Almost a century ago,' he had murmured. 'This is the way my father came – just a kid, fresh out of school and green as a cucumber. Up White Pass to Lindeman and Bennett – you'll see Bennett Lake tomorrow – then down the river and through the canyon to Laberge riding a raft with half a dozen horses, a big stove and a grand piano. By the time he reached Dawson he ought to have known what sort of a man Despera was. Twenty-five thousand of them came down the river in that one year, and everywhere the con men and the grafters. He should have known.' He had laughed then. 'And so should I! Tarasconi, I mean. Like grandfather, like grandson, eh?' It was a laugh without any humour. 'Later they had steamships like the old *Klondike* there, but when he came down the river he was rafted down . . . just a bundle of logs . . .' He had straightened up, stretching himself and yawning. 'That's how they get the timber out of places like the Halliday Arm – rafting it out, or using scows. That's what you told me, wasn't it – ?'

'A barge,' I said. 'That's what the caption to the newspaper picture called it.'

But he had taken no notice of that. 'That's how they got the first load out. By scow. Two months ago it must have been. No, more.' And then, his voice trembling slightly, 'I wonder what's happened to Olsen. Hope he's not dead. Well, a few more days and we'll know the answer – to that and other things.' He had turned away. 'Better go back to the hotel now and get some sleep. God, I'm tired!'

So was I, and very glad to get into pyjamas and relax between sheets. But sleep wasn't that easy, my mind going over and over the events of the last twenty-four hours. I had told him about his son, how he was trying to raise a public outcry against an American company felling a cedar forest planted by a Canadian who had made his money in the Klondike, but all he had said was, 'A lot of good that is, the silly fool. He doesn't know what he's up against.'

Maybe it was the coffee or the chill of the night air, or the fact my room was cold because I had turned off the heat before going out, but I seemed wider awake than ever, worrying about what I should do. I didn't have to go along with him, down to Skagway and the ferry. Instead of the train, I could take a plane from the airport, change at Fort St John and pick up a Ward-air flight out of Edmonton direct to Gatwick. Another twenty-four hours and I could be home. But there was Miriam. And Tom – whatever he had done, I couldn't just leave him.

For a man to be under such pressure that he vanishes almost without trace, dropping out of his whole previous existence and disappearing into an isolated and abandoned mine in the Yukon . . . I was still thinking it was gold, you see, and over dinner I had asked him about the rock slide, whether it had been done deliberately. Yes, he said, he had done it himself. He had got Kevin to bring up a drill and some dynamite, and when I expressed surprise that he could carry out a rock-blasting operation on his own, he had laughed and said quite casually, 'Though my father lived in Vancouver Island he boarded me out, as it were, with an impecunious aunt in Edinburgh. Thought I'd get a better education in Scotland. I went to Gordonstoun and each year, in the long summer hols, I flew back to that big ranch-style house he had just north of Duncan – it had a bit of a beach, a wooden jetty and a fabulous view out beyond the Gulf Islands to the Strait of Georgia and the Rockies beyond. Fishing, water skiing, and sometimes we'd go over to the west coast, the area round Nootka Sound and Friendly Cove where Cook put in on his last voyage.' And he had gone on to talk about surf-boarding among the rocks, nude parties on a rockbound coast where the Pacific rollers swept in from the China Sea five thousand miles and more away, fishing and hunting and camping on the shores of lonely inlets. 'Guess I went pretty wild back there, so Gordonstoun was good for me. And then after Gordonstoun, no university nonsense for this boy, but there was a thing called National Service. 'Course, I could have pleaded Canadian citizenship, but having both, nobody asked any questions when I reported in and signed the form. Can't remember what I had to sign, but something; the whole thing was a bit of a dare as far as I was concerned, and since I was already hooked on stock racing and pretty mad about any bit of machinery that went fast, they put me in the REs and instead of vehicles they gave me explosives to play with.'

He had laughed then and said, 'You mentioned terrorists, back there at the mine. I'd have made one hell of a good terrorist. Anyway, that's how I knew about laying a charge in a rock face. Bringing down that fall was a piece of cake once Kevin had got me the tools. It kept that little bastard Tarasconi out, and anybody else who was just curious to know what was going on. Another week or so . . .'

I don't know whether it was the drink or the coke that made him fantasize so wildly, but somehow he

seemed to have convinced himself that, given another
month or so, he and that Indian would have opened up
a new mine – just the two of them working with that
one tractor and the wooden rocker and sluice box he
had constructed with his own hands. 'I'd've done it,'
he said. 'I know dam' well I would. But for the onset of
winter we'd have got down to bedrock and that's where
the heavy stuff is. Winter, and Tarasconi putting the
finger on me, and those two bastards. I could have
broken their necks, just like that – ' He had snapped his
fingers. 'But I wanted them to talk. And then to find
they were just a couple of hit men hired to deliver that
note and keep tabs on me. They didn't know where she
was.' And he had suddenly seized hold of my arm, his
face thrust close to mine, the pupils of his eyes looking
very odd and his hand trembling. 'Don't you know?
You've just come up here from Vancouver, you've seen
Roy, you've talked to Barony over in Seattle – you must
know something.' And when I hadn't answered – I think
I just shook my head – he said, 'For God's sake, haven't
you any idea where she might be?'

He had stared at me then for a long time, as though
he were in a trance, and when he'd snapped out of it he
had seized hold of the bottle and slopped some more
whisky into our glasses. And because I had thought he
was drunk enough now to tell me what it was all about,
I had begun questioning him again. And instead of
answering my questions, he had flown into a rage,
telling me I was bloody useless and to mind my own
business. After that he had gone suddenly quiet, closing
up on me, silent and morose, his head in his hands.

Once he had muttered, 'I don't know what it's all about and I don't want to know. They're bastards, the whole lot of them. They should be put down, like you put down dogs that have got that rabies disease.'

And then suddenly he had looked up at me. 'Philip. If I don't do what they tell me, they'll kill her. I know they will. There's a lot of money involved, and she and I, we're just pawns. God in heaven! What the hell can I do?' And he had beat his fists against his forehead. But he wouldn't say what it was he had been told to do, and when I asked him if it was a question of the Canadian trees and SVL Timber trying to get him to sell, he'd burst out laughing. 'If it was as simple as that . . . Christ! I'd make my peace with the Old Man and sign the whole thing away just to be rid of them. But it isn't, is it?' And he had reached for his glass and downed the whole of his whisky in one gulp, and then he had sat there staring at me with a vacant look, sad-eyed and his mind locked away in some dark cavern of its own.

I might be his solicitor and out here of my own free will, but if you've rogered a man's wife and been rumbled, it's always there, a barrier between you that crops up at odd, unexpected moments. He had just looked at me, not saying a word, then abruptly got to his feet, heading for the gents. After a moment I had followed to find him standing, his tie loosened and holding in his hand a little gold spoon that was hung about his neck on a slender gold chain. He had taken a pouch from his pocket and was dipping the spoon into it, peering forward to see how much he had scooped up, then putting it to his left nostril and snorting it up. He had done it again with the other nostril, then seeing me his eyes had snapped wide open and he had breathed out a deep, contented Aaah! 'Just to keep me on top, eh?'

'You don't need it, surely.' My voice had sounded very prim.

'No.' By then he had been reaching down to unzip his flies.

'A one-and-one, that's not very much, but if it holds the high – I just like to keep it going, you see, an' because I've not had any for a couple of months, a one-and-one will do it. Christ!' He was staring down at himself. 'And it'll do that too!' And he had added, 'One time Miriam and I used it as an aphrodisiac, but it doesn't work once you're snorting regularly.' He grinned at me over his shoulder. 'Pity Miriam isn't here now . . .' But then he was concentrating and a moment later he was passing water so it hadn't lasted long. And afterwards, while he was washing his hands, he had said, 'Lucky you don't snort. That's all I've got now, just a few grams to last me till my ship comes in.' And he had burst into that high-pitched laugh of his, as though he'd said something funny.

I wondered whether he had got himself involved with some dope pushers, but he shook his head. 'Pushers?' His eyes had sprung very wide as he stared at me in the mirror, all the time running a comb through his bushy mop of grey-white hair. 'No, no. I buy higher up. It's like the difference between always having to drop into the local for a packet of fags and ordering your Havanas in boxes from one of those places in St James's. Only now things are a little changed.' And he had neighed at me again, his teeth showing. 'I need some more, and pretty soon now. I can't face these bastards without it. And Miriam – what have they done with Miriam? All this time . . .' He had been pulling open the door then. 'I'll murder the buggers,' he had hissed in my ear, his breath hot on my cheek as he lurched out into the dining-room.

Back at the table he had gradually simmered down, the rush already dying. 'Maybe Brian will be able to get me some more. Has Brian got any money, do you know?'

'I think so.' But I hadn't told him his son had done what Miriam had done, borrowing things from the house to raise enough to get to Canada. Instead, I had asked him how much it cost to buy cocaine out here. He had shrugged, saying it depended on the quality, didn't it? 'The price has been falling recently. Colombia, Ecuador, Peru, Bolivia, they're all flogging the stuff as hard as they can. They make it up in the mountains, little family labs, but the total of what those peasants produce often provides the bulk of the government's income. It's like those wine lakes in France and Italy. You can buy it cheap if you have to, but the good stuff – that always costs money. And if you don't use good stuff, and you don't cut it right, then you can do yourself a lot of damage. Pure cocaine – that crystalline rock stuff – it's too strong, bad for the membranes of the nose, bad for the gums if you're taking it orally. I always cut my own if I can.' And when I had asked him if Brian was using it, he had shaken his head. 'No, no. He's tried it, but he has his own built-in high. Father to world causes, that's

Brian. But he always knows lots of people. Wherever he is he's got contacts. He'll know where to get it. Indians at Bella Bella probably, or further south at Alert Bay. They're flush with money at the moment. Land sales. So there's sure to be a pusher in Bella Bella, certainly at Bella Coola – that's at the end of the road running in from Williams Lake and the white spruce country, along the Chilanko valley . . .'

They were just names, and thinking about them I fell asleep, having decided to go along with him as far as Skagway and the ship to Prince Rupert. I could always go on then to Vancouver. And in the morning the sun was shining, the river marked by the white of steam rising from the water.

By the time we reached the railway depot the coaches were already waiting, three of them, all rather elderly with little steel platforms at each end and wood-burning stoves. There was a party of Americans with a courier who wore a hat and looked harassed, a small group of Canadian schoolboys humping bagged-up inflatables, and individual travellers kept arriving in cars and taxis, some on foot. A general air of excitement pervaded the area between the depot buildings and the coaches, for there was a small camera crew of three taking close-ups of an actor making his way from one coach to the next.

We found seats and stowed our gear. Tom was travelling very light with the result that the rifle was even more conspicuous than it would have been otherwise. 'What are you going to do about that?' I asked him, suddenly conscious, now that we were in an organized system of transport, that there were such things as customs checks. Skagway was in Alaska, and Alaska was a part of the United States.

'I've got a permit,' he said.

'Under your own name?'

'Of course.' He laughed, a tense, slightly nervous laugh. 'The Americans don't get fussed over guns the way the Canadians do. I remember my father telling me how Sam Steele and twenty Mounties made the Yanks coming up from Skagway hand in their guns. They didn't like it, but that's the way it was up there at that improvised customs post, and the con men sent up by Soapy Smith, the boss man of Skagway, to fleece the thousands staggering up that twelve-mile pass, they got short shrift. Now it's just a train ride,' he added and then fell silent. He was much less talkative now, almost morose.

'What about the holstered gun you took from Camargo?' I asked.

'Under my arm.'

'It may be all right entering Alaska, but we're going back into Canada – at Prince Rupert, I presume. What about the customs there?'

'They'll be so busy checking the rifle, it won't occur to them I've got anything else.' He looked at me, frowning. 'Come to think of it, what did you do with the gun you took from that little rat Lopez?'

'It's in my suitcase,' I said.

There was a sudden flurry of activity, a jolt and people boarding. 'Maybe we better hand them in. Or toss them out as we run through the tunnel at the top of the pass. No, the ravine would be better. There'll be a mist up there today and everybody gawping at the steel bridge.' A lot of clanking and people shouting, then we were shunted back to finish up being hitched onto a long train of oil tankers. The diesel locomotive gave a mournful bellow, a last warning as the couplings clashed.

I was out on the iron platform then and I saw the actor in his blue jeans running as the train started into motion, a battered suitcase in his hand and the television crews filming from the rear of the last coach, the cameraman being held precariously balanced on the outside of the observation platform. Again the mournful bellow, the wheels grinding on the rails, the actor clambering in, and the camera being passed to safety.

The diesel engine was already nosing its way between the river and the government buildings, and looking back I saw somebody had missed the train, a small red car swinging into the depot and a man jumping out. He stopped suddenly, turned and dived back into the car, which swung quickly round and was lost to sight behind some buildings. I looked out the other side, and there was the bridge over the Yukon where we had stood the previous night and the SS *Klondike* looking like a white whale stranded on the grass of the bank, and as we crossed 2nd Avenue, the locomotive still bellowing, there was the little red car coming towards us.

I caught just a glimpse of it, and then there were houses and the steep escarpment rising above us with a small plane taking off from the airport. By air I suppose it would have been no more than a few hours to Bella

Bella, but most of the coast was only covered by local floatplanes and the direct flight distance was almost 800 miles. Too far, and the terrain too rugged, the weather close in to the Rockies too chancy. And by road the distance given to Bella Coola on the map I had with me was just on 2400 miles – 'Rugged driving,' Tom said. He had done it. There was, in fact, no practical alternative but to go by ferry, which meant the better part of a day on the train, two nights on the American ferry stopping at five ports down the Alaska panhandle before Prince Rupert, and finally another day on the BC ferry to Bella Bella.

My first reaction to this slow progression had been one of impatience, almost of disbelief. Tom, on the other hand, took it for granted. 'That's the way it is up here,' he had said with a shrug. 'Travel takes time.' He was used to the journey, had done it several times. For me, to whom the Yukon, Alaska, the Pacific, the Rockies had just been names until now, it was a wonderful experience just to be travelling through this country – except for the feeling I had of being out of my depth and involved in something I didn't understand.

All my training – my conventional upbringing, too – prompted me to report to the authorities. But report what? – those two Colombian gunmen when I was convinced the thing was bigger than that? And there was Tom – you can't just shop the man you represent.

Three days. Three days in close company travelling down the coast. In three days I ought to be able to get some sense out of him, persuade him to take me into his confidence and tell me what it was all about.

Spruce, endless spruce, a copper mine closed by the fall in price, glimpses of the highway and mountains closing in from the right, the train dawdling as though it too was enjoying the scenery. And then, past what is claimed as the smallest desert in the world, we crept in to Carcross at the north end of Lake Bennett where it joins the even bigger Lake Tagish. This was the old caribou crossing – hence the name of the place, Tom said, talking of the huge herds he had seen once on a flight up to the North Slope oil complex. Another of those high-structured, wooden Yukon vessels lay on the shore and one of the railway's early tank locomotives was parked beside the track, bits and pieces of it picked out in white paint, also a freight wagon. We clanked to a stop just after we had crossed the trembling timber swing bridge that spanned the junction of the two lakes and alongside us was the weatherbeaten wood front of the Caribou Hotel with several trucks parked outside, also a small red car. Then I saw them, standing there, just clear of the hotel, outside another clapboard building, Matthew Watson's General Store painted on the front of it, standing quite motionless, their faces without expression as they searched the carriage windows.

I had gone out to the rear platform and was just stepping down with an excited group of youngsters to take a picture when I saw them. I ducked back, but too late. They were already moving towards the coach. 'Those two hunters,' I said as I sat myself down again beside Tom.

He nodded. 'I saw them.'

'What are you going to do?'

'Nothing. They won't trouble us until we get to Bella Bella. Then we'll see.'

The two men were climbing into the coach, each carrying a grip, nothing else. They stood a moment on the iron platform staring at us through the glass of the rear door, the big one frowning slightly, his untidy beard and the moustache seeming blacker than ever in the sombre grey light reflected off the water, Lopez looking tense, his body like a coiled spring as though expecting us to make some hostile move. It was only a few seconds they stood there motionless, but it seemed much longer. Camargo was the first to move, reaching out and opening the door. Then he was pushing through it, and they went past us, not saying anything, not even looking at us.

'It was only an outside chance they'd be fooled into thinking we'd left by air,' Tom said, and he shrugged. 'Maybe it's better this way.'

The train jolted into motion, and though I tried questioning him again, he wouldn't answer, sitting there, staring out of the window at the grey expanse of the lake, his mind apparently locked on his thoughts. And those two men with their coffee-coloured skin and black oily hair sitting impassive and silent at the other end of the coach.

At Bennett we stopped for lunch – benches and trestle tables in a bare echoing hall that was part of the depot, a full-bodied soup brought on in steaming tureens by full-bodied women, steak and bean pudding and apple pie. And when we went out to stretch our legs the mountains had gone, the cloud right down on the deck and a light drizzle blowing in our faces. Lopez and Camargo took turns to keep watch on us and a second engine was shunted on to the train for the long haul up to White Pass.

Bennett boasted the one real section of double track on the whole 110 miles between Skagway and Whitehorse, so we had to wait for the daily train coming in over White Pass from the other direction with another load of passengers for another 'gold rush' station meal. We left just after one-thirty. By then the wind had risen almost to gale force, the rain slashing at the depot buildings, obliterating them almost instantly as we pulled out into the murk. It was like that for perhaps half an hour, then the wind dropped and the clouds thinned to reveal a desolate landscape of bare rock and stunted scrub interspersed with innumerable little lakes. The train was moving now at a snail's pace, the diesels labouring. We stopped by a small building that was like a signal box. We had reached the summit and the border between Alaska and BC.

We were almost at three thousand feet then and through the first of the snow tunnels, an alpine maquis world where a carpet of autumn-gold growth hugged the ground, crouching for shelter amongst bare, black, ice-scarred rocks and beside small pools still skimmed with the night's ice. It was here that Tom, who had seemed lost in a world of his own, suddenly turned to me and asked me to get Lopez's gun from my suitcase. 'There's the first of the real rock tunnels coming up in a moment. You'll be able to get it then without anybody seeing what you're up to.'

'What do you want it for?' I had a sudden vision of him shooting those two down in cold blood. He had been to the lavatory quite recently and I didn't know whether he was drugged-up or not. A man brooding like that . . .

But he just smiled and said, 'You can keep the ammunition. I just want the gun.'

We clattered over a girder bridge, and as we entered the tunnel I got up. I had never handled an automatic, and fumbling in my case in almost complete darkness I couldn't find the catch that would release the magazine. He seemed strangely relaxed when I got back to my seat, sitting there smiling to himself, and when I slipped the gun into his hand I saw him fingering it, then he passed me the magazine. 'Put that in your pocket – for the moment, just to keep your mind at rest.' And he patted my arm, turning and peering back down the coach. He was checking on the seating position of our two shadows and I didn't like it.

The tourist route card we had been given indicated a view of the old steel cantilever bridge immediately after the tunnel, also Dead Horse Gulch and the original White Pass trail of '98. Then there was another tunnel, the original one, and after that we would be into the Glacier Loop with its series of trestles carrying the line along the mountainsides to the Skagway River crossing and Glacier Station at Mile 14, the miles measured from Skagway port where the building of the railway had begun in 1899.

We emerged into the daylight, the mountaintops lost in cloud, everything shrouded in mist, the bridge and the old track looking weird in the veiled light. A few minutes later there was a muted bellow from the engines up front, then the drum of the wheels became louder and suddenly we were into the next tunnel, the daylight abruptly cut off and Tom getting up and pushing past me. The lights were dim, almost non-existent, so that he was little more than a shadow as he made his way down the aisle to where the two of them sat by the cast-iron stove. The big man, Camargo, was on his feet. I half rose at the same time, tense and wondering what was going to happen.

But nothing happened. Tom stood there for a moment, leaning slightly forward as though presenting them with something. Then he had turned and was coming back down the aisle. Daylight suddenly, the engines no longer labouring and the brakes hard on as the world dropped away to our right. 'The Skagway River,' he said as he slipped past me to his seat by the window.

I caught a glimpse of the steel bridge, an old girder contraption straddled from rock to rock across a ravine. 'What were you doing?' I asked.

He was smiling quietly to himself and I suddenly caught a glimpse of the man Miriam had been so attracted by. There was an almost rakish, devil-may-care look about him. 'What were you expecting, a fight?' I waited, knowing by the expression on his face that he couldn't resist telling me. He looked so pleased with himself.

'I bowed,' he said. 'Very formal, very Spanish. Then in their own tongue I said "*Creo que éstas les pertenecen*." And I handed the guns back to them, holding them by the barrels of course.' He laughed gently – not that snorting neigh, but a real, genuine laugh of amusement. 'That was it. They were too surprised to do anything. And now they're stuck with the things. They can hardly thrust them back at me in broad daylight with a bunch of tourists looking on.'

And all the way down to Skagway, which we reached just before four, he was in that same relaxed mood, constantly quoting from his father's experiences as the train wound slowly down the pass, a great loop by the Denver Glacier trail that showed the track and the bridge high up above us on the mountainside, the brakes grinding all the time, and his voice going on and on about how it had been that winter with thousands of men back-packing the minimum of a ton of gear up through the snow, horses lying dead and dying on the trail, blizzards, disease and exhaustion making the climb to the pass a living hell.

CHAPTER TWO

Skagway in the late afternoon of that dismal day was as near to the Styx as I shall probably ever get in this lifetime. The rail tracks, depot and sheds, the quay and the waiting ferry, all lay close under beetling cliffs, the bare rock black with the drizzle that was falling, and beyond was the water of Chilkoot Inlet, grey and flat as polished steel, low cloud cutting everything off, a grey curtain that made it seem the end of the world. And Skagway itself, built on the silt flats of the river and hemmed in by the damp slopes on the far side, was a somewhat phoney version of a gold rush town in limbo, boarded sidewalks and wooden buildings that belonged to the dead world of Soapy Smith.

Since we were booked on the ferry to Prince Rupert, and only in transit through Alaska, customs and immigration clearance was little more than a formality. We dumped our bags at an Edwardian hotel and walked along the Broadway until we ran out of shops and houses. The cloud and the damp were all-pervading and our two friends watched us from the shelter of a doorway. Whether they still had the guns Tom had handed back to them I don't know. He had disposed of the magazines somewhere along the track where the train had crossed a small torrent that ran in from Mount Hefty and the Denver Glacier. Back at the hotel we had a very expensive beer, then went on board, the ferry sailing promptly at 19.45 local time. It was almost dark then and by the time we had had a meal we were docking at Haines, first of the five ports of call on the Panhandle route south.

We had cabins booked and by the time we left, Tom had already turned in. Throughout our cafeteria meal he had seemed to withdraw deeper and deeper into himself so that I was quite glad to be left on my own to wander round the ship. The vehicle deck was still barely half full and the big lounges that would have been crowded in the season looked almost deserted, row upon row of empty seats and only here and there the poorer passengers settling down for the night, our two followers among them. The throb of the engines, the beat of them against the soles of my feet, the knowledge that next day, and the day after, we would be moving through coastal passages that Cook, and later Vancouver who had sailed with him, had first explored – it was all tremendously exciting and it would probably have remained so all the way to Prince Rupert and on down to Bella Bella if I hadn't chanced on something that virtually forced Tom Halliday to open up and tell me the whole pitiful and appalling story.

Some time in the early hours of Sunday morning we

reached Juneau. We left at five-thirty and when I surfaced a couple of hours later I found many more people in the lounges, Indians as well as Americans in every sort of dress, a queue forming in the cafeteria. We were in fog, the air on deck cold and clammy, the sound of the foghorn echoing back from the shore on either side and occasional glimpses of rock and trees, dark walls on the edge of visibility. Tom stayed in his cabin, and when I went to check that he was all right I found the door locked. He was taking it easy, he said. He had a book and he didn't want any breakfast. He sounded half asleep, so I left him to it and spent a pleasant day talking to a variety of passengers: a driller from the oil rigs of the North Slope, two loggers from the Charlottes, a citrus fruit farmer from down near Sacramento, California, and a man who had lived half his life on the slopes of Mount St Helens and had been there during the eruption when it had covered half the state of Washington in a grey pall of ash. By lunchtime we were in Petersburg, the fog thinning and the sun breaking through, so that going through the narrows between Mitkof and Kupreanof Islands we were in a milky haze with the forests on either side glimmering almost silver with the moisture that clung to the needles of the trees. Three hours later we were at Wrangell, and at each of the day's stops one of our South American friends would be watching the passageway that led from Tom's cabin, the other keeping an eye on me.

It was an eerie feeling, not being able to move anywhere on the ship without being watched. Twice I talked to Tom, but only through the door. He seemed to have sunk into a sort of torpor, his voice muffled and surly like a bear disturbed in the middle of its hibernation. Night fell on the 150-mile passage to Ketchikan and he again refused to join me for the evening meal. I had left it till late and after I had finished, when we were already docking at the last Alaskan port, I went down once more to his cabin with the intention of insisting that I brought him something from the cafeteria before it became crowded with new arrivals.

His door was still shut and there was no answer. In sudden panic I beat upon it. A voice behind me said, 'Is all right your friend.' It was Lopez lurking in a doorway further down the passageway. He smiled. 'He is going to the toilet.' And he added, still showing his teeth below the little down-drooped moustache, 'You see for yourself. The door is open.'

I stared at him a moment, then I turned the handle and went in. The reading light was on, clothes piled on the foot of the bunk, the blankets thrown back, no sign of a book and his rucksack on the floor with the contents spilling out, some papers tucked into a plastic folder, letters from Miriam – I recognized the writing – some newspaper cuttings . . . A headline caught my eye:

TEENAGE DRUG MAYHEM
Cheap Coke Floods In

It was from a Chicago paper, the cutting two months old and faded. Another from the same paper was a few days later –

Violence Hits the Streets – Kids Go Crazy for Drug Money

I sat down on the bunk, wondering why he should have kept the cuttings, carrying them about with him along with Miriam's letters . . .

> *Chicago police appear totally baffled by the sudden rush of coke onto the City streets. It's plentiful and it's cheap – cheaper than it has ever been before. And the pushers are everywhere. Samples analyzed show that basically it is good quality, but it has been mixed or cut with anything from amphetamines to borax or even talcum powder. 'You cut coke with speed, which is amphetamines, and you have a killer,' says the eminent toxicologist, Professor . . .*

'What the hell do you think you're up to?' Tom reached forward, snatching the cuttings from my hand. 'Searching my things . . .' He opened the door wide. 'Get out! Get out, do you hear?'

I had stood up, facing him. 'I think you'd better tell me now.'

'Tell you what?' His eyes were very wide, an almost frightened look. 'Why should I t-tell you?'

I reached past him and shut the door. 'Sit down,' I told him. He was bare-legged, his anorak covering his bare chest, his hair standing on end, an unwashed smell and his face looking drawn, almost haggard. 'Sit down,' I said again. 'You've got to tell me now.' And I added,

'If you don't, then I'll go to the police as soon as we get to Prince Rupert. I have to know what it is you've got yourself involved in.' I pointed to the cuttings in his hand. 'What's the connection?'

For a moment I thought he was going to lash out at me, his face gone pale and a wild, violent look in his eyes. But then he discarded his anorak and subsided onto the bunk. 'Yes,' he said. 'Yes, I suppose you'd b-better know.' He nodded slowly to himself. 'I've been thinking about that all day, reading those cuttings, lying here thinking about them.' He put his head in his hands. 'I don't have to read them. I know them by heart, you see.' And after that I didn't have to drag it out of him.

It had all begun very innocently. Almost a decade ago Jonny Epinard had warned him the Ice Cold mine was showing signs of reaching the end of its life. For one thing, starting from the lowest point, they were washing silt at least three quarters of the way up the claim. The yield per ton of silt washed was still very little changed from the first records kept by Tom's father, but the percentage of nuggets, or indeed of anything larger than straightforward dust, had abruptly declined. At first he hadn't taken this seriously, but when the six-monthly profit cheques paid through the Swiss bank had begun to decline, then he had started to take a much closer interest in what was happening up in the Yukon.

This was about the time he had married Miriam, and after a couple of years of unusually heavy expenditure – 'travelling, racing, a plane of my own, parties, concerts – she's very musical, you know – well, it was either cut back or find some additional source of income.' He had started playing the market, with a certain amount of success at first, and gambling, with rather less success. Finally, he had decided to take a look at the BC property. 'I knew nothing about trees, but you didn't have to be a forester to know that there was money standing there in the Cascades, not just in that High Stand down in the bottom along the Snakeskin River, but up on the slopes of the mountains.'

The trees there had never been cut over and some of them were big. 'A lot of scrub, of course, goat's beard, devil's club, teaberry, huckleberry and bilberry, but all through it there was hemlock, cedar and fir that just had to be worth something whatever the problems of getting it out.'

It was the problem of extraction, of course, that had caused the original owners to concentrate on the bottom land and leave the slopes alone. But that had been back in the days of steam-powered saws, traction engines, man-built roads and primitive extraction aids. He had been put in touch with Ringstrop by one of Crown Forest's logging-camp managers and on the basis of the forestry consultant's report he had accepted his advice to sell the timber standing under separate agreements as and when he needed money.

In this way he had been able to control the amount cut, so that the resulting income would roughly match the shortfall from the Yukon mine. But inside of four years the yield from Ice Cold had fallen so low that he was practically dependent on timber for his whole income, so that it wasn't long before virtually everything, other than the High Stand his father had planted, had been clear-felled.

By then several things had happened that were to have a bearing on future events. To increase profits he had agreed with Ringstrop two years before to put Thor Olsen in as manager and instead of selling the timber standing, to sell it felled and delivered. One of the big west coast towing companies was contracted to do the haulage. A year later the towing agreement was with a different company. By then Olsen had informed him that they had virtually run out of all the profitable areas, apart from High Stand, and it was at that point that Barony of SVL had offered to buy it standing, get their own people to do the felling and Angeles Georgia Towing the haulage. The price was a lot higher than any Canadian company had been able to offer and Ringstrop had advised acceptance, Angeles Georgia being a small one-tug company tied to SVL and operating close to cost.

That was when he had begun selling his inessential assets. 'N-nothing would induce me to sell – the old man on my back, his words in my ears.' The flat in Belgravia and the villa in Monaco had already gone. His plane and his stable of old cars, pictures and the best of the silver, that was what they had lived on for the next year. Finally, he had said to hell with it and sold off the first two hectares of High Stand. 'I thought it was the t-timber they wanted. I'd no idea . . .' He sat there, crouched on the edge of his bunk in nothing but his pants, his head in his hands. 'Dad – if he could see me now . . . Christ, what a mess!'

'Are you saying they didn't want the timber?' Even then I didn't connect, didn't see what he was driving at. And his only answer was to turn his head so that his eyes were on the cuttings which I had placed on the top of his rucksack. And when I repeated the question, asking him what they had done with the timber, he said sharply, 'Towed it down to Seattle, you know that.'

'Well then . . .?'

'God Almighty, man – don't you see?' He was staring at me wildly. 'SVL, the towing company, those do-it-yourself and garden shed outfits in Chicago, they're all linked. And that's how the drugs get into the States. Somewhere along the tow route from the Halliday Arm to Seattle, some ship, a cargo vessel, a float-plane maybe – I don't know – but somewhere along the route a consignment of coke brought up from South America is trans-shipped. In Puget Sound a barge-load of logs is a common enough sight, and then, on the long road haul to Mandola's company depot in Chicago, who would think of unloading a great timber truck stacked high with massive tree logs to check what's underneath? An officer would have to be damn sure before he ordered a thing like that.'

He gave a slight shrug, leaning forward, his head in his hands like a man praying. 'Now perhaps you understand. That's what I've been living with. Not just my father's curse. Not just that – but all those kids, all the people who are being sold the stuff. God knows what it's like by the time it reaches them. Something innocent like borax or talcum, that's not so bad, but if it's amphetamines, if it's being mixed with speed, then

G-God help them – speed is the killer – the fastest . . .'
His voice tailed away.

I asked him how long he had known all this, how he
had found out. 'Was it Wolchak?'

He shook his head impatiently, locked in on his own
thoughts and too tense to answer questions. Suddenly
he looked at me, his face strained and that nerve ticking
away on the line of his jaw, the hesitancy in his speech
more pronounced. 'God help me, too,' he breathed. 'Me
– me – I'm involved, you see. That's why they sent me
those c-cuttings, so that I'd know . . . I can't go to the
police, to anyone. And now they want the land, the
trees, everything. They want me to sign . . . and if I
don't, then they've got Miriam. And if I go to the police,
if I blow the whole d-dirty racket wide open – ' He
shook his head. 'I can't do it, can I? Not now. And they
know it.'

And then suddenly he was half down on his knees,
looking up at me, imploring. 'What am I g-going to do?'
And he repeated it, tears in his eyes. 'Help me, for God's
sake. Do I ignore Miriam, stop the whole thing . . .?'

I didn't answer and he shook his head again. 'I can't,
can I? I can't ignore her. The poor kid's down there
somewhere and if I d-don't d-do what they ask . . .'

Even then I didn't believe it. Terrorism, yes – that
was something we in Britain had considerable experience of. But drugs . . . If it had been pushers, or smuggling, the sort of smuggling haul that the customs
periodically unearth, but regular consignments, and on
this sort of scale . . . 'Who's organizing it, do you
know?' I was thinking of Wolchak, dancing into my

office with that set smile of his, and trying to visualize him as a big-time smuggler setting up a drug line that would net millions and millions over the years, destroy thousands of innocent, unsuspecting people, kids a lot of them. But he didn't seem to fit. And the whole thing blown up too big. If it hadn't been for that note, for the fact that both her husband and I had recognized it as her writing, then I'd have thought he had made it all up, an appalling piece of fantasizing to satisfy some psychological need. At least I could have brushed it off as wild exaggeration, the two South Americans and the cuttings from the Chicago press a coincidental basis for wild imagining.

'We'll see what your son thinks about it,' I said.

'Brian?' He laughed and the sound of it was again that snorting neigh. 'Brian is a sort of embodiment of the Old Man's curse, isn't he? That picture you showed me – Man of the Trees, Greenpeace – our friends of the forest killed in action. Self-dramatizing. He sees himself as a sort of Don Quixote.' His voice shook, but whether with anger or despair I wasn't quite sure. And he went on, 'Brian's no use. Trees, whales, seals, the rain forests – that's what he believes in, not people. Me, his mother, Miriam, anybody, we mean n-nothing to him, nothing at all.'

It was at that point that the ship began to tremble, faint shouts and the beat of the engines increasing. Feet sounded on the deck, the thud of a heavy rope against the hull, the blare of a siren. 'The last leg,' he muttered. 'In the morning we'll be at Prince Rupert with Bella Bella only hours away. I've got to make up my mind.'

The anguish in his voice was so real I wished I was out of the stuffy, sick atmosphere of the cabin, out on deck in the cool of the night air watching the Alaska shoreline and the dark of the spruce slide by under the moon, the lights of Ketchikan fading astern. What the hell could I say to the man, what advice could I possibly give him? If he'd read it right, if all that he had said was true – but it couldn't be, surely. Surely what he had been saying of his son was true of himself. He was blowing the whole situation up out of all proportion, dramatizing it so that I would sympathize, so that Brian, when we met up with him, would sympathize. He wanted us to feel sorry for him, to take notice of him . . . He was the little boy Miriam had described, not Peter Pan, but an immature male desperately needing to hold the centre of the stage. Attention, affection, self-importance . . . And then the juddering of the engines caused the cuttings to slip off the rucksack and I was leaning down to pick them up, we were both leaning down, and because they were spread out across the floor we found ourselves staring down at a sort of montage of headlines, and all of them screamed the dreadful toll taken on kids who were becoming hooked, the terrible things they would do to get hold of the money to buy their fixes.

'I don't think you understand,' he said wearily, and began picking them up and stuffing them into the old suitcase he had slung on the rack.

Perhaps he was right. Outside, in the passageway, I could hear people moving about, the sound of voices against the background hum of the engines and the faint murmur of water slipping along the hull. We had increased to passage speed and the normality of it all made Tom's situation seem utterly incongruous, locked in on himself in that stuffy little cabin, a man with a problem no one could solve for him, feeling isolated, utterly alone.

I left him then and went up on deck. Lopez had been standing at the end of the passageway. He had smiled at me, a quick flash of tobacco-browned teeth below the drooping moustache. 'Your friend all right?' And I had nodded, pushing past him and moving quickly, in a hurry to get out into the clean, wholesome air. Just the South American watching, not doing anything, and the gun under his arm without ammunition, and yet it scared me, the present manifestation of a looming menace that was growing larger and larger in my imagination. I was thinking of Miriam, against the background of those newspaper cuttings – the money and the violence – and wondering where she was.

I suppose I got some sleep, but it didn't feel like it as I stumbled out of my bunk at the sound of the ship docking. It was 05.45 hours. Prince Rupert, and we were on time. I shaved and dressed, then went on deck where the glare of arc lights was paling to the first silvery glimmer of dawn.

The BC Ferries vessel was already there with cars waiting on the dock to go aboard. It was scheduled to leave at nine, so we had almost three hours to get through the formalities of re-entering Canada and settle in for a daylight passage that would get us to Bella Bella at eight in the evening. I hoped Brian Halliday would be there to meet us. I desperately needed somebody other than Tom to discuss things with, even though he was probably not the sort of person who would have anything helpful to contribute.

The day dawned sunless and with a low cloud base, so that all but the base of the mountains that rose beyond the flats on which the town was built was obscured. Seaward the port was almost totally locked in by the offshore island of Digby. I don't know why, but I didn't wait for Tom. Just after seven I got my bags and transferred to the other ship. By eight I was breakfasting in the cafeteria, having left my things on a seat up for'ard where I would have the best view of the Inside Passage as we steamed down the BC coast, provided, of course, the clouds lifted.

I was sitting having a cigarette with my second cup of coffee, wondering whether I shouldn't have gone along to Tom's cabin to check that he was awake, and idly watching the trickle of people in the coffee queue, a mixture that I don't think you would see anywhere but in this change-over port between Alaska and British Columbia, when my eyes became fixed on the back of a big, heavily-built man in an olive-khaki shirt and trousers. It was the fact that he was standing with his tray at the cash desk with a little Eskimo woman in front of him and what looked like a Japanese couple behind, though they may have been Filipinos or even from somewhere further south in Asia. He looked so huge by comparison, and something about the way he held his head, the set of his shoulders . . . Then he turned and I called to him.

It was Jim Edmundson. He came over, his tray gripped in his large hands, a brown briefcase under his arm. 'Well, well – how was the mine, eh?' I forgot about Tom then, so glad was I to have somebody to talk to, even if I couldn't tell him the whole story.

'Fine,' I said. 'Most interesting.' And then, as he put his tray down, and the briefcase, and lowered himself into the chair opposite me, I asked him what he was doing, here on a ferry that only went as far as Port Hardy at the northern tip of Vancouver Island. 'You weren't on the American boat.'

'No, I drove down.' He looked so relaxed, so normal, as he tucked hungrily into his breakfast, and in my mind I was comparing him with Tom and the South Americans, the whole background of unreality I had lived with these past few days. 'Road conditions not bad, nor weather, considering the time of year.' His mouth was already full, his jaws working, and he held his fork fisted in his right hand. 'Dumped the car in the parking lot here. From Bella Bella I was expecting to get one of the floatplanes, but now – '

'Where are you going?' I was thinking that perhaps I could hitch a ride if he was headed up the long fjord arms that run into the Rockies in that part of BC. 'Funny thing,' he went on, 'meeting you here. I bin borrowed by the forestry people.' He gulped some coffee, fisted more food into his mouth, the plateful of sausages, eggs and fried potatoes disappearing at a rate of knots. 'They've done it before . . . 'count of the book, I s'pose. I told you, didn't I? . . . I was trained in forestry.'

'Jean said you'd worked for the Forestry Service.'

'That's right.' He nodded, swallowing hard. 'Well,

the guy who should investigate anything in that region . . . he's had an accident . . . went in with a helicopter fighting a fire over beyond that copper mine inshore of Hardy . . . What's odd, meeting you, is that it's the Halliday property. Didn't you tell me something about his son doing a Greenpeace act before the cameras on a bargeful of logs going down to Seattle?'

I nodded. 'And that's why you're here? You mean you're actually going to the Halliday Arm to investigate timber felling in the Cascades?'

He was nodding his head all the time I was putting the question. 'That's what's odd, meeting you here.'

Odd it certainly was, the country so vast. And yet I suppose it wasn't so odd really. BC, the Yukon, Alaska – it was only vast when you were travelling the country. When you wanted something done, though communications were fast and efficient, the people to do the job were desperately thin on the ground; one regional forestry officer injured and who was there close at hand to take over from him?

'They want a full report. Something the media will accept. Just because I had a book published . . .' He shrugged. 'Christ!' he said, 'that was ten years ago. But my bosses agreed . . . So!' He laughed, and I remembered how the sound of his laughter had boomed in that wet, snowy drive from Whitehorse across to Haines Junction, how his teeth had shown white against the black of the forest streaming by. 'Jean's hopping mad. I'd be nursemaid to the children if she had her way, and she don't like sleeping alone.' He grinned, and at that moment Tom came in looking vague, his eyes flicking quickly over the tables. Then he saw me and his face lit up, as though he'd been scared he'd lost me.

He went over to the service counter then and I watched as he got a tray and joined the queue. When he came over to the table all he had on the tray was a glass of orange juice and coffee. I half stood up, uncertain what to do. 'This is Jim Edmundson,' I said. 'You remember I told you how helpful he was after I got to Whitehorse, and then his wife driving me . . .'

'Tom Halliday.' He had set his tray down and was holding out his hand to Edmundson. It surprised me, the first indication that he might now be willing to talk to the Canadian authorities.

'Tom – Halliday?' Jim Edmundson was lumbering awkwardly to his feet, his mouth fallen half open with surprise. 'The Halliday that owns Ice Cold, right?' He gripped Tom's hand as though he were a long-lost friend he'd known all his life. 'There's some people thought you were dead.'

'Well, there's times I'm not sure that wouldn't be a good idea.' Tom managed some sort of a smile and the two of them sat down, Jim Edmundson explaining again why he was on the boat, and Tom staring at him as though fascinated by the way he was being carried along.

'You mean tomorrow y-you'll be f-flying into the Halliday Arm.' The stutter was suddenly quite marked. 'An official visit, as f-forestry adviser – to inspect, then write a report. An of-ficial report?'

'That's right.' Tom leaned back, his eyes closed. He might have been praying, but I thought it more likely he was on the verge of passing out. It must have come as a shock. And then, suddenly, his eyes flicked open. 'I'm going there myself. Philip and I are going there, and Brian – my son – is meeting us at Bella Bella. Can you give us a lift in your plane? No, of course – three is too many probably. But me. I must get there. It's my wife, you see . . .' And then his voice stuttered into incomprehensibility as he saw the other shake his head.

'I won't be flying in,' Edmundson said. 'Not unless the cutter's gone off on a search and rescue.' And he added by way of explanation, 'They're having a Coastguard cutter meet me at Bella Bella.'

'A ship – well, that's better . . .'

But again the big Canadian was shaking his head. 'They don't take passengers, not normally. I guess they're a bit like a navy ship. You'll need to charter one of the floatplanes.'

The engines started up under our feet, a sudden murmur that had the deck, the whole ship, our coffee cups vibrating. Everywhere in the cafeteria people were draining their glasses or their cups, gathering up their things and moving towards the stairs or the glassed-in front of the big saloon to watch our departure. It was one minute to nine and the thump of the first warp coming on board was followed by an increase in the revs and the swish of swirling water as the thrusters came into operation.

'Sometime in the course of the voyage I'd like to put a few questions to you, Mr Halliday, if I may.' Jim Edmundson's voice sounded suddenly remote and impersonal, his formal mode of address very different from the easy sliding into Christian names that was his customary approach to other men. 'Could we have a drink before the midday meal, say about noon. Okay?'

Tom nodded, his eyes flickering uneasily from Jim to me and back to Jim Edmundson. 'What do you want to know?'

Edmundson laughed. 'Don't know yet, do I? Heard so much about you, I'm only just recovering from the surprise of running into you like this. Small world.' He nodded to himself as though he had said something profound. 'Very small world. But that's Canada, eh? Korea. Were you in Korea?' He didn't wait for an answer. 'Last time I was on the Inside Passage run there was a fellow on board – came from a little place up the coast from Ketchikan. An American – Alaskan rather. They like to be called Alaskan. His name was Moses Jallopi. Odd name; odd little guy, too. But there he was and I hadn't seen him since we shared a muddy little slit trench that was more of a shell crater than anything else. We were there two nights, one whole day, not another of our buddies anywhere in sight and the North Koreans, or the Chinese, I never knew which, not fifty metres away, guns banging and shells landing.' He smiled and shrugged. 'Seems like another world now. It's like I say, a small world once you start using our transportation system.' He smiled again, gathering up his briefcase, and at that moment the PA system broke in, loud and metallic. It was a call for passenger James Robert Edmundson to go to the Purser's office and he got to his feet. 'See you in the bar then, around noon.'

We were under way then and within an hour the sun

was burning up the clouds so that the islands and tops of the coast mountains gradually emerged, vistas of tree and rock and water, the sun a luminous glow in the shimmering haze. Noon found us entering the narrowest part of the Grenville Channel, still steaming at something around 18 knots as far as I could guess. I came in from the deck to see Camargo and Lopez sitting three rows back from where I had put my bag. One had a newspaper, the other a magazine. Tom appeared to be asleep, but when I told him it was time we joined Jim Edmundson in the bar his eyes opened slowly, the pupils strangely enlarged, his gaze uncertain.

'You see him.' His voice was a little slurred.

'But he wants to talk to you. A few questions.'

'Tell him I don't like drink, an' I don't answer questions. Tell him anything you dam' well like. I don't wanta be bothered with it. Unless we can hitch a ride on that cutter that's meeting him. If we can do that, then okay – ' His lips were spread in a sly smile as though he thought the decision he had made was a clever one. 'If he'll get us all to the Cascades, then I'll tell him – whatever he wants to know. If he can find Miriam – part'c'ly if he can locate Miriam . . . You think he carries that much weight, enough to get things moving – well, do you?'

'I don't know.'

He sighed, his shoulders lifting in a slight shrug, his head drooping, his eyes closing.

In the end I was on my own when I joined Jim at the bar. He didn't seem surprised. 'That man's on drugs, isn't he?'

'Sometimes,' I said guardedly.

'Takes me back.' He was smiling quietly, his hands still gripped round the beer in front of him. 'Don't know where those Yanks were getting it from. I never enquired. But they were sure getting it from somewhere. You ever tried it, Philip?'

I shook my head.

'Me neither. I'm an open air man. It's city boys mostly take to the stuff. I suppose you need a kick if you live in a concrete ghetto. And in war you need to forget. But a man like Halliday . . .' He shrugged. 'Had everything he wants, I suppose, an' got bored. Now . . .' He opened his briefcase. 'Maybe it's a good thing he isn't here. Much better I show it to his lawyer.' He pulled out a sheet of flimsy paper and passed it across to me. 'Radio message. It was waiting for me when I came on board.'

It announced that the *Kelsey* had orders to pick up an American tug bound for Seattle towing a barge loaded with logs and stand by while customs officers carried out a routine inspection. *You are to proceed on board* Kelsey *with the utmost speed on arrival Bella Bella. Capt. Cornish will brief you to the extent that it may concern your forestry inspection.*

I handed it back to him. 'Well . . .?' I was wondering why he had shown me what was a fairly confidential document.

'Obviously this is another load of timber coming down from your client's Cascades plantation. When the skipper knows you two are landing at Bella Bella with me it's just possible he may want Halliday or both of you with him when he rendezvous with the tug – just in case there is any question of the logs themselves being held for examination.'

'Do you know what it's about?' I asked.

'No. Could be just a question of the export licence. They aren't all that easy to get, all timber having to be offered to Canadian pulp and saw mills first. But a customs inspection of an American tug sounds to me more like a narcotics operation. Last night in the hotel there was some talk in the bar about ferries being gone over for drugs, particularly the American ships coming down from Alaska. At any rate, officers of the narcotics division of the FBI, the Federal Drugs Enforcement Administration, had been staying in the hotel for several weeks.' He lumbered to his feet. 'What can I get you?'

I would have liked a straight malt, something with a kick in it that would steady me up, but I didn't think they'd have a malt. 'Same as you,' I said, my nerves tense, and then, as he went to the bar, I sat back, consciously trying to relax. But I couldn't, my mind overwhelmed by what he had told me, thinking of the tug, which might already have left the Halliday Arm towing that barge piled with felled trees, and wondering when the operation would take place, whether the tug would stop, and if not . . . Anything seemed possible, remembering that note from Miriam and all that Tom had told me at Ketchikan in that sick little cabin of his. I hadn't any doubt, you see. None at all. This was the drug route, though how they got the drugs on board the tow I couldn't guess. But on board either the tug or the barge they would certainly be. That was why

Brian Halliday's protest hadn't stopped them, why they had nearly run him down.

Jim came back with two more cans of beer and as he lowered himself into his seat again he said, 'Something I want to ask you – something that arises from my perusal of the information sent me by the forestry people. My remit, you understand, is to report on the extent to which the environment may be damaged by Halliday signing away more hectares of his father's plantation for clear felling – I take it, with the mine yielding what amounts to a nil return, or what has probably already happened, becoming a drain on his resources, I take it he is now more or less living off the BC forestry land. That right?'

I hesitated, considering how much I ought to tell him. He was no longer a chance-met Canadian being friendly and helpful to a stranger; he was an official asking questions about a client of mine and the answers I gave he would regard as being given in my official capacity as Tom's lawyer and could well go into his report.

'Well?'

'Yes,' I said. 'I think you could say that until a new gold yielding area is opened up at Ice Cold he is quite probably living off the sale of timber he made to the SVL Company in Seattle.'

He nodded, raising his glass and emptying almost half of it. 'As I understand it, he's cut through all the natural growth up on the slopes and what he's left with now is a fully stocked plantation of some four hundred hectares in the bottom. That's not far short of a thousand acres. And this is something I find hard to believe, but it's there in my notes – ' he slapped his briefcase – 'it was planted about seventy years ago.'

'Why do you find that hard to believe?' I asked.

'Because here in BC we only started planting trees in World War II. Before that we relied on natural regeneration. I guess there was some experimental hand planting before then, but if Halliday's father was planting back at the end of World War I, and on the scale of a thousand acres, then he was way ahead of his time. Maybe he was over in England and got the idea from your Forestry Commission. It was around then that Britain started hand planting. And another thing I don't understand – why are the trees being harvested now? We wouldn't normally fell western red cedar under about a hundred and twenty years.'

'I see.' I stared at my drink, thinking about that. 'How much do you reckon the plantation is worth with the trees at their present age?'

He shrugged. 'Difficult to say till I see them, but the timber industry is currently operating on minimum stumpage, so I guess the price would be around five dollars a cube. Say there's two hundred, three hundred cubic metres per hectare, that would make each hectare, which is about 2.4 acres, worth somewhere between a thousand and fifteen hundred dollars. That's the value standing. Of course,' he added, 'the timber would be worth a lot more by the time it gets to market, but even so I find it difficult to understand why it's being cut at this age. They'd be about a hundred feet now and twelve inches diameter at breast height. Leave them another fifty years and they'd be a hundred and fifty feet with the diameter doubled, the yield too, so that the value per hectare would be around two thousand dollars at present prices.'

So the whole property, all the four hundred hectares Tom's father had planted, was currently worth about half a million dollars, and once it was cut, that would be the end of it, his last source of income gone. I checked the figure with Jim and he nodded. 'So why does he disappear?' He stared at me. 'Why go missing as though he were in some kind of trouble – or afraid of something?' And he added, 'Why is he on drugs?'

I had given him the answer to his first query, but now he was asking questions I had no right to answer. Not yet. And in any case, I didn't know the answers, not for sure. It went on like that, Jim putting questions to me and myself parrying them as best I could, until I got us another drink. A dark shoreline was sliding by on either side and the sun was no longer shining as I returned to the table. 'Your drink,' I said, standing beside the table. 'Now look,' I told him, 'either you stop trying to pump information out of me that I'm not entitled to give you, or I leave you to drink on your own. Mostly I'm as puzzled about certain aspects of the situation as you are.'

'Oh, sit down, Philip, sit down.' His face was lit by that large friendly grin of his. 'I understand your situation. But I'm curious, so you can't blame me for trying to get a little nearer the core of the matter.'

'You get us aboard that Coastguard cutter you say is meeting you and I think maybe when Tom sees the search operation . . .' I shrugged and sat down. 'I don't know. I wish I did. But it's just possible he might decide to open up a bit.'

'I take it he's already opened up to you?'

'To some extent,' I said.

'And if he was present when the cutter stands by the tug and its tow, you think it might make him more communicative?'

I nodded. 'He needs help.'

His eyebrows lifted.

'It's his wife,' I said. 'She's disappeared.'

'Left him?'

I shook my head, unwilling to add anything to what I had blurted out. Somebody, sooner or later, would have to hand the whole thing over to the proper authorities, and that person I guessed would have to be me. I had made the first tentative move, but I was unwilling to give any details. The nature of that note of hers had left me with the very real fear that if the matter were handled clumsily it could cost Miriam her life. 'Let's see what happens when you meet up with the tug. When will that be?'

But he couldn't tell me. All he knew about the operation was what the radio message had told him. 'The cutter's skipper will presumably have all the details.' And he added, 'I'll see what I can do about getting you on board. Seeing that the tow comes from Halliday's property Captain Cornish might feel it was better he was in on the operation.'

We went along to the cafeteria for lunch then, sitting at a table with an Eskimo, his wife, who was a half-black American schoolteacher, and their enchanting little five-year-old daughter who had pigtails of black, coarse hair, and eyes that shone blue through the puffy almond slits of coffee-coloured skin.

I could have been happy on that trip down the coast. The sun had broken through at last, glimmering in a milky haze, the Grenville Channel walls spruce-clothed in sombre green, glimpses of small boats, log rafts where there was a timber-loading cove, and here and there on the flats rough timber bunkhouses or dwellings, some on wooden stilts, others rafted so that they looked like the North American version of the ark. And all the time Jim talking, about the country, the people, and occasionally he would turn to the Eskimo, saying a few words to him in his own language, so that the flat smooth swarthy face split in a wide smile, great teeth like gravestones flashing out, the colour of old walrus ivory. The atmosphere was so Robert Service that I almost expected the great characters of the gold rush to come rolling in.

Instead it was Camargo – a quick flash of the dark eyes, and then he was making for the service counter.

'Somebody you know?' Jim asked.

I hesitated. 'Just a hunter. He was up at Ice Cold. South American.'

He nodded. 'We get lots of them. They come for the hunting.' The words came out angrily, between his teeth. 'They enjoy killing. Machismo, I guess – a sort of vicarious orgasm they get out of death. So long as they're at the right end of the gun. Point it at them and I guess machismo gets a little jaded.' I kept my eyes on Camargo's table, expecting Lopez to join him. But nobody joined him. He sat alone, and I guessed that Lopez had been left to watch Tom.

But why? Each night in the passageway outside his cabin, they had taken it in turn. And then, towards the end of lunch, when Jim was talking about the great forest valleys that lay between the ranges of the Rockies and how they had been raped of all the big timber in the early days of the century and right through to pretty near the present time, how the country had only just begun to get to grips with the enormous, costly and lengthy problem of replacement planting, it came to me. They were afraid he'd commit suicide. That's why Camargo and Lopez were watching him turn and turn about. Dead he was no use to them. Dead he couldn't sign the documents they needed that would give them the legal right to harvest the timber on that land.

But still the same question in my mind. Why the hell was the Halliday timber so important to them? If all they needed was an excuse to make towing runs from up north of Vancouver Island to Seattle, then any logging contract would surely do? Or was it because the Halliday Arm was particularly isolated?

In the end I gave up. Jim was talking about Alexander Mackenzie and the rock where he had scratched his name as the first to reach the Pacific overland. 'I never saw it when I was working down south in Vancouver Island. Now maybe I will. The place where he reached salt water after crossing the Rockies isn't very far from the Cascades. In fact, from Ocean Falls it's not more than half a day's run in a canoe with an outboard, or in one of those inflatables. There's hot springs right there, in the Halliday Arm, somebody once told me. Now, you wouldn't think there'd be hot springs down beside an arm of the Pacific with the Rocky Mountains literally standing on top of you.'

His broad, bland face was concentrated on his memories. 'I saw Ocean Falls once. Went in from Shearwater, which isn't far from Bella Bella, through Gunboat Passage, up the Fisher Channel and Cousins Inlet. There's a dam at Ocean Falls to feed electricity to the pulp mill, but now I'm told it's all closed down, finished, most of the people gone. There were some eight thousand when I was there, the rain streaming down and everyone with umbrellas.' He laughed. 'I guess it rains there about 370 days a year. I was there one night and it never stopped, the rock cliffs black and glistening with it, the timber-laid road down from the dam running with water and the clouds so low you felt you couldn't breathe. Now, I suppose, there's hardly anyone there, as the BC Ferries don't go there any more.'

I was trying to follow him on the BC 'Super Natural' road map. 'Where do you reckon your Coastguard boat will pick up the tug?'

But he had no idea. 'Could be right of Waglisia Island – that's the old Indian name for Bella Bella.'

We talked until we had finished our meal and then he excused himself. 'I got to catch up on some background notes. Trouble with driving down from the Yukon like that you can't read at the same time.' Camargo had left by then, and it was Lopez who was sitting alone with a coffee and some food. He stared at Jim curiously as we passed his table. Up for'ard in the saloon it was Camargo who now sat three rows back from us, keeping an eye on Tom who was slumped in his seat, fast asleep.

He didn't stir as I sat down beside him and after reading for a bit I went outside. We were in open water then, the entrance to Princess Royal Channel over the bows, and it had started to rain, big, heavy drops that produced little rings like fish jumping on the flat, leaden-smooth surface of the water.

It rained like that all afternoon, heavy, thundery rain with thunder grumbling over the veiled mountains and occasional flashes of lightning. And then, after an early meal, it suddenly cleared to a brilliant sunset as we turned the winking light on McInnes Island and entered the Seaforth Channel on the run up to Bella Bella. Tom was awake then, his face haggard, and not saying anything. Even when I told him about the radio message Jim had received he made no comment, sitting there watching the approach to our final destination in a state of what appeared to be complete apathy. And then, when the engines slowed, the ship turning and Bella Bella in sight, he suddenly said, 'Did he say when it would be, this operation – tonight?'

'He doesn't know,' I told him.

He turned on me, his eyes staring, his mouth twitching.

'You r-realize, don't you, if it's successful – what it means to Miriam. They'll k-kill her.'

PART FOUR

OCEAN FALLS

CHAPTER ONE

The cutter lay alongside the quay at Bella Bella. It wasn't at all the sort of vessel I had expected. It looked more like a miniature warship with its sharp upthrust bow, rakish black hull and the white-painted bridge structure rising abruptly to the spear-like thrust of the whip aerials either side of the mast, lights, radar, a tangle of high-tech equipment that gave her a very purposeful appearance. And the quay and the village behind sprawled on the hill, houses glimmering in the last of the day and the first of the moon; that, too, wasn't what I had expected of an Indian reserve area. True, I couldn't see any whites on the quay. The few people lounging around, and the little group slinging a baseball, were all dark-skinned. But the quay was solidly timbered, a large area with storage sheds, all of it looking very modern, and the houses behind all modern and quite substantially built.

'You got any place to stay?' Jim asked me as we stood waiting to disembark. I told him I was relying on

Halliday's son, and if he didn't turn up, then at least Tom Halliday knew one of the pilots. There was a little floatplane lying moored to a pontoon buoyed up with empty oil drums. Tom joined us, his gaze fixed on the quay. 'Don't see Brian there,' he muttered.

I, too, had been searching the shoreline. A launch came in from old Bella Bella, arrowing sharp lines across the mirror-still water, its engines breaking the stillness. 'If you do get stuck,' Jim said, 'you can take the launch over to Shearwater, which is round the promontory just east of here. There's a hotel there, and now the main fishing season's over there should be no problem about getting a room.'

'Where the hell's Brian?' There was a nervous edge to Tom's voice and I realized that, like me, he had been relying on his son being at Bella Bella to meet him. 'You sent that cable, didn't you? From Whitehorse? You told him when we'd be here?'

'I said we were catching the ferry from Skagway the next night.'

'Well then – where the hell is he?' And he turned towards the shore again, muttering something about it being typical – 'just typical of the boy'.

There weren't many people going ashore at Bella Bella – a few Indians, the Eskimo and his family, and a young nurse and her husband who was a doctor, both of them working at the hospital. That was all. The Coastguard Captain was on the quay to meet Jim, a short man in black trousers and white shirt with a peaked cap and a beard that was just beginning to show signs of grey. Jim introduced us. His name was Doug Cornish.

An Indian called out, 'Hi!' He was pot-bellied and had a sort of swagger to him, and he stopped to add with a grin, 'Yu, Mustache – yu no like razor eh?' And before the skipper could think of a suitable reply the man was off up the slope to the village with a cheerful wave of his hand.

A young Indian girl standing near moved delicately forward. 'Your name not Mustache.'

'No.' Cornish smiled at her.

'Yu captain of that little boat?' She nodded to the Coastguard cutter, gold earrings dancing to the movement of her head. She had a mass of black hair, breasts just beginning to bud under the red of her T-shirt and she wore a worldly little smile.

Cornish nodded. 'What do you want?'

'Your balls, Captain.' And the smile broadened to a grin, the eyes coquettish as she whisked around with a toss of her black hair and went dancing away to join the youths practising with the baseball. She couldn't have been more than fifteen.

Cornish shook his head, his cheeks red under his beard. 'That's the Indian for you.' He grinned. 'Never could get used to their uninhibited view of the human body.' He glanced at his watch and then at Jim. 'Shall we go on board? I'm all ready to slip.'

'I'd like a word with you first.' He took the Captain by the arm and walked him along the quay past a refuelling pump where they stood in conversation while we waited. Tom was staring down at the launch just mooring at the pontoon. There was a white man at the tiller and Tom called down to him, asking about Brian. 'You seen him?'

'A few days back,' the man shouted back. 'He was here at Bella Bella. Then he got young Steve to fly him up to Ocean Falls. You remember Steve, Tom – he just got in from Bella Coola, said to give you a message if you turned up. Your son's in Ocean Falls and says to meet him there. Okay?'

Tom had moved to the edge of the quay. 'Steve up at his place?' he called down. 'I'd like to talk to him.'

'Reckon so,' the man replied.

It was annoying, Brian not being there. I'd been relying on him, not only for additional information, but to support me in the decision I was gradually coming to and which could not be put off much longer. I was still a long way from the sort of RCMP post where I could get the appropriate high-level action I needed if I was to give the authorities the gist of that note from Miriam. Not any policeman could handle a thing like that, and I still needed Tom's cooperation. That, above all, was where I had been relying on Brian.

My thoughts were interrupted by Jim's voice calling us to get on board right away. The cutter's Captain was already there, hurrying up the ladder to the bridge-housing. 'It's all fixed,' Jim added as he came back for his bag and his briefcase. 'He's taking you both on his own responsibility, and when the operation is over he'll drop you off at Ocean Falls.'

I called to Tom who was still talking to the launch operator. He turned, frowning. 'He'll take us? Why?'

He came back, looking dazed. His eyes had a hunted look as they searched my face. 'Why?'

In telling Tom about the operation I hadn't said anything about drug smuggling. I'd repeated exactly the words of the radio message, a routine search operation. But I could see he had put two and two together. Like me, he had guessed it was drugs the customs officers would be searching for. He stood there for a moment, uncertain what to do. But Jim was already moving away towards the cutter. I had my bags in my hands and could hear the explosive snort of the engine starting up, one of the crew already on the quay moving to throw the bow warp off. The Captain put his head out of the sliding wheelhouse door – 'Hurry up, or I'll leave without you.'

'Come on,' I said. 'There's nothing for you here. Let's get to Ocean Falls and see if Brian can help.' And I turned, half running across the quay, not waiting for him, but sensing that he was following. The beat of the engines was loud as I tossed my bags onto the deck and hauled myself aboard. Tom was close behind me, the bow warp already gone, the props beating the water to a froth as a gap began to open up between the hull and the quay. The stern warp went slack, the bows swinging out and the stern in, and the man on the quay slipped the rope off its bollard and leapt aboard with it. The bows were steadying then, the vessel digging its stern deeper into the water as she picked up speed.

We parked our bags in the mess room aft, which was below deck and empty except for the steward clearing away the last remains of the evening meal. 'You like some coffee, help yourself.' He nodded to the hotplate. 'Coffee's available any time and if you're real thirsty there's the fridge – milk, orange juice, cans of tomato juice. Biscuits in the rack above the table there. Okay?'

I nodded and turned to Tom. 'I'm going up to the wheelhouse,' I said. 'See what the Captain can tell me.'

Tom didn't seem to hear. He was helping himself to coffee, his hair standing up like a brush and his brow creased in a horizontal line. The cup rattled in its saucer, his hand shaking, his mind shut away with its own thoughts and fears. I went up through the hatch and out onto the sidedeck where the wind of our passage thrust at my clothes and I had to clutch my cap. We must have been doing the better part of 20 knots, black water streaming past and the roar of the engines from the open hatch, where one of the oilers sat reading a magazine, almost deafening. A short iron ladder led up the side of the bridge-housing to the half-shut door of the wheel-house. I slid it back and went in, a voice on the radio saying, 'I can't see nuttin'. No lights, no stars, not a fuckin' thing. Where are you, *Naughty Gosling*? This fishing boat *Chick Chick*. Can't see nuttin'. I'm in a fog right up to my eyeballs, boy, an' ah reck'n ah'm lost.'

The Captain reached up and switched stations. 'Poor bloody Indian got himself lost. Next thing is he'll call RCC – that's the Rescue Coordination Centre at Esquimault, Victoria. If he does he'll be out of luck.' And he added, 'Forecast is for fog and that bugger's in it already. Trouble is we don't know where he is. Seaward probably.'

'Thickening up already, Doug.' The Mate was stand-

ing by the radar, peering into the night ahead. He
rubbed his eyes. 'Shit! Why do we have to get ourselves
dealt a bank of fog just when we'd like clear visibility?'

'Good practice, Curly.' The Captain's voice sounded
sour and they grinned at each other. 'Be a long night, I
reck'n.' The Mate was short and fat with black curly
hair and a voice that was hoarse as though he had a
perpetual need to clear his throat and couldn't be
bothered.

'Not going to be easy to locate that tug, is it?' I
asked.

The Mate gave me a startled look as though he
hadn't expected the stranger to voice an opinion, and
certainly not on the bridge. It was the Captain who
answered. 'Soon as we're through the Lama Passage and
into the Fisher Channel we should pick up the tow on
our radar.' He glanced at my battered sea cap. 'You
understand charts?' I nodded and he turned to the chart
table that stretched along most of the rear wall of the
wheelhouse below all the radios, the Decca navigation
and search and rescue equipment. 'She's out of the
Fisher now and into Fitz Hugh Sound and there's a ship
the Defence Forces base at Esquimault has been tracking
by satellite sitting waiting down there by the North Passage.' He pointed a thick hairy finger at the open sea
area to the west of Calvert Island. 'Don't ask me how,
but somebody's bugged her so that they've been able
to track her all the way from somewhere south of the
Californian coast. It's a big motor yacht, I'm told.'

'And what's your role?' I asked him as he stopped

abruptly, leaving me in the air as to what his instructions were.

He hesitated, then said, 'Well, I've let you on board, and since you'll see what happens, no point in your not knowing the role we're supposed to play.' His finger tapped the open water area. 'My instructions are to wait until I've got both yacht and tug on my radar scan and can report they're closing. A chopper is standing by. The expectation is that this is the rendezvous position, that they'll close to let the yacht lie alongside and pass her cargo over. I haven't been told what that cargo is, but as I gather both you and Jim here have already leapt to the conclusion that it's drugs, I can say that that's my conclusion, too. The helicopter will be carrying a rummage party. We stand by in case there's trouble.'

We were in the Lama Passage then, the waterway narrowing to the width of a quite ordinary-sized river, forests of trees green on either side, a pale tide-band of exposed rock close above the surface of the water and our wake arrowing out behind us to surge against it. It would have been too dark to see it if we hadn't had the spotlight trained on it, and as we entered the narrows, our speed unreduced and wisps of fog, Doug Cornish switched on the powerful beam of the 'nightsun' searchlight that seemed to pierce even the fog.

Our speed at that time was just over 18 knots, rocks and lit beacons ahead; I watched Cornish's face for some sign of nervousness, a flicker of hesitation. There was neither.

'Starb'd helm.'

The wheel spun under the helmsman's hand and he repeated, 'Starb'd helm.'

'Helm amidships and steer one-six-o.' And a moment later, the helmsman reported, 'Steering one-six-o.'

After that we just stood there, watching the Fisher Channel shoreline, which on the port side was barely visible, and waiting. The watch changed, the helmsman handing over and collecting the coffee mugs scattered about the wheelhouse.

'Everybody coffee? Milk and sugar?' he asked me. 'No sugar,' I said, and Jim asked for two lumps. The engine beat and the swish of the bow wave, the slop of the water against the starb'd side of the channel, all these were constant sounds. Only the sound from the radio and occasional verbal exchanges between skipper and mate interrupted the monotonous, almost sleep-inducing background noises of a vessel under way.

The Captain was bent over the radar, his eyes glued to the scanner, talking quietly to the Mate, and Jim had pushed open the door and was searching the Channel through a pair of ship's binoculars. I turned to the white expanse of Chart 1933 spread out on the chart table. There was a pair of dividers in the rack and I measured off the distance from where we had turned out of the Lama Passage to Cape Calvert and the open water of North Passage, then checked it off against the minutes of latitude shown vertically on the edge of the chart. A minute is the equivalent of a nautical mile and the dividers indicated just on forty.

'You a sailor?' It was the Captain's voice.

I nodded.

'The tide's with us so we're probably doing twenty over the ground. We'll be up with them in two hours. Sailing boat?' he asked.

He lived at Fulford in the Gulf Islands and kept a small cruiser in the harbour there. 'I named her *Salish* after one of the Indian tribes from the south – like Bella Bella is named for one of the northern tribes; the Haidas and the Bella Bellas were very fierce at one time.' Mugs of coffee appeared on a tray and we talked about boats for a time, then his eyes began to watch the clock. At twenty-three minutes past the hour he switched on the HF single sideband radio and two minutes later he was talking to RCC at the southern end of Vancouver Island. He gave his ETA at the target as approximately 22.55 and it was arranged that unless contrary advice was received from him the helicopter would lift off from Port Hardy at 22.10 hours to be on call within range of the target as the *Kelsey* closed with the tug and ordered it to heave-to. 'Good luck and let's hope this isn't another FBI rabbit that isn't going to come out of the hat.' The radio went silent and he switched it off.

'What was the last tip-off you had, Captain?' There was a wind on our backs and it was Tom's voice.

I turned – we both turned. He was standing in the starb'd doorway, leaning against it, his voice a little high but otherwise relaxed. 'Was it another log tow?'

'No.' The Captain was leaning a little forward, peering at Tom from under his bushy brows. 'I don't think we've met,' he said, the easy-going, friendly manner suddenly gone.

'My name's Tom Halliday.' He came in, shutting the door behind him and holding out his hand. 'You're Captain Cornish, I take it. I have to thank you for taking Philip and myself on this trip with you.' The Captain ignored the outstretched hand. He was frowning as Tom, quite unabashed, went on, his voice tending to slur some of the words, 'I think you know the "target" as you call it, the tow taking logs from the Cascades, which I own, down to Seattle for milling. I would like to talk to the people running this operation if I may. Can you get them on the radio please?'

'No, I cannot.' Doug Cornish's reaction was immediate, his tone uncompromising. 'And you will kindly ask permission before coming on my bridge. Do you understand, Mr Halliday?'

Tom smiled and shrugged, not in the least put out. 'So sorry. Of course. Permission requested, Captain.' It just didn't seem to occur to him his manner and the slightly supercilious tone in his very English voice were not the best way to approach a Canadian skipper on his own ship. And he didn't hesitate, but went straight on, 'You do understand, don't you, this operation, which from all the talk I've been listening to on board is a drugs snatch, could result in a woman's death – in a woman being murdered?'

The frown on Cornish's face deepened. 'Are you drunk or something? What woman? What the hell are you talking about?'

'My wife,' Tom said. 'If this is drugs . . .' He paused, shaking his head and looking suddenly uncertain. 'I want to talk to them. Whoever has set this operation up. I have to warn them – they've threatened to kill her.'

'Who have?' There was disbelief in the Captain's voice. 'What are you talking about?' He sounded exasperated.

Tom started to stutter something, then stopped. 'Ask Philip here. He's a lawyer. Maybe you'll listen to him.'

And so I was brought into it and quietly I told the Captain of the cutter something of what I knew. I couldn't help it. Tom, drugged to the eyeballs, had blurted it out and now I had to back him. In any case, perhaps it was as well, since it made up my mind for me.

But then the incredible happened. They didn't believe it. That Doug Cornish, standing there at the chart table with his Mate watching the scan, on the threshold of an awkward boarding operation with an American tug for target, wouldn't believe me was something I hadn't expected. That he wouldn't believe Tom, whom he clearly suspected of being an alcoholic, was fair enough. Tom wasn't easy to take at times. But that he wouldn't accept it from me, after we'd been standing there at the chart table talking about our respective boats and drinking coffee together . . . 'But the man's right,' I said. 'He's telling the truth. They're holding Miriam Halliday and once they know her husband is on board . . .'

'Then we'll keep him below. That way they'll never know – will that satisfy you?'

I must have been arguing with him for fifteen minutes or more, but he absolutely refused to contact his RCC base. 'You can talk to them afterwards,' he said finally. 'Once we know whether there's drugs on board or not. As soon as the operation's over, then you can talk to them. Not before. Okay?' And that was his final word. I couldn't budge him, nor could Tom, whose tone of voice had changed to one of pleading, tears in his eyes and his voice half-choked with emotion. I could see his change of manner had affected Cornish. He was no longer resentful and there was compassion in his voice as he put his hand on Tom's arm and said, 'Look, even if I accept the truth of what the two of you have been saying, I can't do anything about it. I'm just the skipper of a Coastguard vessel. I carry out orders, and my orders now are to stand by this tug while specialist officers of another branch of government service carry out a search. Afterwards you can talk to whoever you like. And now, Mr Halliday,' he added, 'I suggest you go below and leave me to get on with my job.'

Tom hesitated, glancing at me, and then he turned without another word and went stumbling down the ladder to the sidedeck. 'Better keep an eye on him.' The Captain's hand was on my arm, propelling me towards the door, and as I went out I saw him look across at Jim Edmundson with lifted brows, and seeing Jim nod, I checked and said, 'It's true what he told you. He had a note from her. She's being held hostage – '

'That's a matter for the police.' Cornish's face had suddenly taken a shut look. 'Nothing to do with me. You keep him off my bridge. Understand?' His head thrust forward, his eyes on mine, waiting till I acknowledged his order with a nod. 'Okay, then after this little business is over I'll drop you both at Ocean Falls, or he can go on to the Cascades with Jim Edmundson, whichever he likes.' He turned back to the radio. 'Any sign of that tow?' The Mate shook his head and Cornish thrust him aside and buried his eyes in the eyepiece of the scanner.

Tom was waiting for me at the bottom of the ladder, his hand clutching at me. 'What do I do?' His voice trembled, on the verge of tears.

'Nothing,' I said. 'Nothing you can do – except keep out of sight when we meet up with the tow. They don't know you're on board.'

'That man Lopez, he was with us when we came ashore.'

'So was Camargo,' I said. 'All those two know is that a man you met on the ferry got you a lift on a Coastguard cutter. That's all.'

'But as soon as we reach the tug –'

'That's all,' I repeated. 'All they'll be able to report. And it'll take time for them to contact whoever it is that's employing them. It'll be tomorrow at the earliest before they connect the *Kelsey* and us with the stopping and searching of the tug, and then all sorts of things may be happening.'

'You think they'll find coke on board?' His hand was still gripped tight on my arm. 'Is that what you think?'

'How the hell do I know? But if that yacht makes a rendezvous with the tug and the customs boys search it . . . Then the offices of the SVL Company in Seattle will be raided and the tug boat owners, Angeles Georgia

Towing, as well. If all that happens, then they won't be worrying about Miriam.'

It seemed to satisfy him. He stared at me a moment and I could see his mind grappling with the implications. Then he nodded. 'Ya. Guess you're right, Philip. And the Captain – he'll believe us then, won't he? I mean, if they find one of the ships stuffed with coke, he'll have to believe us, an' then he'll let me talk to this RCC base of his and the authorities will be alerted and they'll start a big search. Ya . . .' He was nodding his head again. 'Maybe it'll all work out for the best. The poor darling – I just hope to God . . .' There were tears in his eyes then and he let go my arm, snuffling into his handkerchief and turning aft. 'Where's the heads?'

I told him where it was and he went aft, balancing himself carefully with his hand on the deckhouse rail. When he returned he asked, 'How long've we got – before we close that tow? An hour?'

'A little more,' I said.

He nodded. 'I'm going to get some coffee then.' I went with him down to the mess-room and with the coffee I had some biscuits and cheese out of the fridge. By the time I had finished he was sprawled on the bulkhead settle half asleep. I got my anorak and went up on deck. The wind of our passage was too great for me to stand on the sidedeck, so I took up a position aft where I could look back from the shelter of the deckhouse along our wake to the vague outline of the mountains and the dark of the shore either side of the broad ribbon of water we were steaming down. The fog was no more than a gossamer-thin veil of mist now that we were out of the narrower Fisher Channel and into Fitz Hugh Sound.

There was a sudden flurry of activity, the engine-room telegraph jangling, the engines juddering and the wake changing to a confused froth as the cutter heeled sharply to port, one engine still going ahead, the other astern as we turned 180ϒ and headed back up the Sound, hugging the western shore, then swinging steadily in towards it to round a lit buoy, land closing in on our starb'd side. I was on the sidedeck then, one of the crew tumbling down the ladder from the bridge. 'What's happening?' I asked.

'We've sighted them, heading seawards through the Hakai Passage. Skipper says . . .' But the rest was lost in the noise of the engines, the rush of the bow wave, his words swept away by the wind.

I went up to the bridge then, thinking to hell with it. He could only throw me off again, and as long as Tom was safe down below . . . The Captain and the Mate were standing shoulder-to-shoulder at the radar, the helmsman rigid with concentration. The Chief was there talking to Jim. I slipped over to the chart table. It was Kelpie Point we had rounded, not a lit buoy, but a beacon on a little rock island, and the Hakai Passage ran north of Calvert and Hecate Islands almost due west out of the Sound to the open sea. A small cross had been pencilled just by a lit beacon north of Starfish Island. I turned expecting to see the flash of it, but there was nothing. 'Steer two-two-five.'

'Two-two-five,' the helmsman repeated.

Cornish moved to the chart table in a couple of

strides. 'Fog's thicker here,' he said, using the sliding rule to pencil in the line of our course through the passage, checking the distance with the dividers, then scribbling 220ϓ – 8m. 'Say the tow is making something over five knots, then we'll be alongside in less than an hour.' Without turning his head he ordered, 'Steer two-two-o.'

'Two-two-o.'

'Your friend all right?' He gave me a quick sideways glance, and when I said he was sleeping he nodded. 'Best thing for him.' Then he was back at the scanner, no word about my leaving the bridge, so I stayed, making myself as inconspicuous as possible. Apparently the tow was visible on the radar. But then the Captain straightened up, stretching and rubbing his eyes. 'Well, that's that, out of sight now round Starfish and Surf heading south beyond the South Pointers. Another hour.' He sighed and turned to me. 'You ever been on this coast before, Mr Redfern?'

I shook my head.

'Show you something,' he said, smiling and beckoning me back to the chart. 'See that reef?' He indicated the Pacific Ocean end of the passage, the southern side. 'The South Pointers. There's a big drying rock there and the tug's gone outside. Had to, of course. But there's a way through between the reef and Surf Island that's marked thirty – that's fathoms on this chart so it's almost sixty metres deep if I've got the nerve to risk it. The fog's thick out there. Have to do it on radar.' He was staring down at the chart, using me as a sort of sounding board for his thoughts. 'Not as bad as the Spider. I took the *Kelsey* through the Spider once. But then it was broad daylight and good visibility, even the little Fulton Passage quite straightforward.' He spread the chart out, and I saw the short cut he proposed to take and all the rocks, it looked about as bad as anything I had ever seen.

But that's the way we went, and the engines going flat out as we steamed south-west through the litter of rubbish, the Captain glued to the radar giving alterations of helm without reference to the chart, and all the time the single sideband radio squawking last-minute instructions as the Mate reported to RCC that our ETA and visual sight of the tow was now less than fifteen minutes away.

A few minutes and we were through, the helm to starb'd as we steered seaward. Cornish reached for the mike. 'Distance off two and a quarter miles, fog fairly thick, sea calm with a slight swell.' We were in fact rolling quite heavily. He had switched to VHF and was talking to the chopper pilot.

The next ten minutes seemed to drag interminably. The Mate was now at the scanner, the wheelhouse dark and everybody staring out through the windshield, searching the void, fog swirling round the bows. 'A light, sir.' It was the helmsman. 'Bearing Green 10.'

'Okay, have got.' Cornish had the binoculars up to his eyes. 'Steer two-five-o,' And then he was through to the helicopter pilot again, talking him down over the target. I could see the towing lights now, all blurred by the fog, and as the shadowy shape of a big barge loaded with logs began to emerge the Captain reached for the engine-room telegraph and rang for slow ahead on both engines.

'God!' the Mate said, peering through the glasses. 'That's pretty ancient, that thing. What is it, an old scow?'

We were passing it close now, moving up on the tug's port side. 'Scows are usually wood.' Cornish reached over and took the glasses. 'That's steel,' he said.

'Yeah, steel. And it's got a wheelhouse – a sort of caboose on its backside. I wonder where they got it – off the scrap heap most like. It's as rusty as hell.'

'Scows are wood,' Cornish repeated. 'And they're flat-sided for on-deck loading. That's a barge.'

'Yes, sir.' The Mate grinned. 'It's a barge – as you say, sir.'

It must have been at least 200 feet long, very low in the water with a little wheelhouse aft and the logs stacked end-to-end so high that if there was a man steering the thing he would have to be constantly in and out of the wheelhouse to peer ahead.

We were past the tow, the tug now visible through swirls of mist. Cornish rang the engine-room to reduce revs still further and ordered the helmsman to close the tug's port side. Then, when there was barely a ship's length between the two vessels, the lights all haloed and blurred in the seething billows of fog, he lifted the loud-hailer mike off its hook and put it to his lips: 'This is Coastguard cutter *Kelsey*. Do you hear me? This is Coastguard cutter *Kelsey*. You are to heave-to please. I repeat – heave-to. Do you hear me?'

And back out of the fog came an American voice:

'I hear you. This is Micky Androxis of American tug *Gabriello*. I am towing. I cannot heave-to.'

'You can reduce speed gradually and turn to port.'

'Why? Why should I reduce speed?'

The Mate's voice cut in then. 'Captain, I've got another blip, just westward of the tow. Looks like it's heading north.'

Cornish nodded. 'That'll be the yacht, I imagine.' The men were moving up the starb'd side of the cutter, automatic rifles gripped in their hands. They took up positions in the bows as Captain Cornish repeated his order to heave-to. The tugmaster pointed out once again that he was in command of an American-registered ship. 'As a Coastguard officer you have no authority to order me to stop – or to board, Captain. You understand?'

Cornish smiled, lifting his shoulders and his eyes in an expression of mock resignation. 'Seems he knows all the answers.' And he added, 'Something I don't believe an ordinary tugmaster would be likely to know.' He told the helmsman to close right in, and repeated his order to heave-to.

'You have to have police on board for me to do that, brother. You don't give me orders. But I take them from an RCMP officer. Okay?'

'A real sea-lawyer,' Cornish muttered as a light glimmered through the fog astern and the faint whoop-whoop-whoop of chopper blades reached us as they beat at the thick humidity. 'Police now arriving,' Cornish snapped over the loudhailer. 'Start slowing down – at once.'

The helicopter was hovering over the barge, lights

picking out the piled-up logs and a man being lowered onto the stern, the rotor blades just visible so that it looked like a ghostly dragonfly, everything veiled, the fog iridescent. Our spotlight held the tug in a merciless glare, the froth of water moving past the two hulls gradually lessening as the speed of both vessels decreased. I saw a second man drop onto the barge, unfasten the harness that had attached him to the winch wire and, as it was reeled in, the helicopter emerging more clearly from the fog, whirls of grey vapour as it slanted forward to take up a position over the tug's long after run, a man swinging down, pushing himself clear of the thick towing hawser, his feet reaching for the steel plates of the deck gleaming wet in our spotlight. Others followed.

'Last man coming down now.' It was the pilot's voice over our loudspeaker. 'I'll be leaving you then, Skip. I'm at call if they want me. I'm to pick them up at Namu, or else they'll send an amphibian up for them. Okay – you got that? You're to collect the bods when they've finished the job and deliver them to Namu. The motor yacht, incidentally, is Colombian-registered. She's hove-to with a Mountie and two customs boys on board. Over.'

Cornish already had the mike to his mouth. 'That's presuming tug, yacht and barge are cleared by the rummage party. What happens if they're not cleared?'

'Then I guess all three vessels will be under arrest,' came the answer. 'Customs will stay on board, so will the police officer. They'll make for Port Hardy most like. Wherever it is, you and I won't have to worry about them. They'll have borrowed their own transport. Okay?'

'Yes, okay.'

'Then I'll get going. See if I can find my way back in this dirty crud. Ta-ta – let's both of us hope they locate whatever it is they're looking for. Out.' And the big chopper lifted away, swinging its blunt nose westward, its landing lights suddenly cut off. Almost immediately it vanished from sight behind the grey, silvery wall that marked the iridescent limit of our own and the tug's lights.

Cornish hung up the VHF mike and turned to the Mate. 'Curly, have the deckies stand by to go alongside. We'll hitch onto the tug and give the engines a rest. The sea's calm enough.'

Not only was the Angeles-Georgia tug called the *Gabriello*, but she was manned by an ethnic mixture of Greek, Mexican and Italian Americans. The captain was of Welsh-Cretan extraction, a dark-haired, dark-eyed, truculent little man, who strutted around the deck of his flat-iron of a ship shouting at us, 'Yu guys are wasting your time. Yu won't find no contraband on my ship. Nothing. D'yu hear? Yu won't find nothing illegal. Yu look on the barge. That bumboat's none of my responsibility. Yu look there if yu think anybody got liquor or drugs. I bring it up empty, yu understand. Empty as a dead man's arse, but what those timber cowboys put in her besides logs, Christ only knows. Not me. It's nuthin' to do with me wot yu find there.'

We were tied up to that tug for almost six hours, right through the night until dawn came and the sun began burning up the fog, our whole world turning from sepia to silver and aglow with the warmth of a hidden furnace. I slept a little. Not much. Tom I don't believe slept at all; by morning his face was haggard, his eyes puffed and slightly inflamed. Once, sitting beside me with a cup of coffee, he had talked about drugs, comparing the operation that was being carried out now with the attitude of US authorities to liquor back in the 1920s. 'Prohibition put liquor underground. It was hoodlums and mobsters that handled it then. Now it's respectable and people accept that there'll be deaths on the road and mayhem on the football terraces as the result of over-indulgence.' He was drawing a comparison between drink and drugs and, though he was clearly trying to justify his own use of cocaine, I knew far too little about it to argue with him.

His point was that it was the outlawing of drugs, the prohibition of them – and he emphasized that he was only talking about cocaine and the coca leaf – that had made the traffic lucrative and driven it underground into the hands of the criminal element. At one time coke had been respectable, the liquors derived from the coca leaf regarded as beneficial as well as stimulating. An Italian had distilled a liquor from it that was like an elixir, sending it to all the crowned heads of Europe, to the President, even the Pope – all had praised it. And there was that great American drink, based on it and still imprinted with the name. 'No coke in it now. Suddenly the medical boys turned against it and the world became teetotal on drugs, coke in particular. Pity!' His hands were trembling, the coffee cup rattling, a nerve twitching the muscles of his jaw. 'If there wasn't so much money in it, then bastards like that – ' he nodded towards the ship's hull plates creaking against the big plastic fenders that separated us from the tug – 'wouldn't have muscled in on the towing contract I had.' He shook his head, his shoulders sagging. 'I never should have sold that timber. So much money . . . Jesus Christ! It seemed such waste – the money I needed just standing there.' Tears of self-pity stood in his eyes. 'Temptation . . . The Devil, if you like – God! You lawyers, you sit there on your bums, smug as the last trump, never stepping out of line, conforming and keeping to precedent, turning your nose up at lesser mortals and passing judgment on them for their indiscretions . . . And now there's Miriam. What the hell happens to her when they've found the drugs and Wolchak hears I was on this bloody Coastguard cutter? He'll think it's my fault. He'll blame me.'

'They haven't found anything,' I said, trying to comfort him. 'They've been over three hours at it – '

'No, but they will. They will.' He was quite certain this was the drugs route to Chicago. 'They virtually told me so. Anyway, it all adds up.'

But the fact was they didn't find any drugs. One member of the tug's crew, a Mexican, had a small amount of cannabis tucked away amongst some socks at the bottom of his suitcase. And on the big motor-cruising yacht, which was carrying a package group of hunters from California up to Prince Rupert, they had found one of the party in possession of narcotic cigarettes. But they hadn't charged either the American or the Mexican, merely confiscating the cigarettes and the cannabis. They had also found three hand guns. But none of this was what they had been looking for.

Almost six hours they had spent rummaging the three vessels and that was all in the way of contraband they had found. It was the two officers on the barge that finished first. 'Guess there's not so very many nooks and crannies on a barge you can hide things.' The man had smiled ruefully, adding that they hadn't been looking for the odd little bag of the stuff.

'The tip-off was that the yacht would be carrying big bags or containers of raw cocaine.' But when the yacht was finally cleared to proceed, and the officers ferried across to the cutter in the inflatable workboat, they admitted that, not only was there no coke on the vessel, but the passengers were all genuine Californian businessmen taking a hunting holiday.

As one of them put it with what I thought was a touch of envy: 'Get away from the wife, get as drunk as a coot, talk smut and do what you dam' well like with nobody around to tell you don't. Reck'n the company running them hunting cruises got it made. They were all as rich as hell and enough booze on board to give any ordinary fella the shakes in a week.' All they had managed to achieve in the three and a half hours they had been on board was to collect the bugging device that had enabled the yacht to be tracked by satellite.

Dawn broke and the last of the customs men came aboard just before seven. They were dead tired and all of them below, drinking coffee and eating into the cook's supplies of sausages and bacon, as Cornish gave the order to throw off the warps, the engines picking up as we got under way and turned our bows to the north, followed by the complaints and curses of the tug's dark-haired skipper. He was out on the sidedeck, shaking his fist. Then, just before disappearing into the fog, he grinned at us and made a rude gesture.

As well as the customs men, and the RCMP officer neat in his uniform of blue blouse and trousers with yellow stripe, there was an American, a short, explosive little man with a crumpled, weatherbeaten face. When I went down for coffee shortly after we had got under way he was holding forth to the others along the lines that the bastards had got away with it this time, but next time they played yachts and barges in Canadian waters they'd be escorted into harbour 'and I'll bloody see that all three vessels are taken to pieces bit by bit.'

'Don't reckon there'll be a next time,' the lanky RCMP officer said.

'Oh, yes there will. For these guys there's always a next time. Once they've got the smell of the money up their nose, you'll see – nothing will stop them.' He was from the State of Michigan, too angry at their failure to find what they'd been looking for and too wrought up not to argue, his feelings running deep. I had barely filled my cup before he was talking about the drugs situation in Chicago and how it had grown as a result of two rival groups of the same mafioso family – the Papas and the Mamas – fighting it out in the streets.

I was on my way back to the wheelhouse, but then he suddenly mentioned the name Wolchak. It was such an unusual name that I stopped, listening as he told how this fat little Polish-Lithuanian Jew, who was the financial brains of the paternal gang, the Papas, had been away in South America organizing the supply side of the drugs racket when the fighting broke out.

'Most of the *famiglia*, both Papas and Mamas, got themselves burned, so when little Josef returns there's only pieces to pick up, and as finance director that had always been his job, picking up the pieces. Jeez! I'd have given anything to have found the little guy right there on board that smug-looking Greek's tug.' And he went on to say there had only been one occasion when anybody had come near to pinning anything on Josef Wolchak and that was long before he had anything to do with the Chicago gangs, when he was trying to raise the starting price to buy in to a half-bust real estate company. He had come in to Idlewild airport – 'it was Idlewild then so you can tell how long ago it was. He had flown in from BA. He had these walking sticks with him, half a dozen of them, the wood all beautifully carved. Souvenirs, he said, and as luck would have it the customs officer dropped one. Then, as it lay, one end on the edge of a weighing machine platform, a motorized trolley drove over the other end of it, snapping it in half. The stick was hollow and a white powder ran out. That was the only time the authorities ever came near to nailing him, and the only time, I guess, he ever ran anything himself. After that he was too big.'

'How did he get away with it?' somebody asked.

'Story is he threatened to sue them for the price of

the stick. Said they were valuable antiques, made by the Quechua Indians up in the mountains of Bolivia, the powder nothing to do with him and probably just lime put there by the Indians to fill the hollow interior and make the sticks heavier and more solid. Maybe it's apocryphal, but even if it is, it's in character, for he's bluffed his way right up to the top of a very nasty, very dangerous heap. And not just bluff. He was the first of the gang bosses to recruit out of South America. But it's like I say; once they smell money, then greed takes over, and if they've got away with it once, they'll have another go at it.'

'Have you got a picture of Wolchak?' I asked.

He swung round from the table, his little eyes narrowed. 'You know him?'

'I've met a man named Josef Wolchak, that's all,' I said. 'It's an unusual name.'

'Not so unusual.' He peered at me. 'You're a Limey, aren't you?' And when I nodded, he asked me where I'd met this man Wolchak. In the end he took my name and address, scribbling it down in his notebook, the connection between the Wolchak who had bounced into my office and the origin of the logs that filled the barge making me even more convinced that the narcotics division had been deliberately set on a false trail.

He asked me a lot of questions, but as I had only met the man that once, and for a very short time, my answers were not very helpful. He promised to send me a photograph so that I could check it against my recollection of the Wolchak who had visited me in my office, and after that I made my excuses and returned to the wheelhouse. By then we were back in the Hakai Passage, having passed seaward of the South Pointers reef, the sun burning up the fog and the salmon leaping. Twice I sighted bald eagles, once in the distance, diving from a dead tree lookout post to seize an unsuspecting fish in its claws, the second time as we rounded Kelpie Point – there were two of them, juveniles Cornish said, standing on the rock right beside the flashing beacon, watching us with complete unconcern. We were so close I could have cast a line at their feet. 'God bless America.' The Mate put his hand over his heart, grinning as he posed to attention.

The big, corrugated iron packing sheds and the power station at Namu shone bright silver in the sun as we ghosted in to lie alongside the wooden jetty and say goodbye to the customs men and the RCMP officers, the American Drug Enforcement officer going with them. They went glumly, knowing their search had been one hundred per cent thorough and yet with the uneasy feeling that somewhere, somehow, they'd been fooled. When they had gone, all of them heading for the hotel, Cornish stretched his arms, his mouth opening in a great yawn. 'Well, that's that. Anybody coming for a walk?'

I said I would, and the Chief also volunteered. His engines were shut down, the crew told they were clear of duty until we sailed at noon. Perhaps I should have slept, like Tom who was flat out, propped against the deckhousing aft, his mouth open and snoring loudly as he lay in the sunshine, his anorak bundled up under his head as a pillow. If I had known . . . But writing about it afterwards one always has the advantage of hindsight. At the time all is in the future and one has no idea what lies in store – otherwise, fortune-tellers, star-gazers and entrail inspectors would be out of business.

CHAPTER TWO

Ocean Falls was little more than thirty miles away, about 2½ hours at 1500 revs, which was our economical cruising speed of 12 knots. By the time we had finished lunch we were back in the Fisher Channel, just passing the entrance to Lama Passage. We continued northwards past Evans Inlet and into the narrows by Bold Point. I was standing on the starb'd platform to the wheelhouse looking at the mountains reared well over two thousand feet above us, bare ice-scoured rock visible on the tops but all the lower slopes clothed in forest trees, their roots bedded into fissures and crevices in the strata. Ahead of us loomed a bald, glaciated mountain, glimpses of snowfields beyond. I was thinking then about Ocean Falls, a dead town they said and the area beyond all high land thrusting deep into the Rockies.

I had caught a glimpse of what it could be like on that walk at Namu with Cornish and his Chief Engineer. It was only a short walk, less than a mile, and all of it along a narrow, raised boardwalk of red cedar planks, and when we had reached the lake there had been a bridge over a torrent outspill and after that we had scrambled along the water's edge. Fish had been rising and there was a bald eagle. Mosquitoes, too. And the going had been rough, patches of swamp, boulders and the roots of trees interlaced – red cedar, hemlock and balsam, a few Douglas fir.

Now the mountains above us were bleak as we followed the King Island shore until we came to the Dean Channel junction and headed up Cousins Inlet. Mackenzie Rock lay only a dozen miles up Dean Channel and I wished I had read his book – the first white man to cross the Rockies and, looking up at the appalling tree-clad loneliness of it all, I wondered how he had had the nerve, what had kept him going.

It was 14.40 when Captain Cornish put Tom Halliday and myself ashore at Ocean Falls. He didn't tie up, simply going alongside the jetty so that we could step onto the wooden planks, then the *Kelsey* was full astern on both engines, and I only just had time to call good luck and goodbye to Jim Edmundson before the cutter was swinging round and heading back down the inlet. By the time Tom and I had humped our bags to the end of the jetty and were walking into the town, the Coastguard cutter looked very small in the giant V of the inlet's rock walls. Soon she would turn north-east up the Dean Channel to pass Echo Harbour and Mackenzie Rock and on towards Kimsquit until they opened Cascade Inlet and reached the Halliday Arm of it.

'A house called Halcyon Days, and it's got a blue

door, that's what he said.' Tom had stopped and was staring about him. Compressed by the mountains, the houses climbing steeply over the rock remains of a giant slide that had gashed the mountain above us, the pale brown bulk of a hotel and the pulp mill sprawled over the narrow flats of the river silt – it all looked much bigger than I had expected. There was a river and we could see its outfall under a bridge, hear the sound of it cascading down from the high lip of the valley.

'You ever been here before?' I asked.

'Once, that's all. BC Ferries called here regularly then. But other times when visiting the Cascades I flew straight in to the Halliday Arm by floatplane from Bella Bella.'

It was mid-afternoon, the streets empty, hardly a soul about, and a cold breeze coming down off the mountains from the north.

'There's a lake up there, about ten miles long. A dam, too, and a hydro-electric power station that once drove the pulp mill. I think I can hear the dynamo. Sounds like it's still running.' There were lights burning, street lights even in daylight – lights, too, on the verandahs of empty houses. 'What was that about Halcyon Days?' I asked.

'It's Brian's address. A friend's place. That's the message he gave Steve Davis, the floatplane pilot at Bella Bella. He'd wait for us there. Trouble is, the launch operator couldn't remember the name of the street. Said we couldn't miss it because it was the board road down from the lake.' By then we were into the town, looking ahead up an asphalt road that climbed beside a tumbling cascade of water. 'Guess we'd better go up to the dam. Should be easy then to find where the board road starts. He said the house was somewhere about the middle of it.'

We dumped our bags on the verandah of an empty house beneath the dull glare of a naked electric light bulb. Clouds had come down and it was starting to drizzle, the cutter gone now and the whole narrow fjord empty of anything but the lowering clouds and the mist. 'Always rains here,' he muttered as we began to walk up the hill. There were hydrangeas blooming and mountain ash bright with berries, and walnut trees – I hadn't expected walnut trees. The higher we climbed the more the noise of rushing water filled our ears, filling the whole narrow cleft of the valley with sound, just as the monstrous ochre-coloured block of the hotel filled it visually – that and the mill, and the little terraced wooden houses clinging to the valley side, bright with peeling ribbons of paint, flowers and lights. And nobody living there, only a few remaining, enough to keep the pulp mill machinery and essential services ticking over.

The dam stood massive, a straight concrete face wedged in the narrow cliffs, a blind wall poised above the town and white with the water streaming down it. Tom went as far as the locked gates that led onto the top of it, a broad dam-top walkway with the iron sluice controls at intervals and a marvellous view down the inlet, half-obscured by cloud mist. The rock-scoured mountain that overhung the town gleamed wet and wicked where the great slide had gashed it, tumbling millions of tons of debris down into the waters of the loch to form the hard standing that reached back from the quay.

But Tom wasn't looking at the slide, or down the inlet. He had his back to the town, staring out across the endless expanse of the lake. 'I went fishing up here once. Seven or eight years ago it must have been. There's a torrent runs into it from another, higher lake. The Halliday Arm and the Cascades almost reach right back to it. In fact, it's from the end of that lake that the water originates to form the falls that give the place its name. The Bella Bella Indians had a log cabin up there, a sort of boathouse for their canoes. A good position with a great rock platform we called the Pulpit. From the top there you could look right down the mountainside a thousand feet or so to the arm of water coming in from Cascade Inlet, the logging camp and the booming-ground.' And he added almost wistfully, 'The cabin was still there when Thor took over as forestry manager and he made it into quite a nice bunk-cum-boathouse for fishing. There's some trout in that lake so big and pink-fleshed I reckon they must be land-locked salmon left over from the last ice age.'

A wind swirled the cloud drizzle round us, suddenly tearing it apart, so that the sun shone and it was momentarily quite warm. The whole head of Tom's hair became silvered with moisture, his features no longer haggard but smoothed out as he looked at the lake, smiling to himself. He seemed suddenly fit and well. I was amazed how quickly he could recover with a little sleep. The weeks spent working in Stone Slide Gully must have hardened him up, for he was a man who lived very close to the limits of his nervous system.

'Let's go and see if we can find Brian.' But even as he spoke we both turned our heads to the sound of an engine far across the lake. Mist still clung to the surface of the water, so that we didn't see it for several minutes, though the sound of it grew quite rapidly. Then suddenly it was there, on the edge of visibility, a rubber inflatable with an outboard engine and a lone man with long, dark hair huddled over it. He ran the inflatable up onto the coarse gravel of the lake edge and a moment later was coming towards us, a rucksack on his back and dragging a little sleigh with two plastic containers on it and a filler can that looked as though it had been used for kerosene. He was flat-featured, his eyes bulging above high cheekbones and broken teeth showing yellow-stained below the black droop of his moustache. If he saw us he didn't show it. He was whistling softly to himself and he went down into the town by another road, the sleigh scraping along behind him.

'One of the squatters, I suppose,' Tom said. 'The cutter's cook told me about the only people here, apart from the mill maintenance men, were hippies up from Vancouver and other ports.'

He had turned and was moving to the bend where the lank-haired man had disappeared. The road looped, swinging down by a different route, the surface of it changed to great planks of cedar, slippery after the rain. There were small verandahed houses beside it, the broad driveway slaloming down in a great curve. God knows how many magnificent trees had been felled to build that road, for it was wide enough for two vehicles to pass, but I suppose with the mountains so full of timber it was cheaper to bridge the tumbled rock slope with sleeper-like planks than to find the infill material to build an ordinary road.

We found the house, the light on over the door and the blue paint peeling. There was a bell, but it didn't work. We knocked. Nobody came and nobody looked out of the windows of the nearby houses; the road, everything, very still, and the only sound the whisper of the water pouring down from the lake above. 'He's not here.' My voice sounded loud, a little strange. 'There's nobody here.' It was like being a visitor from outer space, looking in on a world from which all human life had been expunged. 'Try the door,' I breathed.

It wasn't locked, its hinges creaking with the damp as it swung wide to show the interior of an ordinary little house, everything in place as though the occupant had gone to the post or to the shops and would be back at any moment. We hesitated, both of us standing there, staring at the open door. 'You're right,' Tom muttered. 'He's not here.'

'Maybe there's a message.'

He nodded, but he didn't move. 'Odd, isn't it?' His voice was a little high, a slight tremor in it. 'I don't like it,' he whispered. 'And the town, the emptiness – it's like a ghost town.'

His words, the empty stillness of the place; I didn't like it either, but we couldn't stand there for ever thinking about the strangeness of it. 'There'll be a message,' I said again, and I pushed past him, going first into the

front room, which was lounge and dining-room combined, then through to the kitchen. There was no
message, but the remains of a meal still lay on the table,
there was food in the fridge, which was working, and in
the front bedroom the bed was unmade, clothes scattered around, his grip on the floor.

I called to Tom. 'Looks like he'll be back soon.'

He came in, looked at the bed and the clothes, then
rummaged around in the grip. 'It's Brian all right. Blast
the boy! I was relying on him . . .' He didn't say what it
was he was relying on him for, but I could guess.

We went back into the kitchen. The wind had risen,
tapping the branches of a small rowan against the
window, and it was drizzling again. Above us the sliced
rocks of the great slide hung raw and wet out of the low
cloud base. 'Gloomy sort of place.' Tom switched on the
kitchen light, then went to the store cupboard and began
going through the tins. 'Beans!' he muttered. 'Reminds
me of those weeks I spent up at Ice Cold. Baked beans!
And peaches, canned peaches!' He gave a snorting
laugh. 'Which do you want, beans or sardines – or
corned beef?'

'Any bread?' But I knew it was a forlorn hope.

'Biscuits,' he said. 'And there's coffee, a big jar of
instant coffee.'

'No tea?'

He shook his head. 'You're being difficult.' I settled
in the end for coffee and baked beans. 'A beanfeast,' he
said and gave a laugh that was more like a giggle. 'Can't
call it high tea – no tea. And high coffee, that sounds
daft. So a beanfeast it is.' And he filled the kettle at the

sink, the handle rattling against the tap. 'Where the hell is the boy? Why isn't he here?'

Darkness came early in the narrow, fjord-like cleft into which the town and the pulp mill were clamped, mountain and cloud cutting out the light. I was glad I had had the sense to get spare batteries for my torch on the ferry, remembering the Mate of the cutter saying it rained 370 days of the year at Ocean Falls, and Cornish adding that in winter gusts of 100 mph hit the water from the mountains above, that once he had had a foot-thick coating of ice on all the metalwork on deck, the whole crew out hacking away at it with axes for fear the ship would capsize with the weight of it.

We had our meal, and when we had cleared it up, we dossed down in the lounge. It was still drizzling, so no point in going down into the town; anyway, I was too tired. I was on the floor, wrapped in blankets and an old sleeping bag, Tom snoring on the settee. Some time later he got up and went out of the front door. It was the coffee, I suppose, and when he came back I asked him whether it was still raining. 'Don't know,' he muttered. 'I didn't notice.' And he went to sleep again immediately. It was cold now and I wrapped the blankets close around me, but it was no good. I had to get rid of some of that coffee and when I went out the clouds were broken and lifting, patches of starlight and the wind thrashing in the trees.

I was just zipping up my flies before going into the house when a movement on the road caught my eye, somebody coming up from the town. There was a dark shadow and the scuff of soft shoes on the wet planks. I thought perhaps it was Brian and I was on the point of calling out when the man moved into the pale light from our verandah and I froze, clinging to the shadows beside the house. I couldn't believe it. But there he was, his aquiline features and dark hair clear in the light, his face half-turned towards me, and that same bearskin poncho.

I nearly called his name, but then I remembered how I had last seen him, the anger and the hate in his eyes as Tom had left him beside the mine track. Then he was past me, a shadow moving into shadow, and while I stood there, wondering why he was in Ocean Falls and how he had got there, I saw there was somebody else on the road, a figure slinking along without a sound.

I didn't move and as he passed me I saw it was the same dark, lank-haired man we had seen earlier coming from the inflatable up on the lake. The way he moved, his total concentration on the figure ahead of him, there was no question in my mind – he was following Tarasconi.

I waited till he was well up the hill, almost at the bend, then I went back into the house, grabbed my deck shoes, calling to Tom as I slipped them on, 'Tarasconi just went by. Tony Tarasconi. He's being followed.' Tom grunted as I filled in the details, adding, 'He must have taken the ferry the day before us. He said he was planning to go to Haines.' I had my shoes on then, grabbing up my torch and my anorak. 'I'll just go as far as the lake.'

'What for?' He was still half asleep.

'To see where they go, of course.'

I left him then, slipping out onto the planks of the roadway and moving upwards, keeping to the shadows and half running, my deck shoes making little sound. Blasts of cold air swept down from the mountains, the cloud ragged and edged with moonlight, rents of bright starlight showing. Round the bend the boardway straightened and for an instant I saw both figures. Then Tarasconi disappeared in the brush that bordered the lake. The man following him slipped away to the left, climbing in great leaps till he, too, disappeared, obviously intent on circling his quarry. But why?

I moved up the last of the boardway with extreme caution, keeping all the time to the shadows, and then making a quick dash for it when I reached the open area of rough ground that led to the gate guarding the entrance to the dam-top. There were some bushes and, crouched in their shadow, I had a view along the margin of the lake. The moon was still behind cloud, or maybe it had not risen above the high ranges to the east, but there was enough light from its reflection on the cloud edges, and from the stars, for me to see several hundred yards, as far at least as the point where the inflatable was concealed. I was certain by then that it was the inflatable Tarasconi was after. To steal it, or puncture its fat, inflated sides, or was there something hidden in it, something he needed to find out about?

Crouched there, waiting, my eyes fixed on the spot where I thought the inflatable was hauled out, time passed slowly, the light coming and going with the passage of the clouds, and my eyes straining. Sounds were impossible to hear, even the sound of the wind, my ears full of the roar of water pouring white over the lip of the dam and on down the steep rock-strewn valley to the fjord below. I saw a figure moving along the water's edge in a crouching run, but only for a moment and then it vanished, merging into some bushes, so that I thought perhaps I'd been mistaken. Then I saw it again, but in a different position. The light brightened momentarily. There were two figures. They seemed to be facing each other and at their feet a dark shadow that could have been the inflatable.

They might have been arguing over it, but the light was so uncertain, everything so indistinct, the hands flung up, the step backwards, the splash, all more likely in my imagination for the wind was blowing a veil of cloud across the sky, my eyes peering helplessly as the dark increased.

Had there been two? Had one of them knocked the other into the lake? I looked at the clouds racing across the sky, their passage marked by glimpses of stars. I couldn't be certain what I had seen. Crouched there, close above the lake, the night filled with the roar of water, I began to doubt whether it was really Tarasconi I had seen hurrying up the board road.

I suppose it was only a minute or two, though it seemed much longer, before the clouds were blown away, and then, suddenly, I could see the inflatable. It was afloat and there was a figure crouched over the stern of it. He was working at something, the outboard presumably, and then he was paddling. I could even see the water dripping from the paddle blade as he worked the boat away from the shore, and when he was clear he crouched over the stern again, his arm flashing and a froth of water thrusting him away from me; then more cloud and suddenly the man and the inflatable had vanished, swallowed in the dark waters of the lake.

I was so urgent by then to check what I thought I had seen that I didn't hesitate. I switched on my torch and went running along the path that twisted and turned through the lakeside scrub until I had reached the point where I thought I had seen them. But there was nothing there, nobody, nothing lying in the water. I found the marks of the inflatable, could see where the tipped-up prop of the outboard motor had made a furrow in the black silt of the shore, and there were the marks of feet, but the coarse sand was so loose that there was no knowing whether they had been made by one person or two. It looked like more, for of course, to manoeuvre an inflatable into the water with its outboard engine attached would have been something of a struggle, certainly for one man.

There was a piece of rag there and a short length of nylon fishing line with a knot in it, also a dark stain in the coarse silt that looked as though oil had leaked out from the outboard engine. That was all I could find, though I probed around for some time in the bushes. I even called Tarasconi's name, but my voice was lost in the sound of the wind and the water, not just the dam now, but waves breaking out in the middle of the lake. Nobody answered, so that I was forced to the conclusion that both of them had left in the boat. But where would they go, and why, in the dark with half a gale blowing up on the lake?

I went back to the road then, the wind a little easier as I started down it, and when I reached the house, the verandah door was ajar and I could hear voices raised in argument: 'All right then, there is one guy – probably more. But if you want a fix that bad you do your own haggling, buggered if I will.'

They were in the lounge, Tom still on the couch, his son standing over him. '. . . Mexican, I think,' Brian was saying as I pushed open the door. 'His name's Rodrigo, a gone-to-seed, Che Guevara type with a drooping black moustache and a slinking sort of truculence.' He was wearing an old camouflage jacket and a green baseball hat, and at my entrance he turned quickly, his strange face set, his eyes glaring at me, almost black with anger. 'So you found him in the Yukon and you brought him down here to see the damage he's been doing. Good on you, mate. But now they want to cut more timber, he tells me, and they're using Miriam as a lever.'

'I think, in the circumstances,' I murmured soothingly, 'it would be better if you just sat down, relaxed and we discussed the situation. What are you doing here, anyway?'

'None of your business. And I'm hungry. I've spent the better part of twenty-four hours sitting under a rock halfway up the mountainside.' He had turned and was walking into the kitchen.

I looked across at Tom, sitting slumped on the couch, his eyes half-closed. Clearly he had no intention of standing up to his son. 'He's been down to the Cascades, but they threw him out. Now he's planning to get in by the back door, across the lake.' Tom gave a little shrug. 'He'll only make things worse.'

'How do you mean?'

'I don't know, Brian's always been like that. Puts his head down and charges, no thought for the consequences. His mother was the same. Whatever she wanted she had to have, never mind anybody else. Ruthless,' he muttered. 'There's a ruthless streak.' Apparently Brian had arrived back a few minutes after I had left, coming down off the slope of the mountain above. 'I woke to find him standing over me and you weren't there. Where were you? You were gone a long time.'

I told him where I had been and what I thought I had seen up there at the lakeside. 'What's that?' Brian was framed in the kitchen doorway, a packet of biscuits and some cheese in his hand, his mouth full, 'A struggle, you say?'

'I can't be certain. The light coming and going, everything . . .'

'I know, I know – I was coming down off the mountain. But if there was a struggle, who won – Rodrigo?'

I shook my head. 'The light was too dim.'

'And afterwards?' He wolfed down the rest of the biscuit and cheese. 'Did he go off in that inflatable?'

'I think so.'

'Which way – down the lake, northwards?'

I nodded. 'He kept close to the shore.'

'Yes, of course. He couldn't go out into the middle. Too much wind. You're certain there was only one of them in the boat?'

'I can't be sure, of course,' I said. 'It looked like that.'

'Okay, let me get some food inside me, then we'll go up there again, see if he comes back. And some coffee,' he added, turning back into the kitchen. 'I need coffee if I'm to keep awake. I've got a boat up there, an old canoe I borrowed.' He pulled another can of beans from the cupboard. 'Beans! Windy things and I've had a belly-ful of them. But sustaining.' I had followed him into the kitchen and was filling the kettle while he set the beans on to heat. 'You willing to paddle a canoe with me? Ten miles, a short steep portage, then another mile or so on a smaller lake. Have to make it before dawn.' He glanced at his watch. 'We got just over five hours. That should be enough if the wind goes down.'

'And if it doesn't?' I could hear it thrashing in the trees still.

'Then we'll have to hide up.' I asked him why and he looked at me as though I were being particularly stupid. 'A boat, any sort of a boat, sticks out on a lake like a fly on white paper, we'd be visible for miles as soon as dawn broke.'

'And you don't want to be seen. Who would be there?' I asked. 'Who are you afraid might see you?'

'That's one of the things I mean to find out. There's that Mexican – why's he suddenly headed down the lake at night?'

'It could be Tarasconi,' I said.

'Tarasconi!' He laughed. 'Not a chance. You said only one and he wouldn't stand a chance against a guy like Rodrigo.' He took the beans off the stove and poured them onto a soup plate, then sat down at the kitchen table, eating them with a spoon. 'Help yourself. You'll need something hot inside you.' He reached for another spoon and thrust it into my hand as I sat down opposite him.

'You knew Tarasconi was here, then?'

He nodded, his mouth full. 'That's why he came here – to see me. Flew into Bella Bella by plane from Rupert. Found out from Steve Davis I was up here and he air-lifted him in in his Cessna. A nasty little man. Walked in here just as I was having a late breakfast, sat where you're sitting now – said a South American named Lopez had told him Miriam was being held hostage. Wouldn't say by who, and I didn't believe him. He wanted to trade a half share of a gully named Stone Slide up near the Ice Cold mine for information about where she was being held.'

'And where is she being held?' I asked. 'Did you get it out of him?'

He shook his head. 'No. He admitted in the end he didn't yet know for sure. It was dangerous, he said, but if I made it worth his while . . .' He waved his spoon at me. 'Tuck in, it's the last hot food you'll get for a while if you're coming down the lake with me.' He pushed the plate of beans towards me. 'Anyway, like I said, I didn't believe him. And then he said, did I know my father was alive?' He nodded, smiling. 'I believed that all right. So I kept an eye on the little bugger after that, and when he started moving into positions where he could watch Rodrigo launching that inflatable to go down the lake, I began to think maybe there was something in what he'd told me. Now, for God's sake, Tom says it's true, about Miriam.' He leaned suddenly forward, his face thrust close to mine across the table, his eyes staring. 'Is it true?'

I told him briefly what I knew, then asked him about the man I had seen following Tarasconi up to the lake. 'A dropout,' he said. 'One of the toughest. Likes a fight, so long as he's got the knife. A Mexican or Honduran.' We had finished the beans by then and he slid the biscuits and cheese over to me. 'Middle American anyway, squats in somebody's apartment in a block of flats down by the swimming pool.'

'What's his background?' I asked. 'What's he do for a living?'

Brian shrugged. 'Lives off the other squatters, picks up anything he can. I don't know for sure what he's up to, but he'll sell you beer or hard liquor any time of the day or night, whenever the government liquor store is shut, that is. Drugs, too, if you want them. And he's not a man to cross, very quick with the knife.' He grinned and gave a little shrug. 'That's what I'm told, anyway.'

'By the swimming pool, you say?'

Brian looked up, staring at his father in the doorway. 'Right.'

'What's the number of the apartment?'

His son hesitated. 'Number fifteen. On the third floor. But if you'd been listening to what your legal adviser has been saying you'd realize your pusher has gone off down the lake in his inflatable.' And he added with a little twisted smile, 'Why not break down the door and help yourself?'

I didn't find Brian any more likeable now than I had on the previous occasion when I had seen him in my office. The abrasive energy of the man, the way he assumed I was willing to follow his lead as he rose to his feet and said, 'Well, you coming?' made me want to tell him to go to hell. Instead, I found myself explaining to him in reasoned tones how Jim Edmundson had been sent in by the government to report on the situation.

'What's he going to say in his report?'

I told him I didn't know, that Edmundson would only just have arrived at the Cascades logging camp. And I added, 'The fact that he's been sent there to report indicates that you've made your point and the authorities are now monitoring the situation.'

But he brushed that aside. 'A forestry man, employed by government – he'll look at those trees, work out the value on his little calculator and that'll be that. So long as the land is replanted the government is covered.' He was in the bedroom now, putting his things together. 'Here's a spare sleeping bag.' He tossed a waterproof hold-all across to me. 'We'll need some food, too. You got sweater and anorak? It'll be cold up there – wet and cold, and you'll need a torch.'

'It's still blowing,' I said.

'Thought you were a sailing man.' He said it with a lift of his brows and a little smile, going back into the kitchen and thrusting an assortment of tins and cartons into a plastic bag. 'Okay?'

I hesitated. Tom was back on the couch, his eyes

closed, but I don't think he was asleep. 'You staying here?' His eyes flipped open. 'You're not coming?'

'I'm tired,' he murmured.

'A chance to have a look at the Cascades, check that logging camp – just in case your wife . . .'

He shook his head. 'Edmundson's there now. See what he discovers. No need for me to stick my neck out. Not yet.' His eyes flickered to his son. 'Apartment fifteen, you said?' And when Brian nodded, he smiled and said, 'Maybe in the morning then . . .' He sank back, his eyes closing.

I tucked the hold-all under my arm, picked up the things I needed and followed Brian to the door. 'Is it all right,' I asked as we went out into the night, 'leaving him there on his own? He needs a fix and he might go looking for that Mexican.'

His son shrugged. 'My guess is Rodrigo is down the far end of the lake by now.' And when I reminded him again that it could just as well have been Tarasconi who had gone off in the inflatable he shook his head. 'It'll be Rod, and if he's gone to the end of the lake he won't be back tonight.'

But when we had climbed to the dam and were following our torches along the lakeside path we found the inflatable drawn up among some shrubs well clear of the water, the outboard padlocked into the tipped-up position. 'Where's Tarasconi?' Brian asked, looking up at me, his fingers still feeling the chain of the padlock.

'How the hell do I know?' I was gazing out over the black waters, the two figures blurred in my mind and trying to sort out what I really had seen and what I had imagined. 'Wind's dropped a bit,' I murmured, and then I began searching in the dark silt for the mark where the oil had been spilled, a sudden terrible thought in my mind, but it was all trampled over where the inflatable had been pulled up the steep shore, and anyway I couldn't be sure it had been returned to the same spot.

'Can't do anything about the padlock,' Brian said, straightening up. 'Anyway, there probably isn't enough petrol. We'll take the canoe. Paddling it close along the shore we'll be out of the wind, for the first part at any rate.'

'You're going into the Cascades from the top, is that it?'

He nodded. 'From where I was holed up on the side of the mountain I could see right down the lake as far as the portage, to the point where the falls pour down from the upper lake. I'm told that lake is the water source of the Cascades. There's a hut there, an old Indian hut, and a timber extraction road somewhere below it.' He stood for a moment to look north across the black waters of the lake. 'I don't like being barred entry to my own property,' he said softly. 'And those trees . . . I only saw just the edge of them –'

'They're not your trees,' I reminded him. 'As long as your father's alive –'

'Okay, but it could have been the same if he'd tried to walk round the plantation.'

'Who stopped you?'

'A couple of hulking foresters. They had a power saw with a blade on it as long as your arm. You don't try conclusions with that sort of a weapon.'

'They threatened you?'

'Oh sure, and they'd have used it all right.' He laughed. 'Afterwards they could always say I just walked into it. Wasn't anyone else there to say I didn't.'

I stared at him. 'But surely there must have been somebody in charge. You said in your letter – the one that was forwarded to me in Whitehorse – you said there was a man named Lorient in charge.'

'That's right. The manager, they said. When they saw I was determined to walk down the logging road to High Stand, they called him out of his office back of the quay where I'd parked my boat. He said he didn't care what my name was or who had planted those trees, the whole stand had been sold to an American company and would be felled and shipped over the next few months. I don't know whether he was French Canadian – could be with a name like that. He was a mean-looking bastard and when he realized I wasn't the sort to take orders, that was when they began to get tough. By then, of course, he had figured out just who I was – I mean that I was the guy who had tried to stop a barge-load of High Stand logs in the Georgia Strait. You heard about that, did you?'

And when I told him the Canadian lawyers had given me copies of the press cuttings, he went on, 'Okay, but what you didn't see – what I didn't tell the press, because I knew they wouldn't believe me – and this is just to show how vicious men motivated by greed can be . . .' He stopped there, turning and facing me. 'You saw that picture where the bargeman is leaning over the bows with a boathook in his hands. Looks as though he's trying to fish me out, doesn't it? A kindly seaman trying to save a foolish demonstrator!' The corners of his lips lifted in the little smile that was without humour. 'What in fact he was doing was using it like the Indians used to use whale spears. That boathook had a point on the end and he was thrusting it down to puncture the inflatable, and then to puncture me. That doesn't show either in the TV film or the press pictures, but it's true. That's when I dived into the water. That,' he added, 'was why I didn't argue with Lorient and those two fellows at the Cascades.'

'What about Olsen?' I asked. 'Have you discovered where he is?'

'Bought off,' he said. 'What else? Did the police come up with anything?' And when I didn't answer, he said, 'You lawyers! You want everything cut and dried, a black and white situation before you'll take action. Well, now perhaps you'll see for yourself. Come on!' He turned and started off along the path. 'If you're coming with me I aim to be off the lake and into cover before dawn, so let's get moving.' And as we started off along the path he began talking about the trees. 'You've been to Cathedral Grove, the red cedar and Douglas show-place on the Port Alberni road on Vancouver Island, have you? No? Well, the trees I glimpsed in High Stand will be as big one day. But they're not old primeval forest. They're not museum trees. They were planted this century and there's acres of them standing shoulder-to-shoulder, great stems rising a hundred and twenty, maybe a hundred and fifty feet, rank upon rank, all exactly spaced. They're like giant soldiers stood there on parade.'

He stopped suddenly, turned to me and said, 'I wish to God I'd known old Josh Halliday. He was so far ahead of his time – planting trees like that. Nobody in Canada thought of it then, not for a long time, not out here on the west coast. It's the most magnificent memorial to a man I ever saw, and if this dirty, money-grubbing crowd think they're going to run big chain-saws through it – Christ! I'll get hold of a gun and shoot them down myself.' He laughed then. 'Forgot you were a lawyer, mate. But you wait! Wait till you see those trees. Then you'll understand – something worth fighting for.'

We went on then, the track becoming so overgrown it almost disappeared. A few more yards and he stopped, the beam of his torch thrusting into some bushes to reveal the patched bows of a very battered-looking canoe. We dragged it down to the water's edge where wavelets made little hissing sounds as they broke on an outcrop of rock. It floated buoyant as a cork. 'Ever handled one of these before?' he asked as he stowed the bag of food and the hold-alls.

'No,' I said.

'Nor have I.' He grinned at me. 'Just don't rock the boat, that's all.'

It turned out he had taken a kayak out in the ice when taking pictures of the slaughter of the harp seal pups on the east coast of Canada. But this was an open Indian-type canoe and though we hugged the shore as close as we dared, we were soon taking in water, for the lake ran north and the wind was veering all the time towards north-east. 'We'd be better on the other shore,' I told him.

'Of course we would, but how do we get there?'

The wind was definitely lighter, but the moon, now clear of the clouds, showed the dark of waves out in the centre of the lake.

We made it across the first shallow bay, but when we rounded the next headland we had to turn back and paddle into the shelter of some rocks. Portaging, or even dragging the canoe, was out of the question, the shallows littered with rock and boulders and the lake edge thick with the roots of small trees and shrubs. We rolled ourselves in our sleeping bags and lay listening to the wind and the murmur of the waves.

The surface of the lake gradually quietened, but it took time, so that it was past three before we were able to get going again. By then I had learned enough about Brian's attitude and intentions to have a certain respect for the man, the aggressive, bulldozer approach to any difficulty something of a relief after having spent several days in his father's company. He was a doer, not a worrier, one of those people whose instinct is for action without hesitation. He didn't plan ahead. He hadn't a clear idea of what he'd do when we got down to the logging camp. 'Just have to see, won't we? Maybe if you talk to this guy Edmundson, tell him they're cutting illegally . . .'

'You don't know it's illegal,' I said.

'I saw what they'd cut. I know what two hectares

looks like and there was a clearing there full of stumps that was a dam' sight more than that.'

'If you can see it, so can Edmundson.'

'All right,' he said. 'So he sends in a report and by the time the government gets around to doing anything about it, the timber will have all been cut and shipped. And Wolchak or Mandola, or Barony, whoever is SVL Timber's front man, shrugs his shoulders, says of course they're replanting and everybody's happy – 'cept old Josh Halliday and people like me.'

'So what are you going to do?'

He shook his head. 'Don't know yet. But if I get my hands on one of those power saws – I'm pretty good with a chainsaw.' I caught the gleam of his eyes in the dark. He was grinning at me, and at that moment I sensed something of his father in him, the braggadocio, that devil-may-care sense of the dramatic, and the irresponsible disregard for the consequences.

The wind dropped right away as soon as we reached the point where the lake turned west of north. By then the moon was down behind the mountains and it was very dark when we finally reached the end of the lake, so we had great difficulty working our way up the torrent of water pouring down from above to the point where the portage began, the canoe half full of water and ourselves very wet. The time was 04.20 and we had at least four hundred feet to climb with the canoe hefted on our shoulders. There was a track of sorts, in places more like a rock staircase, the undergrowth all wet and the going slippery. Brian went ahead, probing with his torch. Neither of us spoke, the noise of the water cascading down from the lake above drowning all other sound.

It took us almost an hour to make the top where the water poured in a smooth black rush over a lip of rock and the lake ran away like a pale still path. We could see the outline of the higher peaks of the Rockies black against the stars. No wind now, no clouds and everything very still and quiet, except for the sound of the cascade, which gradually faded to a murmur as we followed a path round to the right, searching for a place where we could safely launch the canoe.

The stars were starting to fade, the first glimmer of dawn beginning to show where the black mass of the mountains rose above the end of the lake. 'Looks like a hell of a lot of water comes into this lake,' Brian said, working his shoulders as he stood staring at the great half circle of peaks. We had stopped for a breather, the canoe resting on a rock slab. 'I'll go on a bit, see how much further we've got to carry the thing.'

He moved off, his torch probing the steep rock slope down to the lake, and I followed. The path dropped down across some tree roots that were like wooden steps and came to a little beach of coarse sand overhung with trees. 'We can launch from here,' I said with a feeling of intense relief, my body under my anorak soaked with sweat, my shoulders already stiffening. And at that moment there was something like a growl or a snarl.

We froze, standing there quite still. 'What is it?' I whispered, remembering Tom telling me how the one thing he'd always feared when out hunting in the

Rockies was accidentally getting between a grizzly and her cubs. The snarl came again and there was the clink of a chain, so that I wondered if it was an animal caught in a trap. Then it began barking. Another joined in, their barks rattling round the rocks.

Brian cursed, seizing my arm and pulling me back along the path, the dogs ripping the stillness apart with their barking and the rattle of their chains. 'It's the hut. It must be occupied.' I could see it then, a dark shape that I had taken for the rock Tom had referred to as the Pulpit. The beam of a torch lit the square of a window as we ducked back the way we had come, the trees closing round us. The casement slammed open and the beam of the torch stabbed the path behind us, a man's voice calling into the night – 'Who's there?' The torch swung across the little beach and out over the water, searching.

By then we were back at the canoe. 'What were they, hunting dogs?' I was thinking we had to get out onto the water before they were loosed to track us down.

'Huskies most like. They sounded like huskies.'

Behind us, and fainter now, we heard the man yelling at the dogs. The barking stopped and suddenly all was quiet again except for the sound of water spilling over the rock sill down into the lake below.

'I hadn't expected them to maintain a watch up here.' Brian had leaned his head so close his cap brushed my ear. 'What do you reckon the depth over that sill? We've got to get to the other side of the lake.'

I shook my head, the water dark and no way of knowing for sure. 'With both of us in the canoe we might just be able to push ourselves across with the paddle.'

I don't think he heard, for he was already working his way along the steep drop to the lake, probing with his torch for a place to manhandle the canoe down into the water. In the end, the only possibility was a shoulder of rock within a few yards of the smooth run of the water over the sill. Somehow we managed to get the canoe safely down to a point where he could slide it over the rock into the water and hold it there. 'You take the bow,' he shouted at me, 'and be prepared to lean right down with your paddle and keep us from going over.' He was up to his knees in the swirling current, the noise of the water deafening.

Somehow I got myself into the bows. Ahead of me was a small jut of rock, and beyond that the dark rush of the spilling lake. 'Ready?' I nodded as he swung the bows so that we faced out into the centre of the lake. 'Now paddle like hell!' he screamed and I felt the stern go down, the frail craft rocking crazily as he clambered in.

I started paddling. There was no time to feel scared. I could feel his paddle dipping with mine as the bows shot out beyond the jut of rock, swinging wildly in the current. 'Hold her!' he yelled and I kept the bows headed down the lake; the canoe swept first sideways, then backwards, the two of us flailing the water with our paddles, heading diagonally across the spill. Suddenly the stern touched rock, the bows swinging out of control, water pouring under us and both of us reaching down with our paddles, pushing the canoe across the face of the lake's outlet, the tug of the water and the noise of it thundering down filling our whole world as we struggled frantically to make the bastion of rock on the far side where a rowan hung a delicate branch towards the water's edge.

Without that branch I don't think we would have made it. I had to stand up in order to reach it and somehow I preserved my balance, pulling us in until we had our hands on the rock itself. Brian passed me a line and I managed to pull myself up onto a wet, sloping ledge. Fortunately the rock was rough and my deck shoes held. Brian followed, and with the canoe riding light and bobbing around in the current, we managed to work it round the shoulder into the quiet of a little inlet that had a bottom of dark silt. It was not much more than a crevice in the rocks, but it was safe.

That was when the reaction set in. My body began to shake uncontrollably and I felt desperately cold. 'We've got to get moving,' Brian said. Dawn was beginning to lighten the tops of the eastern peaks, but I shook my head. At that moment nothing would induce me to get back into that frail craft, not even the fact that I thought I could just make out the dark square block of the hut some two or three hundred yards across the lake, beyond the rush of its waters towards the outlet.

'Come on, for God's sake!'

Again I shook my head, unable to speak.

He stared at me, his head thrust forward. 'Get in!' he hissed. 'If you don't, I warn you – I'll knock you cold and dump you in.' He seized hold of my arm, shaking me. 'D'you want to get shot?'

I shook my head dumbly, not believing him, my teeth chattering.

He slapped me then. Twice, with his open palm, each side of my face, so hard he almost knocked me off my feet. 'Get in!' And this time I did as he said, my cheeks burning, the shakes suddenly gone – only a sense of unreality so that I knelt there in a sort of daze. He thrust my paddle into my hand and the next thing I knew he was in the canoe and we were both of us paddling, thrusting against the current and driving ourselves along the western shore of the lake.

As daylight grew in the sky beyond the mountains, spreading almost reluctantly down into the basin of the lake, Brian stopped paddling and pulled a pair of very small bird-watching binoculars from the waterproof covering to his sleeping bag. We were then about half-way down the lake. 'We'll have to take a chance on it,' he said, his body swivelled round so that he could train the binoculars on the hut, just visible now in the growing light. 'Can't see a soul. Nothing stirring and the two dogs asleep.'

'You can see the dogs, can you?'

'Sure. You might not think it, but these have a magnification of ten.' He stared through the glasses for a moment, then put them down. 'Yes, they're huskies all right, but cross-bred by the look of them.' He picked up his paddle. 'Okay, we'll chance it.' He drove the paddle in deep, thrusting the bows round until they pointed towards a clump of trees on the far side. 'Make for those cedars, and use only your arm – don't move your body, and no splashes.'

The canoe glided out from the shelter of the bank, the light strengthening all the time so that we seemed suddenly very exposed. Every now and then I felt Brian put down his paddle and examine the hut through his glasses, and each time he reported no movement. It was almost five-thirty and we were now right in the middle of the lake, no cloud and the sky turning from green to orange. The cold numbed my fingers, my legs wrapped in the chill, wet compress of my socks and trousers.

'Why are we crossing over?' I asked him. 'We'd have been much safer on the side we were on. We could have laid up there during the day and crossed over after dark tonight.'

'They've got a boat. I saw it, on that little beach below the hut. A boat with an outboard.'

'You say *they* – is there more than one of them?'

'I don't know. But they'll have radio contact with the camp below. It wouldn't take long to rustle up a search party, and once the dogs picked up our scent . . .'

'They're more likely to pick it up on the side we're headed for.'

But he didn't agree, arguing that the cascades were from a series of lake outlets that would make it difficult to search along the shore we were heading for. 'When I landed at the logging camp I counted at least half a dozen cascades. This lake lips over a sort of rim of rock a mile or more long, some of it sheer cliff. But at the northern end the cliffs give way to a much easier slope. I could see the line of a road running up towards it.' He thought it was probably no more than a rough extraction track. 'Just what we want if we can clamber down to it.'

We were almost across the lake now, the clump of trees growing tall and the sound of cascade water beginning to fill the still morning air with a soft murmur. A small headland of rock began reaching out towards the hut, now clearly visible in the strengthening light. An optical illusion, of course, but it looked as though the hut itself was moving, so quietly were we gliding over the mirror-flat surface of the water. And then suddenly it was gone, lost to view behind the low line of rocks. We had heard no sound of barking, seen no sign of any human. Then the bows touched and we were splashing ashore.

The clump of trees stood on a rocky knoll and from the top of it we looked out across a vista of mountains – snow and rock and the green of trees with giant peaks reaching up to a thin layer of cloud, the dawn already reddening to the sunrise. Water cascaded down on either side of us and far below we could see the inlet that had become known as the Halliday Arm, a dog-leg of leaden water thrusting into the wildness of the mountains, curving past a small area of flat land away to our left. There were huts there, the remains of a logging pen, a narrow track snaking up to the top of a low cliff with a truck poised on the edge of it, and immediately below a huge great pole of a tree trunk up-ended to form a primitive crane, another jammed hard against the cliff, and below that a large barge moored against a log-pile jetty. There was no sign of the Coastguard cutter. The barge was already half loaded with timber, the rest of its cargo piled on the quay close beside it.

And in from the quay, filling all the valley right up to the lower slopes, was High Stand, a sea of dark green tops stretching without a break till, just back of the huts, it ceased, the land suddenly bare and dotted with stumps.

'He shouldn't have done it,' Brian said, his teeth clenched. And he added, 'It looks so much worse from up here. Bigger. Much bigger. It's a lot more than two hectares.' He was almost beside himself with sudden anger. 'How could he do it – and with that curse hanging over him?' He turned abruptly. 'Let's see if we can find a way down on to that track.'

The track was away to our left, a rough ribbon of mud, half overgrown and reaching up through rocky slopes of new growth, most of it scrub. To our right was sheer cliff with waterfalls cascading down from the rim of the lake like lace streamers to join up and form a torrent that disappeared into the great stand of trees in the bottom. This main torrent finally emerged as a white froth of fast-flowing water that fed into the inlet over a flat waste littered with the debris of broken trees.

'Come on! No point in standing looking down at what they've done to it.' There was cold anger in his voice, a note of violence. 'Somehow I'm going to stop the bastards.' He had turned and was facing me. Finally he said, speaking slowly, 'What you're seeing down there in the valley bottom has taken over half a century to grow, and look what they've done! Ten minutes with a big chainsaw and . . . crash! Another of them gone.'

He swung round, hurrying back down towards the water and calling over his shoulder, 'Come on or not as you like, but I'm going down there. Now!'

When I caught up with him he already had the canoe launched and was clambering in. I followed, not saying anything. I had no desire to be stranded up there on my own. We pushed off, shoes full of ice-cold water, trousers wet to the knees. There were clouds forming on the mountains as we paddled past the last of the cascade spills, keeping close along the shore and heading towards a gloomy little beach that marked the north end of the lake. A little huddle of cottonwoods ringed the edge of it, most of them dead of age or some disease, the bare trunks and branches covered with a grey lichen. And perched on the tops of two of the tallest were a pair of bald-headed eagles, pale heads above large grey-black bodies.

'There's a boat.' Brian pointed away to our left, and at the sound of his voice the two birds took off, their flight heavy and ponderous, and so quiet they might have been owls. The boat was a semi-inflatable drawn up on the smooth, grey surface of a rock outcrop. We landed at the edge of it, the rock making it possible to scramble ashore without splashing around in the cold lake water.

The boat had no outboard, just a pair of oars, and like the inflatable parked on the big lake by the Ocean Falls dam it looked quite new. There was nothing in it except the oars, a plastic baler and an air pump. I stood there for a moment, looking down at it and wondering about the hut. There was nothing else on the lake that the men in the logging camp below needed a boat to reach, for if they were going in to Ocean Falls the obvious way was by boat direct from the logging camp, not by climbing a thousand feet, then rowing a couple of miles across a lake, scrambling down a portage and hoping there would be somebody at the bottom to ferry them the ten miles to the dam.

'Come on!' Brian was impatient to get the canoe away under cover and start down to the camp.

'What's it for?' I said.

'The boat? Fishing. Or hunting maybe. There's a bit of swamp land over the other side might be good for the occasional moose.' He lifted his end of the canoe, nodding to me to take up mine.

'And the hut?' I murmured, thinking about how we had come upon it suddenly in the night, the dogs barking and the rattle of their chains, the torchlight in the window. 'Two guard dogs and at least one man there – why?'

He didn't answer for a moment as we hefted the canoe up the rock slope. From the top we could see a well-beaten trail leading down through the trees. 'If you'd seen some of the dropouts that squat down in Ocean Falls,' he said, 'and you'd got a fishing lodge up there at the end of this lake, you'd make dam' sure there was some sort of a guard on it. Besides, out here in the west they're most of them hunting mad, particularly townspeople. Hunting is their sport, the outback and all the life that's in it at their disposal, to kill at will.'

We pushed our way into a tangle of what he said

was Sitka alder and scrub birch, up-ended the canoe and stuffed our things underneath it. 'There are laws,' I said.

He laughed. 'Laws! Of course there are laws. But who cares about laws up here in the mountains? You try and haul a moose home in your pick-up or go off with a trophy of antlers without a licence, then the Mounties or the Park Wardens will get you, but up here' – he looked back at me – 'up here, deep in the Rockies – ' He shook his head. 'The law is down there.' He waved a hand south towards Vancouver. 'Not up here. There's nobody to enforce it here.'

He pointed to the logging camp just becoming visible across the little clearing, the dull, blade-like gash of the inlet beyond. 'Even down there, those loggers – they're a law to themselves. Oh, your friend Edmundson, coming in on a Coastguard cutter, may cause a little flutter of anxiety – the long arm of government – but soon as he's gone . . .' He laughed again, and then we were onto the old extraction road, wishing we had gumboots instead of canvas shoes for there was a lot of mud in places and it was heavily overgrown, sloping steeply down along a spur of the mountains.

There was no big timber anywhere, everything felled and only the scrub of new growth – birch and mountain ash and alder, goat's beard, devil's club, and beside the track a trailing evergreen that Brian said was kinnikinick. This was the area Tom Halliday had clear-felled, this was what he had been living on as the Ice Cold mine faded.

The spur stopped abruptly, the track swinging away to the right in a hairpin bend and slanting down towards the green sea of the High Stand tops. At this point the mountainside fell away steeply, the camp and the quay with the barge alongside almost directly below us, the layout, every detail of it crystal clear. It was like seeing it all in an aerial photograph, and away to the right was the bald, stony patch full of brash and debris where a near-rectangle of Josh Halliday's great plantation had been newly felled. The picture was one of utter devastation with the torrent reaching into the inlet from the far side of it.

A broad haulage road ran close alongside the waters of the inlet straight to the quay. A big crawler was moving along it, trailing three of the High Stand stems hoisted by their butts with their tail ends chained to a set of bogies. And right below us a truck was backing off the cliff-edge above the boom crane and starting down the bright gash of that newly bulldozed track to the camp.

Brian was muttering to himself, cursing under his breath. We had both of us stopped, the bend and the drop such a superb vantage point. 'Isn't that Wolchak?' He was staring down at the camp through his binoculars. 'Talking to a big man with a bit of a beard. Could be Edmundson. Have a look.' He passed me the glasses. 'Down there by the mess hut. They're just walking across to the office.'

The magnification was incredible, the camp leaping towards me and so clear I could see individual stones in the dirt road, the red glint of a Coca-Cola tin, and a small cinnamon-coloured bear digging around in a trash can quite regardless of the two men walking past.

'That's Jim Edmundson,' I said. They reached the office, Wolchak talking all the time, quick gestures of the hands, Jim nodding. They paused a moment, looking back towards the clear-felled area. Then they passed through the door of a hut that had a notice on the outside of it.

The camp was deserted then, the only movements the bear still foraging and that truck grinding slowly down the bright yellow gash of the track just above the camp.

It was an odd-looking truck with a lot of piping in it and a big gantry folded down across the cab and protruding way beyond the blunt engine cover. 'It's our mobile drilling-rig,' Brian said when I asked him what it was. 'My father had it brought in when Ice Cold began to peter out. Thought he'd strike oil here.' His grandfather had apparently talked about a bit of a seep he had found at the upper end of High Stand. 'But old Josh, he wasn't interested in oil. He just thought it a joke that he could have planted one hell of a forest on top of an oilfield.' Tom, of course, had seen it as the perfect solution to his growing financial problems. Another gamble that hadn't come off.

The sound of a chainsaw came to us faintly in the wind.

'Can you see where they're cutting?'

'No,' I said.

He reached for the glasses. 'That barge there. Looks like an old cement barge.' It was large and rusty with a little wheelhouse aft. 'And they're loading it dry,' he added, staring down at it. 'That shows what they think of those trees.'

'How do you mean?'

'Well, they're not going for pulp, are they? If it was pulpwood they'd send up one of those self-loading barges, a real big monster with a couple of built-in cranes, and they'd be deck-loading the timber crossways. Then all they do when it arrives at the pulp mill is flood port or starb'd ballast tanks, heel the barge over and slide the whole lot into the water, straight into the logging pen. But instead of that, here they are, loading the timber dry into a barge so that it'll stay dry, and they'll unload it the same way, straight onto the sawmill's quay.'

'Your father is convinced –'

He swung round on me then. 'You don't believe him, do you? He's just trying to convince himself that he isn't responsible for what's going on down there.' And he added in a quieter tone, 'Whatever he thinks they're up to I can tell you this, they're treating those trees as though they're gold. And that's just about what they are.' The buzzing sound was louder now and he swung the glasses towards High Stand, searching along the edge of the clear-felled area. But it wasn't a chainsaw. It was a steadier drone, and suddenly I could see it, low down over the water, a floatplane flying up the inlet. We watched it as it landed in a burst of spray and taxied in towards the quay, cutting a broad curving line through the still water. The pilot jumped out onto a float, leaping ashore with a line and fending off. There were two passengers, one short, the other taller and heavier, and something in the way they walked, their baggage too . . . I got hold of the glasses again and then I knew I was right. 'Camargo and Lopez,' I said.

'The two South Americans?'

I nodded, wondering why they were here. 'They're the hunters who brought that note from Miriam up to the mine. Just left it there for Tom to find.'

'So he told me, but he didn't say anything about hunters. He said they were gunmen, hoodlums in fact.' He had a look at them through the glasses. 'Could be right. They look mean enough.'

'But what are they doing here?'

'What do you think?' He turned on me angrily. 'Can't you get it into your head that that stand of trees down there is worth a fortune. It's thuya, virtually all of it, and red cedar, with its high oil content, is a timber that's in great demand in all countries where the humidity is high – outdoor sheds, greenhouses, window frames, any construction where weather is a problem. Come on! Let's take a closer look.'

He moved off round the bend, starting down the slope into the great basin that looked like the half of a crater, white streams of water falling from the lip and in the bottom that green sea of feathery tree crowns. 'I'm dam' sure,' he said over his shoulder, 'that Wolchak's plan is to fell the whole stand. If he can satisfy the Government, and a clear undertaking to replant would probably be enough, then all he needs is Tom's signature. And if he's got Miriam tucked away somewhere, he's got a hell of a bargaining counter. Tom would do anything for that woman.' And he added, 'Oh, I know he breaks out sometimes – mostly when he's high. Always has done. Except when my mother was around. She kept him fully occupied.' He gave a short laugh as he pushed through a thicket of salmonberry that had invaded the track where water, seeping from the slopes above, had turned it into a quagmire.

In the wet spots, where there was mud or coarse gravel, we saw the marks of rib-soled boots, footprints that pointed both up and down. At intervals other, smaller extraction tracks ran off along the contour lines of the slope. There were no footprints on these side tracks and with the main track getting progressively better we lost them altogether. The scrub growth here was smaller, for we were moving down into the more recently felled areas. Soon we were hearing the murmur of the cascades from the lake above. A power saw started up, sounding like the floatplane taking off, but intermittent, and there was the crash and thud of a tree going down. As the track improved we moved faster, but even so it took us well over half an hour to reach the edge of the high timber.

By then I was hot, tired and very sleepy, stumbling along with my eyes half-closed, my mind worrying only vaguely now about those footprints and the reason for a rowing boat up there on the lake above. Brian still thought it just a recreational facility, the hut too. 'Hunting. Fishing. You got to occupy your spare time somehow, and there's nothing else to do in a place like this.' But why didn't they fish the shores of the Halliday Arm and hunt the flats where the torrent ran out from the big trees? Why climb a thousand feet up an increasingly overgrown track? And those dogs? It was the dogs that worried me more than anything else, my tired brain groping for something that I knew was there at the back of my mind, something I wasn't sure I wanted to know about. God! I was sleepy.

And then we were into High Stand, the air quite still. The humidity was higher here, the cool of a forest, with great trunks, some of them almost two feet across, and rising, rising like the fluted columns of a cathedral, rising up until the branches, like the start of medieval vaulting, fanned out, cutting off the daylight, feathery needles aglint with a diamond splatter of moisture droplets, catching the sunlight that came and went with the passage of the clouds. It was stupendous, magnificent. I'd never been in such a place before, the track we were following all carpeted thickly with the brown softness of dead needles, the quiet almost awe-inspiring, all sound deadened so that the rush of water and the buzz of the chainsaw were reduced to a gentle murmur.

I think that was it – the gentleness. Those huge trees, those giants, were gentle giants. It was a place of peace and my tired brain, grasping that essential, began to understand and appreciate Brian's deep-seated anger at the deadly intrusion of a logging company and its power saws. Every now and then he paused, gazing upwards, an expression of awe. 'Once, when I was going out into the Karakoram,' he said, turning to me, 'I saw something like this. Not far from the base of Nanga Parbat on the way to Gilgit. A forest of great stems that had been planted. That was the only time, but the trees not as big nor as uniform.' And then the chainsaw had started up again and a moment later we heard the crash and thud of another tree going down. 'God! How could he do it?' His voice was trembling and I had the feeling that if Tom had been standing where I was Brian would have gone for him.

He hurried on then, the buzz of chainsaws growing. And then he began moving from bole to bole, the noise louder as we worked our way towards it until we could see the flash of blades backed by the yellow streamer of sawdust and two men bent forward, blades in constant motion as they moved up the long stem deftly lopping off the branches till it lay there, its naked trunk just a piece of raw material for some far-off factory.

The men straightened up, a pause while they talked, the saws silent. One of them laughed, the other smiling as he lit a cigarette. And then they were moving onto the next stem. An arm swung upwards, pulling on the starter cord, the right hand thrusting the saw downwards. It started with a roar, then quietened, the chain still as its operator bent to the base of the tree, turning the blade and checking the angle. Then abruptly he revved the engine to full power, the muscles of his arm flexing as he thrust the blade home, the tortured wood streaming out from the base of the blade like a gout of yellow blood from some great artery of the tree.

'I wish to God I'd got a rifle.'

I was standing right beside Brian and I knew from the expression on his face that if I could have passed him a gun there and then he would have shot them down in cold blood without any compunction at all – an executioner dealing out retribution to a couple of murderers. 'Are those the two that turned you back when you landed at the quay?' I was wondering how many men Wolchak had at the camp.

'They didn't just turn me back. They threatened to take a saw to me.'

We were whispering to each other, but if we had shouted they wouldn't have heard, the sound of the saw so loud and the two so concentrated on what they were doing.

'It was the thin one. The bastard working the saw now – a head like the blade of an axe, dark mahogany features and two fingers missing from the right hand, the white blaze of a saw scar across his forearm. That's the man I'm going to get – somehow.' The anger, the hurt and the hot Peruvian blood . . .

The high pitch of the saw's engine dropped to a faint stutter, the chain still as the blade was withdrawn. A great wedge of timber fell out of the base of the tree, the two inside edges showing the yellow of the wood's cut cells as the feller straightened his thin, tight-muscled body, drew on his cigarette and then moved round to the other side, bracing his legs wide and falling easily into the right stance as he bent down, the blade horizontal and close to the ground. The engine screamed, then slowed as the blade bit, the bright yellow flow of the sawdust streaming between his legs; we just stopped there, rooted to the spot.

I don't know what it was – a sort of fascination, I suppose. To stand there beside Brian watching a tree that had been planted by his grandfather as a small seedling that he had held in his hand, stooping to plant it in the ground, and now it was a hundred, maybe a hundred and fifty feet high, and a man bending to fell it to the ground. The saw was slowing, the engine note deepening as the cut moved in to the full diameter of the butt, the yellow of the sawn wood streaming slower as the engine laboured. A pause, and the second man standing with his hand on the trunk, leaning his weight against it almost nonchalantly.

There was a sudden crack, and looking up I saw the top of the tree sway. A final burst from the feller's saw, then both men were standing slightly back, their hands pressed against the bark as though to push the whole towering weight of the trunk away from them, and the tree moving, moving faster and faster with a great ripping of branches high up. Then it was in the clear, falling away from the men and the uncut forest into the open devastation of clear-felled land.

A thud, a great cloud of dust and debris. Then it was there, on the ground, felled and finished, everything suddenly very quiet, both saws cut out and only the sound of two men talking and the distant murmur of the cascades, the rush of water through the forest.

We watched three trees like that one felled, and then we moved into the timber, working our way towards the camp with the glimmer of daylight that marked the felled area and the inlet just visible away to our right. It was the sound of the crawler's engine that warned us we were getting close. The boles thinned, a breeze stirring as daylight showed ahead, and then we were at the edge of High Stand, the extraction road only a few yards away and the crawler already past on its way to pick up the three felled trees, now trimmed and ready for haulage.

It stopped and I saw Jim Edmundson there, talking to the driver. And when it had gone on Jim continued with his work, pacing out the land, notebook open in his hand. I wanted him to know we were there. I wanted to tell him about the hut, about Tarasconi and the Mexican. God knows what was in my mind. But as I moved out from the brown fluted bark of the tree behind which I'd been standing, Brian hissed at me, 'Wait! There's a truck.'

It was a pick-up, coming fast from the direction of the office. It pulled up not fifty yards from us, Wolchak leaning out from behind the wheel, a battered hat on his head, his glasses glistening. 'Edmundson! Pilot says he can't wait for you any longer.'

Jim had stopped and was making a note. 'Another few minutes. I'm almost through.'

Wolchak jumped out of the cab. 'He's due to pick up some fishermen at Bella Coola midday. He has to leave now.' Even though the ground was rough Wolchak still managed to move over it like a rubber ball, his rotund body conveying an impression of boundless energy. 'I'll drive you back. He's in a hurry now.' He had reached Jim, standing there in front of him with an odd urgency. 'Otherwise it could be a day or so. There's a lot of cloud coming in.'

Jim nodded, staring down at his notebook. Then he closed it, slowly. 'You've felled by my reckoning over four hectares. And you're still felling.'

'We have the owner's agreement.' Wolchak's voice, high-pitched, came to me very distinctly.

'Have you?' Jim looked at the man as he slipped the notebook inside his anorak. 'I asked for it last night. I could see at a glance you'd cut more than the two hectares the forestry people had been notified. You couldn't produce it.'

'No. I said the lawyers had it and we'd send it on. In fact, I've just learned it won't be signed until some time today.'

'You were felling without the owner's agreement then?'

'We had a letter of intent. I told you.'

'But you couldn't produce it.'

'Of course not. It's at our Seattle office. I explained . . .'

The saws had started up again, and at the same time the two of them turned away towards the pick-up. It was then, with Edmundson there, a government-chartered floatplane at the quay, and Wolchak already being questioned, that I started forward. This was the moment to face him with Miriam's disappearance, to find out whether SVL Timber were in any way responsible. That was my reasoning, and I was on the point of calling out to Jim Edmundson when Brian grabbed hold of me.

'No! Not now.' His voice, loud in my ear, was almost drowned by the saws. 'That's a Park warden, not a Mountie. He isn't going to stick his neck into this can of worms.' He hauled me back. 'Can't you get it into your head, that stand of trees represents money, big money. You're fighting greed, men who'll do anything . . .' He shook his head. 'Just wait. Sooner or later . . .' He left it at that and I stood there staring after the two of them, the moment gone. But for Wolchak to tell Jim Edmundson the agreement would be signed today . . .

'Why did he say that?' Brian didn't take it in and I had to repeat the question. 'Why would Wolchak be so sure your father would sign the agreement? And sign it today?'

'Miriam,' he said. 'They'll get hold of Tom . . .' He shrugged, watching as Jim Edmundson got into the cab and the pick-up drove off. 'They'll get at him. Maybe not today. But sooner or later. Meanwhile, your friend there will write a report some time during the next few days and it'll go the round of departments, everybody initialling it and passing it on. It could be a month before anything is actually done about it.' He looked back at the forest behind us. 'A few more fellers and it could all be down inside a month.'

The pick-up went to the office first. The pilot was already down at the Cessna standing impatiently on one of the floats. Then, as soon as he saw Jim come out with his bag and his briefcase, he swung the prop. The engine started immediately, the prop idling as the pick-up stopped alongside. Jim went straight from truck to float and he didn't look back as he climbed into the cabin, though Wolchak had got out and was standing there on the quay. No handshake, no farewell word; I thought that unusual for such a friendly man.

The clouds were right down on the mountain now, the walls of the inlet shrouded, light fading as the

Cessna taxied out and took off, flying straight and low down the waterway. The time was eleven-thirty. Another tree crashed down. The crawler went by again trailing four logs this time. And close under the cliff the great boom crane was lifting the butt of another log, a small winch on the clifftop drawing a hawser tight to hold it into a niche in the rock face, the drilling rig climbing back up the road to the top. We watched as it backed up over a wooden platform erected above the niche, put down pads to hold it in position, then raised the A-frame that had been folded over the cab until it was erect and ready for the drilling pipe. Down on the ground two more men were now working on the log that had been lowered into chocks, manhandling with the aid of a chain purchase what appeared to be a butt-end section of the tree back into position.

I only had a quick look at this work through the glasses, and Brian couldn't tell me what they were doing. His only concern seemed to be Wolchak and he kept the glasses glued on the office. It was about ten minutes later, when the pipe suspended from the mobile rig's A-frame tower was turning, the bit drilling down into the butt of the log up-ended in its niche, that a door of the office opened and two men came out, both carrying rifles slung over their shoulders, rucksacks on their backs. They stood there for a moment, waiting beside the pick-up. Then Wolchak came out and they all climbed in.

Seeing them like that, armed, had taken my mind right back to Ice Cold and Tom, high on snorts of coke, trying to get them to say where Miriam was being held.

I watched as the truck began to move, coming straight down the road towards us. The thought that had been lurking at the back of my mind was suddenly there with a blinding clarity. 'The hut!' I moved across to Brian, shaking him by the arm. 'That dinghy. They're going up there.'

'So what?' He was staring at me uncomprehending, and I didn't understand because now it seemed so obvious to me.

'The hut!' I repeated. 'That's where they've got Miriam. Camargo and Lopez, they're going up there.' Now that it was out, now that I'd said it, it seemed clearer than ever – the dogs, the guard, that Mexican Rodrigo taking in stores. And Tarasconi – it would explain why he'd told Tom he would soon know where Miriam was.

The pick-up went past us, Camargo's bearded face clearly visible as he looked over the tops of the trees at the heights above. 'They're going up there.' I still had hold of Brian's arm, desperately trying to get through to him. 'Suppose Tom contacted Rodrigo after we left? He could be up there now.' But he shook his head, still watching the camp through the glasses. 'What are you looking at?' I demanded. 'Whatever you think of him, he's still your father.'

He shook his head again, and I saw the glasses were fixed on the boom crane that was now manoeuvring the log out of its niche and lowering it to where the two men were rolling another butt-end to the chain purchase. 'I must find out,' he muttered.

'What?' I asked.

'Why they want a log boom. You only need that if you're floating logs down or holding them penned up in a booming ground. But loading them dry, straight off the quay . . . I can't see the point of it.' And he added, 'Tonight. I'll get into the camp tonight.' He lowered the glasses, passing a hand over his face. 'It's the only way. Then maybe I'll have something that'll force the authorities to act.' He yawned. 'You go back up to the top if you want to. See what those two are being sent up there for. I'm going to curl up somewhere, get some sleep, then, when it's dark – well, we'll see . . .'

I argued with him, scared I think to go back on my own, scared of the loneliness – just myself and those two hoodlums, both of them armed. But nothing would shift him. His father, he said, could fend for himself. As for Miriam, if I were right and she was being held in the hut, he didn't see that I'd be much use to her up there on the lake on my own. 'You'd be better employed getting some sleep, then seeing if you can discover something that will stop them pirating a stand of timber that doesn't belong to them and never will.'

In the end I left him, knowing I had no time to lose if I were to get up the lake ahead of the two South Americans. 'Okay,' he said. 'But watch it, mate. Wolchak, and the boys he fronts for, aren't playing for plastic counters. They'll cut you to pieces without a thought.' Those were his last words to me as I turned and started back through the timber at a steady trot. I looked back once, but I couldn't see him. The trees had closed ranks, the great boles a solid wall blocking out even a glimmer of daylight from the open ground.

The saws had stopped again. It was very quiet as I doubled back, searching for the track, starkly conscious that I was alone now, nobody to lead me on, nobody to talk to. High Stand seemed suddenly a hostile place, the tree roots tripping me, the boles hemming me in, and everything very dark.

I found the track and started up the slope of it, the murmur of the torrent a little nearer. It was raining now. I could hear it in the trees, but no rain fell, the canopy shutting it out. Then the saws started up again, the sound faint and far behind me, and I knew Camargo and Lopez had ceased talking to the fellers and were on their way up the track behind me.

In my haste to get back up to the lake ahead of them I barely noticed the increasing dark. It was uphill all the way, my breath labouring. I had nothing to carry, but even so I was exhausted by the time the boles became smaller, faint glimmers of daylight showing through the tops. The rain had thinned to a light drizzle, wisps of white cloud vapour trickling between the trees. And then I was out into the old felled area, the track climbing more steeply, my breath coming in great gasps, and nothing ahead of me, just the mist hanging white and heavy, so that I moved in a pale void where every leaf and twig, every bush glimmered with moisture. I looked back and High Stand had gone, swallowed up in the cloud.

That was when the loneliness really hit. I was slowed to a walk that gradually became a desperate trudge. A lawyer's desk and a small sailing boat were no training for a hike in the Rockies and I hadn't slept for what seemed a lifetime. Every now and then I stopped for breath, eyes and ears reaching back into the grey fog behind me, seeing shadows on the edge of visibility, the rustle of air currents through birch leaves making my heart pump harder. No sound of the saws now, only the growing murmur of the cascades above me.

Noon by my watch and I was back at the hairpin bend, standing at the end of the mountain spur where we had looked down onto the camp and the inlet, and across to the green sea of the forest top. Now there was nothing. I was in a world apart, just myself and cloud vapour. And then I heard a voice.

It came from below me, from back down the track, a voice calling to somebody, faint above the sound of water falling. There was an answer, fainter still. Then silence.

I went on then, climbing the back of the steeply sloping spur, forcing the pace, fear driving me and giving me strength. My shoes squelched in the mud as I forced my way through the thickness of new growth that had seemed so much easier on the way down, my body sodden below the waist, steaming with sweat under my anorak, and nothing to show me how near I was to the top, the clouds solid and all-pervading, but white now, a glimmering iridescence as though I was beginning to climb through it to the sun.

The track, or what remained of it, came to an abrupt end. I turned back then, searching for footprints, found a patch of soft earth fifty yards back and clawed my way up through a mass of alder and some rowans until I was on level ground that sloped away to the invisible edge of the lake. I found the canoe and wasted precious moments trying to right it. It had seemed so easy when there were two of us. Then I remembered the boat hauled out on the sloping rock where we had landed. I grabbed the paddles and the rucksack that contained our food, voices sounding on the track below as I stumbled through the trees to the rock.

It took me only a moment to toss the things into the boat, slide it down the slope into the water and jump in. White cloud vapour clung to the trees, dripped from the branches, the edge of the lake disappearing into nothingness. I rowed quietly, slipping the boat through the water, the rock fading. Suddenly it was gone and I stopped rowing. I could hear the crash of branches, loud above the murmur of water falling away to my right. Then voices. They were talking in Spanish, searching along the lake edge. There was a splash and a curse.

I wondered what they would do, what I was going to do, alone on the lake in thick cloud mist. I was thinking of the hut then, wondering vaguely what would happen when I reached it, my brain grappling wearily with the problem of how to check that Miriam really was being held there.

An exclamation, a stream of half-audible words, the voice harsh and flowing. Lopez. And he had found the canoe.

I began to row again.

PART FIVE

FISHING THE SPIDER

CHAPTER ONE

Following the shore, it was the dark grit of the little beach that I saw first, a scuffed drag-line leading across it to the pale tin gleam of the boat hauled up close to the bushes and tree roots of the bank. I turned my head and there was the hut, a dark shadow in the cloud mist that looked surprisingly large, like a small castle on its rocky mound. The dogs were quiet, the door shut. I back-paddled, dipping the oars with care. The log-built shape faded and was suddenly gone, swallowed so completely by the mist it might never have been there.

I rowed gently to some rocks, found a place where the boat would be partially concealed, leaving it there, half-in, half-out of the water, and making my way cautiously through the trees until I could see the hut again. The trees hung heavy with moisture, no breath of air, everything very still except for the all-pervading sound of water falling.

I don't know how long I crouched there, my legs

cramped, my trousers clinging wetly, eyes straining and the minutes passing. I thought I heard the rattle of a chain, and once I imagined the sound of voices, but nothing moved, the world in limbo, and the boat so near I could have reached out and touched its outboard engine. It was an aluminium boat with a flat ribbed bottom and a bow like a punt. A bald-headed eagle swooped on a fish and I began to shiver.

I couldn't stay there indefinitely. If Camargo and Lopez had been coming up to the hut they'd have launched the canoe by now, and with branches as paddles, or with just their hands, it wouldn't be long before they were here. I rose, trembling, and started cautiously forward. The hut had windows either side of the door that gave it the appearance of a wood-brown Indian face peering out over the lake, the glass of the eyes glinting with the water's pale reflection. There was a side window too, but that seemed boarded up. If I could look in through the windows facing the lake without disturbing the dogs . . .

As though they had sensed my thoughts, the sound of chains dragging was suddenly quite distinct. I froze as one of them gave a little bark that was half-enquiring. At the same instant the door of the hut opened and a man came out, tall and gangling with big ears either side of a long, battered face. I suppose I was within fifty feet of him as he turned and said in English, 'No sign of them yet. They must have missed their way.' He was speaking to the man I had last seen in the early hours of the morning following Tarasconi up the wet curve of the wooden highway in Ocean Falls.

The dogs barked as Rodrigo moved towards the path that led to the portage. 'Ah got two guys expecting me. Canadian whites.' He hawked and spat in the direction of the dogs. 'Remember. You tell that boss o' yours Ah need double, an' Ah need it reg'lar. The market down there's growing fast. Okay?' He looked at the dogs and spat again. 'You got all the protection you need, eh?'

'I guess so,' the other replied, and then I couldn't hear them any more, the two of them moving off into the trees, the mist swallowing them.

My head turned to the hut and the open door, the dark rectangle of it holding my gaze, seeming to beckon. I moved on the instant, almost running. It wasn't a conscious action, my feet moving of their own accord, a reflex action. The dogs began barking as I reached the door. Inside there was a table, chairs, a sort of dresser with crockery, a kerosene stove and a two-tier bunk against the far wall, a walkie-talkie, aerial extended, hanging on a nail on the wall and below it a rifle propped against a small cupboard that had a pressure lamp on it, keys and a powerful torch. There were two doors leading off the central room, both of them held securely shut with heavy double bars of fresh-sawn timber slotted into clumsy wooden brackets.

'Miriam!'

There was no answer, everything very still, except those damn dogs, barking madly now, leaping at the full stretch of their chains.

'Miriam!' I called again and a man's voice answered. He was behind the door to my left. I started towards it with the intention of lifting the bars, but there was a shout from the direction of the lake and I stopped, turning to the open door and the figure of a man running towards it.

I slammed it shut. There was a big key in a lock and I turned it. Seconds later fists pounded on the door's wooden boards, a voice shouting at me to open up and not play bloody stupid games. He thought I was Camargo or Lopez. 'Don't fool around, the High Stand owner is there and he's high as a kite. Don't let him out.'

The dogs had stopped barking, but they were leaping and growling at the full stretch of their chains as the man's face appeared at one of the windows, the two of us staring at each other. Then I had turned and was wrestling with the timber bars to the door, a voice calling from the inside something that sounded like 'shoot the bastard' followed by a string of obscenities. The bars were swollen with damp. I reached for a chair, knocking them up as a rock smashed the glass of the nearest window.

The room door crashed open, Tom standing there, his eyes wild, his face flushed, that muscle twitching at the line of his mouth. 'Where's that fucking Mexican? Where's Rodrigo?' His eyes, searching madly, fastened on the rifle propped against the cupboard. He lunged for it as a dead branch began to demolish the rest of the window, the man wielding it yelling for the door to be opened.

The room from which Tom had emerged was small, no more than eight feet deep, and there was the figure of a man sprawled on a bed at the end. There was a bucket against the opposite wall, the place smelling of stale humanity and excrement. There was blood on the blankets, the man's face swollen and bruised. He looked as though he'd been badly beaten up.

Behind me I heard the click of a bolt. I turned and in the same instant there was the crash of a shot. Tom was at the smashed window, the rifle at his shoulder, smoke curling lazily from the barrel, and from outside the hut the shot man began to scream.

It was a crazy thing to do. If he'd killed the man he would be on a murder charge, and God knows what that would do to him, and Miriam, all the publicity, his name blazoned across Canada and Britain, and myself a witness to it. I could see the expression on the QC's face after he'd read the brief. I can't remember what I said, but when I seized hold of him, trying to restrain him, trying to tell him the consequences, he rounded on me, his face creased with anger, his teeth bared below the beginnings of a new moustache. 'Murder, you say. Are you bloody crazy? That bastard out there, he's the murderer.' And when I stared at him unbelievingly, he said, 'Go and look. On the bed, in there.'

'Who is it?' I asked.

'Olsen. Thor Olsen, my forest manager. And he's dead – dead. You understand?' He was leaning his face close to mine and screaming the words at me. 'Dead!' he screamed again. 'Beaten to death to force Miriam to tell A-Aleksis there – ' he nodded to the man squirming on the ground outside, his hand grasping his left leg, moans of pain issuing from his wide-open mouth – 'to tell him something she didn't know. I should have killed him.' He thrust his face right into mine, the bulging eyes lit by a curious light, violence and excitement vibrating in his voice as he repeated, 'I should have killed him – shot him dead. Instead, I've shot his knee to pieces, nothing more. So don't talk to me of murder.'

A voice called, and he swung round. It was a woman's voice, muffled, but with a high pitch of hysteria. She was calling his name and he lunged for the door at the other end of the hut, clawing at the wooden bars, then hammering them up with the butt of the gun he still held in his hands. The door thrust open and she was there, her arms round him, half laughing, half sobbing, her hair dishevelled, no make-up and her clothes in a mess, blood and dirt and all creased with constant wear. They didn't kiss. They didn't say anything. They just clung to each other, like two lost souls. Then she saw me and she smiled, looking past his shoulder. 'Philip. It was you, wasn't it?'

I didn't say anything and she pushed him away – but gently, almost reluctantly. 'Tom, you've been taking that stuff again. You're high.'

'Of course I'm high. I'm on top of the world.' He laughed, the sound of it a little wild. 'If I hadn't been high I'd never have had the guts to come here with that little Mexican bugger Rodrigo looking for you and walking s-slap into the bloody neat little trap they'd laid for me.'

She came across to me then, holding out her hand. 'Thank you, Philip.' And as I took it she leaned forward and kissed me lightly on the mouth. 'I'm filthy,' she said. 'I'm going down to the lake to clean up.' But she hesitated, staring down at the man who had been her jailer moaning and squirming on the ground, only half conscious now.

'Did he kill Olsen?' I asked her.

'In a way, yes.' She had turned back to the two-tier bunks to grab a piece of soap and a towel that was hanging there. 'Thor wasn't young,' she said, turning to face me. 'Over sixty, he said, and he'd had a hard life. I think it was a heart attack. He was tied up and that sadistic beast was hammering at him with a rough jagged end of a cedar branch, and then suddenly Thor collapsed, and he was dead – just like that. No sign of life. I gave him mouth-to-mouth resuscitation, but no good. He was gone.'

She went out then, stepping past the figure on the ground and going down to the lake, where she stripped off her clothes and began washing herself, her movements practical and energetic, an essential action for any woman who had been cooped up for several weeks in a small room, but I still couldn't take my eyes off the scene. It was so like some of the great pictures I had seen in magazines and books – *Nude Bathing in a Lake*. She looked beautiful.

'You going to gawp at my wife all day?'

I turned to find Tom laughing at me. And then I remembered – Camargo and Lopez. And I shouted to Miriam, a sudden vision in my mind of the canoe emerging out of the grey veil of the mist and one of them lifting his gun to his shoulder. *Swan Lake* and Miriam in the role of Odette, falling and dying there, naked by the quiet, still waters of a lake deep in the Rockies.

She came back into the hut then, her breasts bare and the towel wrapped round her middle, her skin glowing with the coldness of the water.

I started explaining to Tom how his son and I had gone down into High Stand and how we had split up, Brian staying there while I hurried back up to the lake ahead of the two South Americans.

'So they could be here any minute.'

I nodded.

'And they're armed.' He was already moving round the hut, gathering up food, kit, clothes and a torch. 'We must be out on the lake before they get here. You got all you want? Miriam! Bring your blankets, we may have to sleep out tonight, it depends when the tug arrives.' He took down the walkie-talkie hanging on the wall and passed it to me. 'Sling that over your shoulder. Now let's get moving. We'll take the hut work boat and tow yours. Then they'll be stuck here till that dirty little lying pusher of a Mexican comes back for more snow.' I'd never seen him like this, so sure of himself, so in command, not even at his own dinner table back at Bullswood House. But the mention of Rodrigo made me wonder whether the man could have heard the shot, might even now be lurking in the mist at the edge of visibility. Tom was sure not. 'He'd never have heard it, not above the sound of water falling to the lower lake. Ready?'

I nodded and he called to Miriam again. She came out of the room, fully dressed with a bundle of blankets under her arm. 'I've enough here for both of us,' she told him.

'Good.' He went out and I followed.

Miriam hesitated. 'What about Thor? We ought to bury him.'

'No time.' He was standing over the man whose knee was a pulp of blood and bone showing through his trousers. The dark eyes were blank with pain, his breath coming in quick gasps. 'I ought to knee-cap both your legs,' he said, and I saw the man wince, his eyes half-closing and his teeth gritted as he waited in fear for the impact and the agony. Then he passed out.

We shut the door of the hut, locked it and took the key. 'If they land here th-they'll be fully occupied dealing with that guy and trying to get back down to the camp.' Tom was moving across the little beach to where the aluminium boat lay. We dumped our things in it, dragged it down to the water, and while Tom dealt with the outboard, Miriam and I carried the semi-inflatable down, making the painter fast to an aluminium cleat close by where Tom was sitting.

He was pulling the starter cord then, and as we climbed in, the engine burst into life. I thought I heard a shout, somebody calling out of the mist. Miriam had sat herself on the flat platform of the punt's bow and she thought she heard it, too. But by then I was pushing off with an oar, the outboard lowered and the prop biting, a froth of water astern as the boat gathered way.

It was then, as we were moving out from the shore, the hut already gone and the trees fading into mist that Tom saw it, and as I turned it was just emerging from the mist, a canoe's bows and a man's body, ghostly and unreal.

Tom half rose, his eyes widening, his mouth open. The engine roared, the boat skidding round in a tight turn, and he was suddenly singing, bawling out at the top of his voice: '. . . the glory of the coming of the Lord; He is trampling out the vintage where the grapes of wrath are stored – ' The Battle Hymn of the Republic and the boat driving straight for the canoe, which was now broadside to us, the two men in it kneeling and staring at us.

Lopez was the first to react, leaning forward and grabbing his rifle.

'You fool!' I yelled, for Miriam, seated in the bows, was more at risk than either of us.

'. . . the fateful lightning of His terrible swift sword – '

Camargo, too, had got hold of his gun, both of them starting to aim and the canoe so near and clear now I could see the moisture beads on moustache and beard, the frayed stitching of an anorak and their faces set, their dark eyes staring. '. . . sounded forth the trumpet that shall never call retreat; He is sifting out the hearts of men – ' The crunch as we hit the canoe was instantaneous with the crash of their rifles, the flat punt-end riding up on it, trampling it down into the water, the two men falling, their hands thrown up and Tom's voice still drumming out the words, the crash of the shots reverberating, wood splintering . . . 'Our God is marching on.'

He leaned out and grabbed hold of Camargo's rifle, wrenching it out of his hand as the canoe disappeared. 'Swim for it, you buggers,' he yelled at them, lifting the outboard clear of the wreckage, then revving the engine again and heading down the lake, the semi-inflatable riding through the remains of the canoe and their two heads watching us from the water, two disembodied faces staring in disbelief.

'He is coming like the glory of the morning on the waves; He is wisdom to the mighty, He is succour to the brave . . .'

I think I must have said something like, 'You can't leave them to drown,' for he stopped singing long enough to shout above the engine's busy noise, 'Can't I? Don't you know why they were coming up here, to the hut? I heard it all on that thing.' He pointed to the walkie-talkie. 'They were going to play around with Miriam. Do whatever was necessary to get me to sign. And I wouldn't have had any alternative. I'd have signed away High Stand to save Miriam, and you want me to hang around and pick the bastards up.' He gave a wild laugh, the two heads fading into the mist, open-mouthed, their shouts inaudible.

'So the world should be His footstool, and the soul of time His slave. Our God is marching on!' He sat down suddenly, throttling back on the engine and staring into the void. 'I don't care if they drown. I should have killed them, up there at Ice Cold. And Wolchak. What about Josef Wolchak?' His eyes fastened on mine. 'He's down there at the camp, isn't he? And Mandola. What about Mandola and all the others?'

'What others?' I asked.

'I don't know.' He shrugged. 'All the others, the men

who run the pushers, the big boys who pull in the money. Who's down at the camp?'

'Wolchak was the only one I saw, apart from the loggers and truck drivers.'

'And Brian's down there?'

'Yes.'

'They're still felling, then. Have they got a scow there?'

'A barge,' I said.

'Scow, barge – what the hell! Aleksis said something about it having to be loaded by morning. He was talking on the radio. Wolchak had to have my signature to the document by noon tomorrow at the latest. That was when they expected the tug.'

The wildness seemed to have gone out of him, the eyes dead, as though the destruction of the canoe had got some of the anger and the hate out of his system. He was staring along the cascade shore of the lake, trees like phantoms standing in the mist, his eyes blank, his thoughts turned inwards. I didn't say anything, thinking of Camargo and Lopez, two heads in the water beyond the inflatable and disappearing into the void, wondering whether they'd be able to swim ashore or whether the coldness of the water and cramp would drown them first.

Even then I hadn't realized the violence of the world into which I'd been dragged. Only Miriam knew, and she was silent, huddled in the bows, her face tense and very pale. 'You all right?' I asked her and she nodded, no glimmer of a smile, no change of expression, and her eyes on Tom.

'Where did those two come from? There's a way down; at the end of the lake, is it?' He had to shout to make himself heard above the engine.

'Just follow the shoreline,' I told him. 'There's a bit of a bay. I'll point it out to you. It's not far then to the old extraction track.'

'You've been down it, have you?'

'I told you.'

He nodded, but I could see he hadn't taken it in, so I told him again how we'd gone down into High Stand, watched the felling of the timber, and then, when Wolchak had driven Camargo and Lopez to the start of the track, Brian had stayed there while I hurried back ahead of the two South Americans to commandeer the boat and arrive at the hut just when Rodrigo was leaving. 'I suppose he told you he'd take you to where Miriam was being held?'

He smiled then, but it was more of a grimace. 'I didn't trust him, of course, but I was desperate. I wanted to believe him, and then when I saw Miriam ... I'd forgotten they could communicate by VHF, that the whole thing could be stage-managed so that she was there, tied to the door bar; that was all I saw till that bastard with the big ears swiped me across the back of the head.' He put his hand up, feeling it gently. 'I've still got a hell of a bump. Then they flung me into that room with the corpse of poor old Thor ... One day perhaps I'll be able to look Rodrigo in the face knowing he'll spend half the rest of his life behind bars. Perhaps I should have ...'

But I stopped him there, for we were approaching

the end of the lake, the mist swirling to a puff of wind and trees appearing in the gap. He slowed as I motioned him to turn towards the shore and then the aluminium bottom of the boat was bumping on boulders, scraping on the dark grit that ran up to the tree roots. Without being told, Miriam took the painter and stepped over the side, moving slowly, like an automaton, as she splashed her way to the bank. Tom was bent over the outboard, unbolting it from its bracket, and when he'd brought it ashore he looked at me with a quizzical expression. 'Don't reckon we'll be wanting it again, do you?'

I shook my head and he smiled, walking with it to the sloping rock where Brian and I had landed from the canoe and tossing it into the lake. He stood there for a moment, watching it sink, as though in that action he had virtually burned his boats. His mood communicated itself to me, so that as we gathered up our things I had the feeling that whatever lay in store for us down below, there would be no turning back.

It was almost three in the afternoon when we started down that track, myself in the lead and seeing my own footprints in the mud. The breeze was moving the mist, so that the light came and went, strange cloud shapes forming, and there was a rustle of leaves, or was it the distant murmur of the water falling? I felt very tired then, my limbs heavy, my brain numbed with lack of sleep and the unaccustomed exercise. I think we were, all three of us, pretty near the limit of our reserves, Miriam in particular. She didn't talk. Even when asked a direct question she scarcely bothered to answer. There was no expression in her face, and the way she moved she seemed to be in a daze.

We reached the end of the spur, and before following the curve of the hairpin, we stood for a moment looking down at the camp through a gap in the clouds that were billowing raggedly between the rock walls of the inlet. The barge, lying against the quay, was deeper in the water now, the logs stacked in two great bundles, butts facing outwards against the blunt ends of the vessel, the tapering tops laced together like the fingers of some huge hand; there were at least a dozen more logs stacked on the quayside, the boom crane moving all the time as it lifted others from the big tractor transporter. Another log was clamped in the rock niche against the cliff, the A-frame mobile rig drilling into the butt end. 'Your son thinks they're constructing a logging boom,' I said. 'And that that means they're going to fell the whole area of High Stand.'

'Could be.' He nodded slowly. And then suddenly he turned on me and said in a voice taut with nerves, 'So what the hell does he expect me to do about it? What can we do?'

'Get an injunction, I suppose.' I said it without any enthusiasm for the idea, my tired mind thinking ahead to all the work involved in getting an action like that against an American company through a British Columbian court.

'An injunction! That's all you lawyers can think of. Fees for yourself and a court order, a bloody little piece of paper and some poor devil of a bailiff, if there is such a thing, traipsing all the way up here from

Vancouver . . . Have you any idea of the sort of people he'd be dealing with? Well, have you?'

At the time I don't think I really understood what he was talking about, but I could see his point about the bailiff. It would be a civil action and the police would only become involved if there was contempt of court. By then, of course, so much time would have passed that the whole of High Stand would have been felled and shipped, our only recourse the courts again for payment of a proper price for the sale of the timber standing.

The clouds were lifting. For a moment they were above our heads, so that we could look right down the long arm of water, great banks of vapour vaulted over it, the mountains either side cut off, everything looking sombre and very wet. He had turned his head and was staring down at the camp again, men moving around the drilling rig and on the flat platform of the quayside where two of them were working at the butt end of the log that had just been lowered to them. 'What do you think they're doing?' I asked.

He shrugged. 'Brian's probably right in thinking they're constructing a booming pen. They'll need it if they're planning to shift the whole stand out in a hurry. There isn't storage space on the quay and the poorer logs they'll probably raft out anyway.' He had been speaking slowly, as though by putting it into words he could convince himself that Brian's explanation was the right one. 'Why else would they be drilling the butts of selected logs?'

He looked at me then, his eyes staring, his shoulders

sagging. There was a weariness about him that I found disturbing, and my mind flashed back to that lunch at a place near Lewes – it seemed a whole world away now – and Miriam telling me how one minute he'd be on top of the world – 'the stars in my lap', I remembered her words – and the next nothing, a bundle of nerves and temperament, full of insecurity. 'It'll sort itself out, I suppose.' He said it wearily and I saw Miriam watching him, a frown on her face, and there were lines, so that she looked suddenly older, and the expression in her eyes – I think it was pity.

His gaze lifted. They stood looking at each other for a moment and I sensed something pass between them. And then he straightened up, pushing his hand through the wet brush of his hair and squaring his shoulders. 'Let's get on, shall we?'

He gave one final glance down at the camp below, then continued on round the hairpin bend, moving fast. I caught up with him in the first salmonberry thicket. 'What are you planning to do when you get down there?' I asked him.

'See what Brian's up to. Try and stop them if I can.' He shook his head, clearly irritated by my question. 'I don't know. We'll just have to see.'

Miriam caught up with me then, her hand grasping mine, her fingers fastening tight as she held me back. 'Watch him,' she whispered. 'Please. I don't know how much of the stuff he's had. But I know this mood.' She half slipped on a patch of mud, and then she muttered something about his being unpredictable.

'Unpredictable?' I repeated, and she nodded: 'He

could do something stupid, so please – keep an eye on him.'

We were glimpsing the cascades up on the rim of the lake above, the murmur of water filling the horseshoe basin with gentle sound and, below us, the green vista of the cedar tops silvered with moisture, the cloud-topped gut of the inlet beyond. Then the cloud came down again and for a time we could see nothing but the down-slope of the track ahead disappearing into vapour that the breeze rolled around as though it were smoke.

We must have been quite close to the upper edge of High Stand when I thought I saw movement. Tom had seen it, too, for he was suddenly standing very still, his head stretched forward, peering into the mist. Slowly he unslung the rifle from his shoulder, his thumb on the safety catch as he held it poised in both his hands. Faint from below came the sound of a power saw muffled by the trees.

I still held the gun he had snatched from Camargo and then passed to me. I looked down at it, finding the safety catch and wondering whether it was loaded. I'd never fired a rifle in my life. He moved forward in a crouch, and I followed, and then a voice called up to us.

It was Brian.

He didn't look at his father, walking straight past him, his eyes on Miriam. 'So you found her,' he said to me, his face lit by a smile. And then they were hugging each other, and Miriam crooning over him as though she really were his mother. Her reaction, the sudden outpouring of pent-up emotion, was a reminder of the long period of uncertainty and fear she had suffered up there in that hut.

'I told you not to go looking for Rodrigo.' He had turned to face his father, hot anger blazing in his dark eyes. 'I warned you.' He swung round on me. 'What happened?' And when I had told him, he turned on Tom again. 'God, Jesus! You bloody fool! You could have had Miriam maimed for life and those bastards with an agreement signed that gave them the right to do what they're doing. You played right into their hands. Don't you realize there's anything up to a million dollars in the forest your father planted?'

'It's not the trees,' Tom said. 'That's just a cover.'

Thunder rolled down from invisible mountains, a flash of lightning.

Brian shook his head. 'I warned you, and bloody hell, you took no notice.' The sky had taken on a livid hue, the head of the inlet blocked out. 'All you care about is yourself and getting enough coke to keep you high, just so you don't have to face up to the reality of what you've done, letting these people in.'

'I tell you, it's just a c-cover.' Tom's voice was taut as though on the edge of losing control himself.

'Listen!' And Brian went straight on, ignoring his father's attempt to tell him something, 'Do you hear it – those chainsaws?'

They stood facing each other, the echoes of the thunder dying away across the peaks. 'Listen!' he said again. 'Now do you hear it?' And he seized hold of his father's arm and dragged him down the slope of the track. 'Come on, I'll show you. We'll go down through the timber and you can see for yourself.' Miriam tried to stop him, but he waved her away. 'It's time he realized just what he's doing. Once he's seen it, maybe he'll understand.'

The single-purposedness of the man was quite extra-ordinary. He must have been as tired as I was, and yet he could still radiate a sort of demonic energy, his obsession with trees filling his mind to the exclusion of anything else, so that I felt it was a sort of madness that had taken hold of him. And Tom went unresisting, a dazed expression on his face as though he were in the grip of Fate and had no volition of his own.

Only once did he break away. 'Must have a pee,' he murmured. And it was the same as it had been up near Ice Cold. I heard him snorting the stuff up his nose, and as we went on down into the forest, he developed a spring to his step, something near to a swagger in his walk. Miriam was by my side and she said, 'Stop them, can't you? They're so explosive. The two of them together.' She was very tense herself. 'They've always had this effect on each other.'

I shook my head. It wasn't for me to interfere, and anyway we were nearing the end of the track, light showing through the tree boles and the sound of the saws getting louder every moment.

We came to the edge of the clear-felled area, the time 15.55 and the only difference from when I had been there in the morning was that the two fellers had moved half a dozen trees or more northwards, so that our view of the camp was partly obscured by the piled-up brash of lopped branches. Also the thunder was nearer, a closeness in the air and the lowering cloud base getting darker. The sound of the saws was loud here, a small wind carrying it towards us, one man working his way along the bole of a newly fallen tree, snicking branches off with the tip of his saw, the other bent over a standing giant that already had a gaping wedge sawn out of its base to guide the fall.

Brian had hold of his father's arm again, moving him forward under cover of the standing stems. He was talking all the time, but the sound of the chainsaws was so loud I couldn't hear what he was saying. Then timber splintering and the man nearest us looked up from the fallen tree, his chainsaw idling, the other man stepping back from the base of the stem he had been cutting into.

'. . . Stop them.'

'How?'

'For God's sake, you've got a gun.'

Both saws idling now, the top of the tree beginning to move, branches snapping and the three of us staring as the tree slowly toppled forward, the green top of it arcing down across the backcloth of cloud-filled mountainside, black rock and the pale gun-metal flatness of the water . . . Then the splintering crash of the branches, the thud of the stem hitting the ground, an explosion of dust and debris. 'That must be about the tenth I've seen felled today – ten in the few hours I've been here.' Brian's voice was harsh with anger. 'You watch – he'll move straight onto the next in line.' And suddenly he swung Tom round, facing him. 'Remember what you told me, all those years ago – about your father, what he'd written in the deeds. Remember? And now I've read it. And if you won't stop them . . .'

'You can't do it, Brian.' Miriam had moved forward, tugging at his arm, trying to push her way between them. 'He's your father. You can't goad him like that.' She was half-sobbing, her voice vibrant. The saws started up again. The feller had moved and was bending down by the next tree, the saw labouring under full power as the blade cut into the base of it.

Tom pushed Miriam away, his eyes fixed on the man as though mesmerized, watching the first cut made, Brian silent now, and Miriam standing there, her mouth open, her eyes wide. 'No!' I heard her cry that, and then the blade was making the slanting cut, her voice drowned.

Slowly, like a man in a trance, Tom moved out into the open. For a moment he stood there, the gun held ready across his body. The saw laboured, both men intent on what they were doing, the one felling, the other trimming. At last the guide wedge was finished, the feller straightening up, pushing it out with the tip of his saw, the motor idling. Then he was moving round to the rear of the tree, and the sight of him settling himself into position to begin the main saw cut that would fell the tree seemed to trigger something off in Tom's mind. He suddenly started forward, shouting at the man to stop.

The man didn't hear him at first. Neither of them seemed to hear him. By then he was half-running towards them, yelling to them at the top of his voice. The laboured sound of the saw ceased abruptly, the blade withdrawn and the engine dying as the man straightened up, staring at Tom. 'Drop that saw! Drop it!'

'Who are you?'

Tom told him his name and the man laughed. 'You don't give orders around here.' And he bent to the base of the tree again, the note of the saw rising.

I suppose it was the man's manner, his deliberate, almost contemptuous ignoring of him, that touched off the rage that had been building in Tom, so that it became a desperate hepped-up madness. He raised his gun and fired, a snap shot. But the man had seen it coming; he ducked round the end of the tree, slipping the saw blade out from the cut, so that it was held in both his hands as he stood up, flattened against the still-standing stem. The other had also stopped sawing, both of them watching as Tom stumbled forward, working the bolt.

Then he had stopped and was fumbling in his pocket. 'Oh God!' Miriam was close beside me, Brian just starting to move, and I stood there, staring, as Tom started forward again, reversing the gun so that he held it by the barrel to use as a club.

'No!' The exclamation, forced out of her by fear of what was going to happen, rang out in what seemed a desperate stillness, everything happening in slow motion, Tom running forward, and the man stepping out from behind the tree, the engine of his saw revving and the chain of it screaming on the blade.

Tom shouted something, the gun rising in his hands, ready to strike, and the man swinging his saw up so that the blade was stuck out in front of him. Whether Tom stumbled, or whether the man thrust the blade forward and he ran straight onto it, I shall never know. All I recall is the sight of him lunging forward, the rifle coming down and then the thin scream as the blade bit into his chest, bone and flesh flying, blood streaming from it where before I had seen only sawdust, and the poor devil pitching forward, the scream cut off, his body almost ripped in half.

And at the same instant the rifle I was holding was plucked from my hands and Brian had fired it, the crack of the shot followed by the man with the saw being slammed round. His hand clasped at his shoulder. Then he had ducked behind the tree again.

Suddenly all was still, the saws silent, both fellers hidden, and Tom's body lying there, the green of his anorak merged with the green of lopped branches, and Miriam standing beside me, her eyes wide with horror, a low moaning sound coming from her open mouth.

'You got any ammunition for this thing?' Brian's voice sounded half-choked, his face white against the black of his hair.

I shook my head, remembering how Tom in the euphoria of his singing had plucked it out of Camargo's hands.

'The fool! I never thought . . .' He had turned to Miriam, trying to exonerate himself, and she just stared at him in blank horror, glassy-eyed.

The man Brian had wounded was crawling into the forest, dragging his chainsaw behind him. I thought at first he was merely trying to get away from us, but then

I saw he was making for the place where they had left their anoraks and their lunch packs.

Brian had seen it, too. He raised his gun, though there was nothing in it, shouting at the man to stop. But at that moment Miriam started forward. He reached out, catching hold of her arm. 'There's nothing you can do for him.'

'How do you know?' She wrenched herself free, moving fast as she ran the thirty yards or so to where Tom lay, face-down on the ground, his body still. And when she reached him, she called out to him, bending down and turning him over. 'Tom!'

I can see it so clearly, the ripped clothing and the gaping wound, blood still flowing and his eyes fixed and staring. You didn't need any medical training to know that he was dead. Miriam had taken his head in her hands, kneeling there, her face gone paper-white and a sort of croon issuing from her mouth – of love, or horror, I don't know which it was as she clasped that poor, mangled body to her.

At what point Brian and I had moved forward I don't know, but we were there beside her, standing with our heads bent. In such circumstances, it seems, one is too shocked to say a prayer. I had seen injuries before, car accident injuries, dead bodies, too, but always in the cold isolation of a mortuary or a funeral parlour. To see violent death at the instant of dying, the eyes so wide and the teeth bared, the skin of the face still flushed with the exertion of that final rush . . . My limbs seemed suddenly paralysed, my mouth dry as I swallowed desperately.

'Drop it!' Brian's voice was harsh and high, the gun raised. He was pointing it at the man who had been crawling to where they had left their things. He had a walkie-talkie in his hands and in the stillness I heard him say, quite distinctly, 'Hurry! They're armed.' And then he dropped the radio onto the ground, sitting up and placing his hands on top of his head.

I walked over to him. 'My name's Redfern,' I said, 'and I'm an English lawyer.' Lawyer always sounds stronger than solicitor. 'The man you have just killed is my client and the owner of the trees you are illegally felling. You'll be charged with murder.'

'Yeah?' The hard, leathery face cracked open to reveal a row of broken teeth. 'You saw what happened. An unprovoked attack . . .'

'It was murder,' I repeated.

'He stumbled, fell right onto the saw, didn't he?'

'Time we were moving.' Brian had picked up the walkie-talkie handset. 'Wolchak will be here in a moment.'

'Then he can take us up to his office,' I said. 'He'll have an R/T set there and we can get onto the police, maybe get that Coastguard cutter back.'

'Don't be a fool, Philip.' It was Miriam. She had got to her feet, her hands covered in blood, and there was blood all over her skirt, her lips a tight line, her eyes frozen. 'Nothing you can do for Tom. Nothing any of us can do.' There was no emotion in her voice. 'All we can do now is try and get out of here, alive.'

I started to argue with her, but she cut me short, her manner quiet and very controlled. 'I don't think you understand. Either of you. This isn't about forestry. It's nothing to do with trees.' She looked towards the two men sitting there and staring at us. Then she turned abruptly. 'We'll go back up to the lake now.'

I hesitated. Then I followed her, realizing suddenly that her words were for the benefit of the two fellers, that what she wanted to tell us couldn't be said while they were within earshot. Brian stood there for a moment longer. He was genetically incapable of accepting instructions from a woman, but in the end he followed. There had been something in Miriam's tone, and in her manner – a decisiveness, almost a cold-bloodedness in the way she had torn herself away from her husband's body – that was very compelling.

We reached the track, and when we had gone up it a little way, she left it and headed into the dark of the forest. Not until we reached the edge of it, almost at the spot where Brian and I had stood earlier in the day looking out towards the camp, did she turn and face us. She was so choked up, so near to tears that she could hardly speak: 'What I have to tell you – you, Brian, in particular – is that what is going on here has nothing to do with the forest your grandfather planted. Nothing at all.' It had begun to rain, all the end of the inlet blotted out.

'Balls!' Brian's voice exploded in sudden anger. 'Why do you think Tom changed his Will? Why did he leave these trees to me? Because I know the value of them and understand why my grandfather – '

'It's not that.' Her chin was suddenly lifted, a sharp

determined line. 'What I'm trying to tell you is that these people – '

'SVL Timber and Milling? They're sawmillers handling high quality cedar for a specialized market. There's a million dollars locked up in this plantation if they can get it out before I stop them.'

'They aren't sawmillers. They're dope smugglers.' Her face was flushed with anger. 'The trees here are a cover for a drug-importing racket into the States.'

He stared at her unbelievingly, the forest darkening behind him as the clouds thickened. 'Where the hell did you get that idea?'

'Tom – up at Ice Cold.' Thunder crashed, a blinding fork of lightning. 'Why do you think he disappeared? Why do you think he was desperately trying to find gold? These people had their claws into him and he didn't know how to get clear of them. That's why he was back on drugs. He was scared – scared out of his wits.'

'But – ' Brian stared at her, frowning, and then he voiced the question I had been on the point of asking her: 'The SVL Company in Seattle. I went and saw them, a man named Barony. It's an old-established timber company, founded back in the First World War when demand was high.'

'But who's behind it now?' she asked. 'I spoke to Barony, too, I asked him for the name of the major shareholder and he told me to mind my own business. Also, he said his company merely bought timber standing. The people felling and loading it were self-employed, nothing to do with him.'

It was what I had been told, what Brian had been

told, too. We stood there talking it over for a moment longer, but so much of what had happened fell into place that I think even Brian would have been convinced if I hadn't told them about the customs operation and how a barge loaded with logs from the Cascades had been searched, the tug, too, without anything being discovered. If they were smuggling drugs, then the method was not apparent, and Tom hadn't told her how it was being done. Nor had he confided in me, not even on the ferry when he had lain there in his cabin mulling over those Chicago press cuttings.

Finally Brian said, 'Well, there's only one way to find out.' He was gazing out to the quay, where the squat shape of the barge showed drab against the approaching cloudburst.

Wolchak had just come out of his office. He paused for an instant, looking up the valley, the sound of the rain audible as lightning flashed. He wrenched the door of the pick-up open and jumped in, thunder crashing and the office disappearing. The sound of the rain was like surf on a sand shore. The pick-up stayed just ahead of it, so that we could see him quite clearly as he drove past, and the next instant the rainstorm was on us, breaking against the forest tops with a roar that almost drowned the next clap of thunder.

Sheltering behind separate tree boles, the rain such a flood of water and the noise so overwhelming that each of us cowered there in isolation, the horror of what had happened and the motives that had driven Tom to such a point of desperation had time to sink in. I saw Brian glance uncertainly at Miriam, could see what was going on in his mind. His appalled realization that he was to some degree responsible for what had happened to his father was there in his face.

He said something, but either she didn't hear or she didn't want to hear, her face set and stony, no forgiveness in it at all. He looked down at the walkie-talkie, then at the one still slung over my shoulder, and the sight of that means of communication with the outside world seemed to turn his mind to practical matters. The full force of the rain was passing now, but it was still a downpour blotting out all sign of the camp and the jetty as he stepped out from behind his tree. 'Let's go,' he said.

I stared at him blankly, seeing the rain streaming down his face, his black hair plastered to his head. 'Where?' Just opening my mouth to say that one word filled it with water, the fresh sweet taste of rainwater on my tongue.

'The barge. It's our chance now – to get aboard – unseen.' He passed me the handset and turned to Miriam. I thought she would refuse, that he would have to waste time arguing with her. But she nodded and went with him without question, out into the rain, as though, like me, she had realized the logic of his suggestion. If we were ever to get away from the Cascades and the Halliday Arm of the Cascade Inlet our only hope was the barge, and to get on board without being seen we had to do it now while the whole place was awash with rain.

We ran. We ran blindly through the storm, our clothing soaked, water streaming down our bodies. I could feel it cold on my skin, my trousers clinging and my anorak getting heavier by the minute. But somehow we made it, reaching the drowned quay only yards away from the shadowy bulk of the barge. It looked huge close-to; I had never seen such a giant of a barge in my life, not even on the Dutch waterways.

Then our feet were squelching on its wet steel deck plates as we stepped aboard, over mooring lines and the hose of a pump, hurrying aft along the narrow sidedeck to the wheelhouse. It was a small place, the paint flaking and very dirty, sliding wooden doors at each side. There was a wheel and below the windows a shelf with some mugs, a tobacco tin half full of cigarette stubs, an oily rag, some matches, and in the corner a VHF radio, the sort of set used by small boats. It was wired to a battery clamped to the wooden flooring below the shelf, and I presumed it was there to enable tug and barge to keep in contact.

'You reckon it works?' Brian reached forward and switched it on. A little dot glowed red in the gloom and it began to crackle at us. His hand strayed to the mike on its rest at the side of the set, but I stopped him.

'You won't contact anybody,' I said. 'Not in the middle of the mountains here.'

He nodded and switched off. 'At least it's alive and it works.' He ducked his head, disappearing down the near-vertical ladder that led through a trap door to the shelter and comparative warmth of a sort of cuddy. Miriam and I followed him.

The time was 16.39. Another twenty-four hours and with luck we would be out into the Inside Passage headed towards Vancouver. The rain stopped abruptly, footsteps sounded on the deck plates overhead and a voice shouted instructions. They had begun to load another log.

CHAPTER TWO

That first night we spent on the barge I couldn't stop shivering. It wasn't so much the cold – the temperature was nowhere near freezing – but the damp ate into one's bones. Fear had something to do with it, too. At times the whole thing seemed so utterly crazy that, remembering Wolchak seated in the client's chair back in my office in Ditchling, I felt I had only to clamber up to the quay and walk across to his office and the whole thing could be resolved over a cup of coffee. But then the memory of Tom's body cradled in Miriam's arms, her blood-stained hands, and Olsen lying dead in the bunk up at the hut on the lake, and Miriam herself, shut in that room . . . it seemed so impossible, so utterly divorced from real life. My life, at any rate. I'd only read about such things. And now . . .

Listening to Miriam as she went over, slowly and painfully, the eighteen days she had spent in that hut – the loneliness, the fear, the visits from Wolchak, the threats, above all the loneliness, the feeling of being utterly at the mercy of the men who took it in turns to guard and feed her – and the way she told it, in that husky, very matter-of-fact voice of hers. Like us, she had taken a train from Whitehorse to join the ferry at Skagway, determined to have a look at the Cascades before going on to Vancouver. At Bella Bella she had planned to get one of the floatplanes to fly her in, but Lorient had been waiting for her with a boat, Tarasconi having apparently notified the camp of her intentions. He had booked a room for her at the Fisherman's Inn over at Shearwater and would take her on to the Cascades in the morning. Everybody, she thought, was being so kind and thoughtful, but of course, she never reached the Fisherman's Inn. Lorient had given her a drink as they had motored out into the dark waters that led towards Gunboat Passage and that was the last she remembered until she came to in that little room in the log hut on the lake above the Cascades.

As she talked the reality of her ordeal gradually sank in, and with it an acceptance of the fact that I had got myself caught up in something that few lawyers, even criminal lawyers, have to face, other than in the courts.

And for Brian, as well as for myself, what drove it home to us was the realization that a big search was being mounted and they hadn't waited for daylight. Before it was fully dark Wolchak had brought one of the dogs down from the hut. From the wheelhouse we watched the men come out of the dining hut after their evening meal and gather outside the office, a dozen or more of them. Then Wolchak arrived in the pick-up with the dog and the two fellers. Lopez was also with him, which meant presumably that both of them had managed to swim ashore. It also meant that Camargo had been left up at the hut with Aleksis, so that any possibility of our making it down to the lower lake and Ocean Falls was blocked. The floodlights were on, the camp, the quay, the great tree trunk boom-crane, everything brilliantly lit and the hum of the big generator away to our right drowning all other sounds.

Oddly enough, it was the fact that Wolchak had left a wounded employee up at the hut with Camargo to plug that exit from the Cascades that finally convinced me of the urgency and deadly seriousness of the operation.

We watched as he briefed the men, all of them dispersing quickly, the dog and the handler with half a dozen of them being driven off in the truck, back to the spot where Tom had been killed. The rest got on with the job of loading the barge. There were now some twenty or more logs lying stacked at the back of the quay. These looked to be larger stems and they were the ones whose butts had been up-ended and drilled. Now, instead of holding them back to be chained together and launched into the inlet to act as a booming pen, they began to load them. I knew then that Wolchak was pulling out, that this barge would be the last load. To that extent Tom had won. High Stand was safe for the time being. No more trees would be felled.

With the recommencement of loading two men came on board to position the logs. Spiked boots gave them a secure stance on the stacked load as the boom-crane lifted the trunks from the quay and swung them down to be grappled by the curved steel spikes each man held like a deadly extension of the right arm. It was dangerous, difficult work requiring great concentration.

The clouds lifted and the stars showed; a wavering curtain of light above the black outline of the mountains might have been the northern lights. A seal or a whale, something big, splashed a great circle of ripples in the middle of the inlet. And then I saw the dog appear at the edge of the forest, at the very point where we had started our dash through the rain. I watched, appalled, as it sniffed around, searching for a continuation of our scent. But I suppose the rain had been so heavy it had washed away all trace of it once we were in the open. At any rate, after circling around for about ten minutes, sniffing inside and outside the timber, both dog and handler retreated back into the forest. 'The dog knows, but the human doesn't,' Brian whispered in my ear. 'He can't believe we would have left the security of the trees and headed into the camp.'

It was the handler who had pulled the dog away, and after that we closed the hatch and went back down the ladder, to lie huddled together on the single berth, Miriam taking the only chair. It was Brian and I who were short of sleep and we left it to her to wake us just before dawn.

The loading went on most of the night. I must have slept some of the time, in spite of my shivering, for I woke just after four in the morning, no sound on board or ashore, only the hum of the generator. They had stopped loading. I switched my torch on, shielding it with my hand. Miriam was asleep in her chair. I pulled the blankets tight around my shoulders, enjoying the warmth, conscious that my clothes were almost dry against my skin and that I was no longer shivering. I would have been asleep again in seconds, but as I snuggled into a tight ball I suddenly realized Brian was no longer in the bunk with me.

I lay there for a moment, reluctant to leave the little oasis of warmth I had created, then I threw the blankets off, felt my way to the ladder and clambered up to peer cautiously out of the deckhouse window. The barge was now almost fully loaded, the logs stacked higher than the deck. The floodlights were still on, but the only sign of life was a man armed with a rifle walking slowly along the quay, the only sound the generator. Beyond the lights the black of the peaks at the head of the inlet stood sharp-etched against a sky that was paling to the approach of dawn, the moon set and the stars less bright.

I couldn't see Brian anywhere. Had he gone up to the lake? The early hours is not a good time to find oneself alone. Did the silence and emptiness ashore mean the hunt had been called off?

I was just wondering what I would do if he didn't turn up before dawn broke when his head appeared above the edge of the deck plates, peering cautiously out at the man patrolling the quay. He waited until he was well away from the barge, with his back towards it, then he scrambled onto the deck and dived quickly into the shelter of the wheelhouse. 'It's okay,' he said. 'Iron rungs leading down into the hold and one or two quite sizeable gaps where the logs have been carelessly loaded. We can lay up between them.'

'They could shift.' My mind had a sudden terrible vision of what could happen to a human body if we were caught in a seaway on one of the open stretches and those logs started to move.

But he shook his head. 'They're too big, and they're wedged too solid against the side.'

We went back down into the cuddy. Miriam was awake, her eyes wide, almost shocked in the light of my torch. 'Where've you been? I thought – ' But then she got a grip on herself. 'I'd have woken you. It's not time yet.'

'Better make the move now,' Brian said. 'It'll get light early this morning.'

It took time to tidy up the place and leave it with no trace of our having occupied it. Dawn had, in fact, broken when all three of us finally made the transfer from wheelhouse to hold. Brian went first, moving slowly, his body no more than a shadow in the paling floodlights. Then Miriam. I followed her, lying sprawled on the deck plates, my legs swung over the edge, feeling for the rungs just under the overhang of the after deck.

It was to clear this overhang that the logs had been loaded so that there was a gap of almost two feet between the butts and the after bulkhead. And because they had been loaded with their tops interlaced in layers, the butts were slightly separated to present a honeycomb effect and, as Brian had said, some of the gaps were quite sizeable though the logs themselves were undoubtedly very firmly wedged.

Down in the hold it was dark and we had to use our torches, swinging our bodies out from the rungs onto the rounded bulk of the logs, each of us worming our way into a separate cavity. We had divided up the little food we had left. I don't know what the others did, but I ate all of mine in one go. I felt a hearty breakfast would give me strength to cope with whatever the day might bring. But after I had finished it there was nothing else to do and I lay there watching the daylight gradually filter down into the cavernous hold until I could see the shape of the logs, the rough corrugation of the bark and the smooth steel of the rear bulkhead weeping drops of moisture over red flakes of rust.

Time passed slowly. The generator was switched off and after that it was so quiet I could hear water lapping at the hull, the slapping of the house flag on the short mast. Occasionally I thought I heard voices, but so indistinct that I couldn't hear what was said. About eight a vehicle of some sort moved out of the camp. It sounded like the pick-up. Then all was quiet again.

They made no attempt to load more logs. After a while I saw a foot reach out to the rungs facing the gap where I had wedged myself. It was Brian, and about ten minutes later he climbed back down, leaning his head in towards me. 'They've stopped felling by the look of it. The quay is empty. No logs anywhere. And nobody about. You all right?'

'Yes,' I said. 'What about Miriam?'

His head disappeared and I heard her voice, very low and muffled.

'She's okay,' he said. 'Two logs away to your right

and a little higher. I'm two away from you on the starb'd side.' And he added, 'I suggest we all try and get some sleep. And we'd better not talk any more, not until the tug arrives and we get moving. It's too quiet.'

We had over four hours to wait and in all that time we did not dare climb the rungs to peer out over the edge of the deck. Occasionally we heard voices. Once somebody came on board, moving aft to the wheelhouse and down into the cuddy. I could just hear the sounds of his movement through the after bulkhead. Presumably he was the man who would be on the barge during the tow. After what seemed an age his footsteps sounded on the deck again and he went ashore. I held my breath, but there was no shout of alarm. Apparently he was unaware that the place had been occupied during the night.

I think they were all at breakfast. It was very quiet and to ease my cramped limbs I crawled out as far as the rungs, peering up at the log butts. They had shiny little metal tags hammered into them and as I was trying to decipher the numbers Miriam poked her head out of the cavity to my right, her face very pale against the bark, sawdust clinging to her hair. 'What are you doing?'

'I thought I'd make certain they haven't concealed anything between the logs,' I told her.

She shook her head. 'Brian and I checked when it was still dark. You were asleep.'

'And you found nothing?'

'No. If the drugs are on board, then they must have been put there before the barge was towed into the Halliday Arm. In which case they're now in the bottom with the whole cargo of logs on top of them.'

But I thought it unlikely. The previous tow had been loaded and on its way down to Seattle when it had made contact with that other vessel, and anyway, drug enforcement officers would have supervised its unloading. If a consignment of cocaine had been exposed customs and police would have been swarming all over the camp here long before now. Brian joined in the discussion, and it was then, while all three of us were whispering together, that we heard the drone of an engine. It was reflected back from the logs above us, so that it seemed to come from the for'ard end of the barge, but it was increasing all the time and very soon we realized it was a plane flying low up the inlet. It landed quite close to the quay, the engine note dying and then the sudden splash as the floats hit the water.

My first thought was that it might be the police, or maybe Jim Edmundson had returned, but Brian, watching with his head close against the butt end of a log, reported nobody on board the floatplane, only the pilot, and it wasn't anyone he knew. He was wearing a little round woollen cap knitted in bands of red and black, and when I suggested it made him too conspicuous he pulled it off and rubbed it against the butt of a log so that it became coated in sawdust. When he put it back on, head and face merged with the sawn log-ends behind him.

The plane tied up aft of the barge and almost immediately he whispered down to us that it seemed to have come for Wolchak. Wolchak was coming out of the office carrying a bulging briefcase as well as a suitcase and there were two men with a stretcher. It was the man who had killed Tom, the man he had shot. There was a shout and he suddenly ducked his head, clambering quickly down to us. 'The tug,' he said. 'They've just sighted it coming up the inlet. And there's some brash burning down in the clear-felled area.'

We clambered back into our log holes and shortly afterwards there was the resonant clump of feet on the steel decking. By then we could hear the thump of the tug's screws transmitted through the water. The engine of the floatplane started up, the sound of it passing very close to us. Then it took off and some minutes later there were shouts and the thud of a rope hitting the deck, followed by a grinding noise as the tug scraped alongside. Feet clambered over the barge, somebody shouted to let go for'ard, the tug's engines gathered speed, the screws thrashing, and suddenly there was movement as the towing hawser lifted taut out of the water.

The speed of that departure surprised me. I had expected the tug to moor up and the crew to stretch their legs, possibly to have a meal ashore in the camp diner. Instead, the turn-round had been immediate. This, coupled with Wolchak's departure by plane, suggested a certain degree of panic, and there were at least four men on the barge so it had clearly been decided to evacuate everyone. We could hear them arguing in the wheelhouse, an undercurrent of excitement in their voices.

In the circumstances we kept our heads down, each of us holed up and lying flat between the logs, nothing to do but listen for some scrap of information that would indicate our progress down the inlet. The tow rate I guessed at around 6 knots and I lay there trying to recall as much as I could of the details of the Coastguard cutter's chart I had been poring over on the voyage up to Ocean Falls, but there was no way I could even guess at our heading. Maybe at night, if it was clear and I was able to look out, I would be able to identify a star or two. I reckoned by then we should be past the entrance to Cousins Inlet and headed into the Fisher Channel. Presuming they followed the same course as before, midnight should see us approaching the point where we altered course to the westward to pass through Hakai Passage.

Working it out helped pass the time and I played a sort of game with myself, going over and over in my mind the names I could remember on the chart – the Pointers, Surf and Starfish Islands, and, north of them, an area littered with rocks and islets that had stamped itself on my mind because of the name and the way both the Captain and the Mate had referred to it.

Hemmed in by the canyon-like sides of first Cascade Inlet, then the Dean Channel, with the cloud-base like a ceiling above us, the amount of light filtering down into the hold was very limited. By four that afternoon it was practically dark. But then gusts of wind began to play tricks with the sound of the tug's engines echoing off the rocks on either side and it grew perceptibly lighter. Sunset came as an orange glow that shone on the damp metal of the hull and turned the butts of the logs to a colour that was almost salmon pink. Half an hour later it was dark, the wind blattering down from the heights and ragged gaps in the clouds through which I was able to catch a glimpse of the stars.

'Any chance we can reach somebody with this thing?' Brian had joined me, a foot on one of the steel rungs and the walkie-talkie he had taken from the hatchet-faced tree feller slung from his shoulder.

'Short wave?' I shook my head. 'The range is probably no more than five miles.'

'That Coastguard cutter.' We were both of us whispering. 'Could he receive it? Did he have short wave?'

'Yes, but he'd have to be switched on and tuned to the right frequency.'

He nodded. 'So it's the VHF set up in the wheelhouse. D'you know the standby frequency that cutter uses? I've only operated VHF on land with an agreed frequency.'

'Channel 16,' I told him. 'Trouble is it's the standby channel for all ships.'

'And if he's thirty miles away or more, then he's probably out of range, and we're blocked off from any of the inside passages by the mountains, so if he's there . . .' He shrugged, smiling at me, his teeth showing in the pale light that had turned almost green. 'We'll just have to hope for the best.'

It wasn't only that VHF is a direct radio wave, so that if the Coastguards were in another inlet they wouldn't hear us, but something he didn't seem to realize was that every ship within an unobstructed 30-mile radius of us would have the call coming through on their loudspeakers. 'That tug,' I said, 'will be only a hawser-length away – they'll pick us up clearer than any other vessel.'

'So what do we do?'

'Wait till we're a lot further south than we are now. In the narrows between Vancouver Island and the mainland there'll be vessels of all sorts around, lots of fishing boats, more traffic coming in on VHF.'

There was movement on deck then. I think they were probably checking the towing lights. At any rate, nobody even shone a torch down into the hold. We were back in our log holes, and lying there I tried to work out what to say to Captain Cornish if we were able to get into the wheelhouse and raise him on the VHF set. There were other things on my mind too. I had to know whether or not we were taking the Hakai Passage. If we did, then inside of two hours we would be in the open sea, for it was not much more than five miles from Fitz Hugh Sound to the Pacific. The tug would turn south then, and once past Calvert Island we would be within range of the north end of Vancouver Island. If we didn't go through the Hakai and kept straight on down the Fitz Hugh we would save at least a couple of hours.

We decided to wait until the early hours of the morning when the men aft would hopefully be sound asleep in the cuddy and watchkeeping on the tug would be at a low ebb. By then, at three-thirty say, I thought we would probably be in the open sea somewhere in the region of Calvert Island. But it was what I should say when I started calling the outside world on that VHF set that worried me. In the end I decided to sleep on it, having asked Miriam to wake me inside of four hours.

In fact, I woke of my own accord, for by then I was fairly rested. I was also very hungry. There was starlight in the gap between the logs and the steel rim of the afterdeck. I clambered up the rungs until I could see the Bear and had identified the North Star. It was straight above the wheelhouse, so we were still headed south, and it was not until an hour and a half later, when I had come to the conclusion that we were going to continue straight down the Fitz Hugh, that the position of the stars suddenly began to change. There was a light flashing straight over the bows, its reflection on the wheelhouse gradually changing as we turned. It was to port of us then and I stayed there until we were past it, the reflection of it showing the wheelhouse as a dark shape in silhouette, the stars steadying in their new alignment.

We had turned almost 90ϒ to starb'd and were in the Hakai Passage.

Brian poked his head out. 'We've turned, have we?' He had felt the changed motion, something I had not noticed with my mind concentrated on the stars. I went back to sleep, planning to wake every hour and check our course. The time was then 01.12.

I woke again just before two and we were still headed south-west, then again a little after 02.30. I think it was the movement that woke me that time, and when I checked the stars, we seemed to be on a more westerly course. There was a flashing light away to port that intermittently illuminated the wheelhouse. That would be the beacon marking the southern side of the passage into the Pacific. No wonder the barge had started to roll quite noticeably, a lazy, slow, flat-bottomed roll which gradually changed to a corkscrew motion, an occasional jerk on the towing hawser sending shivers through the metal hull.

I checked the position of the stars again and there was no doubt about it, the southerly swell was on our port quarter. We were heading north-west away from Seattle.

I didn't tell the others, and I didn't go to sleep again. It could mean only one thing – that we were on a smuggling run and headed for a rendezvous with the South American carrier somewhere in the mass of islands between our present position and the point where the Inside Passage broke out into open water in Milbanke Sound. I remembered the Spider then, how the Mate had said Captain Cornish had gone in there just for the hell of it, mooring up to a red cedar that was half dead and had a bald-headed eagle's nest in the upper branches. The whole area had been thick with small rock islands, but all of them steep-to, and deep water everywhere. 'Looks much worse on the charts than it really is,' he had said, and now I had this feeling we were being towed there.

That was when I climbed out onto the deck and peered in at the wheelhouse windows. There was nobody at the wheel, the place deserted. Slipping round the starb'd side, I gently slid open the door and went in. The trap door to the cuddy below was open. After listening for a moment and hearing no sound, I released the securing catch and lowered it quietly to the floor. Then I switched on the VHF set.

Even then, as I picked up the mike and pressed the button for Channel 16, I wasn't sure how I was going to phrase my calls, except that I would use Pan, which is urgent but less so than the Mayday distress call. 'Pan. Pan. Pan. Are you there, Cornish? Calling Cornish. Cornish, Cornish, Cornish.' I tried my best to imitate a Canadian accent, my lips close to the mike and speaking very quietly: 'This is fishing boat *Klewarney* calling Cornish.' I had talked to him a lot about the Kluane and Ice Cold – '*Klewarney* calling Cornish. Come in please Cornish. I got fish for you. Ice Cold. Cornish, Cornish, Cornish. Answer by that name only. Okay? Do you hear me, Cornish? Over.'

A fishing boat was the first to answer, the accent so strong I could hardly understand him: 'Yu got fish? Yu tell me where. Where yu are, fella?' And when I repeated my call, he shouted at me, 'Who is this Cornish? Yu tell me where yu lying,' and behind his words I caught the whisper of another voice: 'Coastguard cutter *Kelsey*. Coastguard cutter *Kelsey* – state name of vessel and position. If you want to speak to – '

I slammed in then: 'Get off the air, Coastguard. Shut up, both of you. I want Cornish. Cornish. Nobody else. Do you hear me? Cornish. Over.'

There was a pause, then Cornish's voice came on the air, breathless and tinny out of the speaker as I bent my ear to it: 'Cornish here. Switch to channel 22.' I switched and his voice came up again, but still very faint, asking me what I wanted.

'I have a big haul for you, and I'm keeping it ice cold. You understand? Over.'

There was a pause and I thought I had lost him. But then he said, 'Yes, I think so. Where are you?'

'North of where we were three nights ago,' I told him. 'About ten miles. Your Mate will know. He said you'd been there once. Tied to a tree with an eagle's nest in it. You got that? Over.'

Again the pause, and the indistinct murmur of voices – then: 'Yeh, reckon we got the message. A big haul, you say . . .'

But I shut down on him then, for the tug had suddenly come on the air quite loud demanding to know what my position was and why I was putting out a Pan call. Then abruptly everything went quiet and I switched off, opening up the trap door again and slipping out of the wheelhouse, back to the hold. I had done all I could. It was now up to Cornish.

Just after four a change of movement warned me we were turning. The barge was rolling again, quite heavily, the wind catching us almost broadside and making a whining sound. A glance at the stars confirmed the alteration of course. We were headed almost due east, straight in towards the land, the speed of the tow falling away until we seemed to be barely moving. Then, suddenly, we were under the lee, the rolling abruptly ceased, no wind at all. We were in the Spider. I had no doubt of that, and shortly after that there was a dreadful grating sound, steel on rock as we ground to a halt against one of the islands; then feet pounding, lots of shouting, followed by a hollow thud and the sound of the tug's engines close alongside.

'We've left it too late,' Brian hissed at me. And when

I told him I had already contacted the cutter he could hardly believe me. 'Christ! I was fast asleep. Where are we?'

'At the rendezvous.' And I explained where I thought we were.

Footsteps on the deck again, the sound of mooring lines being made fast, voices calling back and forth, then somebody in authority – it sounded like the Greek tug-master – calling those on the barge to come aboard the tug for breakfast. 'How longa'we got, Captain?' And another voice answered him, ''Bout an hour, that's all.' They were scrambling onto the tug, somebody asking where the supply ship was and a voice answering, 'Holed up in Kildidt Sound.'

'Tha's not much more than coupla miles away.'

'Sure. But they gotta go round – Fulton Passage or else Spider Channel. They ain't gonna fly, that's for sure. So Skip's probably right. You got 'bout an hour. Okay?'

The footsteps died away, everything suddenly quiet except for the slow grinding of the two hulls as they moved to the ghost of a swell coming in through the entrance. I went up the rungs then, peering cautiously out. We were in what appeared to be a lake, rock islets all covered in trees and merging into one another so that there was what appeared to be a continuous shoreline of green all round us. Glimmers of sunlight glinted on the water, the surface ruffled by a slight breeze, and the tug standing over us, funnel and deck housing higher than the logs on the deep-laden barge. The wheelhouse appeared to be deserted. I could actually see right through it to the mountains beyond and a mackerel sky, the scaling of the cloud all silver like a dusting of snow.

The radio had been left on and I could hear a voice, an Indian by the sound of it. He seemed to have got himself and his fishing boat hopelessly lost. 'Bloody Indians.' Somebody had entered the tug's wheelhouse from below. 'Drunk, I bet. Sleeps it off and when he wakes up don't know where the fuck 'is shit-bag of a boat is. Typical.' And another voice said, 'What about that *Klewarney* boat?' It sounded like the tug's Master. 'He wasn't lost and he seemed a lot nearer. Who was he calling?'

'One of the fish company ships by the sound of it. Calling Pan like that. Raised the Coastguard cutter, didn't he? Wonder where those buggers are?'

'Wherever they are, they'll be occupied now, presuming that Indian's put out a search-and-rescue call.'

'Sure. So why don't you finish your meal. We'll be busy ourselves soon.'

I didn't hear the reply, for both of them went out by the other door and all was quiet again, only another fisherman jabbering away on the radio to a mate of his down around Egg Island at the entrance to Smith Sound. I climbed back down to my log hide, Brian whispering to me, 'You reckon the captain of that cutter understood what you were telling him?'

'I think so.'

'How long before he gets here?'

But I couldn't answer that. I'd been going to ask Cornish what his position was, but then the tug had come on the air and I had had to shut down.

'They could radio for a helicopter.' Miriam was rubbing at her left leg as though it had gone to sleep. 'You said they had one on that night operation. If they called in a helicopter – ' But I had to tell her it was most unlikely. It would mean explaining the whole situation over the air to the Rescue Coordination Centre at Victoria and, presuming Cornish had understood my message, he would be afraid the tug might be monitoring his radio calls.

'Then he may be too late.' Miriam's voice was strangely calm. 'In which case Tom's death . . .' I detected a tremor then. 'Isn't there an airbase somewhere you can contact on VHF?' But even as she said it she seemed to realize the impracticability of it – 'No, of course . . . So we just wait.'

'Yes,' I said, wishing I had been able to get their position, or even a rough indication of it. Waiting is bad enough, but when you don't know how long you've got to wait . . . 'They won't be long,' I added, but she knew very well I was only saying that to bolster her courage, and mine too. Voices on the deck of the tug then, one of them cursing the cook for not having served steak for breakfast. 'Bacon, sausages and mash – there's better'n that served in the bloody army now.'

I crawled back in amongst the logs, cursing the man for drawing attention to the emptiness of my stomach. I had had nothing now for twenty-four hours and would have willingly settled for bangers and mash, or anything else I was offered. Other voices emerged from the tug's bows, and then suddenly they were all over the after end of the barge, doing something to the upper layer of logs

– what, I couldn't gather. All I knew was that they seemed to be working their way downwards and there was a lot of straining and cursing. Soon feet came into view, boots braced on the steel rungs and sawdust raining down. A muttered curse and more straining. Something had been hammered in too tight. 'Look at my bloody nails!'

What the hell were they up to? And then, when I saw a boot feeling for the rung right opposite where I lay, I thought it would only be minutes before they discovered us. But that was as low as they came, and after another ten minutes or so they all retreated on deck, the job, whatever it was, apparently done.

We had half an hour of quiet after that, and then somebody shouted, 'Coming in through the entrance now.' Soon the steady thump-thump of a single screw sounded through the metal hull of the barge.

After that everything became very confused. There was a sense of unreality almost, as though it was some radio play I was listening to, for there was nothing to see, only sounds, and these to be interpreted as best I could. As a result, I don't think I was at all scared, my mind being concentrated in my ears, my imagination totally engrossed in trying to convert sounds into visual activity.

The tug's engines started up. That was the first thing. I heard its hull scraping along the side of the barge as it moved away, and then, after a little while, there were voices calling, different voices speaking some sort of Spanish patois, the sound of mooring lines hitting the deck, fenders rubbing and squeaking along the port side as the hull of the barge was thrust sideways, a violent movement that ground our plates against the rock. We were made fast to the new arrival, and as soon as that was done and the movement had subsided there were men all over us.

What they were doing I couldn't make out, but they seemed concentrated at the for'ard and after ends of the barge and their movements suggested they were taking cargo on board. But where they were putting it I had no idea. It certainly didn't come down past the ends of the logs where we were concealed. If it had, we should certainly have been discovered. As it was, I never saw any more of the men working above me than the occasional foot placed on the rung immediately outside my lair, and then only when they started hammering. It sounded like wood on wood, as though periodically one of them took up a mallet and started beating at a log.

The loading and periodical hammering went on for precisely twenty-seven minutes. I timed it, thinking perhaps it might be important to know how long it took to load the cargo. And all the time they were talking, a mixture of English and Spanish that at times was about as incomprehensible as pidgin English. Once I heard what sounded like an Irishman say, 'Jeez, you'd never think there was that many junkies, would you now? Do you think they cleared this lot with St Peter?' And they laughed.

That was the only time any of them referred to the cargo and the only clue I got from listening to their talk. But at least it confirmed what the Hallidays had been saying – this really was a drug run. At no time did I hear anything that indicated what they were doing with the stuff and I could only presume that it was in very durable bags that were being tamped into the interstices between the logs.

As soon as they had finished loading, the lines were let go and the vessel moved away, out into the open water between the islands, the thump of its screw gradually fading. By then the tug was backing up to us, the thresh of water from its stern getting louder, then dying away as men at the for'ard end of the barge made the towing hawser fast. A shout of 'Let go ashore!' then 'Take her away' was followed by renewed threshing that faded until the hawser was taut and the barge plucked sideways, juddering and scraping itself against rock.

The sound diminished, then ceased abruptly, and after a moment we could hear the swish and gurgle of water against the hull. We were under way, the tow's next stop Seattle, unless Cornish had read between the lines of my message and had understood what I had been trying to tell him. I wasn't at all certain he had, also I didn't know how far away he had been. The range for VHF can be very variable, dependent on the terrain and the conditions, and the fact that his voice had sounded so faint that I could hardly decipher what he had been saying did not necessarily mean that he was outside the normal limits of very high frequency transmission.

He was, in fact, over forty miles away, just to the south of Hannah Rocks and heading east for the Alexandra Passage inside Egg Island in an effort to pick up the Indian fisherman who kept coming on the air to say he was lost somewhere in the region of Smith Sound.

They had continued to search for him after I had radioed in, for forty miles to the south of us conditions were very different: the wind had dropped and with it the temperature. They were in thick fog, and with the entrance to Smith Sound littered with rocks and shoals they were concerned for the Indian's safety.

There was, of course, a good deal of speculation in the cutter's wheelhouse about the identity of the *Kluane* and whether there was a fish storage vessel of that name waiting to receive a large haul that was being kept frozen. Only gradually did the truth sink in as they argued about it, remembering how I had talked of Ice Cold as a mine and Edmundson had confirmed it as being in the Kluane. But they still didn't see how I or Tom Halliday could be calling in on the VHF distress channel.

In court, Captain Cornish would read aloud the excerpt from his log recording the message I had transmitted. The time of that message, and the time entry recording his abandonment of the search for the lost fisherman and his alteration of course for Spider Island, would show a lapse of 18½ minutes. That was the length of time they had spent discussing it before finally reaching the decision to abandon the Indian and alter course, and they had only made that decision because of the Mate's insistence that I was the only person to whom he had mentioned the *Kelsey's* navigation of the Spider in at least six months and that he had specifically referred to the cutter's stern being made fast to a red cedar which was half-dead and had an eagle's nest in the upper branches.

However, having made the decision to head north, Captain Cornish in his testimony declared that the more he thought about it, and about the failure of the customs operation when he had been taking Edmundson up to the Cascades, the more he began to appreciate the urgency. His log showed that he was proceeding north at maximum revs and, allowing for favourable tide, was making just on 20 knots over the ground.

We did not know this, of course. Huddled together in the narrow confines between timber and steel at the bottom of the hold, all we knew was that we were headed south at an estimated 6 knots and that another night would have passed before we were into the Narrows between Vancouver Island and the mainland. We knew we were heading south because the sun was shining on the port side of the wheelhouse and we assumed we would be going inside Vancouver Island because that was the normal towing route.

As we steamed south it gradually became colder, the sun's brightness dimming, daylight fading. The tug's siren began to blare at regular intervals. We were in fog, white trails of vapour drifting across the logs, the cold and the damp eating into us.

By then we were convinced that there was now only one man on the barge, for we had heard no sound of voices. Even from the top rung, with our heads in the open, we could hear nothing except the sound of the water rushing past. It seemed that the men from the logging camp, who had been on the barge when loading the cargo, had all been evacuated on the South American vessel. There might, of course, be two men on board, one of them sleeping. 'We'll have to presume that,' I said. Brian didn't say anything. He had heard the man at the wheelhouse singing to himself and thought it was to compensate for the boredom and loneliness of being on his own.

There seemed only two possibilities open to us, and these were discussed endlessly: we could keep watch until the tug was approaching a suitable ship, take over the wheelhouse, then cut the hawser and steer the barge alongside. Alternatively, we could wait until we were in the Narrows, passing really close to a jetty or some small boat, then slip over the side and swim for it. Of the two I favoured cutting the tow and going alongside a Canadian vessel, and in the end Brian agreed. That way it wouldn't be our word alone; we would have the barge and its cargo as evidence, as well as one of the crew. Also it would be dark. I didn't like the thought of swimming for it in broad daylight, nor did the others. Even if the fog did hold, and we were not spotted by the tug's lookout, we would still have to contend with the strong tides running through the Narrows.

So finally it was settled. We would wait till the early hours, when it was still dark and we were somewhere off Port Hardy on the north end of Vancouver Island, then take over the barge. The only problem, of course, was whether we would be lucky enough to have a fairly slow vessel overtaking us at the right time. As soon as we had cut the tow, I would start transmitting a Mayday call in an effort to try and persuade the Rescue Coordination Centre at Victoria to take immediate action. The tug would know, of course, that it had lost its tow and I hoped my emergency call would discourage it from coming back for us.

It was a good idea, but alas, the best laid plans . . . what we didn't know was that the tug was on a bearing west of south, heading for the open sea passage down Vancouver Island's rugged and largely uninhabited west coast. The Coastguard cutter didn't know it either. Nor did the RCC in Victoria. Cornish had contacted them, using his HF single sideband, and they in turn had contacted customs. As a result, the cutter was ordered to wait up for the tow behind Pearl Rocks at the eastern end of the Rankin Shoals. One of these rocks dries as much as sixteen feet, and since it would be low water about two hours after the cutter's ETA, there would be little chance of the tug's radar picking it up, any blip being merged with that of the above-water rock.

Cornish arrived there at 13.39 when the tug was seaward of the Hakai Passage on a course that diverged from the Calvert Island coastline. At 16.00 it was almost due west of Pearl Rocks. The fog was still very thick and Cornish, anticipating the speed and distance run by the tow correctly, had switched his radar scan to very close range, expecting tug and barge to appear in the North Passage between Pearl Rocks and Calvert Island, or just to the west of Watch Rock about five miles away at the other end of the Rankin Shoals.

In fact, at 16.00 we were almost twenty miles west of the shoals.

Two hours later, with the fog still thick, it was almost dark, and it wasn't until then that the cutter came out from behind Pearl Rocks and began a long-distance radar scan. But it had missed the opportunity to pick us up and identify the tow, for by then we were approaching the offshore shipping lane for Prince Rupert and the North and had several vessels within a few miles of us.

That was the position as night fell and the cold increased. A wind had sprung up, waves slapping noisily at the bows, the tow line jerking and the three of us huddled together for warmth. I remember being conscious of Miriam's body close against me, Brian's too, and we were all of us shivering, the breeze and the damp cutting through our clothing, eating into our bones.

Some time shortly after midnight we must have passed Cape Scott at the north-eastern tip of Vancouver Island, nothing near us now except endless forest and the occasional logging camp. I thought we were in Queen Charlotte Strait, heading for Alert Bay and the start of the Narrows, and that we would soon be off Port Hardy. Puzzled by the barge's increasing movement, I climbed the rungs and poked my head out above the line of the deck. There was a light in the wheelhouse, blurred with vaporized moisture, nothing else – nothing visible at all, the night intensely black. Once I slithered out onto the deck and crawled to the side, so that I could look for'ard, but the fog was so dense I couldn't even see the bows, let alone the lights of the tug.

Wind and waves increased steadily until the barge developed a corkscrew motion interrupted periodically by the snatch of the towline. Cold and worried, we let time pass, uncertain what to do. No point in cutting the tow if there was no other vessel in sight and, though I poked my head out above the level of the deck at regular intervals, there was no sign of a coast, no lights, no other vessels, just utter blackness and the fog clinging to the barge's towing lights in a blur of ectoplasmic white.

It was shortly after four that Miriam woke me to say she thought she saw a star. By the time I had sorted myself out and got my head above the level of the deck the fog had gone, the night sky diamond bright, everything very clear – the barge's light, the tug's too, I could even make out the line of the towing hawser dipping into the waves and the whole shape of the tug at the far end of it. But nothing else. No lights where the shore should be. It seemed as though we were being towed through a void. Yet the position of the North Star showed that we were steaming just east of south, the course we should be on for the Narrows.

Now the voyage took on a nightmare quality. We weren't where we should be and I was completely lost. I had no means of knowing that we had altered course at least 45Y to the eastward on reaching Cape Scott shortly after midnight, and that before that we had been heading west of south. Instead I began to feel as the Flying Dutchman must have felt, the voyage going on and on without end. I suppose at some point I reached the conclusion that we were on the Pacific coast of Vancouver Island, but I wasn't conscious of it as a decision, there was no calculation, it just suddenly became apparent to me, and for a time I kept the knowledge to myself.

When I finally told the others the sun was up, but still no sign of the coast and the only ship an empty ore carrier headed north and a long way past us. All to the east was shrouded in fog, a dense bank of it that presented a dark, lowering wall. Once, and once only, I thought I saw something – a darker shadow, high up like a mountain thrusting the wet blanket of the fog skyward. It was there for perhaps an hour, and then it was gone, and by midday we were in fog again, with nothing visible beyond the grey, enclosing walls of it, only the shadowy shape of the tug ahead.

By now the movement had become most unpleasant, a roll and a swoop that combined with the cold, the cramped space that confined our movements and the resinous cedar smell of the logs to produce a sickening sensation that was near to nausea. We weren't actually seasick, thank God, though Brian's face became very white and he yawned a lot. The truth was, I suppose, we had nothing to bring up. We hadn't eaten anything at all for over two days, which was just as well perhaps since there was no way we could empty any movement of our bowels over the side. For myself, I felt constipated and no longer in the least hungry. But thirsty, yes. I presume it was the salt in the air, and nausea. My mouth felt dry and rough, my body at times breaking out into a cold sweat that had me shivering violently.

Miriam seemed the least affected. I think because her mind was locked in on her thoughts, and her memories. She might have slept around occasionally, in an effort to fill the vacuum of her marriage, but the deep affection she had for Tom had always been apparent. Most of the time she seemed asleep – at least, she lay very still, curled up in a foetal ball as though to protect herself – and when she was awake she sat with her eyes wide, staring at nothing. She didn't talk, though her voice was firm and quite decisive when asked a direct question; when, for instance, we had been deciding whether to swim for it or not. Her answer to that had been quite simple: 'You don't have to worry about me. I'm a good swimmer and can probably last longer in the water than either of you. So whatever you decide . . .' And she had left it to us.

That second day at sea, cooped up in the bottom of the barge under a vast weight of cedar logs, seemed interminable, time dragging, the cold unabated by occasional glimmers of sunshine.

Whenever these occurred I would climb the rungs and hang there, my face just above the cold, wet steel of the deck, my eyes desperately searching the opaque brilliance of the humidity, searching for the shadowy shape of a passing ship, and always my hopes dashed. I saw nothing, except once. Once I was lucky and caught a glimpse of the coast away to the east of us.

It was only a brief sighting, and at the time I had no means of knowing where it was. But now, looking at the chart, it is quite obvious it must have been the Brooks Peninsula, which sticks out from the mountainous bulk of Vancouver Island a good ten miles between Brooks Bay and Kyuquot Sound. It looked to be about three, maybe four miles off. The time was then 10.17 according to the entry in my diary.

It was almost ten hours later, at 20.04, that I had my first sight of a shore light. I had poked my head above deck because I had been woken by the deep bay of a big ship's foghorn sounding off at intervals between the higher pitch of our tug's warning note. I nearly missed the light ashore, my eyes fixed on the sudden sight of a vessel coming out of the fog into good visibility and passing so close I could hear the sound of her engines. She was all lit up, rows of portholes, and above them a blaze of lights that showed a great bow wave creaming back to the white water at her wake. She must have been a cruise ship thundering down from Alaska on her way back to California. She was going far too fast for our purpose, and anyway, she was past us.

And then, just as I was about to duck down to tell the others what it was, for the sound of her passage was loud against the hull and they were both peering up at me interrogatively – just at that moment I caught the powerful beam of a light swinging in an arc behind the brilliance of the vessel's stern. After that there was nothing, my eyes following the stern of the big ship now well past us, still blazing with light. They would just be sitting down to dinner and there would be wine and jugs of iced water. I licked my lips, wondering for the umpteenth time what the hell I was doing here, why I had been fool enough . . .

And then, suddenly, there it was again, stabbing out of the blackness well astern of the cruise ship, a powerful beam reaching a white finger of light into a bank of fog, then coming clear as it swung steadily across the ship, reaching out and momentarily illuminating the tug, swinging past it and suddenly blinding me, then on to vanish into fog again. And with the light came the distant sound of what I thought at first was a diaphone, but later identified as a horn. It was a double blast at intervals of about forty seconds and I guessed, quite correctly, that it was sounding two every minute.

I must have watched the beam pass over us at least half a dozen times before I lost it, and the lights of the ship, as the fog rolled over us again. But I could still hear the foghorn. I had been counting the interval between the flashes. It was a powerful light, undoubtedly a lighthouse, and it was flashing white every fifteen seconds, perhaps a little more. If only I had had a chart I would have known where I was.

In fact, it was the San Rafael lighthouse at Friendly Cove in the south-eastern corner of Nootka Island, and Brian identified it as such. Having explored this part of the coast when visiting his grandfather's old home, he reckoned we ought to be about halfway down it, probably opposite where Cook had landed on his third and fateful voyage, the first landing on the Canadian west coast by an Englishman. 'If it's the lighthouse I think,' he said, 'then it marks the entrance to Cook Channel and the fjords leading up to the forestry centres of Tahsis and Gold River. But better wait till we're in the Juan de Fuca Strait.' That was after I had suggested taking over the barge now and trying to raise the lighthouse on the VHF set. There was a bit of a wind and it was blowing onshore, variable, but quite strong in the gusts, and the tide should be making. 'It's about three miles off, maybe less, and we'll be pushed into the land quite fast.'

But he shook his head. 'Not fast enough. And apart from that one ship, and it's past us now, I haven't heard anything passing us close.' He wanted us to wait until we were in the Juan de Fuca Strait. 'There'll be plenty of ships around us then.'

The logic of it was unanswerable and I would have agreed if it hadn't been for Miriam. She had scrambled up the log butts and had seen the lights, had watched the fog roll in again, blotting out even the lights of the tug. 'And suppose the fog holds. Suppose there's fog all the way to Seattle; to the moment we tie up at the SVL Timber quay. We'll never see another ship. And it'll be daylight.' And she added, her voice trembling with urgency: 'We'll never get a chance like this.'

Brian started to reason with her, but she wasn't in a reasoning frame of mind. She was very close to hysteria and it was only then I began to realize what those eighteen days cooped up in that lonely lakeside hut had done to her. 'You can wait if you like. Not me. There's a lighthouse there. I saw it. There'll be lighthouse keepers, a village, people – honest, straightforward, ordinary people.' Her voice was quite wild, the words tumbling over themselves. 'If you won't cut the tow loose I'm going to swim for it.' She was staring at Brian, her eyes very large as she looked into his face.

He wasn't going to budge. I could see that. And so could she. 'All right,' she said and unzipped her anorak.

She was literally starting to strip off. 'For God's sake, Miriam!' I had my hand on her arm, restraining her, my voice tense. 'Don't be silly. You'd never make it.' I could feel her trembling.

Brian tried again, his tone gentler than I had ever heard it before, but it made no difference. Nothing he could say, no pleading from me, had any effect. Her mind was made up and nothing would budge it. She had seen a light ashore and developed a mental block, so that she didn't seem to hear what we were saying, and it gradually dawned on us then that if we didn't do what she wanted and cut the tow, we should have to restrain her physically.

Brian looked at me, a half smile and little shrug. 'So we cut the tow. Agreed?'

I nodded slowly, thinking it wouldn't take long for the men on the tug to realize the barge was no longer attached. Fog or no fog, their radar would soon pick us up, and then what? But when I tried to explain this to Miriam, she simply said, 'You've still got that gun, Brian. You can hold them off for a time, and every minute that passes, we'll be closer to the shore. We won't have to swim so far.'

She smiled then. She actually smiled, a look of triumph on her face as though what she had said was unanswerable. And in a way it was. Darkness and fog, with a lighthouse three miles away, or daylight in the Strait with some vessel passing us a lot nearer. You could toss a coin as to which was the best course of action. Neither was very sensible or necessarily offered much hope.

'So we cut the tow,' I said and Brian nodded.

'Not much choice.' That smile again. Then he turned to Miriam. 'Two rifles, a walkie-talkie and VHF, but no ammunition and that tug a hawser length away. Better get out your prayer mat.' He swung himself onto the steel rungs. 'Okay. Let's go.' And he began to hoist himself up to the deck.

The wheelhouse was empty and we closed the trap door on whoever was sleeping in the cuddy down below. 'I'll leave you to handle things this end,' he said to me, and he laid his rifle on the shelf in front of the wheel. 'Start calling on the radio as soon as I've slipped the tow and get that Coastguard here quick. I hope to God,' he added as he pushed out through the leeward door into the night, 'there's a quick release on that hawser.'

The door slammed shut, his figure swallowed instantly in the black void of the fog, and we stood there, Miriam and I, waiting. I gave him two minutes by my watch to get up for'ard and work out how the release mechanism worked, then I switched on the VHF set and, with the mike close against my mouth, began calling on channel 16: 'Coastguard cutter *Kelsey*. Coastguard cutter *Kelsey*. This is Redfern calling *Kelsey*. Come in please, *Kelsey*.'

To my surprise the *Kelsey* answered immediately and it was Cornish himself, his voice loud and clear. I gave him our position. 'We are on the barge and cutting the tow. The tug won't take long to pick us up and to hold them off we have only two rifles. Hurry, hurry, hurry. It could be a matter of life or death.'

There was a pause, and in that pause I sensed the barge faltering. Then Cornish's voice again, not speaking to me, but to the tug, warning the *Gabriello* to heave to and await the Coastguard escort into Victoria. 'I have you clear and very close on my radar. Do not attempt to make contact with your tow. I repeat – you are not to make contact with or attempt to board that barge. Any such attempt will be resisted by force.'

Fists began pounding at the under side of the trap-door, a man shouting to be let out. The door to the deck slid open and Brian thrust his head in. 'Tow released,' he said. And he added, 'It slipped away over the bows like a whiplash. Can you feel the difference?'

I actually could. The barge seemed to have gone dead, and I thought it had turned slightly to port, broadside to the wind and the waves. The wind force I estimated at about 4, the rate of drift possibly as much as 2 knots – an hour and a half, maybe two hours before we were blown onto the coast below that lighthouse. It was ridiculous. Long before then the tug would be alongside and ourselves overwhelmed, or else swimming for it.

'Did you raise the cutter?'

'Yes.'

'How far away?'

'He was wise enough not to say.'

In fact, the cutter was then about six miles seaward of us, steaming at the same speed and on a parallel course, but keeping several miles astern. When he had failed to pick us up on his radar at Pearl Rocks, or to identify us amongst the traffic west of the Rankin Shoals, he had headed south at full speed with the inten-tion of intercepting and identifying the tow as it entered the Queen Charlotte Strait. Only after he had wasted most of the night lying in the fairway between the BC mainland and the top of Vancouver Island watching for us on his radar did he finally come to the conclusion that the *Gabriello* was taking the open sea route. It had then taken him almost eight hours to catch up with us so that it was well past midday before he had finally taken station to seaward waiting for the fog to clear so that a helicopter could fly in with police and customs.

Knowing it would take him at least twenty minutes to close with us, and having got no reply from the *Gabriello*, Cornish came back to me, asking who was on board beside myself. Then he wanted to know about Tom Halliday, and when I told him he had been killed and his wife had been held prisoner in a lakeside hut high in the mountains above High Stand, he didn't waste time asking for details but began a series of calls, first to the lighthouse, then to any other vessel that might be close to us. As it happened a fisherman out of Friendly Cove was just clearing Yuquot Point heading south-west out of Nootka Sound. Cornish asked him to close us at all possible speed and monitor our drift. All this came out on the loudspeaker of our VHF set. What we didn't know was that at the same time he was in radio-telephone communication with the RC Centre at Victoria and that, despite the fog, a helicopter was being scrambled.

It was at this point that the lights of the tug suddenly loomed out of the fog, her blunt bows thrusting towards us, her superstructure a dim outline. By then the barge was virtually stationary, wallowing in the wind with the waves slapping noisily at her rusty sides. The tug struck us amidships, thumping and scraping as the bows rose and fell, men scrambling for'ard to leap aboard us. Brian had retrieved the rifle and was standing in the open doorway of the wheelhouse so that they could see he was armed.

They paused. A voice shouted to them over a loud-hailer and at the same instant a klaxon sounded very loud and just astern of us. A searchlight beam stabbed the shifting grey banks of fog, white bows and a wheel-house with rods like antennae either side of a short mast festooned with aerials. It was the fishing vessel out of Friendly Cove. The radio was suddenly full of talk as the fisherman spoke to the skipper of the tug and Captain Cornish's voice broke in with instructions to the tug: 'You will stand off from the barge. I repeat, stand off from the barge.'

For a moment everything seemed to freeze as though in a picture, the tug with its bows thrusting against us and three men up for'ard with another coming out of the wheelhouse with a rifle in his hand, and just off our starb'd quarter the white shadow of the fishing boat hanging there in the fog.

It was like that for a moment, then the picture shattered, everything happening at once. We fell off the back of a wave into a deep hollow, the barge rolling and Miriam flung against me. The trap door broke open and was flung back to reveal the heaving shoulders of a powerfully built man in an open shirt with black hair and staring eyes. I kicked out at him, an instinctive reaction with Miriam clinging to me, her mouth open and her face gone white in a blazing beam of light. The fog rolled clear, a gap in the swirling mist and the lighthouse staring at us, one-eyed like a Cyclops, across a welter of breaking waves.

For an instant the scene was lit like a film set, the tug's bows buried under water as they fell against us, the three men on its deck lying in a huddle of tangled limbs and the ghostly fishing boat rolling its gunnels under, mast and rods dipping towards us. 'Philip! I'm going. Come with me. It's so near.'

The grip on my arm loosened. She was turning, reaching for the door. I saw the fear on her face, had the odd experience of sensing her sudden uncontrollable terror transmitted right through me. Then the beam passed on. Twilight for an instant, then blackness. And in that abrupt dark I felt the barge roll back as it was lifted by an incoming comber, saw the top of it curl and break in a blur of grey foam that burst against the tug, slewing it round, then hit us with a crash, spray spattering the wheelhouse and the man I had kicked in the face falling back down the ladder with a cry, the trapdoor banging shut over his head.

Then we were sliding down the surf-flecked back of the wave, falling into the hollow of it to end up with a jarring crash that jabbed right through my body and shook every part of the barge. We were on rock, and until we lifted to the next breaker, we were grinding our bottom plates against its surface, the din appalling.

I don't know whether it was because he realized the barge had struck, and that he was in shoaling water among the rocks, or whether it was the sense of being so abruptly exposed, a gap torn in the fog and all three vessels made visible to the shore by the beam of the lighthouse . . . Whatever it was, there was a sudden rumbling sound as the skipper of the tug put his engines full astern and backed off. Another crash, a splatter of breaking water and then we were lifting, the tug below us and ourselves looking down on it. The lighthouse beam was back, everything lit with blinding clarity, and the tug turning broadside-on to us. And as the beam passed on another light flashed out, this time from seaward.

The cutter was actually in sight. I think I went slightly mad at the sight of the tug hauling off from us and the cutter closing in; I was shouting my head off and doing a little dance. Brian, too – he was making strange war-whoop sounds deep in his throat. And Miriam suddenly burst into tears, clutching hold of me and sobbing, her head bent down as though in prayer, and I heard her say something about stars, and then quite distinctly, 'If only he hadn't taken that last snort – his luck was turning.' Her head was up then and she was looking at Brian with an expression I didn't understand. It wasn't exactly hatred, more an accusation . . . I think if she had had the means she would have killed him then.

PART SIX

MAYDAY!
MAYDAY!

CHAPTER ONE

It was dawn before we were taken off that barge. By then the fog had disappeared and as the sun rose above the tree-clad mountains of Vancouver Island we were able to see how close we had come to disaster, for in the six hours since we had hit that first rock tide and wind had bumped the barge along the iron-hard coast of Maquinna Point and the southern extremity of Nootka Island until it had found deeper water between Maquinna and Yuquot. By then police and customs had boarded the tug by winch from a helicopter and it was the *Gabriello* herself that towed the leaking barge clear of the rocks past Friendly Cove and the entrance to Cook's Channel and into the quiet of the Zuciarte Channel. This took us south and west of Bligh Island to the grey rock of Muchalat Inlet and so up to the pulp mill some eight miles south of Gold River.

That was where we stayed the night, in a motel, and in the morning Cornish came to tell us the customs officers had found no drugs. They had had every log lifted out and been over the barge inch by inch – no trace of cocaine or any other contraband. We were interviewed then, each of us separately, by the police and the customs, and most of the time there was a member of the Federal Drug Enforcement Bureau present. This was at the motel. Statements were taken, not just from us, but also from the captain and crew of the tug, and while the police were chiefly concerned with Tom's death and Miriam's account of her kidnapping and long incarceration in the lakeside hut, the customs officers concentrated on our rendezvous with the South American vessel among the islands of the Spider. After hours of searching, then more time wasted interrogating the crew of the tug, I think they found it very frustrating that we hadn't been able to poke our heads out and see what was going on. What they wanted was confirmation of the nature of the cargo being transferred to the barge and where it had been hidden. 'You state there was a lot of hammering?' The question was addressed to me, and when I nodded, the officer asked me where the hammering had been coming from. 'For'ard, aft, amidships – where?'

'All over,' I said. 'It was loudest aft, of course, but the sound of it was not just confined to our end of the barge.'

He had been one of those on the rummage party when the tug had been stopped the first time, and looking down at my statement, he said, 'You say here it sounded like wood on wood, as though they were tamping something in between the tree logs.' He looked up at me. 'I'm considering, you see, that packages of drugs could have been forced between the logs and then at a later stage – while you people were asleep perhaps – either dumped overboard or loaded into a fishing boat or an inflatable, some inshore craft to be run in to the coast.'

'We would have heard it,' I said, and Brian nodded, adding that though he had slept quite heavily at times during the run from the Cascades to the Spider, he had been awake most of the time after that.

'Wolchak,' the customs officer said, looking down again at the statement spread out on the oilcloth-covered table still littered with the remains of breakfast. 'We've checked with Bella Bella and the pilot of that Cessna confirms that he flew Wolchak and two other men, one of them answering to your description of the man responsible for Mr Halliday's death, out to Bella Coola where there was a hire car waiting for them. Bella Coola is the coastal end of the road west out of Williams Lake and police are making enquiries now to see whether they drove on from there to board another plane. There's an airport at Williams Lake, another at Quesnel, also at Prince George a further eighty miles or so north. In that case he could be in the States now. Alternatively, if he'd doubled back to Namu in a small hire plane he could have organized a boat . . .'

But I was no longer listening, for the mention of Wolchak had taken my mind back to the scene in the mess room of the *Kelsey* with the rummage party sitting there talking over their coffee and that American Drug Enforcement officer describing how a man, who was also named Josef Wolchak, had risen to the head of

those two mafioso families in Chicago. I was remembering the story of how he had made his first drug run from
Columbia to New York. 'Walking stick,' I said.

'What's that?'

I shook my head. It was impossible, of course, and
yet standing there on that hairpin bend, high above the
logging camp, it had seemed so extraordinary to have a
mobile drilling rig parked on the edge of that cliff.
'You've checked the butt ends of those logs, have you?'

'How do you mean?'

'I don't know.' I shrugged, feeling I was on the verge
of making a fool of myself. 'It's just an idea.' And then
I asked the American whether they had had time to
check if the Josef Wolchak involved in the High Stand
selling was the same man his colleague had been talking
about on the *Kelsey* a few days ago.

They were already doing that. 'I guess he's the same
man all right. That's why we're so sure it's drugs.' He
was looking at Brian then. 'I know you think those trees
are valuable, but they're peanuts compared with what's
involved if they were a cover for a regular drug run.' He
turned back to me. 'Walking stick. You said something
about walking sticks.'

I hesitated. A tree trunk was in some ways rather
like a giant version of a walking stick and with the trunk
hollowed out . . . 'Can we go down to the pulp mill and
have a look at those logs?'

I thought they were going to press me to say what
was in my mind, but instead, after a momentary hesitation, everyone staring at me, they got to their feet.
'Okay. Let's go have another look at that timber.' And I

could see that all of them, the two customs officers, the American drugs man and the RCMP officer – Brian and Miriam, too – were mulling over in their minds the idea I had given them, unwilling to put it into words for fear it would prove as nonsensical as it seemed.

We drove down in three vehicles, turned right by the Indian Reserve on the level flats of the Gold River estuary just short of the quay and entered the pulp mill. The logs were stacked in a pile close by a great tree trunk of a boom crane. Across the water the local passenger and cargo ship, the *Uchuck III*, was just pulling out from the pier past the Coastguard cutter which was still lying there. The trunks were very uniform, and in that setting, with the booming ground just below us, the great pile of the mill at our backs plumed with white smoke and the rock walls of Muchalat Inlet to the right and the even narrower gut of Matchloe Bay to our left, clouds hanging black against a shaft of sunlight, they looked so much smaller.

It was the butts I wanted to examine, for I was sure the ones I had seen up-ended against that cliff above the logging camp had been butt-end up. Unfortunately the stacking had been done regardless of the order in which they had been loaded on the barge and they were wet from having been off-loaded into the booming ground first, so that the sawdust clinging to the butts was sticky and very tenacious. In the end, we had to get the mill people to bring in a pump and hose them down under pressure.

The first two dozen or so we examined had clearly not been tampered with in any way, and after that we had to use the back of a truck to give us extra height. All the time large clutches of logs were being brought in from the forests and tipped into the pen, an unnerving bustle of big vehicle activity. And then, when I was beginning to feel I had made a fool of myself, the logging boss who had been clambering over the logs without bothering to use the truck, called for the hose. 'Something here.' He was on his knees, leaning over the round raw wood end of a log, feeling it with his hands. 'Sort of irregular.' The truck was shifted slightly and the hose jet washed the sawdust clear. We could see it then, a slight protuberance and the growth rings not quite matching.

We saw the same thing then in several others. A plug had been inserted. Brian thought it might be just that, having drilled certain logs with the intention of making a boom and then being faced with the prospect that felling would be stopped, they had decided to ship the whole lot out. But it had been very cleverly done, in most cases the growth rings matching and only the slightest crack to indicate that a plug had been inserted in the drill hole. A lot of trouble had been taken to make those plugs fit exactly.

The foreman had scrambled down from the pile and was lumbering across to his office shack. Rain closed off the inlet, grey billows of cloud between the black rock walls. He came back with a big chainsaw. Also a piece of paper, which he handed to the RCMP officer. 'Sign that.' His heavy-jowled features cracked in a grin. 'All right for you, but my people, they wouldn't like it if they got a bill for a damaged cedar log.' The policeman signed and the foreman stuffed it into his pocket. 'Which shall we take first, the one I picked out?'

The officer looked at the rest of us, then nodded. The saw was passed up to us and the foreman began directing the winch winder in the boom crane's cabin. One by one the logs were lifted down until the one that had quite obviously been plugged was fully exposed. The big Canadian was standing with his feet carefully balanced. 'I'll take it bit by bit, okay?' he said as we handed the saw up to him. He pulled the starter cord and the engine roared.

That was when the rain reached us, but he took no notice, though all he was wearing was a heavy coloured shirt, and braces of course. Water spurted from the blade as he leaned forward, the grip claws positioned about two feet from the butt, the engine note deepening as the chain sliced down through the bark and into the wood, pale sawdust pouring out and all of us watching as the rain poured down and lightning flashed somewhere in the hills above us. Suddenly the saw checked and the foreman pulled the blade out, the motor idling, the chain still. He peered down, turning the saw and picking up a smear of dust and oil on the tip of his finger. 'That's not wood.' He held his finger out to us, flecks of white amongst the sawdust, a pale slime, but mixed with the oil and the wood dust it was hard to see the difference. 'Won't do the saw much good if I try and go through it. Have to go round. There's something there.'

He had the crane operator lower the grappling chains, shifted the whole tree trunk several feet, so that the butt hung out over the back of the truck, and then started to cut round the trunk to a fraction over the depth of the saw blade. The rain stopped and at one point, shifting the position of the saw, he said, 'Looks like plastic.' Finally, with the log cut all round and hanging by just a single hinge of wood, so that the end-section trembled at a touch, he stepped back. 'Okay boys, now see what it is.' He paused then, looking at us. The man had a natural sense of the dramatic, holding the heavy chainsaw in his big paw as though it were a sword. Then he leaned forward, revved the motor and snicked the wooden hinge with the tip of the blade, the whole log-end suddenly hanging free.

He gave it a kick and it fell into the truck at our feet, and we were looking at a new butt-end with a hole in the centre of it about eight inches in diameter and white powder dribbling from it. The American reached forward, took some of it in his hand and stood staring down at it. 'Jeez! It's pure. Virgin pure coke. Uncut.'

Customs men gathered round, dipping their fingers in, staring at the powder. 'Let's see how much they've stowed there. Is it plastic bags?'

The foreman shook his head. 'A container more like.' His big hands were already working round the broken edges of the hole. 'Yeah, plastic container – long one by the feel of it.'

It took three of them to drag it clear and lower it to the truck. It was a clear plastic tube measuring 20 cms by 4.5 metres and it was packed from end to end with cocaine.

'Not much difference, is there?' The Drug Enforcement agent had straightened up and was staring at the great pile of logs. 'Why the hell didn't I think of that?' He turned to me. 'Walking sticks! It's just a matter of scale, isn't it? If you can hollow out the one, you can hollow out the other.'

'If you've got the right equipment,' I said, 'and it's available in the right place.' I wondered why I hadn't thought of it, or Tom, looking down on the Cascades logging camp and seeing that mobile drilling rig and a tree trunk up-ended against that cliff.

'Yeah.' He took off his glasses, nodded to himself as he wiped the rain off. 'Neat. Oh, so very neat.' He put his glasses on again, staring at the stack of logs. 'Wonder how much we got in that pile? One hell of a lot, that's for sure. And only a few days back we checked out a barge-load and let it through.'

The elder of the two Canadian customs officers patted his shoulder. 'Not your fault. You'd no means of knowing – '

'Of course I hadn't. I wasn't there. But we had our suspicions – a tip-off. Reliable, too. And we never had the sense to relate that special stand of trees to the drug concealment potential. The barge-load we let through a few nights back will have been trundled through the passes and across the plains and right now it'll be in the SVL Company's timber yard in Chicago, or maybe it's already out in the street... Just think what that means in terms of road accidents, muggings, rape. God! I never thought I'd be faced with something as big as this.' He turned to the foreman. 'Better take me to the manager's office. I need a phone – lots of calls –

Chicago.' He was already clambering down from the truck. The other followed.

Suddenly we were on our own, the police hurrying back to their car, which had a radio, the customs officers heading towards the pier where the Coastguard cutter was now the only vessel. 'I need a drink,' Miriam said in a small voice. 'I feel slightly sick.' And I heard her murmur to herself, 'Tom was right all along.'

There wasn't anywhere to get a drink. We stood around for a while. Then more police arrived to mount guard over the High Stand logs and it began to rain again. We were finally given a meal in the mill canteen and shortly afterwards a police car arrived to whisk us half across Vancouver Island, through Campbell River and down the coastal highway to Victoria, where Brian and I were put up at that lovely creeper-clad relic of Victorian days, the Empress Hotel. It faced the inner harbour and the BC Parliament Building and was conveniently close to the Provincial Courts.

Miriam, after throwing a fit of temperament that was more than justified in the circumstances, was allowed to go out to Oak Bay with the Canadian family she had stayed with before, while Brian and I settled down to drink ourselves into a more relaxed frame of mind. It had been a long journey from Ocean Falls, longer still from the Yukon, and now we were being told we had to wait in case further evidence was required from us when those on the tug, who had now been arrested and charged with drug smuggling, made their first appearance in court.

That might have been the end of it if the authorities,

both in Canada and the States, had not decided to go for Wolchak. It was a mark of the size of the operation that he had been on the spot and running it himself, and as a result he was more exposed than he had probably ever been before. He was arrested at his home in Chicago the day after we reached Victoria, but despite pressure from the public and the media, the courts released him on bail of half a million dollars pending extradition proceedings. Roy McLaren, when I saw him in his office in Vancouver two days later, told me proceedings of that sort could drag on for months. Meanwhile, Barony had already successfully avoided arrest, the SVL Timber lawyers pleading that neither he nor the company was responsible for anything that had been done in the remoteness of the Halliday Arm of Cascade Inlet. The company had purchased the trees, that was all. The felling had been arranged through the owner's representative and delivery through Angeles Georgia Towing.

I was booked out the next day on the Wardair flight back to Gatwick, and feeling I owed myself the luxury of a view over the water, I was staying the night at the Bayshore. Brian had already left for the north again, back to Ocean Falls. That evening, after lazing for an hour in the circular pool beside the parked charter cruisers, I stood in my room with just a towel round my waist, smoking a cigarette and watching the lights come on along the North Shore. I had two windows to my room, one facing across Coal Harbour and Burrard Inlet, the other towards the city where the glass of Vancouver's mini-Manhattan was reflecting the last of the sunset glow. A cargo ship disappeared slowly beyond Deadman's Island and the black silhouette of the trees of Stanley Park.

It was all so beautiful, a floatplane landing, a yacht going alongside the refuelling raft and the lights twinkling right up the slopes to the ski-lift high above the First Narrows. All that was missing was somebody to share it with and my thoughts turned to Miriam, wondering what she was doing tonight, whether to ring her. And then, just as I had seated myself on the bed and started to look up the Oak Bay number of her Canadian friends, the phone rang.

Later, of course, we said it must have been telepathy. She was downstairs and wanted me to have dinner with her. 'Something very exciting. I must tell you.' And she added, her voice bubbling with it, 'You're not doing anything, are you? I must talk it over, and now Brian's gone there's nobody – nobody who knows it all and how Tom would feel. Can you come? Can you join me for a sort of quiet celebration?'

'Of course,' I told her. 'What's it all about?'

'Later.' And almost in the same breath she muttered, 'It's all so ironic. I'll wait for you in the Verandah Room.' And she rang off.

I dressed quickly and went down to find her with a tall glass in front of her frosted with ice and eating roasted nuts as though she hadn't had a meal for weeks. I don't know what she was wearing, trousers I think and a light woollen top, a very ordinary outfit, but she looked radiant. She had another drink with me and then we left the hotel and strolled across the lit driveway to the dim, mysterious labyrinth of the old Coal Harbour quay. She had booked a table at the Keg where I had dined the night I arrived in Vancouver. 'We'll have fish and lots of wine – a lovely, simple atmosphere. Then I'll tell you.' We passed the broken sleeper palings of the old boatyard and went round by a lot of parked cars and the entrance to the marina, laughing at the tow-away signs, her arm linked in mine. I could feel the movement of her hips against me and I was filled with a warm glow, sensing that we would sleep together in my room overlooking the harbour and that it would be a night to remember.

We stood for a time looking down at the boats lying white and deserted against the floating wooden arms of the marina. 'I wouldn't mind living somewhere out here,' she said, the huskiness in her voice more pro-nounced. 'A boat, a house by the shore, and the world – the European world of demos, unions, terrorism, all the mayhem of politics – a million miles away. Or would one find it too peaceful, too removed – too dull?' She looked up at me, smiling.

The Keg, like the ships' chandlery nearby, was a disused boathouse, all wood and bare simplicity. We had another drink, a salad, some fish and a couple of bottles of Californian wine, and we talked – about everything except what she'd come to tell me. It wasn't until the coffee arrived, and with it the two large bran-dies she had ordered, that she suddenly blurted it out: 'Stone Slide Gully,' she said, taking a telex out and pass-ing it across to me. 'Jonny Epinard – he sent that from Whitehorse.' And she went on, her words coming so

fast I could barely follow her – 'You remember that
Indian, Jack McDonald – you said you'd been through
the gully into that grim, volcanic-looking crater beyond
– the time I saw it I thought it looked like an old-
fashioned lavatory pan, the mountains rising up round
it at roughly the same angle. It was always subject to
rock slides – not so much where Tom and the Indian
were beavering away with their tractor and sluice box,
but on the opposite slope. It's very sheer there.' Her
hand reached over, gripping hold of mine. 'You see what
he says. There's been a slide.'

I nodded, my eyes on the telex text: . . . *closing down
for winter. Jack had look at new slide. Picked up 23
nuggets in under an hour, largest 0.4 oz. Looks promising subject evaluation next season. Sorry Tom won't
know. Jonny Epinard.*

Her grip on my hand tightened. 'Gold!' she said.
'And even if it's nothing big it would have got Tom out
of the mess he was in. He'd have been able to tell those
bastards in Chicago to go to hell.' I could feel her nails
biting into my flesh. 'Why didn't it happen when he was
up there? Why now – when it's too late?'

She went on talking about that for some time, what
it would have meant to Tom, how, if it had only happened the previous year, or better still two years ago, he
would never have got in hock to the bank, would never
have considered selling even an acre of High Stand. And
then abruptly she veered away from that line of thought
and began talking about the future, her future – 'Me, a
gold-miner – just think of it!' Her eyes were sparkling,
her face flushed and that Titian hair shining softly in the

dim light. She looked just wonderful as she went on, 'The hours I've listened to Tom talking about his father, about the Klondike and the fever that gripped them all when the Bonanza was discovered. And now, here I am with nuggets in the bank. Not a Bonanza. Of course not. But another Ice Cold perhaps. That would be enough. And when spring comes we can go up there, see if it really is a new placer mine. Would that make me a sourdough?' She drained the last of her brandy, giggling to herself. 'Me, a sourdough!' And she shook her head, adding in a subdued voice, 'I'm glad about High Stand, that I shan't be concerned with those trees. Tom was right – Brian will appreciate them. He understands about trees, and after what happened there . . .' She leaned across the table to me. 'You will handle the legal side for me, won't you? Ice Cold, I mean – you'll come up there with me?' And then on a lighter note: 'I can manage a mine. At least, I think I can,' she added with a grin. 'But it'll mean a company, accounts, a lot of paperwork.' She laughed. 'I never was any good at that sort of thing.'

We talked it over for a while, Miriam building castles, mentally leaping ahead to a full-blown mine, and myself doing the best I could to keep her feet somewhere near the ground. It was all good fun, dreaming dreams and both of us involved. Finally she paid the bill – she insisted absolutely and I let her, because it was her evening, the start of an attempt to build a future for herself from the wretchedness of what had happened. Then we went out into the shadowy world of Coal Harbour quay, the night very still with low cloud so that the water and the old boathouses were lit by the reflected glow of the city's lights.

We reached the uneven, pot-holed surface of the private roadway leading westward to the hotel, walking arm-in-arm, not talking now – just content to let the stillness and the magic of the night work on us, conscious of our closeness and the hours ahead. We were approaching the entrance to the marina and stopped for a moment to watch one of those fast big game fishing boats gliding in towards the pontoon. 'That's what I'd like,' Miriam said. 'A boat like that, so I could explore – ' She walked on.

We were just passing the approach to one of the parking bays when a car's engine started. The lights flicked on at high beam, our shadows leaping across the roadway. Startled, our eyes were blinded. Then the engine revved and in the instant that the car began moving down on us with a squeal of tyres, something triggered inside me, an instinct of preservation. I flung Miriam forward – 'The marina. Run!'

Thank God she didn't hesitate. We made it as the car hurtled past us, scraping the wall and screeching to a halt. The sound of doors and voices calling in the darkness. But by then we were down the ramp and onto the floating pontoon. There was a crack like a backfire and something smacked into the water beside us. Feet sounded on the ramp, the pontoon swaying. I took the second bay, a pontoon full of parked boats, hoping to God I had picked the right one, the boats all dark, not a soul about.

And then I saw it – the high, white bow of that

fishing cruiser gliding in towards the end of the pontoon. 'Jump or swim,' I gasped. 'We've got to make that boat.' I gave one quick glance over my shoulder. 'Can you make it?'

'Yes.' She was close behind me and even then I noticed her breasts, the way she moved. And then we were almost at the end of the pontoon and I was calling to the skipper high on the open bridge: 'Mayday! Mayday!' I yelled. 'Need your help. Muggers.'

He reacted quite instinctively, closing the gap to the pontoon-end just as I reached it. I jumped, landing on my feet and staggering against the wheelhouse. Miriam landed beside me. 'Full ahead – please,' I called up to the man above me. 'They're armed.'

He must have seen them running towards him along the pontoon, for he didn't hesitate, slamming his cruiser into gear, and as the screws bit, he increased the revs, lifting the bows half out of the water and swinging the boat away in a boiling arc towards the pale line of the Royal Vancouver Yacht Club boat sheds.

He was the owner, an American by the sound of it. 'You want the police?' he asked as we joined him on the open bridge. 'I got R/T down below.'

'Did you see their faces clearly?' I asked. 'Could you identify them?'

But of course he had been too occupied getting his boat away. 'If you hadn't called *Mayday* . . .' He shrugged, cutting down on the revs and settling back in his swivel chair, idling across the harbour as I said who we were and told him something of what I thought it was all about. 'So you can't identify them? You're a lawyer and you don't see what the police can do about it?' He sat there for a moment, his peaked cap pushed back on his head, gazing out at the dark outline of the Coal Harbour buildings. A car was disappearing up towards Georgia Street, otherwise there was no sign of movement. 'I'm from California,' he said, 'and down there we get to hear a lot about what drugs do to people, the way kids act – anything to get the next fix; and of course the millions to be made by the men running the racket. You want my advice?' He turned his head sharply, leaning forward and staring at us through his gold-rimmed glasses. 'You get the hell out, back to England, and fast. That's my advice. And if they need you back over here to give evidence, you make damn sure you're under police protection every second you're here. You, too, lady. Okay?' He stood up, increasing the revs again and heading in for the lit bulk of the hotel.

He put us ashore by backing up to the bows of one of the charter cruisers. 'Just remember what I said,' he called down to us. 'I've been in politics as well as business and I know what these boys can do, the sort of hoodlums their money buys them. It may seem all right in England, but over here . . .' He laughed, raising his hand in a casual salute, screws frothing as he eased away. 'And look after the little lady, eh?' The American voice came faintly back to us across the water.

We went up to my room and I did my best, lying there, naked between the sheets, the lights fading, the water blackening, a world of beauty nodding off to sleep. And in the dawn, in the first greying of the light, the hills upside down in the flat mirror of Burrard Inlet and the ashtray beside our bed full of stubbed-out butts, in that dawn reality stood like a silent ghost staring in at the big windows – a golden future for us both, and all I could think of was those bloody hunters waiting up in the Yukon, the two of us lying in each other's arms and the shadow of the drug ring hanging over us . . .

AUTHOR'S NOTE

During the period I was writing *Campbell's Kingdom*, and later *The Land God Gave to Cain*, I came to know more of Canada than all but a handful of Canadians – from the Maritimes to the Rockies and the Caribou Trail, Labrador, too, and north-west across Hudson's Bay to the Barrens and Baffin Island. The one area I did not know at that time, but which has always called to me because of the Gold Rush of '98, was the Yukon.

There was, too, another area of Western Canada that, as sailor and navigator, had a particular appeal for me – those long fingers of water reaching deep into the Coast Mountains of the Rockies between the northern tip of Vancouver Island and the southern end of the Charlottes. To explore that area, which is where Mackenzie scratched his name on a rock as the first overland to the Pacific, I knew I would require the good offices of the Canadian and B C Governments.

Now that I have completed *High Stand*, I would like

to record my thanks to them for arranging for me to be guest of the Canadian Coastguards on one of their cutters carrying out search and rescue duties and generally showing the flag in those little-visited and very remote fjords. In particular, I would like to thank Captain Peter Golden who, as Coastguard Regional Manager, organized the voyage for me, and Captain Peter Kalis of the Coastguard cutter *Rider* who was in a class more or less by himself for high-speed inshore pilotage in very narrow, rock-infested waters. It was he who took me into the Spider and gave me a week of most intricate and enjoyable charting.

In the Yukon everybody is invariably helpful. It is that sort of country, so that in a short space of time I was able to see just what I thought I would need – in particular, a placer gold mine high up on the border of the frozen glacier heights of Kluane National Park. Mike Brine insisted on my wife Dorothy and I being his guest at Dezadeash Lodge and it was he who persuaded Terry Thompson to take us deep into the outback, to the mine he operated high up on the headwaters of a creek named the Squaw, close to the Alaskan border.

Since the title and part of the background of *High Stand* is timber, I should perhaps explain that my knowledge and interest in trees is a very personal one, for in the last quarter of a century Dorothy and I have planted a great number of Canadian trees in Wales where the silvicultural conditions are as good, if not better, than most of the areas of the Canadian west coast where they grow naturally. In fact, it was those early travels in Western Canada that decided me to use some of the money my books were earning to buy otherwise useless land and develop plantations of Canadian spruce and fir.

As they grow into tall timber, they give me an increasing sense of achievement and satisfaction. Not only have we turned small areas of the Ordnance Survey map from white to green, thus providing the country with additional and much needed plantations of what constitute one of the very few renewable natural resources, but in doing so we have at least done something, however small, to offset the destruction of the world's forests, a devastation that will affect the climate in which we all live. This has already happened in various parts of the world, notably in North Africa.

I have for a long time wanted to write a novel that, at least in part, was about trees. But always it seemed as though this aspect of my life was to remain quite separate from my writing, my mind apparently unable to conceive a story in which a forest could be part of the main thread. Then, back again in the Canadian West where I had first dreamed of planting my own stand of timber, suddenly it all came together. *High Stand* is the result.